MW01170148

EYE OF THE NOMAD

"*Eye of the Nomad* is an epic tale of war, love, friendship, and betrayal that will keep readers turning pages anxiously to see what happens to these characters."
—**Grant Leishman, Readers' Favorite**

"A riveting look at the world's first special forces. The novel applies the lessons of Tzu's *Art of War* into a narrative that makes the motivations of Genghis Khan's most elite Mongols part of an accessible and visceral experience. It leaves you enriched but hungry for the second installment."
—**Barry Jesinoski, CEO of the Disabled American Veterans**

"The plot leaves you deeply immersed into a well-crafted and fascinating story. This great piece of workmanship left me curious and excited for book 2: *Moan of the Mountain*."
—**Robert Reynolds, Former Deputy Under Secretary, Department of Veterans Affairs and Past National Commander of the Disabled American Veterans**

"Took me on an amazing journey where I felt like I was actually there. Readers will be captivated by the well researched adventure that Nardolicci takes us on!!"
—**Joey Smoak, CEO of Eastern Carolina Housing Organization**

"Offering a thrilling and immersive historical novel, Nardolicci's detailed and clearly-well researched portrayal of the 12th-century Eurasian Steppe brought the setting to life. Overall, *Eye of the Nomad* is a masterful blend of history and fiction that captivates the reader's imagination and heart, and I can't wait to see more from this exciting series."
—**K.C. Finn, Readers' Favorite**

"An intriguing read that captivates and weaves an alternative narrative, inviting readers to explore a world where imagination and history intersect in fascinating ways."
—**Baasanjav Terbish, Researcher of Mongolia and Inner Asia Studies at University of Cambridge and author of *Sex in the Land of Genghis Khan***

War of Fear is the epic trilogy inspired by the true story of Yasotay, the architect behind Genghis Khan's death squad of special operators... called *The Mangoday*. Yasotay's *Art of War* is influential in building one of the greatest empires in human history. He builds a medieval death machine, only to regret the butchery unleashed upon the world.

Book I, Eye of the Nomad, so begins the legend of Yasotay, a gifted young prince whose search for purpose takes a dramatic turn saving an illiterate nomad from captivity. He embarks on a hero's journey far from home to learn the true meaning of life. Murder, kidnapping, and revenge soon find Yasotay in a thrilling race against time to save someone he loves from a fate worse than death.

Book II, Moan of the Mountain, betrayal, murder, and desperation cause Yasotay to discover how a small special forces team can be leveraged to make an army absolutely invincible. Yasotay builds a band of nomads "consecrated in death" and uses it as a weapon of war that is soon feared across the world. Ultimately, he sees Genghis Khan's ruthless savagery for what it is—pure evil.

Book III, Voice of the Atoned, the pulse-pounding conclusion finds Yasotay chased by his past, watching as Genghis Khan's army kills millions, destroying city after city, seemingly bent on world domination. Transformed through his own personal struggles, Yasotay finally realizes that the monster he unleashed must be stopped. Desperation leads to a plan—but is redemption too late?

For all inquiries, please email Living Beach Publishing at
publishing@LivingBeach.com

UMBERTO NARDOLICCI

EYE OF THE NOMAD

WAR OF FEAR | BOOK I

For information about this title or to order other books and/or electronic media, contact the publisher:
Living Beach Publishing
publishing@LivingBeach.com
WarOfFear.com

ISBN: 979-8-9902451-2-9 (hardcover)
ISBN: 979-8-9902451-3-6 (softcover)
ISBN: 979-8-9902451-1-2 (eBook)

Printed in the United States of America
Cover Design: Kristi Kovacs
Interior Illustrations: Kristi Kovacs, Karina Mingazova, and Catrina Cowart
Cartographer: Mikael Asikainen

Dedicated to my father,
who always loved stories of a long time ago.
"Your love has etched a memory that will
live forever in our hearts."

OUR MISSION

First and foremost is to entertain! Beyond that, I hope to bring awareness and support to the organizations aiding our Nation's Veterans. This book is a historical fiction novel based on the true tales of warriors. It is a tribute to the courage, sacrifice, and resilience all patriots show in the face of unimaginable challenges. As a disabled veteran myself, along with my father, one of my two sons and with several relatives and friends who are veterans or active-duty military personnel, supporting organizations that are close to my heart, such as the Wounded Warrior Project, Tunnel to Towers Foundation, Nardmoor, and, of course, the DAV is very important to me.

All proceeds from the sale of this book will be donated to Veterans' causes. I hope you enjoy the story and feel inspired to give back in your own way, as these heroes deserve our support.

Nardo

CONTENTS

AUTHOR'S NOTE

Umberto's Apologia

1. This trilogy was inspired by the true story of Yasotay. While all characters and events are based on historical figures, places, and deeds, I do not supply a bibliography. I do not doubt that this work's historical and cultural references have several opposing or obscure counter-references. However, I can confidently assure the reader that I used only "those facts" that best helped convey this story. With that said, I have made every effort to use recognized representations of historical people, places, and events.

2. The spelling of all the names of people, places, and things in this work are my contrived adaptations based on the multiple variations that appear in the wide range of reference materials used as sources throughout the writing of this trilogy. These include real historical characters, locations, and objects (or ones entirely made up by me). I chose the easiest to *say*, *hear*, and *spell* wherever and whenever possible. For example, throughout history, a character in the book is referred to as Master Changchun, Master Qiu Chuji, and Tongmi, along with a host of other Chinese and Mongolian phonetically represented names. Since this is irrelevant to the story, I use the simple Master Chang.

3. The differences in speech, tone, inflection, and body language, which are crucial components of communication, vary significantly between the cultures presented in this story.

Unfortunately, many things just don't translate, so I have avoided detailed descriptions and representations of these differences because I am communicating this original manuscript in English. Therefore, these differences are addressed on the few occasions when they are relevant to the story.

4. With respect to measurements, I used several that are Chinese and/or Mongolian. A *chi* is approximately a foot. A *li* is a little less than a third of a mile. Ten li equals roughly 3.1 miles or approximately 5 kilometers. A *shi* is a unit of time equivalent to two hours, so "half a shi" is one hour.

PROLOGUE

Jin, Capital of Zhongdu, late spring, 1165 CE

Feet spread shoulder-length apart, Emperor Shizong, dark-haired and clean-cut, peered down at the ornate stick in the grip of his delicate, privileged hands. "I am intrigued by this... this child and his potential," proclaimed Shizong, appearing relaxed and focused on playing his game of *chuiwan*. The eyes of the sixty or so guests in attendance were glued to the emperor's every move. The tip of Shizong's tongue slightly protruded from the left corner of his mouth as he concentrated on aligning the flat end of his stick with the wooden ball at his feet. He was comfortable performing in front of a crowd. His next move was to strike the ball toward the hole in the lawn, two-and-a-half paces away, all the while trying to converse with Master Chang, which was proving to be a challenge for the priest.

"It's all very interesting, my emperor," responded Chang, mildly irritated by the lapses in their conversation. *This silly game is a distraction; why did he call me here?* "My emperor, I am still unsure how you see this child relating to our efforts?" Chang's formal, deep-red *daopao* robes, tied at his lean waist by a black *dadai* belt, and his simple black hat topped with a round, silver pin made him appear positively priestly. Chang was shadowed by his watchful and silent lead assistant, Master Gao, who was nearly identical in appearance and stance. The priest maintained a respectful tone and a pleasing smile with the emperor, but the beleaguered look on his usually kind face betrayed his frustration.

"He's an amazing young man," said Shizong. Noticing Chang's irritation, a wry smile formed on the emperor's face, whose prickly whiskers ran around his mouth and down to his chin. He mumbled something as if he were talking to himself. Focusing on the immediate challenge, he lightly struck the ball with his jewel-encrusted stick. The perfectly round wooden ball, not much bigger than a walnut, rolled toward the hole in the lawn six *chi* away. The eyes of everyone in attendance were fixated on the ball as it moved across the well-manicured grass toward the impeccably cut round hole, measuring just under a half chi in diameter and depth.

"Go...IN...," playfully exclaimed the emperor. A smile spread from his pursed lips into a broad grin as the ball approached the hole. The emperor quickly stepped forward in unison as the ball spilled into the hole, making a hollow, cavernous noise as it hit the bottom of the wooden cup. Light applause erupted in the south garden from the guests gathered to watch their emperor play *chuiwan* with the elegant Lady Shimo. Only those in his favor were allowed the privilege of observing today's game in the blistering sun. The midday shadows sheltered small portions of the south garden, giving shade to just a fortunate few. Today's parade of gentry, arrayed in their colorful *hanfu*, comprised almost all the fashionable elite of the 12th-century Jin Empire.

"I think he's adorable," purred Lady Shimo, the emperor's kittenish courtesan whose floral-red, exquisitely designed hanfu hung down in the back, making her look as if she had a tail. "I asked him about the Buddha, and his answer was, was...precious." Then, the pretty paramour, whose apple-red cheeks and plump round bottom had won the emperor's favor, brought her stick back and struck her ball toward the same hole.

"See, I think the fair lady is infatuated with the young boy, and I think you will be too, Chang," said the emperor as he admired Lady Shimo's sultry body move sprightly with the roll of her ball directly into the hole at his feet. "Nice shot!" exclaimed the emperor with a playful grin that showed his pearly white teeth. All those in attendance, while subdued, did show their appreciation with nods, hand gestures, and verbal displays of approval.

"You will see, Master Chang, you will see!" chided the emperor as he retrieved his ball from the hole. "Have you ever played *chuiwan*?" he asked the priest. "It originated hundreds of years ago; I think it was called *buda* in the Tang Dynasty…it's great fun!"

"I look forward to meeting him, my Emperor," replied the venerated Master Chang, who was one of the North's seven most respected and venerated Taoist priests. As a disciple of the most revered Master Wang Chong, he was no ordinary priest. "And no, my Emperor, I have never had the pleasure of playing *chuiwan*."

"That's three hits for you and four for me, Wulu. You always win," Lady Shimo teased in a playful voice. Hearing her use his intimate name, never used in public, made his cheeks flush just a little. The emperor handed his ornate stick to one of the eunuch assistants among the crowd of those waiting to serve him. Eunuchs attended to his every need, from consoling him on military machinations to wiping his nether region. They were a valued commodity within the imperial palace.

"Oh, here he is now!" exclaimed Lady Shimo loudly, her baby face bubbling and body bouncing while she excitedly clapped her hands in a light and rapid fashion.

Princess Jia and her son Yasotay entered the sun-soaked south lawn through the Moon Gate, a large circular opening in the garden wall covered in tangled green vines and adorned with hundreds of little white flowers. It was one of the main entrances to the emperor's residence. A woman, who appeared to be somewhat older than the princess, followed two paces behind the pair, a governess to the young boy.

Princess Jia was radiant in her flowing, floor-length, deep royal-blue silk hanfu. The gold-colored piping around its edges matched the intricately folded gold sash around her middle. Her delicate foot-wear, also gold with royal blue stitching, rounded out the stunning and well-planned presentation of the twenty-year-old princess as she walked through the Moon Gate. With every intricate detail of her beautiful face, thin lips, large brown eyes, and attire fashioned to present a very delicate, refined, and contrived look, her natural beauty was almost obscured.

"Princess Jia and young Yasotay, I would like to introduce you to Master Chang," said the emperor.

"It is my pleasure to meet you, Princess Jia, and certainly you, young Yasotay!" greeted Chang. "I have already heard so much about you."

While he deeply bowed, a small pair of round hazel eyes, those of the five-year-old child's, calmly held Chang's gaze. The child's face had been dusted with a thin coat of white powder, making his eyes and their startling hazel hue stand out. Dressed in a plain cream tunic with a blood-red sash around his middle to match his silk trousers, the young boy responded, "It is also an honor to meet you, Master Chang."

Princess Jia, reflexively fussing with and straightening the bottom of Yasotay's jacket, noticed the prized dragon figurine held tightly in the boy's hand. Princess Jia hissed and whispered in an aggravated tone, "Yasotay, give me that." The green figurine seemed enormous compared to his tiny hands. The boy refused, tightened his hold, and looked to his governess instead. Mana held out her hand and smiled kindly at him with warm eyes, and Yasotay handed the dragon over. Chang looked on at this exchange and smiled.

"Good, now we'll show what this young boy can do. Let's see," the emperor paused, thinking, "What can I ask him?" Cupping the palm of his hand under his chin with his fingers on his cheek, he was thinking intently, getting straight to the task at hand. Yasotay looked to Mana, and she responded with a slight affirmative nod and another warm, encouraging smile. The young man turned his attention back to the emperor and Master Chang.

"I have one," proclaimed the emperor to Master Chang. "I have a question for young Yasotay, which will honor you and your interest in ethical matters." Chang bowed in appreciation. Then, the emperor looked directly at Yasotay and said, "I would like you to recite section seventy-four of the *Tao Te Ching*."

"Stand up straight and answer the question!" ordered Princess Jia to her son, who was already standing perfectly straight.

Yasotay took one small step forward and began to speak, "If men are not afraid to die, it is of no avail to threaten them with death. If men constantly fear dying, and breaking the law means a man will be killed, who will dare break the law? The official executioner kills. Substituting him is like substituting the master carpenter who carves; you can do so, but one rarely escapes harm."

"Very well said. Well done, young man!" responded Chang with a broad smile, mildly surprised that this child, whose appearance and doll-like performance conjured thoughts of a trained monkey, could articulate so clearly from the great works of Master Lao Tzu.

"But do you know what it means?" asked Chang in a jocular tone bordering on sarcasm.

"All creatures fear death," said Yasotay matter-of-factly. "Master Lao knows that each of us fights our own internal war of fear. Once cornered by death, both man and beast do but one of two things: fight with fury or cower in fear!" The young man paused for a moment in thought. "Plagues, wars, and famine make death a daily reminder; people lose faith…they cower. Master Lao was speaking to those in authority, those leaders who choose to kill deviants, and others who disobey the law. Leaders must be careful not to create too much fear within those they lead, lest they become immune to death as a deterrent, which makes them more inclined to strike out in response. Their yearning for a supreme god and the hope for something or someplace better renews *faith*! Therefore, the belief in a god is both useful and difficult when managing the affairs of state."

His young voice changed tempo when he expressed the after-thought, "The closing point, referencing the master carpenter and the executioner, merely argues that those trained and conditioned for kill-ing are best kept to their calling."

Chang's long, clean-shaven face began to change color, turning vis-ibly red. His visions of a trained monkey were long gone. Not sure what to say, mouth gaping wide, totally surprised, he instinctively responded, "Yes, well, I agree, interesting, and thank you for that!"

"He's a bit of a know-it-all," proclaimed the emperor, breaking up the awkward moment. "But I believe that if you are building this library of all known knowledge, as you put it, to discover some supreme singular..."

"My Emperor!" interrupted Chang, speaking over him. One of the eunuchs drew his breath in loudly at this breach of protocol. No one ever interrupts the emperor.

"Yes, I know, Chang, secrecy and all, but someone like young Yaso-tay here could be a valuable addition to our efforts." The emperor did the signature twirl of his chin whiskers with the side of his left index finger.

"Your staff seems less than satisfactory for this effort! Have you considered bringing on others?" asked the emperor, giving Yasotay an affectionate pat on the back while extending a dubious glance at the less-than-satisfactory Gao. The emperor's slight was received loud and clear by Chang's principal assistant, who just stood there, silently observing their interactions. His teal-colored daopao, typical Taoist attire, was aged and slightly faded but with perfect folds and creases.

"Yes, Emperor, I understand your point," said Chang with a nod, not actually comprehending the point or even thinking about an answer. Still, the bewildered look on his face revealed much. Chang was strug-gling to understand what he had just witnessed with this child.

"He is still too young," said Princess Jia hesitantly. "The emperor must be talking about once he is *of age* for such things."

"Yes, obviously, Jia, I'm not looking to pull the baby from the breast," the emperor conceded. After expressing an odd look of surprise and confusion with his brow furrowed, he continued, "It seems that for now, Master Chang will have to rely on understudies who are hopefully smart enough to understand what we are handsomely paying to collect." Then, as an additional intentional insult, the emperor mocked Chang, whispering, "…and, more importantly, for what purpose we labor."

"How old is he, four or five?" asked Chang incredulously.

"He was five just two weeks ago," said Princess Jia.

"Five years old!" Chang hesitated for a moment to bring his emotions under control. "Young Yasotay is many years away, and I would certainly welcome him when the time comes, Emperor…I deeply apologize for any misunderstanding." Chang's long face softened. "But if there is nothing further, I must take my leave." Chang bowed deeply and awaited the emperor's dismissal. The emperor feigned a nod of assent and quickly turned away, which told the priest, *You are fine, leave.* Chang bowed for the last time toward Princess Jia and Yasotay. Then, giving the boy one long, last look, he slipped out quietly with his shadow, Gao, trailing closely behind.

"I had heard of this child, but I wasn't expecting THAT," whispered Gao to Chang, dumbfounded, as they walked quickly through the Moon Gate and out of earshot from the gathering.

"What was *that*?" Chang exclaimed in a low, exasperated tone, seemingly speaking to himself. "That child spoke as if he possessed the intellect of an ageless master! His tone and the confidence in his voice sounded more like those of a very mature and learned person!"

"Who is he?" asked Gao, whose low tone and mannerisms seemed to replicate Chang's, just in a younger version.

"He is the second cousin to the emperor, Princess Jia being the emperor's first cousin."

"Who is his father?" asked Gao, "that child looks different!"

"I don't know." Chang's eyes narrowed, his brow furrowed in confusion. "Princess Jia's husband died soon after she was wed. All I know is she left Zhongdu for the port city of Pingzhou after her husband's death and returned a year later with his child."

"His facial features look a little odd," added Gao, "he almost looks foreign."

Chang ignored this comment. "That had to be some sort of trick," mused Chang out loud. "I could swear I've read a similar opinion of Master Lao's work."

"Are you saying he memorized some obscure commentary on section seventy-four of the *Tao Te Ching*?" asked Gao. "Who would do that?"

"I don't know what I'm saying. Maybe the emperor gave him the question in advance," said Chang. The priest hesitated momentarily, then continued, "Gao, I want you to talk to our friends and find out as much as you can about this child prodigy. Who his father is, his history, everything."

"Yes, Master Chang, I will attend to it!"

"What of the emperor breaking protocol and mentioning our project in public?" asked Gao.

"What of it?" replied Chang sharply. "He can tell what we do to everyone if he likes."

"I don't trust those around him! They latch on to him like parasites stealing crumbs from the sides of his mouth," said Gao.

"Those fools know what we do, but it doesn't matter. It doesn't change anything!"

CHAPTER ONE 一

Wudang Mountains, spring, 1175 CE

The two revered masters sat facing each other in the precisely prescribed positions. The mats upon which they sat were set to an exact location. The grand room had a musky scent of tung oil and jasmine, with its walls, beams, and rafters made of cypress and poplar. It had an ancient and almost magical look and feel. All who entered this room realized they shared an experience, a union with those from the past. Various elements of mysticism were part of the room's original design, from the dragon heads meticulously carved into the beams overhead to the beautifully sewn tapestries hung from the walls. Three small wooden benches comprised the extent of the sparse furnishings in this main hall.

All preparations had been made, and the decorum established, checked, and then checked again. The two priests in full formal ministerial attire had just taken their seats in Dragon Hall, located in a remote mountain temple on the border of the Jin and Song Dynasties. Their flowing robes crafted from silk, Master Chang in blue and Master Jing in green, echoed harmony with nature. But, if a facial expression could speak, Master Chang's face was screaming, "FINALLY!" Having just suffered through the myriad of Master Jing's tiresome rituals, introductions, and prayers, Chang was weary and sincerely desired an end to the pomp and circumstance.

After three weeks of travel and little sleep due to the anticipation of this meeting, Chang had been patient long enough and now wanted to proceed to the long-awaited reunion. The round-faced man across from him was Master Jing, the lead Daoshi of the Purple Cloud Temple. The formal ceremonial greeting, reserved for esteemed and honored visitors, seemed to drag on until Jing finally concluded and gave Chang his full and undivided attention—in silence. There was a long pause as Chang wondered if they would be interrupted by another perfunctory *Book of Rites* ceremony.

Chang finally spoke in a low and slow voice, "Where is the young gifted one now?"

Jing's brown eyes lit up, knowing very well to whom Chang referred. "Yasotay is currently in the east courtyard with his fellow students, my Daoshi," Jing spoke with proper tone and pronunciation, crisp and clear, as any subordinate would speak to his superior on such an occasion. As head priest of the Purple Cloud Temple, Jing was held in high regard within the Taoist order. The arrival of the venerated Master Chang to his mountain temple created opportunities for Jing. Someone like Chang, who holds favor with the emperor and the elite cabal alike, could substantially help his temple's cause. This fact gave Chang province and Jing the impetus for all the perfectly executed pomp and circumstance.

"I would like to see him now!" Chang's statement was more of a command than a request.

"Why, yes, my Daoshi, right away, Daoshi." Jing was on his feet with a quick bow before finishing his sentence, eager to show Chang the way. "Please, right this way, please," he gestured as he walked with his right arm outstretched and head bowing several times.

"This temple is blessed with your presence today, Master Chang, and I was wondering if there was any way that you could help us get the materials necessary to complete the planned additions to the temple," Jing respectfully asked as he led their progress toward the temple's east courtyard.

"Humph," grunted Chang.

Jing was surprised and confused by Chang's brusque manner. This request was within Chang's power to grant, and Jing was trying his best to please his superior with very exact adherence to the Taoist rites he performed. Yasotay, the gifted one, had helped Jing prepare and rehearse weeks before Chang's arrival. Every minute detail of these rites was practiced multiple times to ensure absolute precision.

They walked in silence, their bright robes flowing in the late afternoon breeze, arms tucked inside the fluted sleeves of their intricately decorated garments. Their appearance was designed to indicate intellect and a higher standing in the Jin court—rather than the lowly drab cotton and hemp daopao that those beneath them wore. The temple's main building was ornate with large decorative columns and a bright berry-red roof. The main temple was situated in the shadow of a large and wide cliff face rimmed with gigantic rocks, and this building was part of a series of buildings scattered across a large mountainous area.

Their path to the courtyard snaked through what felt to Chang like an endless garden of well-manicured foliage with brightly colored, sweet-smelling flowers of narcissus and jasmine. Flowering Yulan branches hung across the path in numerous places. Ivy-covered trellises were scattered amongst numerous matching well-built buildings. The flowering plants made a living tunnel in certain spots along the trail. A rush of memories suddenly reminded Chang that *the Purple Cloud Temple in the Wudang Mountains is simply...beautiful.*

The foliage exploded with intoxicating scents and vibrant living colors that Chang recalled from years past. While Jing's students and staff kept the facility immaculate and operational, the fifty-year-old temple frequently required maintenance. The surrounding hills were covered with a lush green shroud of spruce and pine trees. The scent of the spring flowers and trees seemed to chase them as they walked along the path, catching up with their nostrils now and again.

While Chang had enjoyed many spring walks through this same lush green valley, he needed to put those thoughts aside and focus. What should he expect? What has become of *the gifted one?* He and Jing came upon a narrow path between two buildings, emptying into a smaller courtyard on the eastern side of the temple compound. They stopped beneath an overhang, where they could see the whole courtyard but were not visible to those in the yard. Chang could see twenty-five to thirty students in the throes of different activities. A handful or so sat at desks, writing. A couple of students worked on canvas and easel, painting, while others toiled with bamboo dizi flutes. They were attempting to play—*Not so well*, thought Chang to himself, as he winced at a misplayed note.

Chang was tired and frustrated. He didn't know what he was expecting, but it wasn't this. Looking at Jing, his junior, he broke the silence between them and, in a rapid fashion, asked, "What is this? What are they doing? Which one is *HE*?" Chang's stern voice rang out.

Jing sputtered, vainly trying to answer all three questions at once. He was obviously confused. "They, they, this, he is…this is their open practice time, my Daoshi," Jing stumbled over his words as he tried to answer in a rushed voice.

Not waiting for Jing to elaborate further, Chang continued, "And what are they doing?" He waved his hand toward two young men facing each other in combat stance, one clearly taller than the other. Each had one hand up and one behind his back, doing some odd form of hand wrestling with their forward hands.

"I believe he calls it the *hand-dance*, and that is Yasotay on the right," replied Jing, referring to the taller of the two hand-dancing students.

Jing noticed the quizzical look on Chang's face. "It's something he's been working on." Shrugging his shoulders, he continued, "Yasotay says it combines Tao Yin and the Eighteen Hands of Luohan. As he explained to me, it's a training technique focused on balancing energy equally between Yin and Yang. It trains you to exploit your opponent's energy by bringing it into balance with your own. Thus, no matter how slight or fierce their blow, you can bring their expended force into harmony and under your control. It starts with body position. Then, you place your hand against your opponents. You begin with balancing your force with another's. They press hard, you respond with soft..." recounted Jing in an unconvincing tone that tapered off, "the merging with...I'm sorry, my Daoshi. Yasotay can explain it far better than I."

Chang watched Yasotay silently for a long moment, thinking. Finally, Chang said, "Yes, I believe I will speak with him alone in my quarters. Bring him to me immediately!"

They both turned and slowly began the walk back toward Dragon Hall. "As you wish, my Daoshi," said Jing in a submissive tone, realizing something had changed in Chang's demeanor.

"How long has he been under your care?" asked Chang.

"Yasotay arrived at the temple three years ago. Quite an amazing young man. He has a visual acuity and memory, the likes of which I have never seen or even heard of before!" exclaimed Jing.

Chang said, "Yes, I met him once...he was just five years old. His mother paraded him around like a trained monkey to entertain the elite. He recited detailed passages of great works from memory. Initially, I was amused, then quickly confused when he gave his astute opinion. In the end, I concluded it was some sort of staged trick. The emperor likes to play his games. We were formally introduced, but I doubt he remembers me...he was so very young at the time."

"Yasotay's ability to recall what he reads is no trick, my Daoshi," said Jing, "and he certainly maintains his opinions! So, when he first arrived, having heard of the talents of this twelve-year-old boy, I wanted to see this for myself. I put him to the test! Within moments of his arrival, I gave him parchment and pen and instructed him to write the Thirteen

Classics from memory. I assumed this was an impossible task for one so young. But, to my surprise and delight, in a short amount of time, the first book appeared on my desk, then the second. Within the year, he perfectly transcribed all thirteen books from memory, with handwriting so articulate I had them bound, and they now sit in a place of honor in my library. He made me a believer."

"…and what of his studies here?" asked Chang.

"During his first three months, he read every manuscript in our library and organized, transcribed, and annotated every secret *fulu* in the temple. Many of which he had already set to memory. His role here, ever since, has been more of a student-teacher and head librarian." In an exasperated tone, Jing added, "Too young to be a priest and too knowledgeable in the ways of the Tao to be a student. He's so unlike any of my other students. What else was I to do with him?" Jing paused and looked over at Chang. "He still has the curiosity of a child's mind but not yet the maturity to match his intellect. Nor does he have the self-awareness one would expect his brilliance would afford, something he will hopefully gain in time."

"Yes, well, he has studied in several unique and unusual places from what I've been told," added Chang. "I was told he knows more than most scholars but with a child's diffidence."

In a reflective tone, Jing continued, "He's certainly not shy. I can assure you he has lived a very monastic life. I was told he studied under Master Zhizain, the great Buddhist monk from the Song Dynasty."

"I know of Master Zhijain," Chang repeated his name, correcting Jing's pronunciation in a respectful tone.

"Master Zhijain…Yes, well, it is rumored that Emperor Shizong sent Yasotay to Master Zhijain to make a statement to those in the South: *We are smarter than you!* While we have peace, there is still great rivalry between the Jin and Song Empires. The Song Empire put Yasotay to work. He spent two years with the Zhenren, Master Zhu at the White Deer Grotto Academy, transcribing and annotating manuscripts. It is said he worked side by side with Master Zhu right up until he came to me. Can you believe it, a child working alongside a Zhenren, a person

6

considered perfect in every way?" Jing continued, "The story, as I was told, is Emperor Shizong directed Master Yasotay to be returned to the North. Upon hearing this command, Master Zhu was very displeased and expressed his displeasure. They say he lost his head figuratively, and from what I heard, he almost lost it literally too. To everyone's surprise, Master Zhu traveled here to deliver Yasotay, delivering him to me personally. He has an obvious affection for the boy, traveling all this way. His parting words, and only words to me for that matter, were, "*Challenge him!*"

They arrived at the entrance to Chang's quarters, where Master Gao, his assistant, stood just outside the door and awaited their return. "I appreciate your candor…I will retire for now and do not wish to be disturbed. Have Yasotay brought to me when he reaches a break in his studies," instructed Chang, softening his insistence on seeing him immediately.

"As you request, my Daoshi," Jing answered. He and Gao bowed respectfully, and with the slightest bow from Chang, Jing was off to deal with pressing temple business. Chang entered his chambers, with Gao following closely behind. He sat and took a moment to clear his mind.

Gao interrupted his silence, "What crazy circumstances this young man creates wherever he goes."

Chang explained, "I'm not the only one interested in him!"

"The rumors of his abilities are ridiculous. He has become a legend, a myth among the common folk. They say he can conjure the words of the divine himself."

"…simple fools!" Chang spat. "But I think he may help us truly understand 'The Way,' the deepest truths, and real knowledge of the unknown. I think this is possible!"

Gao added, "Convincing the emperor to have this flesh-and-blood *parable* returned was a risk. The peace between Jin and Song is fragile already. Why are you risking your reputation? Your life? He's still just a young man."

"My main goal with young Yasotay is to prove what I already believe to be true."

"Which is?" inquired Gao with a puzzled look.

"If someone possessed a working knowledge of most of the known written facts in human history, could that person answer the big and seemingly impossible questions that plague mankind?" Chang's eyes were filled with passion as he spoke, "How to turn rock into gold? The divine purpose for man on earth? Would he know which god figure is the real God, or is there one at all? What are the stars, and where do they come from? Does man have to die? And most important, can man achieve singularity with the divine, and if so, how?" Chang's eyes looked up, searching.

It was apparent to Gao that Chang truly believed Yasotay made the answers to these inextricable questions within reach. Gao couldn't help but feel like Yasotay was casting a spell on Master Chang.

"It seems a very lofty goal for someone, for anyone, even this protégé!" responded Gao.

"If through knowledge and his gift, Yasotay can help to answer just one of these questions!" Chang leaned forward, speaking in a low, intent voice, "That's why I need Yasotay at my school. And, as an ancillary benefit, we will use his amazing gifts to establish the White Cloud Temple as a great learning center. Riches will flood in from all the handsomely paying students. He will help me grow White Cloud into the greatest learning temple on earth!" Chang paused in thought, then continued in a different tone, "He should prove very helpful for my aim if he is as they say…respectable, imaginative, creative, likable, and most importantly, gifted."

The master shifted slightly in his seat and continued, "I guess we will see!"

"I am told one challenges his accuracy about any manuscript at their peril," Gao declared.

"If that is true, I can't imagine what it's like to have all those manuscripts in one's head, especially for one so young. For me, it would be like having Lao Tzu, Confucius, Buddha, Mohammad, Jesus, and every well-informed sage arguing for space in my head…competing for the words from my mouth…*I have to think*," he said in a much louder voice than he intended. Chang added, "Well now, wait, hold on, think…why waste time questioning him the way I would any other understudy?"

"We know he's smart, but he's still just a child."

"Let's see what I can do to challenge him, as Master Zhu so aptly put it," said Chang. "It will undoubtedly help answer my main question… is he more than just memorization? Were his comments as a child just rehearsed? Can he bring together all the lessons, knowledge, and truths he holds on the tip of his tongue?"

Chang was interrupted by the sound of a board creaking outside his door. "We will find out soon enough!" he exclaimed with bridled excitement in a lowered tone, giving Gao his leave. He quickly and quietly slipped behind a partition wall out of sight, knowing he had planted the seed he intended to cultivate.

"Come," bellowed Chang before any knock or arrival announcement was made.

In walked the young man, barely fifteen years old, who was already taller than the average height of most grown men. He appeared a little lanky, but at first glance, nothing would make one think there was anything unique or different about him.

"It's a pleasure to see you again, Master Chang," Yasotay said with a smile and respectful bow at the entrance. He wore the same simple hemp daopao as most young students.

"Yes, come in and sit, sit," invited Chang. "I would like to have a conversation with you."

"Yes, Master Chang," replied Yasotay respectfully as he straightened his back and walked toward where Chang pointed for him to sit. One fluid motion from standing to sitting, and Yasotay was eye to eye with Chang. The priest noticed Yasotay's hazel eyes; they seemed to have a green hue—something odd that he hadn't remembered.

Chang began awkwardly, "I would like to discuss…"

A thumping sound from the quarters' decorative, carved-tiger wooden door knocker stopped the conversation before it began.

"What is it?" Chang barked in an exasperated tone.

A timid voice from the other side of the door could be heard. "Master Jing asked me to offer you ... would like some tea, sir?" Yasotay recognized the voice of Yichen, a young assistant whose current purpose in life was to run errands for Jing.

"I would like NOT TO BE DISTURBED!" Chang's voice rang out. "And since you've already done so, bring us some tea!"

"Yes, Master," Yichen's voice quivered.

Chang regained his composure, took a deep breath, and asked, "What I would like to discuss with you, Yasotay, is your future," said Chang. "But first, tell me about yourself."

Thoughtfully, Yasotay began, "Well, Master Chang, I was born in Tianjin. I never met my father. My mother and I moved to..."

"No, no, no," interrupted Chang. "I'm well aware of your history, where you were born, where you have lived." Chang hesitated, thinking, *I know more than you probably know.* He took notice of Yasotay's slightly rounded eyes and uniquely different facial features, which brought to mind Gao's report on what he learned digging into Yasotay's past. Then, finally, Chang blurted out in reaction to that thought, "I have recently spoken with your mother. I don't doubt you miss her very much!"

The expression on Yasotay's face noticeably changed. Yasotay imagined he had been sent south to the Song Dynasty *for his own good,* just as his mother had insisted. But he later guessed that it was to benefit the Jin Dynasty. Chang noticed the change in his facial expression, realizing he'd hit a nerve. He quickly switched back to his original line of questioning. "No, I am interested in hearing about *you. What* do you like to do for fun? Who are you? What about friends? Who is your favorite writer, poet, or philosopher? That type of thing!"

"Well, Master Chang . . ." Yasotay shifted in his seat and looked to the ceiling for answers. He had never been asked these questions before. Over the years, he had been asked ten thousand questions about all the spiritual masters, past empires, tactics and wars, weapons, and magic. This is what had always been expected of him, but not this, not questions about himself. There was a long pause, and Yasotay began to feel as though the air in the room was stagnant.

A wry grin slowly spread across Chang's face as the moments ticked by. *I stumped the miracle boy on my first question,* he thought, feeling triumphant. Then he said in a dry, sarcastic tone, "I expected some rehearsed commitment to the *Tao Te Ching* and Master Lao Tzu."

Still in thought, Yasotay sat motionless. Finally, he sighed and responded, "I respect Master Lao Tzu, of course, but you asked me: who am I personally? I guess I am someone who loves to learn. My passion is learning, applying what I can learn, and discovering how it relates to my life." Chang sensed his response was given based upon significant consideration and deep thought.

"But you retain so much knowledge; why the passion for more?" asked Chang, whose body language conveyed a genuine interest in the answer.

"I am amazed by what men say, do, and write and how this relates to me. Regarding having a gift, the visual acuity with manuscripts…its origins and purpose are a mystery to me." Yasotay's voice trailed off, and his body language was open and relaxed, showing vulnerability. Chang sensed this change. "I love running through the woods all along the mountainside with my staff, as Master Jing says, 'bounding about over creeks and logs.'" Yasotay imitated Jing's voice as best he could.

Chang snickered at the boy's imitation. "Interesting. Coming to the White Cloud Temple with me will be good for you. There are many trails through the woods, and you will be near your mother. That should be a good thing," suggested Chang, changing to an upbeat tone and acting like some hard-fought agreement had already been reached. Finally, Chang exclaimed, "Good, it's settled. I have much to teach you, and there are many things for you to explore!"

Something occurred to Yasotay. "Yes, I would very much like to see my mother again," he whispered, almost to himself.

But it was loud enough that Gao could hear, still spying from behind the screen. *Yasotay forgot to mention the additional privilege of learning from the great Master Chang,* thought Gao while shaking his head.

"Great, you're going to be working with me for the foreseeable future, and we will do wonderful things together," proclaimed Chang. "We leave the day after tomorrow, and we will stop to see Master Yang, pick up the ceremonial fireworks, and do one more errand before we make our way home."

"Master?" Yasotay said in a questioning tone.

"Never mind young man, now give me your leave. I am tired and ready for rest. We will talk tomorrow," Chang stated as he stood and removed his outer jacket.

Yasotay stood and bowed, and as he opened the door to leave, there stood little Yichen, holding a tray with tea and cups in one hand while the other was on the door knocker. The motion of the door opening, along with the unexpected appearance of Yasotay, startled Yichen. His involuntary shudder caused a teacup from the tray to fall. Yasotay, moving fluidly, reached down to pluck the cup out of midair. He placed it back on the tray and patted Yichen's shoulder in a friendly gesture as he walked past him into the night air.

The night was calm and cool. Yasotay walked back to his sleeping quarters. As he did, he stopped to gaze in wonder at the thousands of stars in the sky. He contemplated his upcoming change, the journey ahead, seeing his mother, and working with Chang. And most importantly, seeing Mana. It had been a long time, too long.

As Chang walked along the path with Yasotay the next day in the brisk morning air, he announced, "I have made all the arrangements; we will be off at dawn tomorrow."

He looked over at the young man. "Are you prepared to leave?" queried Chang as they moved toward a small outbuilding designed similarly to all the other structures in the temple, just smaller.

However, this building was different in one material way: it was a ritual display case—a shrine. Multiple talisman posters hung on either side of the front pillars, with written quotes and ritual prayers. In the middle of the display sat a *guandao,* a large crescent-shaped blade with a long wooden staff-like handle. It had a spiked metal pommel, and the guandao's blade had a dragon's head on it. Yasotay knew this weapon well; he had cleaned and polished it many times. It was old and well-maintained, and he knew the blade was still very sharp.

"I have made all my preparations; what little I have to prepare," said Yasotay.

As they walked up to the building, a plump frog jumped from the path up ahead into a small pond alongside the path.

"Chicken of the Field, I believe it's called," said Chang.

"Yes, Daoshi, the Tiger Frog, also called 'Chicken of the Field.' I assume the name is because it's large and plump like a chicken, or maybe because it tastes like one," said Yasotay with a childish grin.

"So, I'll wager I know something about this blade that you don't!" Chang said playfully, nodding toward the display as they approached.

Yasotay gave him a questioning look. "What is it you know about the Green Dragon Crescent Blade?" asked Chang, gazing upon the display with its extensive assortment of prayers and talismans piled around it.

Both men paused and performed a perfunctory bow and quick prayer in front of the display.

"Same as you, Master. The Green Dragon is a weapon celebrated in the story of Guan Yu and the famous Battle of Yiling between the states of Shu and Wu," reported Yasotay. "Every child has sung the story of this reclining moon blade."

"Yes, Yasotay, but unlike all of those who only know the song, you and I know the secret that Guan Yu never used the blade in battle," continued Chang.

"Yes, Master…though most scholars who read history know this as well," added Yasotay, enjoying the friendly conversational dance with Chang regarding this renowned piece of weaponry.

"So, it appears to me that the child only knows what the song tells them, and the scholar only knows what books reveal," said Chang with a smile. "So, if books are the truth beyond the song, what truth lies beyond the books?"

"Only reality, Daoshi. What one can see, hear, taste, smell, and feel," replied Yasotay.

"…and what of the truths of the Tao?" asked Chang.

"As a Taoist, for me, that truth is in the teachings of Master Lao Tzu," answered Yasotay.

"Did he tell you these truths himself?" asked Chang in a sarcastic, rising tone.

"Yes, my Daoshi, as written in the *Tao Te Ching*," responded Yasotay.

"Is the *Tao Te Ching* not a book?" asked Chang. "What are the truths beyond its words?"

"How would one even answer that question, Master?" After a long pause, Yasotay pondered it and said, "Coming at it in reverse, I guess, since every culture in the world has its truth…their 'enlightened ones' are the ones who tell them what's true. Those enlightened ones are their truth, or at least in their followers' minds."

"Then the truth lies within one's followers?" enquired Chang.

"No, that's not what I am saying. The truth lies within the enlightened ones."

"Yes, now it sounds like you're asking more than you're stating," said Chang, and after a pause, he added, "To both of us, the *Tao Te Ching* and the teachings of Master Lao Tzu are the truth…the stories we've been told, the books we have read, the prayers we recite, the songs we have sung, this is *our* truth."

Shifting his body posture, Chang continued, "I was here the day that blade was placed where it now sits. I was also here thirty years ago as a student when I was startled awake by a tremendous noise. I ran out toward the commotion. We found the weapon in the rubble of the temple. The shaft had been broken, and the blade bent….It had been destroyed beyond all repair. You see, a large rock had dislodged from atop the cliff face and rolled down to fall where the blade sat. The weapon was damaged, and it was taken away. One day, it returned. And here it sits, repaired, all decorated with talismans and signs that state, 'Here is the Green Dragon, the famous weapon of Guan Yu.' So, I ask you: What did we bow and pray to when we arrived in the presence of this blade, this physical object? Do we hold it as the truth? Or did we bow and pray to the story about Guan Yu and the Green Dragon told here in these talismans?" asked Chang, waving his hand toward the shrine.

Yasotay looked at the proclamations of the phrases around the weapon. The blade appeared different in some way, changed.

"There are several errors," said Yasotay. "The sayings about Guan Yu are wrong; that is not how they are officially recounted." He was referring to the prayers, statements, and talisman hanging on signs around the blade.

"Oh really?" said Master Chang in a curious tone.

"Mistakes jump right from the page for me, like the frog jumping across our path moments ago. They jump out from most things I read, at least ever since I can remember. I didn't have the heart to tell Master Jing. He's so proud of this display. Many come to see the Green Dragon. They give their respects; they leave gifts. As Master Jing told me when I arrived, he wrote these quotes, prayers, and talismans with his own hand."

"I didn't notice…jumping frogs, you say?" asked Chang. "Does this happen with all things in error that you read?"

"Yes, my Daoshi," said Yasotay.

After a long pause, Chang said thoughtfully, "I want you to do me a favor, Yasotay."

"Anything, my Daoshi," he immediately replied.

"If I write something erroneous, and it jumps out at you, I want you to tell me," said Chang. "If I say something wrong, some misquote, or incorrectly stated historical fact, I want you to correct me."

"Yes, my Daoshi," said Yasotay, in agreement, "but what if you say something that *makes the frog jump* when we are among subordinates? Pointing this out would be disrespectful!"

"I would rather be the fool that misspoke and now knows the truth than the fool that proceeds in his own foolishness, not knowing any better," answered Chang. "Although, remember my young sage, both are better than the wretched fool who misspeaks to deceive."

"Even the most wretched of fools teach the most learned sage how not to be!" added Yasotay.

"Agreed, well, wait, who said that?" asked Chang. "Was it Master Sun Tzu in *The Art of War*, or was it Confucius in *The Spring and Autumn Annals*?"

"I am not sure…" Yasotay replied, fully knowing the answer.

"I don't believe you," said Chang. "We're going to need to work on this. We'll have a signal, you and I. You will bring your right finger to the side of your nose on the rare occasions I misquote the masters whose thoughts and writings you appear to possess at the tip of your tongue," instructed Chang. "In this way, you will speak outside the knowledge of others."

"Yes, my Daoshi…as you wish," replied Yasotay.

The party gathered at the temple gate the following day and prepared for the journey ahead. Master Chang wore his thick cotton travel daopao, bright berry-red in color, and was sitting on his horse fussing with a small wooden bowl with an intricate carving on the rim. Yasotay sat on a young mare and wore a simple *shanku*, a suit made from coarse, dull-white fabric. As with all shanku jackets, the left side was wrapped over the right to prevent one's sword from tangling in the clothing.

Master Chang traveled with an entourage of three priests, Master Gao, Master Kang, and Master Chao. All three were dressed in immaculate, teal-colored robes to signify their ordained life in the priesthood. The priests tended to the extra horses, ladened with all the necessary supplies for the long trip. Additionally, Master Chang had four armed men wearing the emperor's colors and carrying his flags. Upon orders from the emperor, the men were tasked with guarding Master Chang and seeing him return safely to the White Cloud Temple. The warriors carried everything they needed for their own personal comfort and sustenance. Yasotay guided his horse close to where Chang sat upon his horse.

"What is that, Master Chang?" asked Yasotay, nodding at the wooden bowl Chang held.

"It's a compass. If I have put enough water in the bowl, the turtle's tail should be pointing south," informed Chang.

Yasotay stretched his body and lengthened his neck to peer into the bowl. He saw a small wooden turtle floating in the water with its tail pointing south.

"The tail points true, my Daoshi, to the south!" confirmed Yasotay, motioning in the same direction.

"Yes, well, this little turtle has come in handy several times on journeys such as these," said Chang, placing his index finger on the little bobbing turtle. Then, while still hanging onto the bowl and the turtle, he flicked the bowl, emptying the water, and placing the bowl and the turtle into a small brown leather pouch, he pulled the drawstring shut in one swift and smooth motion as if he had performed this ritual ten thousand times. But this time, instead of tucking it away in his saddlebag, he handed it to Yasotay. "Keep this; I have others."

"You are most gracious, my Daoshi. Thank you," replied Yasotay gratefully.

Master Jing was there to see them off and checked and rechecked with the three young priests to ensure their supplies were all in order.

"Master Jing," Chang said as he bowed respectfully at the priest. "Thank you for your hospitality. It was a delight to see the temple in such pristine order. You do this temple great service. I give you my word that I will investigate helping you with the supplies you need for your additions to the temple. Oh, and one last thing … you might want to check the Green Dragon display; I noticed an error in one of the quotes."

"Yes, my Daoshi, right away," nodded Master Jing as his eyes swiveled to look directly at Yasotay, whose surprised look could not help but divulge the truth. Yasotay noticed Chang briefly make the gesture of touching his nose with his right finger before he spun his horse around and trotted off down the path just as swiftly and seemingly practiced as he had put the compass away. The remaining entourage began to follow behind him, one at a time in single file, with Yasotay lingering behind.

"You will be missed, Master Yasotay," insisted Master Jing, with a rueful smile on his round face but a fondness in his voice.

"Congratulations, it looks like you'll get the supplies you need, and thank you, my Daoshi. I am fortunate to have spent time here and learned so much from you. Thank you for that gift."

"It's kind of you to say that!" declared Master Jing, "safe travels." Jing stood at the gate and watched them until they were well out of sight.

They moved briskly on the relatively flat terrain for most of the first day. By early evening, the path had become much more challenging to travel. It led them up one incline and down the next, deeper and deeper into a dense forest. One of the warriors rode ahead and returned shortly after reporting he had found a site close enough to camp for the evening. Due to concern about bandits, the emperor had insisted on Chang's military escorts. The group arrived at the perfect spot for their purposes, unpacked their belongings, and set up camp for the evening.

The morning sun rose on a colorful collection of four-pole canopies, which the travelers used as shelter. The simple tents of various heights were set up in two separate groups. One group had a small tent for each of the four warriors. The other had three larger canopies for the five remaining travelers. The three understudies shared one shelter, while Yasotay and Chang each had their own. Their camp was situated just a short walk to a small creek where everyone could refill their water skins and water their horses.

The party began their second day traversing a steep mountain trail headed directly north near the Wafang River. The mountain pass became narrower and narrower to a point where there were only two directions to go: forward or back. Passing someone coming the other way would be tricky, if not impossible. This narrow, hazardous pass had been carved out of the mountain hundreds of years ago. Tumbling collections of small rocks regularly spilled onto the pathway, making the mind anxious, but the terrified looks revealed that it was the switchbacks that scared everyone to death. Erosion had made them the narrowest and most perilous part of the path. Unfortunately, while it was a commonly used route, it had a dangerously steep drop-off to their immediate left and a sharp incline up the mountain to their right. Suddenly, one of the horses dislodged a large rock that tumbled down the side and out of sight. They all watched it fall in silence. The path, carved into the middle of the mountainside, ran along a string of mountains, eventually arriving at the Luohe River basin area. Traversing this pass was always breathtaking and nerve-wracking at the same time.

The twelve horses walked along, in single file, in the middle of the narrow path. The two warriors led the way, followed by Chang, then the three priests, and the other two warriors who led the pack horses. Yasotay, on his horse, brought up the rear. The dull monotony of a long journey was starting to set in. The sun was out, with no breeze and not a cloud in the sky; it was a scorching day and a brutally hot ride.

Suddenly, a large crack rang out. A thunderous noise engulfed them, and the mountain appeared to be moving. Yasotay's horse reared, and a cloud of dust enveloped him. He could hear the warriors cry out. Their screams were seemingly drowned out by the tons of rock and shale sliding down the mountain. Yasotay started coughing and choking. His eyes were burning. He was momentarily unable to see. Smaller rocks pelted him as he struggled to calm his horse, which was dancing restlessly in place. The view of the ground directly in front of him, where two of the warriors had been sitting on their horses, was there one moment and *gone* the next. All Yasotay could see was a cloud of dust. The backside of the pack horse immediately in front of him had magically disappeared. All that was left where the two warriors and handful of horses had been moments ago was nothing but large rocks that hadn't been there before. As the dust began to settle, a stream of dirt could be seen trickling downhill. Yasotay thought he caught a glimpse of one of the warrior's red banners out of the corner of his eye. It was like a flash in his eye, and then it was gone.

As soon as the rockslide started to subside, he heard Chang yelling, "Yasotay! Are you SAFE?!" as a handful of small straggling rocks tumbled playfully down the incline, the main torrent complete.

"Yes, Master, I am fine," replied Yasotay as he exhaled heavily, realizing he was still holding his breath. Stunned and a little off-balance from all that had happened, he wiped away a film of dust from his forehead. Looking to his left over the ledge, down where the two warriors must now be, Yasotay proclaimed in a youthful, naïve tone, "I guess I should thank all the gods of every faith." Coming this close to his mortality made him uncertain about what else to say or how to act. Everyone had heard what he said and, for an awkward moment, just stared at him across the remaining path while a few smaller rocks were still dancing down the mountainside.

The seven stunned and disoriented riders dismounted from their horses. Most were looking down to where the bodies of their fallen companions must now lie. Others looked up at the mountain, concerned about the potential for more rockslides. All wore expressions of surprise and disbelief. The group was in shock, and after a moment, the awful realization of what had happened fell upon them. The two remaining warriors continued to stare downward, looking for their companions. One of them was on his knees at the edge of the trail, bits of dirt and rock crumbling away beneath his palms as he peered over the edge. He coughed into his shoulder, his eyes never leaving the ravine where he could just make out the twitching, twisted remains of a horse half protruding from a pile of dirt and stone.

"Can you make it across?" asked Chang, looking at the debris pile on the trail, separating Yasotay from the rest of them. Though the trail was intact, many rocks lay directly in Yasotay's path.

"I think I can," responded Yasotay hesitantly, who appeared more shaken than before as he looked up the mountainside at where the rocks had come from.

"Let me send someone over to help you," Chang insisted, his voice trembling with the stress of the situation.

"No, I'm fine," answered Yasotay, taking his first step on the debris-covered trail. "Be careful, Yasotay," directed Chang. Yasotay held the horse's reins in his hand as he and his horse deftly crossed to the other side. His horse walked behind him, stepping among the debris as if nothing was amiss. The two remaining warriors began to look for a way down the steep slope to see if they could offer any aid to their comrades.

The remaining travelers stood at the trail's edge, peering over the side. There was a long pause; the two warriors who went to look for the others were gone from view.

"It must be six hundred chi to the bottom," reported Gao.

"I'll bet at least that," said Kang.

"It's down so far. I can't see anything," stated Chang.

"Who were they?" asked Kang.

"I don't know their names. One spoke to me briefly; they have kept to themselves the whole trip," said Chao.

"One gave me some water when my waterskin ran dry yesterday… before we stopped to set up camp," Kang shared.

"The one who always carried the red banner was Liu Ao, and the other was Liu Bang," added Yasotay nonchalantly while peering over the side.

"You know this how? I haven't heard you speak to anyone since we left the temple," said Chao.

Chang immediately answered the question for Yasotay, "Powers of observation, Master Chao, powers of observation!"

"Respectfully, Master Chang," said Gao, "my powers of observation tell me we have sunlight just long enough to get off this ridge. We can still make it to the caves and Master Yang's fireworks by sunset if we leave now. Otherwise, we will be camping on this ledge," explained Gao, looking directly at Chang.

"I have read about rockslides of this type. They are common in this region," Yasotay reflected aloud to no one in particular.

"I can't see the other two warriors down there," said Chao, peering down the incline. "Are they trying to find them?"

A short while later, the two warriors returned, and one of them, Wein, spoke directly to Chang. "We climbed down to a good vantage point and could see remains….They are gone….To reach them, we must set up camp and join our ropes together."

Chang interrupted, "What could you do for them if you were to reach them?"

"I don't know," said Wein, wearing the stress of the situation on his rugged face. The large scar on his right hand became noticeable as he seemed to wrench at the hilt of his sword. "We can make a lever with some tree limbs to move some of the boulders, but it will take two or three of us. The rocks are many in number and size. But I'm sure they did not survive, Master. I believe…" Wein dropped his head in respect and sorrow. "I believe they are gone!" The strain in his voice made those last words crackle from his lips.

"Describe what you observed, Wein," Chang requested in a calm and soothing voice.

Wein took a moment, gathered himself, and began, "From where we stood, we could see a large pile of rocks. One horse was atop the pile of boulders, clearly dead, his neck broken, twisted in an unnatural way." He paused a moment, took a breath, and then continued, "Liu Ao and Liu Bang couldn't have survived," he shuddered, envisioning again the severed arm at the base of the pile and one of the warrior's legs, bent at an unnatural angle, protruding from the rubble.

Wein continued, reaching for the rope on his saddle. "We will need ropes to climb down…"

Chang interrupted him, "We will do no such thing because there is nothing to be done!"

"But, Master, I am responsible for…" said Wein.

Chang interrupted him again, "I will explain to your leadership what happened." Chang spoke louder so everyone could hear, "We must continue on! Everyone, let's prepare to leave!" The warriors and priests dutifully began to prepare to remount their horses and continue their trek to the caves.

"Wein seems disturbed, and Master Chang appeared unmoved," said Kang to Chao in a hushed voice as they both observed Wein fussing with a leather bag connected to his saddle.

"He acts like a wounded puppy," said Chao.

"One of the fallen warriors was his brother," said Yasotay, having overheard the hushed conversation while standing right behind them.

"What was that?" asked Chao, who turned to face Yasotay.

"Liu Bang, one of the men taken by the rockslide, was Wein's younger brother," replied Yasotay.

"And how do you know this?" asked Chao.

"I heard them last night," responded Yasotay, "when Wein relieved Liu Bang for guard duty. They talked for a while. I was awake and could not help but hear. They were brothers, and I could tell they were very close from their conversation."

"Powers of observation, Master Chao, powers of observation," whispered Kang to Chao, mockingly saying it in the same tone and tempo as Master Chang.

The travelers were back on track, single file once again, moving forward, more acutely aware of their surroundings, and at a slightly quicker pace than before the landslide. The path traversed downward and widened as the day wore on. The procession continued, traveling in silence toward their destination, and soon, the woods began to enclose them more and more with every step. The long shadows formed by the trees told Yasotay that the sun had reached the unseen horizon. Then there was an intermittent popping sound, *pop, pop—pop*, and suddenly, the trees around them rang out with a large BANG! Two horses reared on their hind legs, the others rustling with anxiety. Snorting and stomping, they were nervous. The considerable noise seemed to shake the trees and the ground beneath them.

"No fears. That's just Master Yang testing his creations," chuckled Chang with a wry smile.

"His creations, Master Chang?" asked Yasotay.

"Yes, Master Yang didn't invent fireworks, but he has certainly perfected them," said Chang.

Everyone's focus was ahead, toward where the considerable noise had come from. Soon, they could see a large clearing and a collection of about twenty-five to thirty tents of all sizes, with many canopies and odd makeshift structures, forming a small village. Behind and to the left of them was a large cliff face; the weathered shale wall towered over the village, two-hundred chi in the air. A large cave entrance was visible at the base, while hundreds of smaller caves and cut-ins were visible along the rock face.

Chang led the group, still in single file, as they crossed a small field toward the tent village. To their left was a garden with a small fence enclosure and several plants that appeared well-maintained. A wheelbarrow and hoe leaned against the fence that looked old but sturdy. Chang led the group to a large gray tent and dismounted from his horse.

"We will be staying here tonight," Chang instructed the group. "Kang, you and Chao can set up camp over there," pointing to an area to the right of the giant gray tent. The two warriors kept walking toward the main collection of tents.

"Where are they going?" asked Yasotay.

"We don't need their protection here; they are going to stay with their people, a very ethnically oriented group," replied Chang. "Yasotay, Gao, join me. We're going to find Master Yang."

They walked into the tent and were instantly assailed by a strong and unusual smell. It was a thick, stale, stagnant odor from a fine smoke floating in the air that burned the inside of their noses. The tent had many makeshift shelves filled with large ceramic vessels, each with odd markings. Toward the back were many tables covered with bowls, scales, and various instruments for grinding, measuring, and cutting. An old man sat on a small wooden box behind a bunch of odd-looking tables configured in an *L* shape; he was busy reading something.

"Master Yang!" Chang called out.

Startled by the intrusion, he looked up and said, "Yes…well, hello, good to see you again, Master Chang." A big smile formed across his old, weathered face and in his small, kind eyes. He let out a friendly chuckle for a friend not seen for a long time. It seemed to Yasotay everything about him was gray: the box-shaped hat on his head; his robe, the sash; his straight, unkept long hair; his beard and mustache; the old skin on his face and hands; even the nails on his fingers, all presenting different shades of gray.

"This is Yasotay, and you remember Master Gao," said Chang, introducing the two young men.

"Yes, yes, and it is a pleasure to meet you, young Yasotay," Yang said eagerly, greeting the young boy excitedly. "I have heard great things about you. Your reputation proceeds you, young man, yes, yes it does." Gao shifted uneasily as Yang ignored him.

"You honor me, Master Yang," responded Yasotay, giving a deep bow of respect. He noticed Yang's right hand was missing an index finger, and his thumb on that same hand appeared to be malformed.

Gao scowled, his face reddening with jealousy as he did his best to contain his emotions.

"I will have Master Gao prepare my carriage," said Chang. "I assume you have completed making the fireworks?" Suddenly, a considerable crackling noise could be heard outside the tent, pop—pop, pop, pop, pop.

"Yes, Master Chang, I have everything prepared. All the items are assembled and boxed. They just need to be loaded," Yang said.

"We plan to leave at daybreak tomorrow. Our aim is to reach the crossing by midday, four days from now," explained Chang. "I have one more errand to perform."

"Li Wo!" bellowed Yang, and moments later, a young girl no older than ten stepped into the tent from the back and joined Master Yang behind the tables. She had long knotted hair, a dirty little face, and, ominously, was missing her right arm.

"Yes, Master?" answered the girl in a gentle voice.

"Li Wo, would you please show Master Gao to the carriage and help him load the fireworks? They would like to pack up before dark," requested Yang.

"Yes, Master," she answered and looked toward Gao, who was already making his way toward her. They slipped out through the back entrance together.

Yang yelled to them, "And Master Gao, don't forget to ensure the carriage is away from cooking fires and covered from the rain." He said in a low voice, under his breath, "You could lose more than a finger if you're not careful!"

"Yes, Master Yang," said Gao, who could be heard through the sides of the tent.

"Good, good…good," responded Yang. He now turned back to them. "So, Yasotay, do you know much about explosive displays?"

"I have seen them before."

"Do you know how they are made?" asked Yang. "It's mainly about the recipe, the precise mixture. That is the key to it!" He raised his digit-missing hand to emphasize the point.

"I am going to check on Gao to ensure those fireworks are stored properly," Chang said. "Yasotay, Master Yang would love to show you his craft. This will be good for you to learn, so I'll leave the two of you to talk." Yasotay nodded in understanding while the enthusiastic and eccentric Yang ignored Chang and continued. "You see, Yasotay, the trick is to slightly alter the mixture of the three base ingredients, which yields different combustion results."

As Chang walked away, he could hear Yang's voice trailing off. "There are other ingredients one can add to effect different results, but the purity of the three main ingredients is of critical importance. Let me show you the…"

While Yang and Yasotay spent the rest of the day together, Chang did his best to relax under a canopy and read a manuscript. The three priests had seen to loading the carriage, tending to the horses, and preparing their food for the evening. "There must be fifty people who live here," said Chao as he brushed the mane of Chang's horse. Chao was the shorter of the three assistants, and all three wore the same-colored teal pants, jacket, and hat.

"I would guess closer to seventy," observed Gao, the older of the three.

"Do you think they all work for Master Yang making fireworks?" asked Kang.

"I don't know," said Gao.

"Where is...the gifted one?" asked Chao sarcastically, emphasizing the word *gifted.*

"He's with Master Yang," Gao said, then pop—pop, pop, could be heard throughout the camp.

"Yes, and no doubt Yang is divulging all his secrets," mocked Chao. "There are many secret talismans that even you, Gao, a head priest under Master Chang, have not earned the right to learn. So why does everyone treat him as if he's Lao Tzu himself? He seems no different than us, except younger. He hardly speaks, and when he does, it's often a snide comment, which others always excuse. They don't treat any of us that way."

"And what's with this *gift* everyone keeps talking about?" asked Chao. "Other than his ability to eavesdrop on people's conversations, I am..."

"Well, that's Master Chang's prerogative now, isn't it?" interrupted Gao. "Why don't you quit fussing about things that aren't your business and..."

Suddenly, Chang's voice interrupted the conversation as he approached them. "Yes, Master Chao, why don't you!" he reprimanded, surprising the three priests tending to the horses. Chang's eyes fixed on Chao, who reflexively cowered in silence.

To Chao's relief, Chang diverted his attention to Gao. "Master Gao, is all ready for an early departure?"

"Yes, Master Chang, the carriage is loaded. I assume you and young Yasotay will ride in the carriage for the remainder of our trip," replied Gao.

Yasotay appeared from around the corner. "Master Chang, I have been working with Master Yang and made a firework. Would you like to come and watch?" Yasotay had overheard what Chao had said, which put a slight damper on his original enthusiasm.

"Yes, excellent, I would like that. Master Gao, you may join us." Yasotay led the way toward the large gray tent.

Late evening shadows had set in behind the tent where there was a large clearing. As they approached, they could see Yang and Li Wo in the center of it. Li Wo held a small stick at her side that glowed bright red at the end. Yasotay joined Yang, whose attention was fixed on a brightly colored, green cylindrical device sitting on a small, charred table. Li Wo handed Yang the stick. "Back, back," said Yang, taking the stick from her. And she quickly left the center.

Yang motioned for Yasotay to follow her and back away. Yasotay and Li Wo continued their backward retreat. Once at a safe distance, Yang looked back at the device and then placed the glowing stick on the ground next to a tail that extended from the device. Then, he, too, quickly retreated. Everyone was now staring at the sizzling tail in anticipation. Then, the cylinder took off with a flash and a searing hiss. It screamed straight up through the air, as high as the surrounding treetops, and then it sputtered. After hanging in the air for a brief moment, it suddenly turned and shot violently downward on a path straight toward Yasotay and Li Wo. Yasotay instinctively lurched toward the young girl, protectively covering her and diving to his left while holding Li Wo on his way down. The cylinder streaked over them, took another abrupt right turn in flight, and shot off toward the tree line. Then, just before reaching the trees, there was a massive explosion. Everyone flinched in unison. Thousands of little red embers shot out in all directions, lighting up parts of the forest not otherwise visible in the low light of dusk in a brilliant display of colored trees and shadows.

Standing unnoticed on the outskirts of the clearing, four men ran into the forest and began stomping on fallen embers. Others carrying buckets of water followed. There was a concerted effort to ensure the forest didn't catch fire.

"Yes, well, I think the way you packed the mixture in the cylinder wasn't right, Yasotay; we can't have any air pockets. We will have to try again. Come!" instructed Yang as he bustled past Yasotay and Li Wo, still lying on the ground. Yang headed back toward the tent as if nothing had happened. Gao, Chang, and Yasotay were stunned. Adding to the surreal situation was the fire brigade stomping out the embers among the trees. It was apparent that they had done this before. Yasotay got up from the ground, rubbing his hands together.

His smile clearly expressed what he was thinking: *Making things explode is exhilarating!* Yasotay hurried to follow Yang toward the tent to try again.

The next morning came quickly for Yasotay. Yang was excited to show him his skills in mixing powders and had kept Yasotay up till late at night, concocting different combinations. Then, well past midnight, they embarked on a torch-lit tour of the caves that provided some of these incendiary ingredients. Finally, in a slow and tired state, on a short amount of sleep, Yasotay began preparing his horse for the trip.

"Yasotay, come here. You'll be riding with me," Chang informed him. The priest was already seated atop the carriage bench. "Come, sit here…leave the horses. Chao, take Yasotay's horse and tie it to the others."

"Yes, my Daoshi," replied Yasotay and Chao together in perfect harmony.

"Master Yasotay…Master Yasotay, I have something for you," Yang called out, quickly walking up to the carriage where Yasotay had just found his seat. "It has been a pleasure meeting you, my young man."

"The honor is mine, Master Yang," replied Yasotay.

"Here, I want you to have this. Keep it for later." Yang handed him a small wooden box with intricate writings carved into the wood.

"Thank you, Master Yang, you have been most gracious," Yasotay responded, bowing his head in gratitude.

"Safe travels, young man, safe travels," Yang said warmly.

The traveling party departed once again in a single file. The two warriors who had camped separately from the group reappeared in the morning as they prepared to leave. They rode on for two full days of uneventful travel in a methodical and deliberate traveling routine. The mornings were cool, and the days were hot and sunny. Master Chang and Yasotay were comfortable sitting in the carriage thanks to its roof, which kept the beating sun off their heads. The road was wide and flat, and they only passed an occasional person on horseback or foot, all traveling in the opposite direction.

"We are headed west now, Master," said Yasotay as he balanced the turtle inside the bowl.

"The road takes us west here and bends around to the north. We will reach the bridge by midday," confirmed Chang. "I have one last stop to make. After that, we will be off toward home as soon as possible."

They came up over a rise to see a long series of rolling hills that trailed off into the distance. The Great Wall cut through the landscape and rode along the tops of those rolling hills.

"This view is absolutely breathtaking," exclaimed Yasotay as the carriage slowed to a stop. Taking in the view, Yasotay ran his eyes along the dips and curves of the wall that stretched as far as he could see. Yasotay was seeing this part of the Great Wall for the first time.

"Master Gao, do you know when the first section of the wall was built?" asked Chang of his underling, who had pulled up beside the carriage.

"Was it during the Han Dynasty twelve hundred years ago?" answered Gao.

"Yasotay, tell him about the Great Wall," said Chang.

"The first section of the Great Wall was originally constructed during the Warring States period roughly sixteen hundred years ago," said Yasotay. "This particular section of the wall was built during that period and then rebuilt five centuries later around the end of the Han Dynasty. It's a magnificent creation, having been built, rebuilt, and repaired over hundreds of years. They used the *hangtu* method of wall-building. This ancient technique used a form and tamping process to build wall material up one layer at a time."

"There's your answer, Master Gao," said Chang with a smile. He was having fun antagonizing his underlings with how smart this young man really was.

With the Great Wall looming before them as they proceeded, they came upon a bridge beyond which was a small village. They crossed the bridge and entered the village. The aged and weathered two-story houses lined both sides of the road. Each was as similarly built as the next. Finally, at the fourth structure on the left, Chang pulled back on the reins and slowed the carriage to a stop. A short, dark man with a large roll of fat under his chubby chin came out from under the canopy that jutted out from the front of the structure.

"Master Chang, it is good to see you again," said the man, revealing a black-toothed grin.

"Have you had any luck, Buwei?" asked Chang.

"Yes, yes, I have," said Buwei, the chubby little man with his large, charcoal smile. "As I told you, I can acquire whatever you seek from the Silu…horses, camels, silk, slaves. It doesn't matter; it's all available." Then, he turned his head and barked, "Me Win! Bring those manuscripts here."

"What's the Silu?" asked Kang in a low whisper to Gao.

"The Silu is a network of roads that connects the Eastern world to the West. Most all trade transpires on the Silu!" whispered Gao.

Gao jumped from his horse and stood next to the carriage. A middle-aged man with gray hair and exceptionally large eyebrows pushed a large wheelbarrow filled with books, manuscripts, and various parchments out to them. "I was able to purchase most of these from a man who came on the Silu from the West. He required a high price…others traded for much less, but his manuscripts were of the highest quality."

"Fine, what is it I owe you?" asked Chang.

"Three hundred *kuan* for the lot of it," said Buwei.

"Ridiculous," exclaimed Chang. "I will give you two hundred and not one coin more."

"I paid more for them than you've offered. I cannot do it for less than two hundred seventy-five," said Buwei.

"Fine, keep them," spit Chang, who motioned for them to leave.

"Fine, fine, fine…two fifty, and they are yours," Buwei responded. Everyone else stood there watching the two haggle over the price.

"I have two hundred and twenty-five kuan, and that is fair. Otherwise, you can keep them," said Chang dismissively.

"What good are they to me or to anyone for that matter? They're covered with chicken scratches in a foreign language. You asked me to buy foreign books and manuscripts, which I have, and now I have these things which are of no value to me," moaned Buwei, then thinking for a moment, "...fine, two twenty-five."

"Done," said Chang with a smile, happy with the results of the negotiation. He hastily reached for a square wooden stick on which round coins with square holes were perfectly strung. Chang started to count out the coins. Having agreed to the price, Gao began placing the contents of the wheelbarrow into a large chest in the back of the carriage.

"I prefer paper money. It's not as difficult to carry and count as coins are," said Buwei.

"I have no paper money. I know it's the new way; I do things the old way. Would you rather give me these manuscripts for free? I would hate to inconvenience you with my coins," said Chang in a sarcastic tone.

"No, Master Chang, payment in coins is fine," said Buwei.

"Here, Master Chang," said Gao, handing Chang one of the books from the pile. It had a coarse leather cover and a leather cord binding. Master Chang took the book from Gao and handed it to Yasotay.

"Here, take this," ordered Chang.

"What is this?" asked Yasotay.

"It's a book from the West, and I'm pretty sure it's a holy book. I believe it's called a Bible!" replied Master Chang.

"A Bible? What is that?" asked Yasotay.

"It's a religious book," replied Chang. "I know many Westerners consider it a holy book and worship it. The faith, Christianity, is spreading here as well." Yasotay looked up from the book. "That's what we'll be doing, my young friend," Chang informed him. "For the past twenty-five years, I have been collecting books, manuscripts, and artifacts of all types not only from the West but from the South too. I have one of the largest collections you will find anywhere."

"It has some odd markings in it," observed Yasotay, flipping through the book. "I have never seen symbols like this before."

"I'm pretty sure it's called *Greek*...I believe, or Hebrew. I'm not quite sure."

"Interesting!" mused Yasotay, looking closely and turning the large book over in his hands.

"Glad to hear you find it interesting! Because we are not only going to decipher what language it's written in, we're going to discover what it actually says!"

"So, you're collecting all these manuscripts to build a library?" asked Yasotay.

"Yes, WE are going to build a great library," answered Chang. "*Real knowledge is to know the extent of one's ignorance*,...wasn't that Confucius?"

"Yes, yes, it was Master Chang," said Yasotay.

"With this library, I intend for us to learn the true extent of our ignorance," said Chang.

As the travelers progressed on the last leg of their journey toward the city of Zhongdu and the White Cloud Temple, the Great Wall on their left snaked up and down the rolling hills to the north.

"I look forward to the challenge, Master Chang," said Yasotay as he inspected the manuscript closely. A wave of apprehension washed over him...*understanding this will take a lifetime! Do I want a life of study? Is there a deeper meaning or purpose to my life? Is a life of nothing but studying my path?*

Zhongdu, last day of the year, 1176 CE

Fireworks, feasting, and family reunions marked Zhongdu's Lunar New Year festivities. Preparations for the year's most important day had started weeks earlier with a thorough cleaning. Every household worked diligently to clean out the previous year's bad karma. Buildings throughout the city were adorned with bright red decorations to collect good luck and ward off misfortune. Homes were ornamented with red lanterns and symbolic paper cutouts, encouraging the arrival of wealth and good fortune. The city crackled with the sound of firecrackers, which caused ears to ring and the odor of sulfur to linger in the air and sting the nostrils. The constant barrage of sights, sounds, and smells was believed to scare away evil spirits. As with every year, the night would conclude with a giant fireworks display by order of the emperor himself. Throughout Zhongdu and the whole Jin state, it was widely believed that the emperor held the most impressive fireworks display in the world.

Preparing the ceremonial feast was the most time-consuming activity of the New Year's festivities. Dumplings, noodles, pork, poultry, fish, *baozi*, and various fruits and vegetables were cooked and consumed in large quantities; eating was a significant part of the celebration. The most popular foods were sticky rice cakes, symbolizing success, and dumplings, which supposedly brought great wealth to those who ate them. Various traditional Chinese desserts were served along with tea and other drinks. Rice wine and all alcoholic beverages were consumed in moderation, as public drunkenness was deemed highly inappropriate.

Yasotay knew that the fireworks, food, and parades were the focal point of the festivities. But, what stood out for him was the most cherished aspect of the day—the time spent with family. He knew of people who traveled hundreds of *li* to be with their families. Additionally, the Lunar New Year was when this largely agrarian society took a break from the daily farming routine. The New Year's tradition has existed for over a millennium. Its history was well documented, and each family had their customs that reflected their social status. Everyone looked forward to being with family and friends, whatever their social standing, but not Yasotay.

The royal family's New Year was full of formal rituals performed by Emperor Shizong and the rest of his family and staff. Yasotay was required to attend the grand feast at a minimum. He begrudgingly put in an appearance for the least amount of time necessary to appease his mother and cousin. He wore his one formal *magua* silk robe—royal blue and ankle-length with wide sleeves and a leather belt. Yasotay would rather have stayed in the Daochang, teaching a *wushu* class, than dealing with the pomp and circumstance of the day's activities. But he always enjoyed seeing Mana, so there was at least one positive benefit to this dinner.

Fame preceded him in every introduction and every public appearance. Mostly, people liked to test him, having prepared a question or two, hopeful to stump the walking bookworm. Most were questions on specific facts from ancient stories, and he answered the questions as best he could.

This year, sitting beside his mother at the imperial grand feast, Yasotay waited for the silence to be broken after the formal royal greeting and seating.

"So, Yasotay, how do you like the freedom of living at the temple instead of here with your mother?" asked the emperor.

"While I prefer the royal palace, my Emperor, I like the temple; I am closer to my studies," said Yasotay, not because he felt that way but because it was the answer his cousin wanted to hear.

"Next, we need to find you a suitable wife!" said the emperor.

Princess Jia chimed in, "That's a good idea, my Emperor. I think he spends too much time with his nose in a book." She turned to Yasotay. "Most of the writings you're working on make no sense to me. A good woman might be the best thing for you."

His mother had arranged introductions to several young women, who were all rather plain and uninteresting. Yasotay felt alienated and distant from most people his age, no one more so than his thirteen-year-old cousin, Wudubu, who sat next to him. His cousin, the emperor, would have the final say about who was chosen as his wife. Women were viewed as chattel to sell off for influence or power. However, for the royal family, both men and women were viewed in this light. The emperor and the rest of the elite would never miss an opportunity to further their own interests. And marriage to anyone in the royal family was priceless to any Jin noble.

Yasotay was intentionally ignorant of most of this power-positioning nonsense. He was familiar with the cultural custom of using marriage to curry favor and cultivate power. Yasotay respected others who participated to better themselves or their families, but his personal thoughts were clear: *If I am to be married, whom I marry will be my choice.* He was resolved to choose his own wife and his own life.

"The books may make no sense to us, my princess, but they are essential to other cultures. That's why young Yasotay's work is critical to the Empire," said Wudi, the emperor's counselor. Wudi was a eunuch with cunning ambition who had advanced his position in the court. He was a short, chubby, bald man wearing a bright red magua silk robe with a magnificently embroidered dragon on the front. It was difficult to see unless you were standing at the perfect angle due to the bulge in the fabric created by his protruding round belly. The robe was of the highest quality, a clear sign of the wearer's esteemed rank in the emperor's court.

"If I may, my Emperor, I would like to tell the princess something," said Kang, standing and bowing to the emperor. "I have worked as an assistant to *The Master of the Manuscript*," Kang paused and respectfully nodded a slight bow to Yasotay, "...for over a year, and doing so has been my great honor. Your son's work is vital to the Empire, my Princess. Soon, I am afraid he will have to continue without me. My father has secured my billet to attend Officers' School...I leave in two months." There were low murmurings of approval from the group of twenty-five intimate guests of the emperor.

"Congratulations, Master Kang," said Emperor Shizong. "Your father, General Zhou, is my most trusted commander. I have no doubt you will make a fine officer."

"Pfft, from the pen to the sword, Kang will be dead in a week," Wudubu mumbled quietly under his breath.

Yasotay ignored young Wudubu's smug remark; he was genuinely happy for Kang. He was a valued assistant whom he had grown to trust. Looking at all those at the table, he realized someone was missing. He turned to his mother. "Where is Mana?" asked Yasotay in a low voice. "Is she not welcome to eat with us anymore?"

"She was your nanny, your milk mother, Yasotay. Aren't you a little old for that?" his mother replied with a sneer. "And she's not family," Jia added. "We had to make room for others at the emperor's table." Princess Jia began nonchalantly picking and tugging at the sleeve of her robe.

Yasotay knew what the sleeve tug meant. It always meant his mother was nervous and was being elusive or barefaced lying. "She may not be part of your family, but she's part of mine," said Yasotay with a raised voice.

The loudness of Yasotay's voice caught the attention of everyone at the table. "Is anything wrong?" the emperor asked with eyes on Yasotay and Princess Jia.

"Everything is fine, my Emperor!" Yasotay and Princess Jia said in unison. The dinner guests returned to their conversations.

Yasotay sat through the remainder of the dinner without saying another word. He was displeased with his mother's attitude toward Mana but felt it best to stay quiet. Waiting the appropriate amount of time, Yasotay finally asked, "By your leave, my Emperor, Mother, I must attend to obligations at the temple," said Yasotay.

"You will miss the fireworks!" said Princess Jia. "You have barely eaten anything."

The emperor gave a nod of dismissal. Yasotay rose from his seated position, bowed respectfully to him, and quickly departed the feast.

It was well past midnight, and while the smoke from the fireworks had dissipated, the sulfur odor still hung in the air. It was two *shi* before dawn, and the air felt cool and moist on the skin. The *ninsha*, all in black, stole down a dark alley and rounded a corner at the back of the palace compound. Hidden in the shadows, he searched for the specific tree he had previously identified as useful for his mission. The massive *duanshu* tree was a favorite of bees, and those that frequent it produce a highly valued, white-colored honey from the tree's nectar. This one was located on the south side of the compound near the palace wall. The tree's close proximity to the fifteen-chi-high wall that encircled the palace complex had been noted as a security risk, but because of its value, it was spared the axe and kept neatly trimmed so that no branch hung too close to the wall instead.

He found the tree and began his agile and noiseless climb to its highest branches. Reaching a height much higher than the palace wall, he looked around closely, ensuring his movements had not been watched.

He knew the guards would torture and kill him if he were caught. Wudi had paid him handsomely for this operation, and his success was imperative. He reached into his jacket, removed a long rope, and tied it with a quick-release knot around a thick branch. He then climbed down the tree roughly six chi, so he was almost level with the top of the palace wall. Gripping the rope tightly, he swung out and caught the top of the wall with his feet without making a sound. He quickly landed on it and rappelled down the inside wall. He found himself inside the royal compound, neither seen nor heard by anyone. He crept through the shadows. His movements were slow and calculated; he aimed to kill the target without leaving a trace. Fortunately, the sleeping quarters of his victim were just a short distance from the compound wall.

He was told her room was the third on the left in the servant's barracks at the compound's south end. A modest building, the servants were housed outside many of the layers of security afforded the emperor. Entering the room, he waited motionless for his eyes to adjust to the limited light. He could see the outline of a single bed in the small room, with a prone figure, sleeping, their body rising and falling in sync with the sound of their breath.

The ninsha was a paid assassin whose patience and thoroughness were necessary for his work. Slowly and stealthily, he placed himself into position. His prey was sleeping on her side. He could make out her shoulder. His movements needed to be quick and deadly. With an almost gliding motion, he was on top of her. He quickly flipped the woman onto her back and covered her nose and mouth with a sturdy, thick cloth. His knees pinned down both her shoulders. He could see her eyes staring at him in terror as she finally realized she couldn't move—or breathe.

She tried to fight back, kicking her legs wildly; she was making noise, kicking something made of wood. He could hear it, which was a problem. She might draw attention to the attack. He tried to slide his legs down her body to stop her from kicking out. It wasn't working. It was supposed to look like she died in her sleep, not murder. He couldn't just slit her throat. He pushed down harder with his hands on the cloth that covered her nose and mouth. Suddenly, he heard a crack and felt her neck give way. She went limp. The ninsha waited a long moment, then slowly folded the cloth and placed it in his pocket. He checked the vein in her neck and then climbed off his victim. She was dead. Using two fingers, he closed her eyelids and straightened the blanket and her body to make her look peacefully asleep. He found the small wooden altar table she had kicked over and returned it to the foot of the bed. The ninsha quietly left the room and slipped out of the palace compound without a sound.

The White Cloud Temple was located in the city's southwest corner, just a short horse ride from the Imperial Palace. It was early morning, the first day of the new year, and Yasotay was practicing in the courtyard. His weapon this morning was a *guandao*, though somewhat modified. Yasotay called it the "Training Dragon" because it was a replica of Master Jing's Green Dragon, except the blade was made of wood. While he enjoyed training, teaching was his passion, yet his busy schedule only allowed him to teach one daily class for a half-a-shi. He had started teaching last year; the first two days, his class was held in the large courtyard of the temple. Master Chang appeared both mornings; he watched keenly and listened from the balcony above. After the second day, Chang approached Yasotay and proclaimed, "You may use the Daochang to conduct your class; I have had Gao clean out a space in the back where you can store your weapons and training equipment."

"Thank you, my Daoshi," said Yasotay. Since then and shortly after dawn, the Daochang would host Yasotay's wushu class.

The Daochang was the main hall that opened to the temple's courtyard. Yasotay had initially thought it would be the perfect spot to train those who wanted to learn his version of wushu. The room was large, with an eighteen-chi high ceiling and bamboo flooring made from thin reeds woven into a parquet pattern. This made the floor somewhat springy, which Yasotay's students were grateful for since it helped to soften their falls. Large wooden pillars surrounded the perimeter of the room. Finely crafted lattice doors and windows, all with the same intricate pattern of large and small interlocking rectangles, were situated around the room. White translucent paper was layered behind the latticework of each panel for privacy and to mute the sun's rays.

One large window high up on the wall of the Daochang was round and encircled a large Yin and Yang symbol. The curve between the two halves was fashioned of carved wood, with black paper behind the Yin half and white paper behind the Yang. When the morning sun reached the perfect spot each day, it would cast a bright Yin/Yang shadow on the opposite wall that moved across the wall with the seasons.

Yasotay kept the etiquette during his class very simple: respect everyone. He believed it so important that he made a placard that said, "All who enter here treat each other with respect."

He started each of his classes by hanging the placard on a hook. He would return it to the equipment room at the end of class. Having trained under Master Lu Chong of the Song Dynasty, Yasotay based much of his class on Master Lu's approach. His hand-to-hand practices mimicked the striking techniques of animals, so each training level was named after one: tiger, snake, monkey, and others. All weapon training also progressed in levels, beginning with the staff.

"Good morning, my Laoshi," said Chao. Everyone who attended Yasotay's class called him Laoshi, which means teacher.

"I've come early today to request again that you train me on the *kusari*," said Chao.

"And I will tell you what I told you the past three times you have asked: It would be my honor to teach you the kusari…once you have mastered the staff. It's the one weapon every pupil of mine must master *before* moving on to other weapons," said Yasotay.

"My Laoshi, I cannot complete all the forms with the staff," said Chao.

"You cannot complete all the forms *yet!*" corrected Yasotay. "The staff is the most basic of all weapons…you need to learn its use first!"

"I think I will be working toward mastery of the staff for the rest of my life!" said Chao with a dejected look.

"All true sages make it their life's work to strive for mastery. This is something you should take on as one of life's challenges. When I trained with Master Lu, I approached each of his programs with conviction," said Yasotay. "Each program required achieving perfect form at each level and then the approval of Master Lu to move on to the next. Many of my classmates would work at one level for three to five years, and I heard one had worked for over seven years on one level!"

"Yes, and how long did it take you to complete the program?" asked Chao.

"That's not what I am talking about. It is true that when I was thirteen, I was scolded by Master Lu for progressing through his programs too quickly. He then tasked me with other duties, which dramatically slowed my progress. One of these was to document as many different predators and their tactics as I could find in nature. Master Lu taught me how to observe the predatory nature of various animals and discover how those lessons could be applied to one's own approach to wushu," said Yasotay. "The time and effort I spent taught me to slow down and better understand his teachings."

"Yes, and how long did it take you to complete the program?" asked Chao.

"I completed all the levels of Master Lu's training within one year," said Yasotay.

"I have been attending your wushu class for over a year," said Chao with a look of frustration.

"From what I can see, you are very close to completing your current level," said Yasotay.

"Yes, and yes, I do understand standards must be met before one moves on." Chao paused, then added, "Will you at least show me your practice techniques with the kusari? I've watched you, and there must be some trick. You are so precise with your strikes and amazingly quick with recovery. Please at least explain the basics to me," he said.

Yasotay had become good friends with Chao; he and Kang worked as his assistants. "Fine, Chao, I will tell you a secret…it's in the chain," said Yasotay.

"What?"

"All you see is a chain with a metal ball at the end. Do you not?" Chao nodded. "But there are small metal bumps in the chain at certain distances apart so that I always know how far the ball is from my hand." Yasotay produced a kusari from a leather pouch on his hip. "Here, run the chain between your thumb and finger." Yasotay held it out to Chao. "Feel the bumps in the chain."

Chao fingered the Kusari's chain. "Yes, here's a little bump...and there's another," said Chao, running the chain through his fingers.

"The training involves learning different moves while holding the chain at each *bump*. Striking, swinging, pulling in, letting more out.... This makes it easier. Knowing how far the ball is from your hand gives you the foundation for all the throws and spinning movements everyone finds so impressive," said Yasotay.

"I knew there had to be an explanation!" said Chao with a satisfied grin.

"And now you need to put in extra practice on the staff so you can complete that training. Once completed, I can show you all my drills with the Kusari." Yasotay rolled up the ball-and-chain weapon and placed it neatly in its pouch. "So let's talk about your training with the staff. What's your problem with mastering the moves?"

"The 'monkey climbing the tree' move is my only problem," Chao said.

"Yes, that is tough, yet one of my favorites. We can work on it together after class," said Yasotay.

Students began to arrive and take their places. Yasotay preferred the lower-rank students moved toward the front, the higher rank in the back. The small class of fifteen stood in three rows of five. Yasotay walked around the formation as the class began to perform their warm-up forms. The class proceeded through Yasotay's exercise regime. Halfway through the class, two of the emperor's royal guards entered the Daochang.

"Can we help you?" asked Yasotay of the two guards in full formal attire.

"Prince Yasotay, the emperor has requested your presence," said one. "Will you please come with us?"

Yasotay signaled his second-in-command to take over leading the class, then followed the guards out of Daochang. After a short horse ride, he followed the two warriors into the south end of the Imperial Palace. His curiosity was beginning to grow as neither warrior looked at him on the short trip. Then he realized they were taking him to where Mana lived. His stomach began to twist, and with every step, he felt more ill as he sensed something terrible had happened. Once inside, he noticed the servants kept their eyes averted from him and had grim expressions. Something was very wrong.

Before he entered her room, Yasotay stood outside the threshold, frozen in thought, trying to understand the situation. Inside the room, he could see the emperor, General Zhou, Wudi, and his mother all standing over a bed. On it was Mana, lying peacefully, hands on her chest.

Yasotay was stunned and didn't know how to respond. He slowly walked into the room. No one said a word. Everyone was staring down at Mana.

"I'm so, so, sorry, Yasotay," said Princess Jia. "I know how much she meant to you!" The princess's eyes were watering.

Yasotay looked down and saw the simple wooden altar table he had made her when he was very young. It was sitting there at the foot of her bed. Mana used this little stand to hold her bedside candle. The candle was missing; he bent down and picked up the table.

"It appears that she passed away in her sleep," said Wudi.

"That is obviously the case. I am sorry for your loss, Yasotay," said the emperor.

Yasotay was feeling like this was all a dream. He bent down and took Mana's hand. He looked at her cold, dead hand in his. Then he noticed a small amount of smeared blood on his fingers.

"What is this?" asked Yasotay, looking at the blood on his palm. He moved to examine the altar table; there was blood on that too.

"There is blood on this table; what do you think it means?" asked Yasotay, who looked confused and grief-stricken. He held up the small wooden altar table with the blood on it for everyone to see.

"Where could that blood have come from?" asked General Zhou. He looked around the group. "Do you think she was hit with that wooded table?"

"She looks peaceful, and there are no marks on her face and hands!" said Wudi, standing there with his arms crossed.

"I just picked this up; it was at the foot of her bed," said Yasotay, who reflexively placed the altar table where he found it.

The general reached down and pulled back the blanket covering Mana's feet. Her left heel lay in a small pool of blood. When General Zhou lifted her foot, everyone could see a cut on her heel.

"If she passed in her sleep, then why the cut on her foot?" asked Yasotay.

"Well, that wound certainly didn't kill her," said the emperor. "Are you saying this is not a natural death?"

"No, my Emperor. I am simply wondering why she has a cut on her foot." said Yasotay.

"Who would kill Mana?" asked Princess Jia with raised eyebrows.

"Could she have kicked the altar table while struggling?" asked Yasotay.

"It doesn't mean she was killed!" said the emperor with his signature twirl of his chin whiskers.

"I'm not saying it means anything. I'm just saying there is a wound on her foot, and that's not what killed her!" said Yasotay.

Wudi hurriedly added, "I've seen people dying from natural causes who thrashed about with their arms and legs in their last moments."

"Yes, that explains it." The emperor thought for a moment. "Wudi will conduct an inquiry, but for now, a heart problem is what we will call this death."

Yasotay still seemed uncertain. He leaned over and examined her foot, then the table's edge.

The emperor put a hand on his shoulder. "You understand, we must be very careful not to misinform the masses. I mean, *what would people think*...somebody killed in the palace compound." He muttered under his breath, speaking to himself but loud enough to be heard.

"Who cares what others think?" asked Yasotay.

"It makes the Emperor appear weak," General Zhou added.

"I'm sorry, my Emperor," said Wudi. "I will have this unfortunate situation cleaned up shortly."

"And what of the truth?" asked Yasotay, who appeared indignant, "Will you clean that up too, Wudi?"

"Yasotay!" yelled Princess Jia. "My Emperor, you must excuse my son's irrational behavior. He is obviously distressed; he cared very much for this woman."

"I am not irrational, Mother; I just want answers," said Yasotay with a heavy sigh.

"I, too, want answers!" assured the emperor. "And Wudi is going to get them for us."

"Yes, yes, I will, my Emperor," said Wudi obsequiously.

"Does that ease your concerns, Yasotay?" said the emperor in a voice that sounded more like a statement than a question.

Yasotay collected himself. "Thank you, my Emperor," he said, taking a deep bow. Yasotay knew this was what the emperor wanted to hear. "If you will excuse me, I should return to my class."

"Yes, I, too, must attend to other matters," said the emperor. He looked at his counselor. "Wudi?"

"I will handle everything, my Emperor!" said Wudi.

The emperor turned and walked out the door, with General Zhou following close behind. Yasotay began to leave behind them.

"Yasotay!" blurted Princess Jia. He turned to his mother with a blank look and waited for what she had to say.

"I'm so sorry! I know you cared for her very much," said Princess Jia, "and I am truly sorry."

"Thank you," said Yasotay, who bent to pick up the small altar table. "I made this for her when I was a child; Is it okay if I were to hold onto it?" He looked at Wudi, whom the emperor had put in charge of the inquiry.

"I think you should," said Wudi.

Yasotay turned and left the room.

Wudi and Princess Jia remained after everyone had left. The princess stared at Wudi with an incredulous look on her face. Wudi stood there and seemed to shrink under her gaze. After a very long and silent moment, she turned and left the room.

It was late afternoon, and Yasotay was in the Daochang, repeatedly striking a hanging bag with a staff. He was moving quickly and striking with two- and three-hit combinations, whack, whack—whack, whack, whack. As Chao walked up, he could tell something was bothering Yasotay by how ferociously he was striking the bag: whack, whack, whack—whack, whack.

He just stood there watching him for a while, admiring the speed and the footwork. Finally, he spoke to his teacher. "Yasotay, I heard about your friend; I'm sorry!" said Chao, his arms crossed his chest.

Whack, whack. "I appreciate your condolence," he said and continued—whack, whack, whack.

Chao watched him for a moment longer. "Excuse me, but can I speak to you?" asked Chao, staring down at his feet.

Yasotay stopped, leaned on the staff, and turned to his student. "What do you need?" asked Yasotay as he caught his breath.

"I have something to tell you that is hard to explain," said Chao, while his arms unfolded and his hands nervously fidgeted at his side.

Yasotay was intently observing Chao. He sensed that something was wrong. "Please, go on."

"Yesterday, I overheard Gao telling Master Chang that *Wudi hired someone to fix Princess Jia's problem.*"

"What problem? What does that mean," asked Yasotay.

"I don't know," answered Chao. "I could tell that they were speaking of something important. I'm telling you this because of how Master Chang responded."

"Which was…"

"*She had to be silenced. Leaking secrets like that can bring down an empire*," said Chao.

"And what does that mean? Who were they talking about?" asked Yasotay.

"Yes, and when I heard that your Mana had suddenly died…I just thought you should hear about it," Chao blurted out.

"But what secrets could be so important?" Yasotay asked. "What does it mean?"

Chao shook his head. "I would have dismissed it if it weren't for your Mana's sudden death."

"Are you saying, or are they saying, that Mana was killed to keep her quiet? About what?" asked Yasotay.

Chao shrugged his shoulders.

"I know there are many unanswered questions. The emperor is conducting an investigation. He's concerned about appearances and how it would look if someone had been killed on palace grounds. How did you overhear this conversation between Gao and Master Chang?" asked Yasotay.

"Now you're demanding to hear all my secrets," Chao said with a smile. Yasotay stood there motionless, waiting for an explanation. "All right. There is a magical spot where, if you are completely still, you can hear everything being said here in the Daochang; it's the closet in the other room." Chao said and added with a smile, "I nap in there!"

"Let me see if I understand: you were eavesdropping from your secret resting spot on Gao and Master Chang when you *think* you overheard them talking about how Wudi hired someone to fix some problem that involved my mother and keeping a big secret?"

"Well…yes!" said Chao.

They both just stood there staring at the floor. Yasotay didn't know what to say or do. He knew that he needed time to think!

"Thank you, Chao, for your honesty," said Yasotay, who flipped his staff in the air, caught it, and proceeded to whack at the hanging bag again. Chao lingered for a moment, watching him beat on the bag, and then he left without saying another word. Yasotay continued to hit the bag long after Chao left. He seemed to be in a trance, thinking about everything else while striking it over and over again.

Yasotay couldn't believe all that had happened. *Did Wudi have Mana killed to bury some secret?* Wudi had once worked as his mother's assistant for many years, and they shared a strong bond. After the emperor's previous assistant passed away due to old age, Wudi, the next, most senior eunuch, was chosen as the emperor's new assistant. It had been just over a year since this transition occurred.

Yasotay's mind was spinning. *What's the big secret they want to protect? And why do I even care? With Mana gone, why should I stay here? She was the only one I cared about. These people are all liars and schemers…Gao, Master Chang, my own mother. They are deceiving me, lying to me, using me. Do I want to spend the rest of my days suffering all this palace intrigue? My studies have revealed a whole new world out there. If I stay here, I'll have no choice but to keep my nose in a book. Do I really want to know what happened to Mana? It won't bring her back….Now, who's afraid of the truth?*

These thoughts rambled around in Yasotay's mind until, after much internal debate, he reached a resolve: *I need to find my own life, my own way! Stop reading about what others have done, and go live my life!*

The moon was so bright and full in the night sky that the Yin and Yang image in the window glowed perfectly on the floor of the Daochang. Yasotay was sitting there, covered in sweat, staring at the perfect symmetry of the symbol in the center of the room. He had pounded on that hanging bag to exhaustion. Yasotay could hear a group of people enter the side door and walk toward him.

"Yasotay, there you are; your mother is here looking for you!" said Chang. With him was his mother, Gao, and Wudi.

"Yasotay, Yasotay, you're all wet. Are you all right?" asked Princess Jia.

"I am fine," said Yasotay. "Why are you here, mother?"

"Because I am concerned about you, Yasotay," replied Princess Jia.

"There is no need to be concerned," said Yasotay. He stood up and straightened out his tunic. "Unless you have come to tell me about this secret everyone is hiding?"

"What are you talking about? What secret?" said Princess Jia. She turned to Wudi and asked, "What secret is he talking about?" Wudi shrugged his shoulders with a puzzled look, and Princess Jia began picking and tugging at her sleeve.

He turned to the others. "Master Chang, Gao? Do you know what secret I'm talking about? Who did Wudi hire?" They both looked at each other and then back at Yasotay.

Chang noticed Yasotay bring his right finger to the side of his nose, which signaled to Chang, *Don't be a fool and try to lie!* They all stared down at the floor like something was drawing their eyes to a spot.

Except for Yasotay, who carefully considered each person, looking them up and down. He realized, *at a minimum, they all withheld the truth, which made them all liars!* There was a long, quiet silence. His mother stood there like a statue carved in stone.

"Chao, if you're wondering, that was one long, silent pause. You didn't miss anything...." Yasotay took a deep breath in, then exhaled loudly. "Since I'm not going to hear the truth, I do prefer to hear nothing at all, so I thank you for that!" He was clearly irritated but calm, not irrational. Yasotay noticed Gao looking around in wonder, no doubt searching for Chao. He now turned and walked past them toward the temple door. Princess Jia quickly inhaled a breath like she was going to say something, paused, and then seemed to think better of it.

At the door, Yasotay turned back to them. "I understand why you are all here," he said, trying his best to hide his true feelings. "I appreciate your concern. Everything is fine, I am fine. Mother, please have Wudi take you home. Master Chang, Gao, we can speak about this later, but if you will excuse me, I require a bath and rest...it's been a long day!" Yasotay bowed, turned, and headed through the doorway. Walking out that door felt like the start of a new life for Yasotay. No sooner had the door closed behind him than Princess Jia turned to Chang with anger in her eyes.

"We said nothing to him!" protested Chang with a trailing voice. He had a perplexed look on his face and was showing his palms.

"Humph," Princess Jia spit out, spun around, and walked toward the door.

Wudi spoke in a low and cold voice, "If the emperor learns of this, it could become a problem for all of us."

"When you originally came to me for help, you didn't tell me your purpose," said Chang.

"You said you didn't want to know!" protested Wudi.

"I did not, but now I am entangled," said Chang.

"You are…due to your own fault; you and Gao gossip like school-girls," Wudi gave them both a long, hard look and followed Princess Jia out the way they came in.

Chang and Gao exited the Daochang in the opposite direction, away from listening ears. "What just happened here?" asked Gao.

"I don't know. Do you think Yasotay knows the truth?" asked Chang.

"What? That Princess Jia is not his real mother or that she had his real mother killed because she was going to tell everyone?" said Gao.

"Gao, don't say those words aloud. Wudi is right; the emperor would kill anyone who knew the truth and didn't tell him."

Later that evening, Yasotay entered the Daochang for the last time. He had taken a long hot bath, dressed, and packed some necessities in a simple cloth sack. The Yin and Yang symbol glowed brightly on the floor as he walked into the Daochang with the bag thrown over his shoulder. It was well after midnight, and he needed to retrieve one last thing he had almost forgotten. Looking around the building, he was overwhelmed with the feeling, *I'm going to miss this place!* But he knew this was the right thing to do. Yasotay didn't know what secret was being kept from him or what it had to do with Mana's death, and he didn't care. *I have no interest in staying here and listening to their lies while trying to figure it out! It won't change the fact that she's gone. It won't bring her back. I need to get away. I need to LEAVE!* So that was his plan; he was leaving them without saying another word. *No chance for more lies!*

His last stop, which he had almost forgotten, was to retrieve his kusari from the weapons closet. He opened the closet and grabbed the small leather pouch. Pausing momentarily, he noticed all the training weapons neatly hung in the closet and thought, *I'm really going to miss this place.*

Yasotay was unsure of where he was going but was comforted by the thought that there was an amazing and mysterious world out there just waiting to be explored. *Going to the edge of the empire sounds like a start! There's no telling where fate will take me from there.*

CHAPTER THREE

Northern reaches of the Jin Empire, summer, 1178 CE

Yasotay sat on a large tree stump, taking a break from chopping wood. He watched as a handful of goats chewed at the sparse ground growth on the barn's east side. Once a fenced-in yard, he was working in a three thousand-square-chi area now occupied by the massive remains of a fallen juniper tree. The once-beautiful tree had, days ago, stood tall and proud outside Hangu's fence. Hangu's property was a large farm that had been handed down from generation to generation. Unfortunately, the tree had been hit by lightning during a fierce storm just the previous week. The pile of broken and burnt remains from the enormous tree required days of work to remove. The fence, damaged by the fall, had been partially repaired and was currently strung together with a makeshift patch of tree branches tied together.

Hangu, a short, middle-aged farmer who had initially built the fence, asked Yasotay to keep an eye on his goats while he ran an errand—just in case.

Nomads were in the area, and Yasotay sensed that Hangu clearly did not trust them. He told Yasotay just before he left: "Watch out for them because they steal; they are more like animals than men." Yasotay had never met a nomad, but he was more than mildly curious; he had read about them in Chang's library. They were characterized in most stories as half-baked humans who were extraordinarily vulgar, incredibly dirty, and had no culture or morals. This was quite similar to Hangu's previously stated impression of them. Hangu had been talking about the nomads all week in anticipation of their arrival. Yasotay was interested in meeting these people to form his own impression. From his experience, he knew what it was like for people to have their preconceived notions. He intentionally took people at face value and let their actions help him form his opinion.

Yasotay went back to his work. He couldn't help but think how foolish Hangu was being. He was, in fact, looking forward to meeting these strange and wonderous wanderers. Yasotay was profoundly enjoying his new life and experiencing whatever it brought him. He had been cooped up in Zhongdu for far too long.

I'm done with THAT LIFE! This gift is a curse! I must leave! Those words rang in his head for the hundredth time since his departure. At the time, his mind was made up. He desired something different, away from his controlling mother, devious emperor-cousin, headmaster Chang, and all the Empire's shallow elite had to offer him. They were all hypocrites to him; the veil had been lifted in his mind. Yasotay walked out of their controlling, manipulative world with no immediate plan for the next day, let alone the rest of his life. And then he met Hangu.

"I take it you didn't see anyone?" asked Hangu, returning from his errand. His diminutive stature, small, thin face, and beady little eyes appeared from around the corner of the barn.

"No one," answered Yasotay, looking up briefly and then returning to chopping a large branch off the fallen tree.

"Well, someone at the market said that nomad traders will be at the Four Corners tomorrow morning," added Hangu. "I need a large felt blanket. Will you go with me?"

"Yes, Hangu," Yasotay said, swinging his axe at a large branch. "Right now, I am busy working on clearing this tree."

"Yes, let me help you!" offered Hangu, who got the hint and began picking up branches, assisting Yasotay in the cleanup.

"I'm glad you'll be coming with me," said Hangu. "Make sure you bring that thumper thing along too."

Yasotay stopped in mid-axe-swing, and with a puzzled look, he asked Hangu, "Thumper thing?"

"Yes, you know that metal ball, the one on the end of the chain, that thing you used to thump those two men causing trouble last month."

"Oh, yes. Let's hope we don't need to do that again," exclaimed Yasotay as he bent over to pick up a branch from the fallen tree. Then, he slid his hand down the handle toward the axe blade and began to clear small shoots off a perfectly sized staff about six chi tall. When done, he held it up and exclaimed, "I will bring this," Yasotay said playfully, holding out a perfectly straight staff.

In a frustrated voice, Hangu said, "A stick? Not sure how that will help with a lawless band of nomads. Better bring the thumper, just in case." Yasotay could hear the apprehension in his reply.

"Don't worry, Hangu, we'll be fine," said Yasotay reassuringly. Smiling to himself, he set the stick to the side, away from the carnage of the fallen tree, and continued working on clearing the juniper tree.

Morning came early for Hangu. He was awake before Yasotay, which was a first in the seven months since Yasotay arrived on his doorstep. At the time, Yasotay had the idea of trading his labor for room and board.

Hangu and his wife Lian had no children, and Lian's father had just passed away six months earlier. As luck would have it, Hangu needed additional hands with all the chores, and he anxiously agreed to the arrangement. Taller-than-normal stature, Yasotay was initially intimidating to the farmer. Then, after Yasotay had been there for a few months, sleeping in the barn, he offered the young man more recompense and space in his home. He had proven to be beyond helpful around the farm. But he refused any additional compensation while graciously accepting the sleeping space in Hangu and Lian's home.

"You're up early," chirped Yasotay.

Hangu spoke in a hushed and nervous voice, "Yes, well, I couldn't sleep; I don't trust these nomads. I was thinking maybe we shouldn't go. Last time I traded with these barbarians, I couldn't understand them… and they were very aggressive." Hangu was wringing his hands, overly agitated; Yasotay had never seen him this uneasy.

"We'll be fine, Hangu. I'm familiar with their language. Don't worry, I'll watch out for you," said Yasotay reassuringly. "Is Lian coming?"

"No, I want her to stay here and keep an eye on things," replied Hangu.

As instructed, Yasotay began preparing the lesser of the two carts Hangu owned. "Just in case they try to steal our cart, I would prefer we use this one," Hangu said as he pointed at the older wooden cart Yasotay had labored to repair four months ago. Raising it from the dead, he had taken the broken-down useless pile of junk, replaced several boards, fixed both wheels, and added a bench and canopy. It had an old and well-worn look, broken down but usable.

"And let's take that wild ass you like so much instead of one of my horses, you know, just in case." Hangu had no interest in dealing with that stubborn beast, but he knew Yasotay could control her. She was a wild female Mongolian ass, given in a trade. Hangu thought Tata was a mule, but Yasotay had recognized that she had the long ears of an ass. Tata was mostly dark brown with white markings and had four black socks.

"You know, I don't particularly like that beast. It kicked at me once," said Hangu.

"I don't think she meant anything by it." Yasotay scratched between Tata's ears, knowing full well she loved it. "She's a good girl."

"Humph, good girl," Hangu grunted. "I sense an odd malice in her eyes. I think she's evil!"

"Nonsense," Yasotay replied while giving Tata a big hug around her neck.

He had quickly bonded with Tata the instant they met, so much so that Hangu had insisted that Yasotay consider the indomitable beast his own. After hitching Tata to the cart and throwing a bag of millet in the back, Yasotay tied off the goats behind the cart and departed for the Four Corners.

It was early in the cool, sunny morning as Yasotay and Hangu headed east on the main road. Yasotay had initially installed a canopy on the cart to protect riders from the sun. But on this cool morning, the canopy was rolled up and stored away as the sun on their faces was a welcome travel companion.

It was a short distance to the Four Corners, but Yasotay guided Tata to move slowly due to the three goats trailing the cart. He had initially tied four of them to the back of the cart, but Hangu said to take only three, "Just in case!"

It was midmorning as they rounded a bend in the road, and their destination came into view. It was the intersection of the region's two main thoroughfares. Everyone who lived within a day's ride knew of the Four Corners. At the northwest corner was a large field of low-growing grass. Hundreds of people were gathered in small clumps in the field and along the road. He recognized a couple of them from town and many strangely dressed people he did not know—people with long, thick, flowing robes, hair, and beards—the nomads, no doubt. A strong odor, which got fiercer as they approached, gave off a distinct stench. It was powerful and pungent. At first, Yasotay thought the smell was from the many animals gathered there, but as one of the nomads walked past, he realized the assaulting, fusty, earthy scent of spoiled milk and body odor came from the nomads themselves.

To his surprise, his scanning eyes noticed one man who stood out. He was standing with a small group and was bound by a cangue. This device was a wearable wooden pillory locked securely around the man's neck and resting on his shoulders. The flat wooden framework panel had a hole that secured each hand in place. This particular prisoner had only his right hand bound within the cangue; his left hand remained free. The man was covered in dirt; his dark blood-red hair hung knotted and tangled from his head down to the cangue around his neck. His clothes were torn and ragged, and he seemed to be staring at Yasotay.

Curious, Yasotay steered the cart toward the group of four, two standing and two on horseback. He told Hangu, "Let's ask these people if they have that blanket you're looking for."

"I don't know, Yasotay," whispered Hangu as they approached. "They look rough, with that one wearing the 'cangue of shame,' I don't think…"

"Don't worry, Hangu. We'll be fine," Yasotay said, pulling gently on Tata's reins. He guided her toward the group and drew her to a complete stop. Addressing the nomad on horseback closest to them, Yasotay spoke in a foreign language Hangu didn't know. "We are looking for large felt blankets and are willing to trade goats for them," He was undeniably well-spoken, which surprised Hangu.

For some reason, the prisoner was still staring at Yasotay. The man had a broad face with a prominent chin, and for a brief moment, Yasotay met his gaze. He could feel this man's glowing green eyes, like two islands within his otherwise dirt-covered face, wordlessly screaming, "*Help Me!*" Yasotay could feel it in his bones that there was much more to this prisoner than met the eye.

The nomad standing beside the prisoner wore a bright green hat and said, "We have no blankets for trade." The prisoner continued to glare at Yasotay. Up close, you could see dried blood and dirt caked over multiple cuts and abrasions on his wrist and neck where the wooden contraption had left marks. The two nomads on horseback were noticeably larger; one wore a grubby red robe, and the other wore a dark brown robe. The red robe nomad held the end of a chain that attached to the cangue device. Suddenly, he reached down from his horse and violently smacked the prisoner's head with the part of the chain in his hand, ordering, "Stop staring!" It was a fierce blow, and Yasotay and Hangu flinched while Tata stirred at the commotion. The prisoner stumbled, lost his balance, and fell to the ground hard, awkwardly twisting his ankle. Lying on the ground, he clutched his right ankle with his free hand in pain.

"We do have horses and goats to trade for blades, depending upon the quality," said the nomad holding the prisoner's chain as if nothing had just happened.

"No, we have goats and a bag of millet to trade. We are looking for blankets," said Yasotay.

"We don't have any blankets for trade," repeated the nomad wearing the green hat.

Yasotay nodded and gestured his thanks, pulling on Tata's reins, which caused their cart to lurch forward. As he rode away, Yasotay could hear the nomads arguing about who would help the prisoner walk if he was injured and unable to do so. Yasotay and Hangu roamed around to the different groups of people, asking about blankets for trade. They did get a couple of offers from traders interested in their cart. It seemed Yasotay's canopy, which he had unfurled in preparation for the trip back in the midday sun, interested several of them. Hangu thought better since he had no interest in what was being offered. Soon it became apparent they wouldn't find what they came for, and Hangu decided they had wasted enough of the day.

"I think we should go; we can try our luck again tomorrow," Hangu said despondently.

"As you wish, Hangu," replied Yasotay, pulling on the reins and guiding the cart to his left, back toward home. As they drove off, he could see the prisoner watching them depart.

As soon as they returned home, Yasotay went back to work clearing the fallen tree from the yard. Hangu fed the goats and performed chores about the farm, intentionally avoiding the hard manual labor of removing chunks of the large tree. Yasotay worked feverishly, and in the back of his mind, he was still haunted by the image of the green eyes of the prisoner wearing a cangue.

Hangu helped Lian with the fire to make dinner, checked on the horses, and occasionally brought Yasotay some water to enjoy while on a break. The day was slowly ending, and Yasotay was resting, sitting on a log, still thinking about the prisoner whom he couldn't get out of his mind, when he noticed an unpleasant odor. It was very faint, and he couldn't quite place it. Scanning the area, he saw nothing unusual or out of the ordinary. But he could definitely smell something, something familiar. Then it popped into his head: *That's the smell of those nomads!*

Due to the winds, which were gentle and blowing in from the east, Yasotay mused out loud, "Their smell does carry!" Then, he noticed a bush sway in the grove of trees at the far edge of the field. He went to investigate. Carrying the two-handed axe in his right hand, Yasotay walked toward where he had seen the movement. As he got closer, he slowed his pace and moved deliberately and silently. He could hear something, a scratching sound, and the smell had gotten much stronger. Raising his axe to shoulder height, he was ready to strike if necessary. Yasotay stepped through the bushes, and there was the green-eyed nomad wearing the cangue, seated on the ground, poking at the yoke around his neck with a stick.

He was startled by Yasotay holding the axe. "Don't, NO…I mean you no harm," the nomad said, throwing his one free hand up along with the palm of his other hand.

Yasotay lowered the axe to his side to allay his fears. "What are you doing?" he asked.

"I'm trying to remove this damnable thing from around my neck," the man said, throwing the stick to the ground. "My name is Temujin. I am being held hostage over a dispute between clans."

Yasotay stood there and looked more closely at him. He couldn't help but feel pity for this young man having to wear such an ungodly device. Yasotay was faced with the question: *What shall I do?* And then, *what would my Taoist teaching ask of me?*

Yasotay had seen peasants forced to wear a cangue in the streets of Zhongdu to shame them for some inappropriate behavior. Most dangerous criminals were just put to death; generally, only those committing minor offenses were placed in a cangue. Yasotay was happy to help, but he had no experience with putting one of these things on or, more importantly, taking one off.

"Well, Temujin, it appears you're in luck. I will help you to remove that…thing. My name is Yasotay. Let me take a look at it." He moved closer to the device and the odiferous nomad.

Still sitting, Temujin leaned back until the back of the cangue rested on the ground to give Yasotay a better view of the device.

"It appears that this thing has four main cross-members holding the flat top boards together," said Yasotay as he examined the construction of this diabolical device. "Whoever built this thing made it hard to slip off or be easily removed."

"Yes, I know. And I've been wearing this contraption for what seems like an eternity," said Temujin indignantly. "If I ever get my hands on the old man who put me in this thing, I'll…"

"I think if we can remove two or three of these cross-members, we should be able to separate the main boards enough to remove it from around your neck," explained Yasotay, murmuring to himself. "Whoever made this thing was thorough."

Yasotay tried to wedge the axe blade between a cross-member board and one of the top boards, but he couldn't get leverage, and it wouldn't budge. Using a rock, he tried to bang on the back of the axe head to wedge it between the two pieces of wood. No luck. Then, holding the top of the cangue with his left hand, Yasotay slid his hand down on the axe handle and made a small chopping motion on the bottom cross-member.

"Hold still. I would hate to miss!" teased Yasotay with a reassuring smile. Then, noticing the extent of the scars, blood, and scrapes around

Temujin's neck and hand, he added in a calming tone, "It looks like you have been wearing this for a while!" Temujin said nothing.

After repeated strokes, the bottom cross-member split in two along the length of the board, making it easier for Yasotay to wedge the axe in between the boards, pry them loose, and remove the two remaining pieces of the first cross-member. Realizing that it was easier to remove the cross-members if he split them first, Yasotay split and removed two more of them, leaving only one holding the device together. Temujin, now able to squeeze his right hand from the cangue, instantly tried to lift the yoke off his neck with both hands. With the last cross-member still tightly in place, Yasotay went behind the nomad, placed his foot alongside Temujin's head, and lifted one of the top boards. The last cross-member split, and the cangue fell into pieces around the man's lap. Temujin laid back with his head on the ground in total relief, looking up at the sky.

"Thank Tengri, the Eternal Blue Sky! I cannot express how good it feels to lay my head and shoulders flat on the ground—finally! You have performed Tengri's will, my friend. Thank you," said Temujin with a deep sense of gratitude.

"Happy to be of service," replied Yasotay, reaching out a hand to help Temujin to his feet.

He stood up and winced immediately upon putting weight on his right foot. "I stumbled on the way here and twisted it again." Both men looked down at his right ankle, which had swollen to twice the size of his left.

Yasotay knelt and held Temujin's right foot in his two hands. "It doesn't look broken, but it's most certainly a nasty sprain. You will need to stay off this foot for a couple of days. Then, with time to heal, it should be fine."

"I must go; those ass-licking dogs who imprisoned me will be out looking for me," said Temujin.

"How did you escape?" asked Yasotay.

"I hit that big one in the head with that contraption and hobbled away as quickly as possible. It was odd because the one in the green hat saw me hiding and let me go. I think he was tired of dealing with me. This isn't my first time escaping from those wretched fools, but I intend for it to be my last."

"It's almost night. The sun is setting now; why don't you come to Hangu's farm with me? It's just across the field. We can eat, and you can rest. I will wrap your ankle, and you can be off before sunrise in the morning with a good night's sleep," Yasotay proposed.

"No, I think…" Temujin hesitated, and with a nervous look, he took a step and winced again in pain. Then, dropping his shoulders and resigned to his situation, Temujin sighed in relief and said, "Yes…I appreciate your help!"

"Here, let me give you a hand," offered Yasotay. Bending at the waist, he took Temujin's right arm and placed it around his lowered left shoulder. Then, he wrapped his left arm behind his back and supported the wounded man as they walked gingerly out of the brush and across the field. They had to go roughly three hundred paces to the barn, which required multiple rest stops along the way.

"I suppose you would like a bath?" Yasotay suggested.

"Bath…. No!" exclaimed Temujin, almost in horror at the thought. "There are evil spirits in the water. But I would like a bucket of water. I am thirsty and want to remove the dirt from my face and hands."

"I think we can see to that," explained Yasotay, thinking it very odd that Temujin wouldn't accept the offer to take a bath with some of his freshly scented bath beans. Yasotay couldn't help but think, *this man smells!*

The duo slowly progressed across the field toward Hangu's farm, a collection of ten small structures connected to each other, along with a separate barn building for the animals. Hangu's family has owned this farm for generations, and every building has a specific purpose. The structures were arranged in a rectangular shape, creating a protective complex with two inner courtyards. The front courtyard was designed for receiving guests, while the back courtyard was reserved for family use. The brick structures appear to be a single building from the outside, with their backs connected and facing outward. Each structure has small windows but no outward-facing doors, except for the main entrance facing south. This entrance leads directly into the first courtyard, which serves as the receiving area. Yasotay usually sleeps in the corner to the right of this courtyard. A large, detached barn separate from the primary collection of buildings had a fenced area just one hundred paces east of the main complex. The two of them slowly approach the barn, with Yasotay aiding Temujin around the fence to where he had been working on the fallen tree.

"Over there is a bucket of water I have been…" said Yasotay, motioning toward a large bucket next to the fence where he had been working. But before he could finish, Temujin took three big hops on his good foot and knelt in front of the bucket. He plunged his hands into the water and splashed it on his face. The blood and dirt ran down his neck, chest, and back as he repeatedly splashed water on his face, gulping down a few handfuls before he finally grabbed the bucket with both hands and dumped the remaining water over the top of his head with his mouth open wide. He spitted, then coughed loudly, shaking his head. He looked up toward the sky as he dropped the bucket at his side.

"There is a small creek where you can get more water and clean up more if you like?" said Yasotay, helping Temujin to his feet. The nomad stood there with closed eyes and streaks of dirt and blood running down his face and neck. He took big breaths in and out.

Finally, after a long moment, Temujin said, "Yes, that would be good." Yasotay put his left arm and shoulder under Temujin's right arm as he again helped him walk. They hobbled around the front of the complex toward a small stream that ran along the west side of the building. In the first month of his arrival at the farm, Yasotay had created a small dam on this stream and built a sluice of wood and bamboo that channeled water from the creek to the back west corner of the farm complex where the kitchen was located. Originally, Hangu marveled at his invention, thinking Yasotay must be some sort of magician.

Approaching the dam, Yasotay cautioned, "You must drink slower this time, Temujin; you will get sick if you drink too fast."

Temujin said nothing as he knelt at the water's edge and splashed the caked-on dirt and grime from his face, neck, and hands. Standing over him, Yasotay could see the extent of the cangue's marks and bruising on his neck and wrist. He wondered about the filthy nomad's belief in water demons. *How could his silly belief be so strong that it keeps him from jumping into the stream when he so needed it?* Then, Yasotay could faintly hear Hangu's voice. "Yasotay." In a louder and more shrilled voice, while standing at the doorway to his house, Hangu called out again, "Yasotay, Yasotay."

"Give me a moment; I'll be back," he told Temujin, acknowledging him with a wave and leaving Temujin where he knelt.

Walking up to meet Hangu, but before he had a chance to say anything, Hangu whispered in a concerned voice, "Who is that?"

"He is one of the people we met earlier today at the Four Corners," replied Yasotay.

"What does he want?" asked Hangu. "I don't remember meeting him. Why is he here? Is he a threat? Is there a problem?" Hangu was obviously nervous about Yasotay's newfound friend.

"He is injured, hungry, and thirsty, and I offered to help him."

"Lian has made some food. So, you should send him on his way and come and eat," ordered Hangu.

"I would like to offer him a meal and a place to rest for the evening if that's all right with you and Lian?" asked Yasotay. "If there's not enough food, he can have mine. I'm not hungry."

"I don't know. He looks dangerous," said Hangu, with a concerned look. "I don't think it's wise. How do you know he won't slit our throats while we sleep?"

"You took me in," said Yasotay. "I didn't slit your throat."

"You were dressed like a priest; he is dressed like a bandit!" said Hangu.

Temujin had finished drinking and rinsing his wounds and was trying to walk toward where they stood in front of the farm's main door. They watched as he did his best to limp the twenty-five to thirty paces to where they were. He moved slowly and painfully; after covering about half the distance, Temujin stepped on a small rock with his bad foot and went down like a sack of stones, shuddering involuntarily in pain.

"He won't make it past that row of pine trees tonight with that foot," said Yasotay, motioning toward the row of large trees bordering the field.

"I don't know, Yasotay. He's a nomad; he can't be trusted," said Hangu. "This is bad, really bad!"

"I wish to help him, nomad or not. It's the right thing to do, but I respect that this is your home. I suppose I will have to take him…" said Yasotay.

But before he could finish, Hangu blurted out, "He can stay in the barn. You can bring him food there, but I don't want him in my home!"

"As you wish, Hangu. You are most gracious; I will see to it that he's gone in the morning before sunrise. You have my word!"

Yasotay walked over and helped the nomad up, putting his arm around Temujin's back to support him as he walked once again. The two hobbled past Hangu, who looked closely at Temujin, trying to place him. The nomad's eyes remained fixed on the ground before him, watching each step he took. He glanced up at the farmer briefly, his green eyes meeting Hangu's for an instant. Hangu's mouth dropped open as he suddenly remembered where he had seen those eyes. Then, not saying a word, Hangu turned and retreated through his front door, closing it behind him. They could hear the wooden slide locking it tight.

Yasotay helped Temujin into the barn and organized an area for him in one of the empty stalls by adding fresh straw. He had Temujin lie down and prop up his leg; he insisted that Temujin keep it elevated to alleviate the swelling. Then, leaving him, he told the nomad that he would return with food and water, which he did. When he handed him the bowl of rice and meat, Temujin devoured the contents as though he had not eaten for days, spilling rice down the front of his torn and dirty *deel*.

"I leave you to rest and will return before sunrise to wrap your ankle," said Yasotay.

Having eaten and lying back, Temujin had closed his eyes, was already half asleep, and said, "I must return to my clan." He raised his arm at the elbow, palm out, then let it fall back down next to him, and he was asleep.

Yasotay turned to leave but hesitated and looked down at him for a moment. Noticing once again the scars on his hand and around his neck, with his foot swollen and propped up in the air, Yasotay realized for the first time how young and truly vulnerable the man lying before him was.

After contemplating a moment, Yasotay walked outside to where Tata was standing. He removed her harness and began stroking her neck. "What do you think of him, Tata? He doesn't seem to be an animal the way most people claim about these nomads. Though, the others were certainly treating him like one with that thing around his neck." Yasotay spoke to the ass as to a trusted friend. He pulled half an apple from his pocket. "Here you go, girl." Tata took the apple in one bite. "It seems to me that helping him is the right thing to do! These nomads are interesting…smelly, but interesting; Temujin seems very different than the few stories I've read about the nomads," said Yasotay, who enjoyed speaking from the heart to Tata. He placed his head up against hers. "I know there's more going on in your head than you let on." The ass whinnied.

"Come on, girl, time to go inside; I need to finish up and get to sleep. We must get up earlier than normal and help our new friend get on the road. I wonder what it would be like to learn more about these people. Who knows, maybe we'll go with him. I have always been curious to learn their ways, so little is written…and this one could certainly use our help. What do you think, Tata?" Yasotay petted her head and then walked her into the barn. He guided Tata to her stall, hung her harness on the wooden peg, and checked again on Temujin, who was asleep in the next stall. He quietly closed the barn door on his way out.

Yasotay had to see that Temujin was on his way well before sunrise, as he had promised Hangu and Lian. It was clear that they were both very uncomfortable with the nomad sleeping in their barn. They didn't want any trouble and repeatedly stated that to Yasotay. So, he planned to wake up early, wrap Temujin's foot tight for travel, hand him some extra clothes, along with a small bag of grain and some dried meat, and send him down the road.

Yasotay finally fell asleep. It was extremely early in the morning when the BANG, BANG, BANG sound of someone striking the main door startled him awake. It sounded as if they were trying to break down the door. Then, BANG, BANG, BANG came again. Yasotay was on his feet and grabbed his staff from its place. Hangu and Lian appeared at the doorway between the two courtyards; both had ghost-white faces and robes that were hurriedly thrown on and looked disheveled.

"Do you want me to answer the door?" asked Yasotay in a hushed voice, standing closer to the main door than Hangu. Light, obviously from torches, could be seen glowing above the courtyard wall.

"No, I will," said Hangu, already moving across the courtyard toward him. He opened the door, and there stood three hulking nomads. Their pungent stench accosted Hangu in a wave, forcing him to step back. His stomach immediately turned, leaving him with an acidic taste in his mouth. Each nomad held a fiery torch in their hand. With the door wide open, Yasotay could see three or four more nomads on horses and several riderless horses loitering about in front of Hangu's compound.

"Have you seen a red-haired devil wearing a cangue around his neck?" menacingly barked the big nomad wearing a red robe. He had a torch in one hand and a sword in the other. Yasotay recognized two of them from the market. The one wearing that green hat said, "We tracked him to the woods around here."

Hangu strained to understand them, and before he could say anything, Yasotay said, "It is just us three here; there are no others."

Lifting his torch so the flames were licking the top of the doorway, the nomad in the red robe said, "Check over there," motioning the others toward the barn. With that, the three of them turned and walked away. Hangu closed the door and quickly slid the latch to bolt it shut.

"I knew that nomad was trouble!" said Lian in a whispered voice. "When they find him, they will return and won't knock next time!" Then, she turned to Yasotay. "This is all your fault."

"If they find him, they will just leave with him. If not, we'll say he must have hidden in the barn." Yasotay stepped over to the small window and looked out at the barn. He could see shapes and shadows moving within the torchlit barn.

"They are going to burn down my barn," Hangu said anxiously, peering out the window over Yasotay's shoulder. "If they do, will they come after us next?"

"I'll go out there and do what I can," replied Yasotay. He went and grabbed his kusari from his belongings, then carrying his wooden staff, he crossed the courtyard and went out the main door.

As Yasotay slowly walked toward the barn, a loud voice shouted from across the field. "Here, here, here," The nomads on horseback took off, headed toward the voice in the darkness. The other three came running out of the barn, and Yasotay heard one of them whistle. They were soon atop their horses, also heading across the field, quickly following the others. Within moments, they were all gone.

Yasotay stood there momentarily, thinking about what was happening. He realized one of the nomads had found the remains of the cangue in the woods and had called the others. It was night and very dark out, but Yasotay had no doubt they would figure it out and return to Hangu's house. It was time for Yasotay to choose a path; there was no time to waste. *The common thread is to do the right thing and help someone in need*, he said to himself. Yasotay ran into the barn.

"Quickly, we must leave NOW! Temujin, where are you?" said Yasotay as he went to Tata's stall and put a harness over her head.

"I am over here," Temujin said, hopping out of the shadows at the same time as Hangu showed up at the barn door. "They are going to return!"

"I know," exclaimed Yasotay. "Temujin and I have to leave, *NOW!*"

"I can ride," said Temujin eagerly. "Just give me a horse, and I will go," He saw which animal Yasotay was bridling and said, "Not that animal, anything but that one. It is ill-tempered. It pissed on me while I slept! That beast is evil!" Hangu didn't know what Temujin was saying, but his body language was clearly stating, *not that animal*, which brought a nod of agreement from Hangu.

"Don't worry. I'm going with you!" said Yasotay.

"You can take your cart," Hangu said. "You fixed it from junk; it's yours. Just get him out of my barn and away from my home."

"Thanks, Hangu. I greatly appreciate your offer," replied Yasotay, leading Tata over to the cart and attaching her bellyband to the breaching rods on both sides. Then, finally, she was ready to go.

"Get in the back of the cart. You can't ride with that ankle," Yasotay told Temujin. "I'll be right back." He left the barn in an all-out run and headed back toward the house. Yasotay ran in and grabbed a wooden chest from his sleeping quarters, which held his few meager belongings. He wrapped a blue sash around his waist, covering the pouch that held his kusari, and headed for the door. Lian stood at the doorway between the two courtyards. Noticing her, Yasotay set down the chest. Then, he bowed gratefully and purposefully to Lian. "I have greatly appreciated your hospitality over the past months."

She returned the bow and said, "I take it you're leaving with him?"

Yasotay replied, "Yes." And he hastily gathered up his chest and bolted out the door toward the barn.

"Safe travels, Yasotay," whispered Lian softly to the young man's back as he left. "I wish you good fortune. May God bless your path!"

Yasotay looked across the field as he quickly traversed the distance between the house and the barn. He could make out the faint lights from the torches that danced about in the forest, where the remnants of Temujin's cangue were. He knew if they were skilled enough to track him this far, they would likely pick up his trail again and head back this way within moments. It was dark, but a half-moon was hanging in the sky, enough to light their way.

"Hangu, I doubt that I will be able to return," Yasotay said as he placed the wooden chest under the cart seat. "Thank you for all you have done for me." Yasotay bowed.

"You must hurry, my boy; leave now before they come back," answered Hangu in what sounded like a fatherly tone to Yasotay.

"I want you to do one more thing. I am taking the road west. Once I am around the bend and out of sight, you must start waving a torch and yelling to get their attention. Then, when they return, tell them someone has just stolen your cart and headed west."

"But that's the way you are going," said Hangu.

"I know, but if you help them, they won't suspect your involvement. Otherwise, they may burn down your house and harm you and Lian. So don't worry about us. I know these roads better than them. They will be hard-pressed to catch us," stated Yasotay, climbing up onto the cart seat.

"Wait, what did you just tell him?" asked Temujin.

"I told him once we're gone to save himself by telling them someone just stole his cart and which way we're headed," Yasotay calmly explained.

"No, don't send them our way," yelled Temujin, lying in the back of the cart. "That's a bad plan!"

"We'll be fine; you'll see that Tata can run like the wind. In this way, we all have a fighting chance!" With that, Yasotay said a word to Tata, and they were off at a quick pace.

"Hold on, Temujin. As soon as we reach the bend up there, I'm putting Tata into a full gallop." The nomad, who was already bouncing around in the back of the cart, adjusted his grip on the side panel of the cart.

"Understood," said Temujin in an apprehensive tone while testing the cart's other grab points, looking for something better to hold. He bounced around and felt like he was already about to be ejected from the back of the cart! Finally, finding a piece of rope attached to the cart, he wrapped his right hand around it multiple times and did his best to brace himself.

As the cart began to round the bend, Yasotay looked back and saw that Hangu had a torch in his hand and was waving it back and forth.

Yasotay guided Tata around the bend, and then, when directed, the ass sped off like the wind. Her blustery pace was considerable, considering she was hauling a cart with two riders on board. Fortunately,

Yasotay's eyes had finally adjusted to the darkness. He could see well enough to know exactly where they were, even at their blistering pace. Time seemed to stand still as Tata rode hard. Then, finally, Yasotay turned left, leaving the well-marked main road onto a lesser-used road with the cart sliding through the turn. He was well aware that the main road twisted and turned and ultimately went through a small town up ahead. This path wound southwest around the town and connected back to the main road on the town's far side. Yasotay pulled lightly on the reins to slow their pace. The road sloped down gently and bent slightly toward the right. He remembered a turn that would lead them down to the river and a remote fishing spot. He turned down a dark, narrow path, hidden from view, and emerged on the riverbed. They could go no further with the cart. With no easy way to turn around, he pulled back on the reins.

Yasotay jumped from the cart and immediately went to Tata. "Easy girl, easy." Yasotay did his best to speak with a calming tone. He knew Tata had run as hard and fast as possible and that exhaustion would now set in! Her head hung low with fatigue, alternately coming up for air and then falling once again. Yasotay praised and soothed her, quietly trying to ease her as she strained and gasped for air.

"I don't think we should…" Temujin stopped in midsentence because Yasotay raised his index finger to his mouth. Tata's left ear had twitched, and then she raised her nose and sniffed the night air. Yasotay was very familiar with her exceptional hearing and knew that tic all too well. It told him that something or someone was coming! Sure enough, a few moments later, he could hear the faint sound of horses moving closer at a gallop. Yasotay put his index finger up to his lips again. Even Tata seemed to understand the situation; the group became noticeably sensitive to every sound. Then Yasotay crept off very quietly with his staff in hand and slowly climbed up the riverbed's embankment to a position where he could see yet was still hidden. The scant light from the partial moon was enough for him to make out three riders headed toward them. Yasotay looked down to where the cart stood and saw that Temujin was now crouched, partially hidden behind the cart.

Yasotay could now see the three riders approaching the turnoff, which was nothing more than a narrow trail, little more than a game trail. Even during the day, it was easily missed. Yasotay climbed farther up the embankment and crept low along a tangle of thick bushes until he had an even clearer view of the road and the turnoff. The riders stopped abruptly just a few strides past the hidden trail. The leader's black stallion snorted and pawed at the ground. He spun the stallion around, looking back up the road they had just come down. Pausing, he peered intently through the dim light. It was dark, so no one noticed Yasotay stepping out onto the road.

"That looked like a path back there; I think I saw marks in the dirt," said the leader in a low, harsh tone.

"I will go look," said the big nomad in the bright red jacket as he slipped off his horse. It was dark, but Yasotay could see that one of his legs moved awkwardly when he put weight on it. At that moment, the third rider, the one who wore the green hat, spun his head around. "Look over there." Nodding down the road, the other two turned their heads, squinting to see.

"I think you should get back on your horses and leave!" said Yasotay, his body outlined by the moonlight. He was standing with his left hand on his staff, and his right hand rolled into a fist, sitting on his hip. He spoke in a very slow and clear voice. The nomads' eyes all turned his way, but they could only see his silhouette.

"Where is the red devil?" bellowed the green-capped nomad from atop his horse. "Give him to us now!" With that said, there was a loud and hollow CRACK. The green hat went flying as the nomad fell from his horse with a giant thud. Not seeing any reason for this fall, the nomad leader, still on his stallion, looked down at his fallen comrade. "Get up, you fool," he shouted. Then he heard a loud buzzing sound as if a giant bee was flying around; he looked around, and then came another CRACK! He, too, went down in a pile to the ground. The two lay on the path, motionless. The third nomad stood there frozen for a moment; you could see his mind trying to comprehend what had just happened. *Everything was happening so quickly; it just didn't make any sense.*

Yasotay tried desperately not to break the mesmerizing moment. He slowly pulled on the chain with his right hand, reeling it in. The last nomad standing, the largest of the three and wearing the red robe, finally realized what had happened and screamed, "Aarrgghhhh," as he charged Yasotay, axe in hand. But it was too late; with a quick jerk on the chain and a snap of his wrist, Yasotay sent the small metal ball flying directly toward the charging nomad's head. *CRACK!* The man's legs appeared to be still moving forward as his head seemed to retreat. With a large thud, the third nomad was on his back, dazed.

Temujin came limping out from the underbrush. Having witnessed the first nomad fall from his horse, he had limped down the path to get closer. He hobbled up, snatched a sword from the hand of one of the unconscious nomads, and thrust it into the fallen man's chest. He placed his injured foot on the trunk of the body and, with a wince, withdrew the blade. He next limped over to the second nomad, the last to go down, who was already starting to regain consciousness. Temujin raised his sword.

"No... Don't!" insisted Yasotay, but it was too late; Temujin thrust his sword deep into the chest of the large, red-robed nomad, which hammered his torso back to the ground. Then, he again placed his injured foot on the nomad's chest and withdrew the blade. While it was still dark, Yasotay could see Temujin's face contorted in a half grin, half grimace. He asked, "Why not? Do you think they would have spared you?"

"We could have made it so they couldn't follow," replied Yasotay in an exasperated tone.

"Which is what I am doing...making it so they can't follow!" insisted Temujin as he moved toward the third and final nomad.

"No," demanded Yasotay, moving forward and placing his staff across Temujin's chest, blocking his way. "I will deal with this one."

"As you please; today, you are the wolf, and they are your prey. You may do with the last one as you wish," snapped Temujin with a bow and a smile. Hopping around, he stooped down and began rummaging through the belongings of the nomad he had just stabbed, looking for anything of value. He pulled a long dagger from the man's belt.

Yasotay walked over to one of the nomads' horses and removed some coiled rope from one of the saddles. He then stepped back to the still-living nomad, bent down, grabbed the front of his jacket, and pulled him into a sitting position. Then, Yasotay got behind him, lifted his body from under both arms, and dragged him about seven paces to the nearest tree. He sat him down against the tree, tied one hand and then the other behind the man's back and around the tree's trunk. Next, Yasotay found his green hat, which had fallen off, and placed it back on his head and over his eyes. The man was sitting there, looking like he was taking a nap. Except for his two dead friends, no one would be the wiser. Yasotay rolled the other two bodies into the brush while Temujin took inventory.

"I've got three bladders of water, some dried meats, a small bag of millet, two swords, one axe, one bow with a quiver of arrows, and four daggers." Temujin yanked on one of the boots from the dead nomad's foot. "These might fit me," he added.

"Fine," said Yasotay with a sigh, realizing the situation was out of his control. With only two dead and a third unconscious, they could assume at least four or five more nomads were still searching for them. Yasotay walked down the narrow path to where they had left Tata and the cart. After some maneuvering, Yasotay led Tata and their cart back up to the main road.

"We need to leave," explained Yasotay, "the other nomads will still be looking for us. In which direction are your people?"

"My people are a long way north and west, essentially northwest from here," said Temujin, throwing a warm-looking sheepskin over his shoulders that he had removed from one of his pursuers.

"Do they know of your clan?" asked Yasotay.

"Yes. I am my clan's leader like my father was, as was his father. This is why they imprisoned me, to weaken us," said Temujin. That statement stirred up many questions in Yasotay's mind, but he thought, *set them aside; we must get out of here!*

"So we can assume they know which direction we're headed. The main road we split off from goes through town and continues west, so they will probably be looking for us along that road. This side road connects back to the main road on the other side of town. So, I figure the search party split up, back at the turn, with these three following this road and the remainder of them headed through town, assuming we went that way." Yasotay looked to the horizon. "The sun will be up soon, so we should go!"

"I can't get my foot into this boot!" exclaimed Temujin in exasperation, sitting on the ground with his new boot on his left foot while trying to get his swollen right foot into the other.

"It appears to have swollen even more," observed Yasotay. "We never had a chance to wrap it again, and the hobbling around on it hasn't helped. Come, let me wrap it quickly."

Yasotay helped Temujin to the back of the cart, where he could sit.

Looking down at his foot, Temujin said, "This foot gets larger every time I look at it…" He paused and pointed to Yasotay's pouch. "So, what is that thing?"

"What are you talking about?" asked Yasotay, sounding annoyed. He was preoccupied with wrapping Temujin's foot.

"That ball-and-chain thing?" answered Temujin. "You know that humming bee you stung those three with?"

"Oh, my kusari," said Yasotay, "or at least that's my informal name for it. It's a weapon I had read about. I believe it was invented in Nippon." He pulled the end of the kusari out of the leather pouch secured around his waist and handed it to Temujin.

"Ni-pon?" repeated Temujin with a confused look, holding the metal ball at the end of the chain, bouncing it in his hand and considering its weight.

"Yes, it's a foreign land, across the great sea, called the 'Land of the Rising Sun,'" explained Yasotay. "A blacksmith made this for me, and I've practiced with it ever since. There's an ancient story of a Chinese warrior who was deadly at throwing rocks. Many tried, but all failed at besting him. His deadly aim was renowned throughout the empire. Many great swordsmen fell at his hand. I discovered a description of this weapon and remembered the rock-throwing story. So, I decided it might be an interesting weapon to learn."

"You taught yourself how to throw a metal rock connected to a long chain at people's heads and knock them out?" Temujin lightly threw the ball in the air, catching it and laughing in approval as he flipped the metal ball back to Yasotay.

"Ahh, yeah, I guess you can say that," smiled Yasotay, catching the metal ball and putting it back in its leather pouch. "But someone trained in its use can do much more than hit someone in the head. It's a useful tool in combat if used properly."

"Yes, well it did the deed here quick enough! I may not have seen it, but I did hear its bee buzz," laughed Temujin. "The one you tied to the tree looks dead too."

"He'll have a bad headache when he wakes, but he's still breathing," added Yasotay. "We need to leave here. This foot is in no condition to walk or ride. So best you stay in the back of the cart for now."

"I think I can ride…" Then, sliding off the cart, he winced and almost fell. Temujin's face sagged with that same resigned look as yesterday's. He hopped to the rear of the cart on one leg and pulled his body up onto it.

Yasotay tied two of the three nomads' horses off to the back of the cart. Then, he took the reins of the third horse and tied him to a tree by the lifeless but still-breathing nomad. Temujin was inspecting the blades and supplies he had confiscated as Yasotay climbed up into the cart and whispered to Tata, who began slowly ambling forward.

"This bow looks well made, but the edges of these swords are dull, and they're made from inferior metal," observed Temujin thoughtfully as he looked at the small haul of weapons. "No wonder they were looking to trade for better blades," with disgust, he tossed the best of the low-grade blades against the inside of the cart.

They rode along quickly in silence for a good while. Their pace was not too fast to draw attention. They rode at a comfortable trot for Tata as Temujin watched the light from the rising sun illuminate the clouds high above, creating an orange and purple fluff. The collection of low-hanging clouds blocked the direct sunlight; they appeared dark blue on the horizon and bright white just above it. Other than these random wisps of clouds, the sky was bare blue in between them and a canopy of multicolored thicker cloud wisps high in the sky.

Yasotay looked back and noticed the beautiful sunrise that Temujin was enjoying. "The new day dawns with a beautiful display for your first day of freedom…how long has it been?" asked Yasotay.

In deep thought, Temujin stared at the magnificent display, transfixed by its fleeting beauty. "Eight long months, seven tortured in that damn yoke. I don't know why you helped me or how I will ever repay you," said Temujin in a low, clear, conjectural tone filled with appreciation. "I pledge this: for long as we share the road, I will do anything within my power to ensure no harm comes to you, as you have done for me."

Yasotay stayed quiet, thinking, *Why did I do this? While his sincerity seems real, where am I going when we finally escape danger? The common thread is me helping those in need, but when does it end? Am I actually traveling with him into the wilderness?*

"'For as long as we share the road …'" pledged Yasotay, pausing for a moment, "We will be back to the main road up ahead shortly. Let's get you hidden under cover," instructed Yasotay, who pulled on the reins and brought Tata to a stop. He hopped out and reached into the back of the cart. He grabbed one of the swords and, walking over to the side of the road, began hacking at some high, leafy plants with star-like yellow flowers.

"You were right; these blades are dull," Yasotay stated as he hacked and hacked. Finally, he had gathered enough, and he began spreading the long stalks over the back of the cart, covering Temujin lying down inside the back of the cart.

"I am exhausted and will try to nap," said Temujin as he fluffed the pilfered sheepskin under his head. "Between animals pissing on me and those bastards trying to kill me, I just need some uninterrupted sleep."

"That's good. You stay down out of sight," said Yasotay, throwing a rope over the top of the heap of bushes and cinching it down.

"Not too tight," came Temujin's voice from under the stalks. "If there's trouble, you let me know. I can't think of anything I would rather do than jump up out from under these weeds and cut down those miserable bastards," he added, tightening his grip on the dull sword he held closely in his hand. Yasotay, done with securing the pile of plants, put up the cart canopy. After all his handiwork, Yasotay and Tata looked like any other traveler today, with Temujin hidden from view.

"Let's see if we can get around the town and on our way without getting killed or killing anyone else," Yasotay said as he jumped back up onto the cart's bench, and with a word to Tata, they were off.

After a short ride, Yasotay broke the silence. "We're coming up to the main road in a moment, and I don't see anyone; hopefully, we won't stand out. But it would be better if more people were on the road!"

"Maybe you should have listened to me and not had Hangu say anything. I remember you told him to say, "Someone stole my cart," Temujin said. "So, they are certainly looking for a cart!"

"I think we'll be fine. There are many carts on the road. You just lay low and out of sight," said Yasotay, whispering a word under his breath that made Tata pick up her pace as they merged onto the main east/west road. The road was well worn with only the occasional rock or pothole, so smooth that it made the infrequent bumps feel more insufferable. They traveled almost half a shi without seeing anyone. At times, Yasotay thought he could hear a light snoring coming from the back under the plants.

"We have someone coming toward us," said Yasotay. "Stay down and be quiet."

Up ahead, there were two people and a mule walking toward them. The mule was loaded down with two large bundles of sticks on either side, and one of the two people was a young boy, the other an older man holding a rope leading the mule. Yasotay nodded and smiled as they passed. They rode on, passing the occasional fellow traveler. Several people seemed to be headed into town this morning. Yasotay did his best to avoid the intermittent bumps when he noticed Tata's ear twitch. Seeing no one ahead, he glanced behind him and saw two men on horseback a good way back, approaching them at full speed.

"Looks like we have a couple of nomads coming our way," reported Yasotay. "Best you just stay quiet and let me deal with them."

"Understood, but if it's going to turn into a fight, you let me know *before* you start hitting them in the head with your metal rock," said Temujin, who was anxious to get revenge against his captors.

"They're here," said Yasotay under his breath, trying not to move his lips. The two horsemen overtook Tata and the cart since Yasotay hadn't changed their comfortable pace. They pulled up on either side of the cart, and one with a sword in his hand used it to motion for Yasotay to stop. He obliged and pulled back on the reins.

"What do you want?" asked Yasotay, who intentionally spoke the nomad language in an awkward manner as he had noticed many from Hangu's village did when speaking to the nomads.

"We're looking for an escaped prisoner, red hair. Have you seen him?" asked the man to Yasotay's left. The one on the right was closely inspecting the cart.

"No," said Yasotay.

"What are these plants for? Why is your cart filled with weeds?" asked the man to his right.

"It's not weeds, it's woad!"

"It's what?"

"It's woad, used to make a blue dye ... for dyeing cloth. I sell to a trader who pays well," responded Yasotay.

"Blue dye? It's a green plant with yellow flowers?" questioned the man.

"They boil the leaves. It makes a bright blue dye," informed Yasotay.

Suddenly, the man to Yasotay's left pulled back on his reins. His horse backed up, giving him a clear view of the pile of plants. He noticed a hint of blue on the outer edges of the flowers. He took his sword and stabbed into the pile of woad in the back of the cart, once, twice, three times.

The nomad stepped forward and gave Yasotay a long, hard look. He noticed a blue sash around Yasotay's waist. He looked back at the plants and again at Yasotay. "Let's go!" An instant later, they wheeled their horses around and headed back down the road from where they came.

"Temujin…?" asked Yasotay.

"He just missed me," he replied. "The first stroke ran right along my leg. So, I guess they're gone? I need to sit up!"

"Yes, it's clear." Yasotay jumped down and loosened the rope. Temujin sat up with his head popping through the foliage, not daring to expose himself further.

They continued on the main road and picked up their pace, traveling west for the rest of the day. To their left was the vast expansive grasslands of the steppe, and to their right was a sloping hill with islands of trees dotting its broad undulations. Finally, around mid-day, Temujin emerged from his hiding place and moved to the front with Yasotay. Sitting on the bench, he propped his swollen foot on the wooden front ledge of the cart at Yasotay's insistence. The two parallel dirt tracks of the road seemed to cut through the broad grassy plain of the countryside as if it had been traversed every day for thousands of years. They stopped only twice, once to relieve themselves and another time when Yasotay noticed mushrooms and herbs growing near a shaded area. Fighting with Tata, who also found value in some of the herbs, he picked what he needed and placed them in a small leather bag for keeping. It was late in the afternoon. The sun would set shortly, so they decided to stop, eat, and rest for the evening.

Temujin was tending to a small fire he made from sticks and some horse dung that Yasotay had found. Still favoring his injured foot, Temujin was in obvious pain. "You were very quick on your feet with that story about blue dye," he said with a grimace.

"It is all true," replied Yasotay, hopping down from the cart after digging out a small pot from his wooden chest underneath the bench. "This plant is, indeed, used to dye cloth blue. It has served this purpose for hundreds of years," continued Yasotay while unhooking Tata from the cart. Free of her harness, Tata walked twenty paces to the bank of a small stream and drank. Yasotay joined her to get some water for his pot.

"You never cease to amaze me. How do you know about this dye?" asked Temujin, poking the fire with a stick as Yasotay walked back from the stream.

"I am full of a great deal of useless information," responded Yasotay with a smile. He sat next to Temujin near the fire.

"Not so useless after all," Temujin said with a grin.

"It was my life's work for several years. I studied under a Taoist priest named Master Chang. He is a man of great worth, a learned man who has been collecting documents, manuscripts, and writings from all over the world for many years. His library is very large!" Yasotay looked closely at the amount of water in the pot. He poured a little water out, then a little more, and finally placed it near the fire, close enough to heat the contents.

"Li-barr-y. What's a librarry?" asked Temujin, watching Yasotay as he threw in some of the mushrooms he'd picked into the pot, and then, reaching into his small leather bag, he began pinching some herbs into it as well.

"It's a large collection of writings, all kinds of writings, that tell stories, all kinds of stories. His collection was extensive, from many different lands. Many are written in foreign languages. There were thousands of documents, religious manuscripts, drawings, and maps. I have a gift for reading and remembering things. I have read all about the different gods of the West, the many gods of the South, and all the major writings from the different dynasties that previously held control here in the East. That was my position when I worked for Master Chang, reading, cataloging, and interpreting documents all day." Yasotay paused for a moment in thought, then said aloud a thought that crossed his mind for the first time. "I enjoy learning, and Master Chang used this fact toward his own ends."

"Cat-a-log?" repeated Temujin in a questioning voice, watching and listening closely, trying his best to understand.

Yasotay had meticulously measured the herbs and mushrooms he had thrown into the pot, which had now begun to boil. He responded, "Yes, sorry, catalog means to arrange in an orderly way, to group things together that are similar into a list or ledger." Temujin still looked puzzled but changed the subject.

"And what is it that you're throwing into that pot?" asked Temujin.

"Just some herbs and stuff," answered Yasotay. He paused. "Let's see. We have some yan hu root and some hojari, a tree sap for pain and soreness, and then some chives, curry leaves, and lingzhi to relax you and for taste."

"You talk of these things like a shaman," said Temujin.

Yasotay quickly added, "I know how I can explain catalog!" He paused for a moment. "If you were to remember everything I threw into this pot, it would be a list of things in your head. Do you understand?" Temujin just stared back. Yasotay continued, "Do you know how you took inventory of the knives, blades, and bows that you took from the three captors we subdued? That's a catalog or a list.... Do you know how to write?"

"Symbols, characters, pictures.... I know of these things; I have seen them, but nomads have no written words," said Temujin.

How can that be? The written word is one of the fundamental building blocks of a culture. It enables the documentation of one's history, thought Yasotay. *This is fascinating.*

"Let me see if I understand you. So, your life was learning; is this true?" asked Temujin.

"Basically, yes."

"So, why did you leave if you loved learning so much?" queried Temujin.

"I guess...it's because...I don't know how to explain it!" Yasotay paused for a long moment. "I left because I felt there was more to life than learning from others. I wanted to experience life, to live it myself, on my own terms," he said, more certainly, as he stirred the boiling pot, then removed it from the fire to cool.

"I don't understand," replied Temujin, shaking his head slowly while looking at Yasotay with interest.

"When you learn primarily from others—what others write or say—you're learning about their experiences, thoughts, and deeds. I appreciate the value of that knowledge, but I wanted to experience these things for myself. For instance, I had read about the cangue and how it was used throughout history. In the Tang Dynasty, the cangue was worn by all prisoners sentenced to death as defined by the Ten Abominations of Crimes Law, which was subdivided into four major categories. I know all the history of the cangue, but I never really understood the torture of wearing one until I met you! When I saw your pain, the utter frustration of being forced to wear that device, your cuts and scars, your inability to sleep or feed yourself, only then did I truly understand it and its cruel purpose."

"You can trust what I say. Knowing it from stories instead of wearing one is truly much better," stated Temujin, rubbing the back of his neck with his hand instinctively.

They sat silent for a while, eating dried meat and sipping on the hot broth Yasotay had prepared. The sun was setting, and evening was settling in. Temujin knew how to ration food to make it last, so there was very little meat shared between the two travelers that night. He had calculated it would take roughly three weeks to reach their destination. Finally, with the pot empty and the night's rations gone, they sat back and relaxed. An apparent calm settled over them, and for a while, the two laid back and enjoyed the moment, looking into the night sky. Lying on either side of the small fire, they both gazed at the heavens. Their minds drifted, watching shooting stars move across the sky against the backdrop of thousands of more stars glowing brightly. One traced across the sky, then another. After a while, all the stars seemed to move faster than usual; everything in the universe seemed in motion.

"That's it, like the stars in the sky. I left because I needed to be in motion," declared Yasotay with a satisfying grin.

"So, you learned what a cangue really was, but that doesn't answer the question of *why did you help me*?" asked Temujin in a serious and sober voice.

Yasotay paused briefly. "I guess it was your eyes that told me to!"

"My eyes?" responded Temujin, surprised by his answer.

"Yes, your eyes. When we first met, you stared at me, and I felt like your eyes were speaking to me, telling me something beyond what I have read about nomads and cangues. I can truly say I don't need to wear one to understand what it feels like. It was in your eyes. When I returned from town, I thought about helping you…finding you and setting you free. For some reason, I shared your pain and wanted to free you of it. When I found you in the woods, I had already decided to go back to find you," explained Yasotay. He reached over with a stick and stirred the embers of the fire. "So, tell me about you and your people. I know very little about the nomads of the steppe." He paused and looked at Temujin. "Tell me. Why were you being held prisoner?"

"My name is Temujin of the Clan of Borjigin. I am the son of Yesugei. My father was the son of Bartan, the son of the great Khabul Khan," said Temujin proudly.

"I read about your great-grandfather. He was received at the Jin court and was recognized by the Jin as a leader of the Mongols," said Yasotay. "There is little written about the Mongols, nothing I can recall beyond depicting your kind as barbarians, especially Khabul Khan. As the story is told, he offended the emperor, and they poisoned him." Temujin unconsciously lifted his chin and stuck his chest out, which Yasotay noted and hurriedly added, "So, you are the great-grandson of the historic Khabul Khan."

"Yes, I am of a royal bloodline and will take my rightful place as leader of my clan…a Khan!" boomed Temujin. "This is why those worthless ass-licking dogs kept me prisoner. The Taichiud once ruled the Mongols and are unwilling to recognize my claim. I am the true ruler of all those Mongols who dwell in felt tents!"

Yasotay remembered reading about numerous nomads who claimed to descend from royal blood. It was Yasotay's impression that the nomad leaders rose as quickly as they fell. "Your father was murdered? By whom?" asked Yasotay in a low, calm voice, trying to subdue his passion. *This one seems very excitable,* thought Yasotay.

"By the Tartars, poisoned by cowards, the same way a woman would kill!" Temujin's voice became lower and noticeably reverent. "I was with him at his last breath. I traveled for a week to reach him in time. He had waited for me to come to him before dying." Temujin choked and cleared his throat. They were both quiet for a long moment.

Yasotay didn't know what to say; he felt sad for Temujin, who was so touched by this tragedy that he blurted out his real pain about his father's death.

"I never knew my father, never met him…my mother told me he died before I was born. I don't believe her."

"So, you didn't know your father?" Temujin frowned and started sitting up, felt light-headed, and laid back down again.

"No," said Yasotay. "And I can't explain it, but I just don't believe her."

"My father was my rock, my foundation," responded Temujin with feeling, displaying his deep love, which surprised Yasotay. "I am sorry you don't know of this bond."

"But I do," remarked Yasotay. "I have my foundation…a thread as strong as any family bond!"

"A thread?" queried Temujin.

"Yes, a thread," Yasotay said.

"You are confusing most of the time, but I have no idea what you say now!" Temujin blurted with a soft laugh.

"I believe there is a thread, a sutra of truth that carries through every religion, every god, every deity that man currently worships or has ever worshiped in the past," explained Yasotay. "Yes, there are differences, but the key lies within the similarities among those truths. This is my rock, my foundation…my thread!"

Temujin, on his back with his gaze fixed on the night sky, sat up, leaned on one elbow, and looked at Yasotay, "So, you're saying some bigger god is your father?"

Before Yasotay could reply, Temujin blinked several times, shook his head to clear it, and then laid his head back down. "What was in that broth you made?" asked Temujin. "My head is spinning. Whatever it was, it makes you sound even more confusing."

Another flurry of shooting stars streamed across their field of sight. Yasotay responded, "No, not a…bigger god…not like some god of gods!"

Yasotay hesitated for a moment, beginning to feel the effects of the broth himself. "Let me ask you. In what god do you believe?"

"Tengri is the god of all things under the eternal blue sky," replied Temujin without hesitation.

"What makes your god more right, true, or better than any other?" asked Yasotay.

"My father's blood brother, Togru, believes in his Jesus God," quipped Temujin. "Says he's *of Christ*, whatever that means. He says that he fears only God the Almighty."

"Is Togru a good man?" asked Yasotay.

"Yes. Togru is a man of honor. He has been and remains a good friend. He's like a second father to me," said Temujin.

"There are many *good men* who worship many different 'gods.' However, I believe a common thread of truth connects them all. This pursuit—to identify this truth across all the religions—was the mission I abandoned when I left Chang. I left because I could not learn the truth through books alone. Instead, one must experience this truth."

"So, again, you're speaking of some…other god out there?" asked Temujin, waving his upraised arms, which left a swirling image hanging in the night air.

Yasotay laughed aloud, genuinely enjoying the banter, and asked, "Why is Tengri God to you?"

"I was raised to know this truth; it is in my heart," answered Temujin without hesitation. "My father believed in Tengri! And so did his father!"

"Which is why it is true…for you," confirmed Yasotay. "Because those who are your foundation believed it, and those who were their foundation believed in it! It was passed on to you…but what of those raised on the God of Buddha, or of Jesus, or Muhammad, or any others that the host of sages and prophets claimed to be *The True God*? Wasn't their belief implanted into their hearts as Tengri was in yours?" Yasotay let him absorb this idea. "So, they are as heretic to you as you are to them. We all, whatever our tribe, are defined by a desire to believe in a higher being, a bigger purpose. We are beings of worship and belief, and that urge must be sated in each of us in some way. One may worship possessions, people, gods…whatever the case, but we each must focus this urge on something or someone."

"What did you say? What does that mean?" asked Temujin, confused. "I think you have drunk too much from that pot! I know I have…"

"Seneca, a very wise man from long ago, said: 'A higher being is regarded by the common people as true, to the wise as false, and to those who rule as useful.' Everyone has such beliefs; it's part of being alive…of being human. Your beliefs are as different to others as their beliefs are to you," continued Yasotay. "We are all born with a passion drawing us toward…something greater." Yasotay waved his arm, leaving a visual trail. "We all want to be part of that *something greater*! A true leader recognizes this fact and unites those of different beliefs to a noble cause shared by all."

"It's their trust in *your* common cause that matters, not their god!" confirmed Temujin, with a hint of intrigue and satisfaction.

"Yes, the key to uniting a diverse group of people is to vigorously encourage a shared cause," replied Yasotay. "No matter who they bow their heads to in prayer, if they raise their hand to your cause, you can lead them!"

"That makes sense," proclaimed Temujin. "By uniting all the tribes of the steppe under one banner, no matter their religion in heaven, be it Tengri, Buddha, or Jesus, they can be taught to follow one leader! "

Neither spoke for a long while, lost in their fanciful flights. Then, finally, Temujin broke the silence. "If you like to learn, my friend, tomorrow I will teach 'the southern wolf' all about those 'northern wolves' who live in felt tents."

"I would like that," said Yasotay with a smile. They both looked up at the starry sky. "Star light, star bright, last star I see tonight, I wish I might, I wish I may see the stars throughout the day!"

"Whatever you put in that pot…it went right to my head," remarked Temujin. "Plus, my foot doesn't hurt now." This was followed by light laughter from both of them, which quickly rose into roaring, uncontrollable laughter.

CHAPTER FOUR

South of Lake Hulun, late summer, 1178 CE

It was early morning, and Yasotay was busy preparing for the day's journey. Temujin sat there doing his best to sharpen the blade of a sword using a flat stone he had found.

"Wrong type of stone, bad metal. I think I'm making the edge worse!" said Temujin, throwing the blade and rock down in frustration.

"I wouldn't bother with it," responded Yasotay. "You could rub that metal on a rock for years and never get it any sharper than it is now."

"Though winter is coming very soon," declared Temujin. "I know exactly where my people are grazing their herd. Do you see that mountain range far off to the north?" Temujin gestured to the distance.

Yasotay gazed out across the boundless expanse of the steppe. The plains sprawled out as far as the eye could see, pulling the horizon in all directions. Initially, Yasotay saw no mountain range while scanning the unbroken vastness. The sky seemed to stretch down to meet the earth at the edge of everywhere he looked. Then, barely discernible on the remote edge of the horizon, Yasotay could see a slight smudge against the vast canvas of the steppe.

Temujin was gingerly attempting to pull on one of the boots he'd taken from the nomad they had killed, but his swollen ankle was making it impossible. Over the past few days, the swelling had decreased considerably, but his ankle was still a collection of black, orange, purple, and red bruises this morning.

"Yes, now I see it," Yasotay exclaimed as he gazed off to the north. "I also notice your ankle is beginning to look better." Yasotay had been keeping an eye on it.

"My people are grazing their herds west of those mountains," said Temujin, yanking on the boot with a grimace. "There, it is rich with grass for the animals, and the weather is not too harsh yet, so my people are still there. Soon, they will leave for the valley in the shadow of Mother and Father Mountain. It is there we stay for the winter."

Looking down at the boots on his feet, he liked what he saw. Temujin stood up, grabbed the sword he had thrown down, slipped the bow sling over his shoulder, and tied the arrows to his side at the ready—he then slowly and gingerly mounted a horse.

"My ankle is feeling much better today," said Temujin. "I think I will ride!"

Yasotay noticed the stark contrast between Temujin's appearance now, tall and proud on his horse, and the image of him lying vulnerable and frustrated while wearing the cangue. Temujin looked like a *formidable nomad*, as told of in the tales, much more so than the other nomads Yasotay had met. Temujin carried himself with an air about him that you couldn't help but notice.

They rode on for most of the morning. The sun was warm on their faces, the temperature mild, and the blue sky was dotted with large, white fluffy clouds. By midday, Temujin's ankle throbbed in pain, and he had returned to riding in the cart. They had left the worn path days ago for open grasslands. Temujin seemed to be directed by an internal compass, while Yasotay regularly checked his little turtle compass.

"What is that?" asked Temujin, looking over Yasotay's shoulder.

"It's a compass. See the turtle's tail? It always points to the south," said Yasotay, holding it up for him to see.

"I don't need the stars during the day to tell me in what direction we go, nor do I need a turtle's tail," boasted Temujin. "I know the way!" he said, pointing ahead.

Yasotay remembered that first night they spent together with a soft laugh. "That children's rhyme comes to mind—stars in the day—and the turtle compass was a gift from my master. It helps when you get turned around."

"Master, my master," chirped Temujin teasingly with a grin. "You speak of him like a whipped dog. But I know which way to go," said Temujin, mixing jest with a pointed opinion. "And up ahead is a river we will need to cross."

"Master is a sign of respect, not blind obedience," replied Yasotay, mildly amused at his friendly "master" jab. Over the past several days, Yasotay had grown accustomed to Temujin's jovial nature. He lifted his head high in an exaggerated motion as if to see further ahead and said sarcastically, "I see no river!" He was doing his best to jest back at Temujin, who didn't notice.

"Do you see how the land slopes?" asked Temujin with seriousness, moving his hand downward. "That usually means there's water ahead! I know Lake Hulun is north of here, and the river runs west from the mountains."

Yasotay looked ahead but couldn't quite make out the landscape contours he was pointing out, and then said, "I need to draw a map!"

"I can see. I know where we are and where we go!" Temujin said, with the self-confidence of experience.

At that moment, setting the man's lame jesting aside, something became very clear to Yasotay. His ride with Temujin had become an immersion into the nomadic world—Temujin's world. It was evident in his every move and gesture, from how Temujin rode to how he rationed food and water to what he said and did. He could see this place was, indeed, a nomad's world, and he seemed to know things only those who had survived in this vast wilderness knew.

While Yasotay had spent many nights on the trail, he was always well-provisioned and had an intended timeline for returning to civilization. This was a very different experience for him. Yasotay couldn't help but feel a deep sense of liberation, relief, and freedom from the trappings of his previous existence—*finally experiencing life!*

As they drove along on a plush green turf that extended in all directions, a section of the river came into view. The river had cut through the landscape, slicing into the rolling grassy plain as it snaked across the terrain, creating a significant drop-off along its banks. Yasotay guided their cart alongside the riverbank, careful not to get too close to its edge.

"This is the Kherlen River. If you look downstream," pointed Temujin, "this river feeds into the lake. So, we are entering the great Three River Valley!"

"I see no lake?" remarked Yasotay, lifting his head high, a smirk on his face, with another awkward attempt at humor.

"It's a long distance from here," Temujin continued with a grin. "We should be fine; we are a day or two of travel to my people if we can find a shallow part of the river to cross. It looks deep here, and there is no way to get your cart down to the water or even across it. Let's continue, and we will find a place." So, they drove on a short while and came upon a spot twice as wide and half as deep with a clear sandy bottom.

"This looks like the spot!" said Temujin to himself. "We can cross over here if you like or wait till the morning. Either way, I am hungry, and we need to eat!"

"It's late in the day. Let's camp next to that tree up there and cross in the morning," acknowledged Yasotay as he jumped off his cart.

A routine had formed between the two regarding travel duties. Yasotay did most of the foraging for either wood or dung for the fire, and Temujin tended to the horses, which most definitely did *not* include Tata. Temujin made it clear that he would not deal with that beast!

"Every time I get near that animal, I feel in danger," complained Temujin. "When I come near, her leg is up, ready to kick me. She has stepped on my sore foot and nipped at me like she was going to bite me several times!"

Yasotay smiled and said, "She's just funny around almost everyone. You should just stay clear of her!"

As a rule, Temujin did just that, saying on multiple occasions, "If that ass could slit throats, she would have slit mine by now…. *She is evil!*"

Temujin was still hobbling, getting around as best he could. His ankle was healing but very slowly. Though limping, he could still hunt and was deadly accurate with the bow. He also tended the fire in the evenings, keeping it as low and smoke-free as possible without letting it go out.

Yasotay was usually the one who prepared what food they could find. Temujin noticed that Yasotay ate very little but was always drinking hot water. It seemed like a regular morning and evening ritual.

"So why do you constantly drink hot water?" asked Temujin. "This is very odd!"

"It helps balance me," answered Yasotay. "So why are you constantly eating?"

"Because I am hungry," said Temujin, chewing on the latest morsel of food he'd found.

"There once was an emperor who drank boiled water. He believed that boiling the water removed the evil spirits, which may sound odd, but it's been a habit of mine for years … I much prefer tea!"

"That doesn't sound odd, but there are evil spirits in the water," said Temujin, "Tea, what is tea?"

"As the story is told, one day, a leaf accidentally landed in that emperor's boiling water. Unaware of the leaf in the water, his attendant served his master the boiled brew. He noticed a pleasant aroma coming from the water and liked the taste. Thus, tea was invented."

"I have some leaves right here if you like," quipped Temujin, grabbing some random foliage on the ground and then motioning toward Yasotay's cup.

"No, I'm fine," said Yasotay with a smile while covering the top of his cup. He enjoyed Temujin's jovial approach to things, a welcome relief from Hangu's high state of anxiety.

For Yasotay, this whole experience was a new and unique encounter with a distinctly different culture. He was being exposed to the many odd quirks of this nomad. The first time he noticed Temujin *doing it*, they were packing up, readying for the day's travel.

At first, he thought Temujin was kissing the horse's neck for some reason. They had been on the road for several days, and water and supplies were getting low. Yasotay caught him doing this several times, and he finally realized what was happening. Temujin was taking a sharp edge, cutting the horse's neck veins and suckling on the blood from its neck. It was obviously an ancient nomad survival technique. Once done, he would smear something on the cut, arresting the bleeding. Yasotay had read of this practice, but seeing it performed firsthand made it seem even more peculiar. He thought with a devilish grin: I *would like to see him try that on Tata!*

The first rabbit Temujin killed was with a remarkably long shot; his arrow flew straight and true. As they approached the fallen rabbit, just as Yasotay was about to commend the fantastic shot, Temujin bent over, picked up the rabbit, and brought the carcass to his mouth. Yasotay was startled and assumed he intended to eat it raw on the spot. He smiled and said, "Maybe we can shoot another one; I prefer my meat cooked!"

Temujin stopped sucking the blood from the rabbit and looked up at him with a long and awkward look. Finally, after a protracted pause, Temujin declared, "We can cook this one!"

While Temujin didn't mind eating raw rabbit, he was clearly familiar with skinning and cooking it properly over a fire, which he did very efficiently. Yasotay noticed that the nomad ate the gizzards raw while preparing the kill for cooking. He would take them, squeeze out all offending matter, and devour the rest. He offered some to Yasotay, who politely declined.

The travelers crossed the river the following day. The waters breathed life into the flora and fauna that called the region home. Patches of willow trees and reeds created a haven for a diverse array of bird species, their songs and calls filling the air with a melodious chorus of sounds.

Temujin was leading Yasotay and Tata into the heart of a vast expanse. Fertile grasslands stretched between the Onon and Kherlen Rivers, and Yasotay was awestruck by the beauty of this seemingly untouched land. Soon, they crossed the rolling grasslands and were in rolling hills teeming with fir and birch trees. Animals for hunting were readily abundant, and streams with fresh, clear water sweet to the taste were full of fish. Yasotay thought in amazement: *This realm is touched by the divine!*

"Among my people, these are the most desired lands in all the valleys," explained Temujin as he rode his horse alongside Yasotay and Tata. They were moving along at a comfortable pace in the late afternoon when a small group of round white-felt tents came into view. The tents had a smoke hole in the middle of the roof. Despite having never been in one, Yasotay knew they were called *ger*. Or at least that's what the Mongolians called them; they were also known as *yurts* by the Turks. Yasotay had read about these structures, but having never seen, let alone been in one, he was curious. He noticed one ger stood out from all the rest and dwarfed the others scattered on the hillside. It had a black panel in the front, marking the entrance.

Temujin whistled what sounded like a short, high-pitched bird song, and suddenly, one, two, and then three horses grazing in the field to their right started galloping toward them. He whistled again, and Tata reared back on her hindquarters this time. "Easy, girl, easy," said Yasotay in a soothing voice. He was just as wide-eyed at the scene unfolding before them. Moments later, Yasotay could see four more horses join the approaching fray from behind the gers. Seven horses now ran toward them at full gallop, clouds of dust billowing behind them as their manes and tails whipped the air.

Temujin hopped off his horse and walked proudly forward, his arms spread wide toward the approaching herd. Yasotay noticed he still had a slight limp as he moved toward the advancing pack of prancing ponies. As they approached, Temujin greeted each one, rubbing low on the neck of each horse as it came to meet him. Amazed by the tender scene, Yasotay didn't know what to say. Just then, a giant eagle flew over their heads; it was quite the homecoming. People began pouring out of their gers, and moments later, roughly forty men, women, and children were standing outside, ready to greet Temujin—and his travel companions.

Temujin hopped bareback onto one of his horses and rode toward the crowd. Left behind, Yasotay and Tata trudged along at the same pace as before the spectacle. As they slowly approached the group of gathered people, Yasotay couldn't help but notice the pungent smell of the assembly as they chanted and cheered his name, "Temujin, Temujin, our leader Temujin is back, praise Tengri! Temujin, Temujin." Having traveled with him over these past couple of weeks, Yasotay had become accustomed to Temujin's malodor, but this was a whole new collective stench that would take some time to get used to!

Outside the large ger stood an older woman. Yasotay noticed a standard of nine yak tails was displayed proudly on a thick black pole next to the entrance of the ger. Each of the nine tassels consisted of a skirt of light-brown yak-tail hair gathered with red leather bindings, which were connected individually to the pole.

Temujin slowly walked up to the woman, who had been joined by a little girl standing close to her side. With arms out, elbows at her sides, the woman exclaimed loudly, "Temujin, my dear boy is home!"

"How are you, Mother?" asked Temujin, placing his arms under hers in his embrace as a show of respect.

"I am well now that you have returned," answered Temujin's mother, who had a streak of gray on the right-hand side of her otherwise brownish-red hair.

"Yasotay, come. Let me introduce you," insisted Temujin, extending his arm and waving for him to step forward.

Yasotay made a clicking noise with his tongue, and Tata clopped forward. He was reluctant to interrupt the idyllic scene of Temujin being reunited with his mother. He immediately noticed the intimacy between them—something he had never had with his mother.

"The Blue Wolf has returned. I knew they couldn't hold you forever," interrupted a young man who had arrived and was now standing next to Temujin's mother. He wore a plain-colored, unadorned *deel*, similar to everyone else, except he had a large bow slung across his back. This bow stood out from any archery weapon Yasotay had ever seen. It was clearly well crafted and comprised of both bone and wood. Additionally, he noticed the quiver of equally impressive arrows at his side in a leather container hanging from his belt.

"Hassar, you look as ugly as ever!" said Temujin with a big smile as he engaged in a smack of hands and a vigorous handshake with the man. Then, all seemed to join in with hearty laughs of warmth and respect. A young child of nine or ten years ran up and wrapped his arms around Temujin's waist. "Ah, Temuge, it's good to see you too," responded Temujin, patting the young man on his back.

"Yasotay, I would like to introduce you to my mother, Houlun," said Temujin. "This is Yasotay, the southern wolf who freed me from the cangue and helped me to escape from those miserable pissants."

"Yasotay, you are always welcome among us. Thank you for returning my son," proclaimed Houlun.

"You honor me," he said, dropping his head slightly in respect to the older woman.

"Southern wolf? I believe there must be a story behind that name," said Hassar.

"Yes, maybe that story will explain your limp," Houlun said.

"…this is my brother Hassar," said Temujin. "And this little one here is Temuge."

"We must celebrate your escape and rejoice in your return. Tonight, we will hear all the tales of your bravery," said Hassar, "for tomorrow, we move south to the valley between Mother and Father Mountains. That is, of course, as long as you approve, my elder brother and fearless leader?" said Hassar bowing with a joking grin.

Temujin playfully slapped him on top of his bowed head. "Maybe a beheading, mother? To commemorate my homecoming? I have just the person in mind!" Temujin said, playfully sizing up his brother's bowed head for removal.

"He is still our best hunter and the deadliest and most accurate warrior with a bow in the valley," said Houlun, "so don't hurt him. Why do you two have to play so rough?"

"My other brothers, Hachiun and Belgutai, are here somewhere," said Temujin to Yasotay, "along with my mother's youngest, Temulun." Temujin reached down and hoisted up high the little girl standing next to Houlun, who had been silently awaiting his attention and was now squealing with joy.

"Yasotay, I would like you to meet Temulun. Temulun, this is Yasotay the Southern Wolf."

"It is nice to meet you, Temulun," said Yasotay.

She squealed as Temujin tickled her, playfully repeating, "Well, say something, come on, say something." Every time she went to speak, he tickled her harder, so much so that she couldn't say anything. She had long brown hair and looked and was dressed like her mother, just a smaller version.

Yasotay noticed Tata getting restless, her head bobbing up and down, so he asked Temujin, "I need to get some water for Tata and find somewhere to place my cart?"

"Hachiun, fetch some water for Yasotay," barked Temujin, finally spotting him among the crowd. It was said more as an order than a request.

"This is what is left of our clan," Temujin told Yasotay, waving his arm toward those around them. "My father led thousands, and now those following the Nine Tails of the Yak are less than fifty."

"Yes, but we are strong in our support of the Nine Tails of the Yak," said a large, burly man stepping forward to give Temujin a big welcoming hug. The homecoming ebbed and flowed from quiet embrace to boisterous laughter as the throng of welcoming nomads continued to stream past their leader. After their greeting, many of them went back to work in and among the collection of gers. Temujin's grin remained, though, and a glimmer of joy sparkled in his eyes.

At one point, Temujin turned to Yasotay. "You can sleep with my family until I figure out a better arrangement."

"I am just spending the night and will be off in the morning."

"Nonsense, you must stay," insisted Temujin, "at least for a couple of days."

"I am grateful for your offer, but I…" Yasotay was thankfully interrupted in midsentence by Hachiun thrusting a large bladder of water in his face. And just then, his mother pulled Temujin away to greet someone else in the small crowd.

"Hachiun." Yasotay slightly bowed in appreciation, took the bladder, and walked over to Tata. All told, twenty-five gers were scattered around, and roughly forty-five to fifty people had greeted or were waiting to greet Temujin. These people loved him, as was apparent from the deep appreciation shown Yasotay for aiding him in his time of need. The group was full of joyous laughter and merriment. It greatly contrasted his own personal experience with family gatherings and reunions, which were generally ceremonial and somewhat perfunctory. Yasotay could see the genuine delight of these people with Temujin's return, and he couldn't help but think, *So this is a nomad family!*

Yasotay removed the straps that secured Tata to the cart and scratched between her ears. He whispered to her, "How are you, my friend? You need to watch your neck around these ones! Would you like a drink?" He began to pour water into his hand for her to drink, but she wasn't interested. Tata lifted her head and slowly walked away to Yasotay's right. She circled the outer perimeter of the boisterous crowd that had gathered to greet the two travelers.

Yasotay splashed the water in his hand on his face and said to himself, *She can fend for herself.* He took a big swig from the water bladder. Then, he noticed an old man standing with a beautiful eagle on his shoulder. It was the same eagle that had flown out to meet them when they arrived. The bird had a small leather hood over its head and was a fantastic creature and amazingly well-trained. Curious, he walked over to take a closer look. "That is a beautiful bird you have there," said Yasotay as he approached.

"She is," responded the man, who appeared to have specks of dried bird feces all over his deel and had an oddly different yet still stunningly powerful new odor. "This is Qadan, the best hunter in the valley!"

"She appears to be obedient," Yasotay said, "You send her out, and she comes right back?" The man nodded. "How long does it take to train an eagle to hunt?"

"This eagle was very young when taken for training. She first learned to catch a rabbit pelt dragged behind a horse," explained the old man. "Each time she did, she was given a morsel to eat. Once she develops a skill, you move on to other skills all the way up to live prey. The key to training a hunting bird is to keep it from eating its prey. You always feed them by hand and never let them eat what they catch, you see…"

"Yasotay! Where is he? YASOTAY!" yelled Temujin, his voice ringing out amongst the gathering.

"Excuse me; it was nice meeting you."

"Yes, the young master calls; you must go!" said the old man with a crooked smile.

He walked up to where Temujin stood, who immediately put his arm around Yasotay's shoulder while he continued to direct his attention to the couple standing before him. "Yasotay, I want you to meet Altan and his wife, Sarnai." He turned to the married couple standing there, the woman holding a small child. Out of the corner of his eye, Yasotay saw something odd. Tata's head was resting on the shoulder of a beautiful young woman, standing a bit behind and to the left of the couple. Her left arm was bent around Tata's head as if she had her in a headlock, except her hand was gently stroking between her ears.

After a momentary pause, Yasotay proclaimed, "How are you. I'm glad to meet you," taking a moment to gather his wits about him after that unexpected sight.

"Temujin says good things about you. This is Erden," said Altan, referring to the child on Sarnai's hip, "and my daughter, Tera," he said, gesturing to the woman with Tata. The short, stout man had piercing, steely-gray eyes. "She is betrothed to Baatar, from the Jadaran clan," Altan proudly explained.

"Altan has gracefully offered for you to stay with him, his wife, and his children," said Temujin. "While you would be welcome in my family ger, it currently overflows. Altan has more room to accommodate you!"

"It is an honor to meet you, Yasotay," said Sarnai. "We are proud to welcome you to our ger."

"It is my honor, and thank you for your hospitality," replied Yasotay, bowing in respect. As Temujin's arm fell from Yasotay's shoulder, introductions were concluded. They moved to the side as Temujin began to speak with Altan about hunting in the east valley.

Yasotay stepped over toward Tata. "It appears you have made a new friend," he said, patting Tata on the nose while looking into Tera's warm caramel eyes. "How are you, Tera?"

"I am well, thank you."

"Tata seems to like you," said Yasotay.

"Yes, kindred souls are naturally attracted to one another," responded Tera with a smile. Tata had snuffed up a strand of her long reddish-brown hair that had fallen across Tata's right nostril.

As soon as they began speaking, all the other voices and sounds seemed to become dull background noises.

"Tata doesn't like many people," explained Yasotay, "but she certainly seems fine with you!"

"Why shouldn't she? Do I appear unfriendly to you?"

"No, no, no, it's not you. She just doesn't like most people,"

"Well, maybe I'm not like most people to her," explained Tera. "I was standing here speaking with my mother when, to my surprise, this head appeared from behind me and rested on my shoulder. She seems so gentle and loving to me. Why do you say such mean things about her?" asked Tera, all the while rubbing between Tata's ears.

"Well, to be honest, she's generally ornery to everyone…except you. Now, why is that?" asked Yasotay with a broad smile, making the small scar on his chin slightly red and noticeable.

"You have a good smile," noted Tera, "when you smile, you smile from the heart."

"Thank you, as do you."

"So, are you saying Tata is mean to you?" asked Tera.

"No, Tata is my best friend; she is my partner," replied Yasotay as he ran his hand down Tata's back. "I know her quirks well, and she knows mine."

"I was told the stranger who traveled with Temujin was a wolf from the south without a wife," said Tera with a teasing smile. "It seems like an odd marriage, a wolf and an ass!"

"Well, she is very good to me," explained Yasotay. "You see, she chose me the same way it appears that she has chosen you."

"Oh, really," asked Tera.

"Yes, Tata was originally given to a friend in trade, but he couldn't control her. When I first met her, she took an instant liking to me, so he was kind enough to give her to me. Actually, he was terrified of Tata and wanted nothing to do with her." They spoke comfortably as if they had been friends who were just reacquainting themselves with one another. Time seemed to stand still.

Suddenly, Temujin's large arm was back around his shoulders. "Come, Yasotay, and drink with me. I want to introduce you to the rest of my family," he announced, holding a bladder of fermented mare's milk called ayrag.

"Stay away from that beast, Tera," warned Temujin. "She's as mean as they come. I hate her almost as much as I hate dogs." Tata snorted as if she knew he was talking about her.

"Easy, Tata," said Yasotay in a soothing voice.

"Come," urged Temujin, pulling him away from Tera and Tata.

"It was a pleasure meeting you," Yasotay yelled back to Tera as Temujin's sizeable right arm wrestled him away.

Tera could hear him saying to Yasotay, "Why do you keep that miserable animal that hates…"

"I will see to feeding Tata and place your things in my father's ger!" Tera yelled in response with a beaming smile, which she quickly hid due to a searing glare from her mother.

"No, don't worry, I can take care of it," he said and was gone.

Tera answered her mother's glare, "What? I'm just being helpful to our guest with his belongings!"

"That is not what is bothering me," barked Sarnai. Tera shook her head and led Tata away.

The evening wore on with Temujin introducing Yasotay to every clan member—some of them twice. Everybody repeatedly heard Temujin's harrowing story of captivity and escape, accompanied by plenty of food, drink, and laughter. Yasotay found his first taste of ayrag extraordinarily bitter and not very good. But as the night wore on, it began to take on a more tolerable tart yet sweet flavor. Temujin was very forceful all evening, regularly declaring, "Everyone must drink!" which usually resulted in Yasotay having a bladder of ayrag thrust in his face.

Overall, it was a pretty memorable evening. A chanting shaman danced around the large bonfire, banging on a drum and singing strange words Yasotay had never heard or read in his life. That was surprising since he knew at least ten different languages. The shaman was an elderly woman whose prophetic abilities included forecasting the weather. When she did speak words Yasotay could understand, she predicted the rise of a great chieftain. Leader of all those who dwelled in felt tents, an apparent reference to Temujin. The clan's people were mesmerized by her every word, their mouths open and eyes wide. They were captivated.

After much dancing, banging her drum, and chanting, the woman fell silent. She suddenly stopped. All eyes were on her, awaiting her next move. After a pause, she rubbed her eyes and appeared to wake from a long, deep sleep. She then began greeting everyone as if she had just arrived at the celebration. This ritual act was followed with copious amounts of additional ayrag. Yasotay bounced around from one conversation to the next all evening. It went on late into the night until Altan and Yasotay were the last two to leave the fire. As Yasotay slowly walked with Altan to his ger, he could tell that something was on the man's mind.

"So, the stories tell me you are an amazing warrior," observed Altan. "I know what Temujin says about you is true…as true as if seen with my own eyes!"

"Yes, but I'm not all of what he says of me. I have learned things and do my best to apply what I've learned. But, to me, a *true warrior* is someone who has seen war and fought for the lives of those they love. I have not!" The howl of a wolf far away to their right lightly echoed through the encampment, and a howl in response could be heard far away to their left.

"I don't think you understand our situation…we fight every day…" Altan stopped walking and raised his open palm to the side of his face to emphasize what he said. "Each day, we fight for survival. Sometimes, it's the wolf on four legs and other times; it's the even more dangerous wolf on two legs," he said forcefully while slowly bringing his hand down. "Every day is a battle for us! There is no rest for us here. You sleep in my ger tonight, but we could be attacked, and within moments, you are fighting for your life!" His steely eyes opened wide. He was worked up and a little more than a little drunk. "That is not a story. It is real; it happens all the time! Because in these lands, you die if you do not fight."

"I understand," replied Yasotay in a calm voice, attempting to bring the intensity of the conversation down. "I understand the struggle of life and death."

Altan paused and gathered himself. "Do you like my daughter?"

"Yes, she's very pleasant and smart," replied Yasotay. "Tata likes her." He paused. "You have a wonderful family, Altan. In the few moments I spent with them this evening, I could tell your wife is delightful, and your son Erden is strong as an ox and loves to play."

"Yes, but my wife said she felt that you and my daughter seemed *too familiar* together," explained Altan, "as if she likes you too much. Also, she did not like how my daughter looked at you."

Yasotay thought for a moment. "Please be assured, I have only the utmost respect for your family, Altan," said Yasotay sincerely, but he was also aware of the effects the ayrag had on him.

"Children are difficult. You are too young to understand this, but believe me, it's true," Altan said and continued, "She is promised to Baatar. He is a good young man, but she is unhappy with this decision. And now, with the blessing of Temujin, I am bound to honor this promise."

Yasotay thought for a moment, then asked, "You are faithful to Temujin, are you not?"

"Yes, I am, and my father faithfully followed Yesugei, his father. My grandfather, Buka, was blood brothers with Temujin's grandfather. Our families have been with the Borjigin before the great Khabul Khan," said Altan. "My family is faithful to the Borjigin."

"I respect your loyalty to the Borjigin. I, too, know allegiance, honor, and devotion…the type that is steadfast. I pledge to you that if trouble comes to your tent tonight, I will be ready to fight with you to protect your family," said Yasotay. "This promise includes the honor of your daughter and your commitment to her betrothed."

"I appreciate hearing you say that, Yasotay. I don't have the intuition of my wife, but I did notice Tera's attachment to your ass," Altan stated with a wry grin.

"Yes, Tata rarely makes friends, and she is as stubborn as they come. There is little we can do about that relationship," explained Yasotay with a grin. "I think that I will go check on Tata now."

"So you know, a place was prepared for you to rest to the left as you enter our ger. Sarnai told me that Tera placed your chest and a blanket there for you. Our ger is over there," he said, motioning to their left. "Your animal should be tied up to the right of it," he waved his hand, obviously drunk. "I am going to retire; the ayrag has gotten to me."

"Thank you. I will be joining you in a moment," said Yasotay.

Yasotay walked over to where Altan had indicated, and there was Tata with her head down, nosing through the roughage at her feet. She lifted her head when Yasotay approached. "How are you, my friend?" Yasotay asked in a very low voice, looking around and seeing no one. "I have no apple for you tonight, but I brought you some sea buckthorn." Yasotay pulled out a small clump of five or six large orange berries attached to a stalk and placed them under Tata's nose. She gave them one sniff and took them in her mouth. "They say that they will make your coat shine. Of course, you don't have to shine for me, Tata, but you might want to impress your new friend. I was surprised to see you so friendly with Tera. That is not like you, my girl. What do you see in her? Yes, she is pretty and very smart, but surely you don't like anyone except me?" Yasotay enjoyed his private conversations with Tata, rubbing between her ears just like he noticed Tera had. "You like all this attention after all, don't you?"

"Remember, she is betrothed to another, so you must respect that!" insisted Yasotay with a grin. "So, what do you think of these nomads? I know you don't like Temujin, but he is gregarious, bold, and somewhat fascinating…and has grown on me. He certainly has the loyalty of all those who follow him; they love him. My question is, *what kind of leader is he?* Both religious and political leaders share two immutable traits: they have the trust of those who follow them and the ability to manipulate the truth, shape it to their desire, or use it as a weapon against those they lead. They seduce the weak and stupid and confuse the smart and sophisticated. They hide behind big words like knowledge, wisdom, and tradition while they control, manipulate, and use fear to their advantage. We are all just puppets playing our roles in their game! Ahh, I apologize, Tata. I ramble when I drink."

Tata had finished with her berries and returned to rummaging around at her feet for something to eat. Yasotay gently stroked her neck and said, "I am sorry, Tata. I hate to sound so negative. Temujin has asked me to stay and learn their ways, and I think I will. What makes their ways any better or worse than those of my people or any other people for that matter? There is nothing written about their ways; maybe I will write about them. We'll see!"

Yasotay paused. "They will break camp tomorrow to move further south. Temujin will leave to retrieve his wife and has asked me to join him on his journey. It's a two-day trip there, and I will leave you here with Tera to help with the move."

"I will ask her to drive my cart, and I want you to watch over Tera for me. You can help Altan protect his family while I'm gone. Will you do this for me, my Tata?" She snorted and jostled her head up and down, as she always did when he asked her a question. "Good, you are always agreeable! I should go. I am an outsider, and the last thing I need is to be caught talking to an ass in the middle of the night. Good night, my friend."

Yasotay was tired; it had been a long day, and the ayrag had gotten to him too. He found Altan's ger and tried to be quiet while entering it for the first time. It was dark inside; the only light was from the embers of a small fire that glowed red in the center of the room. Yasotay could see the outline of Altan, who was still awake. He looked around and found his wooden chest up against the side of the ger. On the floor, lying next to his chest, was a large woolen blanket. Seeing it brought Yasotay back to what seemed like years ago, but which was just a few weeks, when he and Hangu had gone looking for a large blanket. That search had led him here. He took the folded blanket, laid it on the floor of the ger, and lay down, closing his eyes, and then heard Altan quietly ask, "Did you see Tera out there?"

"No, I did not," answered Yasotay, "would you like me to go look…"

No sooner had he finished speaking than Tera walked through the entrance to the ger.

"Where did you go?" asked Altan, "it is late, and you are still out wandering around the steppe!"

"If you must know, I needed to perform my necessities," answered Tera. "You have nothing to worry about; Tata will protect me!"

"What are you talking about?" responded Altan in an irritated voice. "Oh, just go to sleep!"

Yasotay was thinking how this blanket was so much better than the branches and plants he and Temujin had foraged each night to keep from sleeping directly on the cold, hard ground. He had slept on such makeshift beds under the stars every night since leaving Hangu's warm house. As he lay on the floor with half the blanket underneath him protecting him from the cold ground and the other half folded over his body, he was comfortable, and his eyes began to close. Suddenly, a thought hit Yasotay, and his eyes opened wide. He almost said aloud, *Did Tera overhear me talking to Tata?*

CHAPTER FIVE

Northern Grasslands, early fall, 1178 CE

hy am I freezing? Yasotay's mind screamed from his lucid dream to being wide awake. He looked around the ger, trying to remember where he was. The past few weeks all snapped back into the present moment. Instantly, he realized the obvious answer to that vexing question. Morning came cold and rough this far north of the Yellow River basin. The weather had suddenly changed, and Yasotay could feel the cold in his bones. Had it not been for the thick blanket Tera had given him last night, he surely would have frozen to the ground. Yasotay rose from the floor of the ger. Wearing the blanket over his head, he walked out the door made from thick black felt and plunged into the brutal frozen tundra of the steppe.

The inescapable fact was *it is freezing cold out here*! Clouds of white steam billowed from his mouth. It was much colder than inside the ger. *Maybe I made a mistake*! Moving helped get his blood flowing, but the bitter cold stung his skin with what felt like sharp, pointy little icicles. Finally, after a few moments of walking toward the outer reaches of their camp, he found the perfect spot. After a big step-up, Yasotay sat down facing east atop a large flat rock, about knee-high above the ground. There was no wind, which seemed odd, and only the chirping of a single bird rang out through the valley. Half the blanket was under him; the rest was wrapped over his head and around him. The blanket was large enough for him to make his own personal cocoon. Everything was tucked in except for his glowing hazel eyes, which peeked out from the blanket and were fixed upon the skyline's dark shadows where, within moments, the sunrise could be seen.

Using his breath to fill his cocoon, he began his morning ritual: sitting in a comfortable seven-point meditation posture and controlling his breathing in and out. After some time, he would start to sort things out in his mind and plan his day. He truly loved the solitude of these moments right before the sun crested the horizon.

While focusing on his breathing, Yasotay thought he saw a silhouette moving across the black floor of the valley. It was a slight movement, there and gone, then moments later, it appeared again to his left. The dim light seemed to be playing games with his sight. The rising sun's red glow on the underside of the clouds began to reveal vibrant hues of orange, which outlined a series of blood-colored clouds with yellow veins in bulbous patterns in the sky. It made for a picturesque morning view, coupled with the dark shadow of the mountains and deep valleys below. Controlling his breathing, in and then out, he felt a tingle on the back of his neck; the view was awe-inspiring.

As Yasotay sat there, each passing moment revealed more detail within his field of view. Ahead was a large rock formation far to his left at the bottom of a long sloping hillside. To his right was the wide-open realm of the steppe grasslands, currently a cold and desolate tundra. The fertile land between the Onon and Kherlen rivers showed a marked temperature difference between yesterday and this morning. Thinking of stark contrasts, his previous life of study in Zhongdu with his mother and Master Chang was much different from this frozen wilderness. It was, indeed, a different world, a much harsher one. For some reason, it felt like *this* was his first morning of real freedom. Not that he wasn't free when he lived with Hangu, but it was always in the shadow cast by his past life at the temple. Now, in the wild grasslands of the steppe, he was in a world he would learn about through living here instead of reading about it. This fact excited him. *But*, he thought ruefully, *I didn't know it would be so cold!*

There! Now, with the sun rising, he caught a glimpse through the glow. It was the silhouette again, then two others—one in the middle of his view and another to his left. Finally, staring into the shadows, something came into full view. It was a sizeable canine shape, stealing toward him with slow, measured steps in a lurking posture, head bowed, eyes a fiery white glow, fixated on his steaming cocoon. Yasotay noticed her breath, the seething steam coming from her nostrils. What startled him was seeing the other two shapes flanking him, white eyes staring as they crept forward in the same fashion—advancing. The chirping of the single bird was ominously gone; only a heavy silence pierced the morning chill. The three gray shadows moved as one, all with their ears lying back flat and their tails pointing straight out, parallel to the ground. It was as if they each had a role to play in their attack performance, one which they had seemingly enacted numerous times with perfectly timed discipline, *slowly, methodically, menacingly advancing!*

Still sitting in his cocoon, Yasotay moved purposefully, taking the ball of the kusari in his right hand. He slowly reached out of his cocoon and began spinning the small steel ball in the air. The three hesitated in their advance, the two mirroring the alpha female leading the pack. Her ears flattened further back as she hunched lower to the ground. She was the smart one; Yasotay could see cunning in her movements. She was still advancing but considerably slower, which seemed even more menacing if that were possible.

The chain of the kusari was designed to make a humming sound that began low and increased in volume as Yasotay released each link into the spinning whirlabout. Six white eyes were now transfixed on the spinning ball, and Yasotay's was equally transfixed on their movements. He thought that he could hear a low, rumbling growl. Finally, the approaching wolves stopped, all three frozen in time.

Yasotay sensed something behind him and was starting to feel boxed in. He let the blanket fall from the top of his head behind him; the wolves flinched, leaning back in unison. He began spinning the ball in the air faster and faster, letting out more and more of the chain, and within moments, it was spinning in a large radius in front of him. A radius as tall as Yasotay's sitting frame, whistling a loud buzzing sound. The wolves just stood there listening to the noise and staring—hypnotized. A moment later, the trance was broken when an arrow whizzed through the air and almost hit the lead wolf. It missed its mark and skidded away in the dirt, startling her, so she bolted back down the slope. Yasotay leapt to his feet, still spinning the kusari. All three wolves were out of sight in the blink of an eye, after the arrow hit the dirt.

"Those wolves are harmless; they were just curious. You need not worry. There's plenty of easily gotten game available; their bellies are full," explained Sarnai in a raspy morning voice, coming up from behind Yasotay. "I guess that's the weapon that Temujin talked about in the story of his escape next to the river!" Sarnai said, beguiled by the sight of Yasotay, who was now standing atop the rock, letting the kusari spin out, with the rising sun setting him aglow. She looked at him in amazement.

"Yes, it is, and they certainly seemed curious, especially the one you shot at," replied Yasotay, who made a quick motion with his arm, further slowing the spinning ball's movement. Then, reaching out, he grabbed the ball out of midair and reeled in his chain with the proficiency of one who had done the act thousands of times, placing the kusari away in its pouch.

"If food were scarce, you would've had a fight on your hands. I didn't shoot at her; no need to kill. The shot was to scare them away." Sarnai's red hair looked like it had frost on it this morning. "They hunt our herds when game is scarce and only hunt us when our herds are thin."

Yasotay bent over and picked up his blanket. "Curious or not, it felt like a very dangerous dance," he said as he hopped down off the rock.

"Temujin called you a wolf last night. The wolf is an emissary of Tengri, God of the Eternal Blue Sky, and the wolf bears the will of Tengri," Sarnai explained, her expression softening as she placed her right hand on her chest. "I woke up, came outside, and followed the sound of the odd noise you were making doing the dance of death with the wolves of the steppe. What does this foretell, Tengri?" Sarnai asked, looking up. She seemed to hesitate, awaiting a response. "Your presence is a great omen. Both Temujin and the emissaries of Tengri seem to agree…maybe you were sent to us for a reason." She held another long pause, then finally said, "Altan told me he believed you could be trusted; I will trust you, Yasotay!" Sarnai slightly bowed her head and lowered her big brown eyes. They both stood silently gazing at the beautiful sunrise for a long moment.

"Thank you. I greatly appreciate your kindness in sharing your ger. Is there anything I can do for you?" asked Yasotay, folding his blanket.

Sarnai paused momentarily and then, aroused from her daze, said, "Go find Tera and ask her what to do. She needs help dismantling and packing the ger." Sarnai's tone signaled that her mind had returned to the many tasks at hand. "I must help Altan with the herd. We leave today, south to the valley, to feed our herds in the shadows of Mother and Father Mountains."

Yasotay walked back toward the ger while Sarnai went to retrieve her arrow.

"Come, you can help me!" called Tera with a wave upon seeing Yasotay as she exited the ger.

"Where are we going?" he asked, swiping his right hand across his face to brush his sandy brown hair away from his eyes.

"We need to take down our ger; that is our job! Father said he is busy with the herd and that you would help."

"Yes, your mother volunteered me too. It appears I am to do as you command," said Yasotay in an accommodating tone.

"The first thing we need to do is remove these three ropes that hold the outer ger cover in place," explained Tera as she started tugging on one of the knots in a thick rope encircling the ger.

"How can I help?" asked Yasotay.

"Untie that rope there!" Tera motioned with her head toward a different rope. As they worked, Tera said, "So, they say you will travel as an escort with Temujin to retrieve his bride?"

"Yes, that is the plan," answered Yasotay, placing his blanket aside; he tried to untie the knot holding the other rope around the ger.

"Have you ever ridden a horse *all day*? Multiple days in a *row*?" Tera inquired with a noticeably severe tone in her voice. She had made quick work of the third and final rope and started to peel off the multiple pieces of the layered outer wall covering. "Here, grab this," she said to Yasotay, who had already begun to pull on the corner of the tarp; he was attempting to shadow her every action with a helping hand.

"Yes, it's been several years, but I traveled by horse great distances in my youth. Why do you ask?" Yasotay was curious about her question as he dropped a folded wall section into the pile.

"Those you ride with have been saddled since birth. They will ride all day and part of the night with limited rest, and they know only one speed...*full speed*! Are you ready for that?" asked Tera, folding the front quarter of the roof up with Yasotay helping on the other side. "Why I ask is simple, you arrived by cart. You can't take your cart, Yasotay; Tata won't be able to keep up!"

"You would be surprised at Tata's speed," answered Yasotay, "but yes, the terrain is too rough, and because of the cart, Tata will move too slowly. I was planning to ask if you would take Tata and my cart with you?"

"Yes, I will. I noticed you are oddly protective of her," said Tera with a smile.

"Well, she is one of my few friends."

"I ask about your riding skills because the terrain will sometimes be steep and dangerous, and you will be traveling at full speed. My point is, are you ready for that type of ride?" Tera asked. Then, pausing briefly, she bit down on her lip and quickly asked, "Am I one of those friends too?" she blurted out with a sheepish grin.

"Yes, any friend of Tata is a friend of mine, and I guess I'll just have to do my best to keep up and not fall off my horse," said Yasotay, oblivious to her flirtatious question. He saw that someone had already loaded his chest onto his cart, and Tata was sniffing the grass at her feet.

After an awkward pause, she added, "Yes, I guess you will!" then Tera flashed a knowing smile. "I will take Tata and your cart...next, we remove the layers of the roof cover."

Yasotay sensed her mocking tone and asked, "What do you think I should do?" He then reached over and helped her with a layer of the roof cover.

"You're young; you should be able to keep up if given a good horse, but know this: you are not accustomed to this type of ride. On the third day, your bones will ache unlike anything you have ever experienced," warned Tera.

"I will keep that in mind," said Yasotay.

"Once we remove the remaining top layers, we must remove the inner roof poles, called *uni*, from the *khana* side wall. If you look, each uni pole is secured to the khana lattice wall on one end and slides into the *toono*, or the central crown wheel of the roof, at the other end. The roof's center is also held aloft with two posts, which makes the ger strong. And the center of the crown is a window where the fire's smoke is drawn out, and fresh air is let in," explained Tera. "This design has been with our people for centuries and can withstand the highest winds!"

"I see, so the toono is the center of the wheel, and uni poles are the spokes!" repeated Yasotay, removing another uni pole. "But what happens to the crown once we remove all these poles? Won't it fall? What will keep it in place?"

"Yes, it would fall, and *no*, we're not going to let that happen!" she stated emphatically. "Since there are only two of us, we will remove most

114

of the uni poles, and then each of us will take one of the two *bagana*." Tera pointed toward the two tall decorative posts holding up the toono. "We will lift up, which will release the remaining uni poles, and then carefully lower the toono down to the ground," explained Tera. "A ger is often given as a wedding gift and is kept in the family, with crowns gifted down from generation to generation. We must be careful. This is our home!" Tera paused, gathering her energy. "Loosen that uni, but don't remove it." Yasotay did as instructed. "Now come here. Remember, we must not let the toono fall."

"Got it," confirmed Yasotay.

Tera was now standing in the center of what few pieces remained of the structure. She held one of the two center posts and directed Yasotay to the other. "Grab the other bagana, help me; we are going to both lift these posts at the same time." She had a very serious look on her face and said, "Remember, the remaining uni poles currently holding the toono in place will fall away, and the toono will be free. Once free, we will carefully lower it to the ground."

"I've got it."

"Are you ready?" asked Tera, but before he could answer, she added, "Lift up," but Yasotay wasn't ready and lifted much slower than Tera, then he overcompensated and jerked his post up. A couple of uni poles fell away on Tera's side, but not all of them. This caused the toono to become unbalanced; they found themselves trying to balance a tilting wheel in the air at the end of two long posts. The remaining uni poles fell away, and the two began shifting their posts back and forth, up and down, trying to coordinate their movements and control the wheel from crashing to the ground.

"You got it, wait…wow." Yasotay contorted his body, moving his arms back and forth to balance his side of the toono. Tera was doing the same, moving her feet like in a dance, trying her best to hold it steady, but the toono slipped and flipped. Both Yasotay and Tera let go of their posts and put their arms out to catch the falling wheel. Amazingly, the toono flipped upside down and landed in their outstretched arms. It was a perfect catch.

Yasotay and Tera smiled at each other in victory. Meanwhile, the two bagana posts stood in the air as if someone still held them, but no one did! Suddenly, Yasotay's bagana pole fell backward behind them and hit the ground with a big thud, which startled them. Though Tera's pole had remained upright for a moment longer, it was now slowly falling. They both saw it coming in slow motion, watching helpless as it bounced with a hollow "clunk" off the top of Yasotay's forehead. His smile turned into a grimace of half pain and half surprise. Tera began laughing and howled even harder at the shocked look on his face. She noticed the small scar on his chin beamed red when he was embarrassed. Tera was so distracted that she didn't see one of the poles on the ground, tripped over it, and fell to the ground. Her fall elicited even more laughter.

"Let's set this down," said Yasotay, now holding the full weight of the toono and placing it safely on the ground, "before someone gets hurt." He then extended his hand to help Tera get up from the ground. Still smiling, she accepted the offer and noticed the scar's red glow had disappeared.

"You two are like children at play," said Altan, whose head had popped up over the still-standing Khana wall. "Yasotay, Temujin is looking for you! Tera, let's quit playing and get this ger packed; we have a long way to go today!"

Tera turned to Yasotay. "You can go. It was that hard part I needed help with."

"Hard part! I would have rather missed that!" proclaimed Yasotay, rubbing his head where the post had struck him. "Glad that's out of the way!"

Tera laughed again. "Yes, and don't forget to bring that horse blanket I gave you, or the next time I see you, it will hurt in a much different place."

"YASOTAY, let's *GO!*" bellowed through the air.

"Temujin calls. You must go," exclaimed Tera. "Ride well."

"Thank you, and please take care of my Tata," said Yasotay, grabbing his blanket.

"I will watch over her like my own child," responded Tera with a big smile.

"Thank you, but be aware, she always seems to find trouble."

"Don't worry. I will watch her. *Go!*"

With an ever so slight bow, Yasotay was off to find Temujin.

He found him outside his ger, standing there with Borchu, Belgutai, and five horses, all packed and ready to go. Borchu was short, stout, and muscular, with a protruding forehead, prominent puffy cheeks, and a face that looked like he was constantly squinting. He carried a crossbow at his side and a sword on his hip. Yasotay had been introduced to him days earlier, and at that time, he sensed that Borchu served Temujin's every whim like most of the clan, except more so. Belgutai was Temujin's half-brother, smaller in stature than him, and also seemed to idolize Temujin.

"We are not taking any additional horses, only this one for Bourtai, so we will have to watch our horses closely for exhaustion," explained Temujin. "I prefer to travel with at least one additional horse per person, but there are no spare horses now because of the move. You ride that one, Yasotay…and what happened to your head?" he asked, walking toward a gray-and-white horse whose marks changed from gray with white marks to white with gray marks at its midsection. Its legs, tail, and mane were all solid gray, making him stand out from the three brown horses and the all-white mare bearing a sacred red scarf called a *khadag*, specifically chosen to carry Bourtai, Temujin's bride.

"Ahh, it's nothing," claimed Yasotay, rubbing the bruise on his forehead.

"I had Borchu pack you supplies. He put strips of meat under your saddle for you, don't lose them. Come, we must leave now!" exclaimed Temujin. Yasotay quickly rolled up his blanket and tied it to the back of the horse. Then he leapt onto the saddle, and the group slowly began to stroll out of the camp.

Stroking Tata's neck and watching them leave, Tera took one last look at Yasotay and the others departing. Then, she spoke to Tata the same way she had overheard Yasotay, speaking privately to her, "That blanket isn't going to save his backside tied to the back of that saddle…

and its not going to be the only thing tenderized this trip, now is it Tata?" she grinned. Tata nodded dutifully, closely watching the small wild apple that had appeared in Tera's hand. "You are easily bribed into agreement!" proclaimed Tera, scratching between Tata's ears and feeding her the apple.

The pace of the four horses picked up from a slow walk out of the camp to a quick trot. Temujin, Belgutai, and Borchu were well-armed with swords, daggers, bows, and large quivers of arrows. Yasotay realized a large sword with a simple wooden handle was hanging from the saddle of his horse. Their pace was quick but comfortable over the flat, open terrain they currently traversed. They rode all day, stopping only for brief necessity breaks now and then. The terrain varied more in the afternoon, and their natural pace changed with the landscape. They fluctuated from walking and trotting to cantering, then slowing down again. All five horses seemed to naturally follow the same gait or pace with little direction, which was somewhat odd to Yasotay. Their open-field gait was what Yasotay called *the fifth gait*. It was when the horse traveled at a running-walking pace that seemed to produce the least amount of bounce. It was not a gallop, and Yasotay had never ridden a horse that moved this way. He had read about and experienced the four gaits of a horse but never this fifth gait.

The Mongol approach to riding and the distance they covered on the first day were, by Yasotay's standards, very impressive. The four travelers mostly rode in silence over the next two days, each focused on the ride. Yasotay had traveled by horse many times but had never covered this much terrain in such a short time. The well-made leather stirrups connected to the saddle made for a better riding experience than he had previously known. He could easily stand up in the stirrups and turn his torso to look behind. The ride was reasonably comfortable, but he felt like he was in a long-distance horse race. Tera's questioning of his riding prowess kept ringing in his ears. Yasotay was always in the rear of the group, and his horse seemed jittery, which he finally mentioned to Temujin.

"Quiet your hands!" explained Temujin. "They are moving too much and pulling on the reins when we go faster; you must keep your hands in front of you and move them less. Also, stop telling the horse where to go. It knows where to go; the less direction you give, the better." Yasotay did as Temujin told him and worked on quieting his hand movements, not jerking the reins as much, and giving the horse less direction. The ride was noticeably better over the remainder of the first day and all of the second.

Yasotay awoke on the third day, and it, indeed, felt like every bone in his body ached. He wasn't sure if it was due to the long, fast ride or to Tera having placed the notion in his head, which *willed* it to be true. Either way, his inner thighs were raw, and he dreaded getting back on that horse for another whole day of riding.

"So, Temujin, when do you expect to find Bourtai's clan?" asked Yasotay as he walked gingerly toward his horse.

"Do you ask because you are sore and need a break from riding or because you are just mildly curious about our progress?" asked Temujin, laughing, his tone dripping with sarcasm.

"Both," answered Yasotay with a grin. "I should have listened to Tera and used that blanket; the insides of my legs are raw!"

"We should find them today," answered Temujin. "They camp along the Senggur River, which is just ahead. And yes, the blanket will help!"

It was sunny and warm by midday when they finally came upon a river and, shortly after that, Bourtai's clan. Two riders came out from the large encampment of thirty or so gers to meet them.

"My name is Temujin of the Clan of Borjigin. I am the son of Yesugei. I am here to claim my betrothed, Bourtai," proclaimed Temujin to the two riders.

Upon hearing this announcement, one of the riders immediately spun his horse around and galloped back toward the camp.

"Everyone is very tense here. There have been raids by the Taichiud. We were told that they were holding you prisoner," said the remaining rider, who was escorting them at a slow walking pace toward the camp.

"Yes, and obviously, I have escaped!" responded Temujin. "Why do you say things are tense?"

"Both the Taichiud and the Merkit have been raiding smaller clans, taking their women and animals, and killing those old enough to take revenge," explained the escort.

"Mongols killing Mongols. This is wrong. Someday, the clans must unify and bring peace to our people," said Temujin.

"I can tell you those who live here support peace," said the escort, "but we will fight if we must."

They slowly rode up to the collection of round white gers, all facing south, that dotted the hillside. With the sun high in the sky, the chill of the morning had dissipated. Sweat beaded on Yasotay's forehead as they approached. This collection of gers looked very similar to Temujin's encampment, though there were more gers and a larger herd of animals. The encampment sat in the shadow of a large grass-covered hill with sparsely scattered rocks and a few trees and shrubs. A family of five, three adults and two children, stood outside one of the gers, toward which the escort ushered Temujin and his men. Of the five people, it was obvious that Bourtai was the young, round-faced, pretty girl with brown hair and brown eyes who clearly stood out from the others. A large herd of goats to the right of the ger sang a chorus of oddly harmonizing bleating sounds. It appeared to Yasotay that they were announcing their arrival.

Bourtai's deel was a long one-piece jacket of blue and orange material that closed with the left side over the right and was secured just below her right armpit with a tie. It had a pocket on the right hip and sleeves down to the elbow. The outer lining of the robe looked as if it were made of silk, and its inner fur lining was exposed at the sleeves and hem. A black sable fur trim around the collar highlighted the girl's bright, young olive skin tone. It was one of the most colorful and intricate articles of clothing Yasotay had seen since his uncle's palace.

"Welcome, Temujin. You certainly have grown since we last met!" said the older man. Standing with him was a middle-aged woman with a young boy at each side, holding an oversized black fur jacket. One looked to be about ten or eleven and the other a year or two younger, both dressed in matching deep-blue deels with decorative yellow branches embroidered onto the fabric. Both deels had yellow trim and looked to be lined with fur as well. Bourtai's parents wore simple gray deels; her father's was tied with a bright yellow sash, and her mother's a faded red sash.

"It has been many years, Sechen," replied Temujin.

"Please, you and your companions are welcome in our home," answered Sechen. With that invitation, Temujin and the rest of his companions dismounted and followed Sechen and his family into their ger. Once everyone was inside, Belgutai stepped forward and proclaimed formally, "I am Belgutai, son of Yesugei and brother of Temujin. Your daughter's hand is sought by many, but she will go to only the one who is destined for her. Many years ago, you made a promise to our father. Therefore, I come to ask for your daughter's hand for my brother."

"Yes, with pleasure, we will honor that promise, but first, we must feast," said the older man. "My name is Sechen, and this is my wife, Tacotan." Sechen then introduced the rest of his family, and Belgutai and Temujin introduced Yasotay and Borchu.

The introductions were followed by a quiet, almost eerie moment. Suddenly, a low and very light rumble could be heard in the distance. Yasotay looked around the room and first noticed the wide-eyed fear on the faces of the children. The women quickly ushered the two children and Bourtai to the back of the ger as the men immediately filed out. At first, as he followed them out, Yasotay was blinded by the sun's rays. As his eyes adjusted, the source of their uneasiness was revealed. Across the rolling green landscape, Yasotay could see dozens of horses riding in a broad line toward the encampment. The line of horses seemed to stretch on and on without end. Hundreds of Mongolian warriors came into clear view on the not-too-distant horizon, riding up the valley with great haste toward their small camp.

The moment changed from apprehension to dread as the ground trembling beneath their feet seemed to indicate that the earth itself recognized the might of the approaching force. At the forefront rode the vanguard; one of the twenty riders in it held aloft a blue banner, snapping proudly in the breeze and emblazoned with an insignia that Yasotay couldn't quite make out.

Temujin and Borchu pulled their swords from their sides in unison. Belgutai removed his bow from his back and notched an arrow. An initial streak of terror ran through Yasotay's mind. He wasn't quite sure what to do. He stood frozen, running various scenarios through his mind all at once. Behind the vanguard, the main body of the horde extended as far as the eye could see, and it appeared that it was headed directly toward them. Each warrior had at least one other horse tied off behind him, so the sheer volume of the stampeding herd was immense. As they approached, the thunder of the horse hooves created a drumbeat that echoed across the valley.

Just the horses were a sight to see: magnificent beasts of varying sizes and colors. The group moved together so seamlessly that it resembled a flock of birds in flight. The bond between man and horse, forged through thousands of years of intimate interdependence, was palpable.

At that moment, Yasotay found himself on the precipice. Anticipation was mingled with anxiety, admiration with humility, and wonder with pure terror. The world seemed to hold its breath as time stood still, allowing him to fully grasp the majesty and significance of this irresistible torrent, a testament to the history of these people not yet written in any book. This moment was absolutely unnerving!

Then, all of a sudden, Temujin cheered, "It's Jamka!" Sheathing his sword back in its scabbard, with a big smile, Temujin walked forward—alone—toward the advancing horde. One warrior rode ahead of the vanguard and clearly stood out from the others. He was wearing a bright red deel with gold trim. He had a tuft of hair down the center of his head, bordered by shaved skin. Some of it hung down over his forehead and reached a point between his eyebrows. The unshaven hair on the sides of his head was braided into long queues that hung to mid-chest, and adorning the ends of the braids were gold metal rings that bounced while he rode. His long mustache was braided tendrils on either side of his mouth, and a small clump of hair garnished the middle of his chin.

"Temujin, my friend, it is good to see you!" exclaimed Jamka. He dismounted from his horse with a graceful hop and stood face-to-face with Temujin. The vanguard and the rest of the horse riders slowed to a stop, with the main body of troops holding at a short distance from the camp. Their handshake, which appeared rehearsed, consisted of grasping each other's right forearm with their right hands and, at the same time, putting their left hands on the other's right shoulder. This, done all in unison, made a smacking sound and looked more like a wrestling hold than a hug. With big smiles on their faces, Jamka asked, "I heard you escaped!"

"Those miserable ass-licking dogs couldn't hold me forever," explained Temujin, still holding Jamka's forearm, whose face turned from a smile to disgust, revealing his feelings for his friend's captors. Both men still had their left hand on the other's shoulder.

"That does not surprise me. Now it's rumored those same dogs have attacked an encampment of the Jadaran," explained Jamka, releasing the wrestling-style embrace. "We are following the river to see for ourselves." Jamka paused momentarily, then, throwing a hair queue over his shoulder, he said, "Come, ride with me. They should be but a short distance north from here. It would be good to ride with you, my old friend."

"I would like that, but I am here to claim my betrothed, Bourtai," explained Temujin, as his eyes darted back and forth as he thought about the two options. His eyebrows knitted together while tension gathered at the corners of his mouth.

"I will have you back to your bride before sunset," promised Jamka. "Join me, and let's see what kind of trouble those Taichiud ass-licking dogs are up to. Together, we can control this valley and burn their gers to the ground!"

With a sudden look of resolve, Temujin turned and walked back to where Bourtai and her family stood. He said, "I am going with Jamka. Yasotay, Borchu, Belgutai, join me," commanded Temujin as he gracefully hopped up on his horse. "We will return before sunset!"

"And we will prepare a celebration and request that Heaven's protection be granted to the union between our two families," asserted Bourtai's father, Sechen.

In moments, with a thunderous departure, all that remained was a fine brown dust plume hanging in the air. As it slowly dissipated, it revealed the white horse, with the red khadag scarf wrapped around its neck—the horse that Temujin had brought as a gift for his bride was all that remained.

Yasotay realized as he rode with the group that *This is the first time I have ever ridden into battle with a large group, let alone a horde of Mongols!* The thunderous noise heightened his awareness. Chunks of mud and dust were flying about the swarm of shifting souls riding free. Some warriors held bows; others grasped swords and axes.

Feeling the sheer magnitude of the formidable force that engulfed him made stories of historic battles skip through Yasotay's mind. He recalled how the forces of Liu Bei stormed toward the Red Cliffs and victory, a turning point in the Three Kingdoms period. Yasotay felt a fantastic rush of adrenaline, and over the booming rumble of the pounding hooves, something occurred to him: *There is camaraderie among these riders…a brotherhood that seems to transcend spoken words as the hundreds ride as one.* After a short ride up the Senggur River, they could see smoke up ahead, and the pack's pace quickened in anticipation. With the river to their left, Yasotay noticed a slender plume of black smoke rising into the blue sky from the rolling green meadow stretched out before them. As they approached, Yasotay could see a small collection of gers and several bumps or rocks in the field surrounding them. Once closer, he realized those weren't rocks.

Some gers still stood; several were torn and battered. Bodies were strewn throughout the campsite. Many gers were burned to the ground. For Yasotay, the scene was surreal, like time had slowed, and his view narrowed everywhere he looked. Headless bodies were scattered around a wagon. Their heads had apparently been cleaved off in the same spot next to it. Yasotay noticed all the heads had rolled to the bottom of the small gully, where they sat in a pile. He estimated that about twenty gers were initially set up in this small enclave beside the river. *This was a horrible massacre.* The horde of riders slowed and then stopped on the outskirts of the encampment. The vanguard, which Yasotay was part of, continued into the heart of the camp. Clearly, this fight was long over, and all that remained was carnage.

"I had to see it with my own eyes," said Jamka with a look of disgust. "They took the women and children and beheaded the rest. Some fought, but they were overrun…. Look, it was Taichiud." He pointed to a nomad lying face up on the ground with two arrows protruding from his chest. "The arrows in his quiver tell me he is Taichiud!"

Temujin spitted out, "Those ass-licking bastards."

There was a long, silent pause. Finally breaking the silence, Yasotay asked Borchu in a low and respectful voice, "What makes those arrows Taichiud?" His short, stout frame sat naturally on his horse a short distance from Yasotay's.

"The different colored feathers used to mark different types of arrows. The fletching on those arrows uses the colors of the Taichiud," explained the young man sitting on a white-gray mare between Yasotay and Borchu.

The three watched as Temujin and Jamka slowly rode side by side, talking privately while their horses walked around the perimeter of the camp's shambled remains. Some of the other warriors dismounted and began scrutinizing the carnage, looking for anything of value. Multiple bodies lay littered among the debris of what yesterday was a mirror image of Temujin's own camp. Having witnessed enough, Yasotay turned his horse and began to amble away from the remnants of the camp. Putting a little distance between himself and that grisly scene seemed like a good idea. He slowly rode toward the main body of riders, who were still keeping their distance a couple hundred paces back.

"Hello, I am Baatar," said the young man on the white-gray mare, who had lightly trotted up to catch him.

Yasotay noticed the young man was slightly built compared to the others in Jamka's horde, clearly one of the younger riders. His thick brown hair covered his head, and he had two braided tendrils similar to

Jamka's, but his were hanging on either side of his eyes. The rest of his hair was pulled back into a short, braided queue that hung down just past his shoulders. He was apparently trying to grow facial hair, even though it resembled just a trivial shadow on his face. He wore a gray deel with a leather sash around his waist. His sword had an emerald green grip and a large white pommel, which looked to be ivory. The top of his leather scabbard was trimmed with gold, similar to Jamka's.

"Are you the Baatar betrothed to Tera, Altan's daughter?" asked Yasotay.

"Yes, yes, I am," answered the young man with a big smile.

"But you are still a child!" responded Yasotay in disbelief, realizing after seeing the young man's angry expression that his comment would have been better left unsaid.

"I am thirteen years old," blurted Baatar, his young face contorted and shoulders slumped, betraying his hidden desire to be considered a man.

"Yes, I meant no disrespect, and thank you for the education on fletching colors. I did not know that. I am friends with Altan, Sarnai, and their daughter Tera. My name is Yasotay."

"I am pleased to meet any friend of my betrothed's family," said Baatar.

"Are you related to Jamka?" asked Yasotay, interested in learning more about this young man and trying to block out what he had just seen.

"He is my cousin," explained Baatar. "He just started letting me ride with him after I proved my ability to shoot a bow accurately from a moving horse."

"While I have used a bow, I have not yet learned the nomad's ways," Yasotay said and paused. "What is the purpose of that ring-like piece of bone several of you wear on your thumb?"

"This?" asked Baatar, holding up his right hand to reveal a ring made of bone on his right thumb. "It's used as a string release for your thumb…" Using his forefinger, he showed how it moved, smiling with an innocent, childlike expression. "If we get the chance, I will show you how we shoot a bow…if you wish."

126

"I would like that, thank you," replied Yasotay, noticing that Temujin and Jamka's horses galloped lightly toward them.

"I have spoken with Temujin. Baatar, take three warriors and escort Temujin and his betrothed back to his clan. I plan to attend the celebration of Temujin's wedding, which will be in ten days. In the meantime, we will hunt down the Taichiud dogs who committed this atrocity. After the celebration, you can return home with me." Jamka's expression of his desires was clear, concise—and final.

"Yes, cousin," answered Baatar as he turned his horse around and walked it toward Jamka's first captain. After receiving his instructions from Baatar, the captain ordered the warriors to mount up and prepare to leave.

"Yasotay, Borchu, let's head back to Bourtai," directed Temujin. "Jamka, my brother-in-arms, be safe." They grasped each other's forearms, and Temujin continued, "May your golden way be filled with fortune. I will see you in ten days when we will finally drink and celebrate together. We haven't shared a *Naadam* festival since we were children."

"Yes, well, there will be no wrestling or riding for you since you are the groom…unless you count what you do with your bride!" Jamka laughed heartily and released the clasp of his friend with a big smile. "Safe and tireless travels, my friend!" Both men were laughing as they parted ways, each with his right hand raised. Yasotay could sense how heartfelt the bond was between these two.

With a loud whistle, the horde seemed to disappear, with nothing left but a low-hanging column of dust trailing off to the north. Yasotay fussed with Tera's blanket, trying to get it folded just right to cover his saddle and ease his suffering. Having observed the impressive sight of hundreds of horses thundering away, Baatar, accompanied by three well-provisioned riders, each of them having two horses, reunited with Temujin, Yasotay, and Borchu. Together, they began their journey south, retracing their steps back to Sechen and his family's camp. They rode back in silence to the small yet spirited celebration that awaited them. They planned to enjoy the evening and depart in the morning to join Temujin's clan, where the wedding would be held. Tacotan, Bourtai's mother, would travel with them to attend the wedding, but her father, Sechen, had to remain and tend to his herd.

After dinner, it was with much fanfare that Bourtai's parents gave Temujin a long black sable overcoat as her dowery. Temujin tried on the beautiful coat with three oversized, sturdy clasps made of metal and leather. *For someone who was wearing a mobile pillory just three or four weeks ago, the coat is a very large and warm contrast*, thought Yasotay, admiring the quality of the fur.

With its fifteen horses, the party of ten headed southwest toward the valley of Mother and Father Mountains shortly after dawn. The group was settling into the long, slow trek back to Temujin's clan. They had been traveling all morning, and the sun was high when Baatar noticed something ahead and raised his hand. The group of horses slowed their pace.

"What is that?" asked Yasotay.

"It kind of looks like a bear, doesn't it?" said Temujin.

"That is a Ghost of the Mountains!" interjected Tacotan, describing the usually hard-to-find light brown *Mazaalai* bear currently blocking their way. "It is believed that the bear's bile has healing powers, so the shamans use it for medicine." As they slowly approached, the group drew closer together. They could see a large brown bear with a white stripe under his neck pawing at the dirt.

The party stopped. "I have heard the tales of these ghost bears," said Temujin. "This is very odd. These bears are rarely seen, yet this one sees us and is not running away!"

"Why is he slapping at the dirt like he's killing ants?" asked Bourtai. Temujin looked around at the others in bewilderment, then steered his horse to walk slowly, carefully toward the bear. The other riders mirrored Temujin's movements as they slowly approached. In a flash, the bear ran off up the hill to their right and between a large number of boulders scattered on the hillside.

Cautiously, they approached the spot where he had been "killing ants" to find nothing other than the bear's paw prints in the dirt.

"This is some kind of omen," proclaimed Tacotan. "The ghost of the steppe was…"

"Wait…I think I hear something!" proclaimed Baatar. Everyone reined in their horses to stand quietly and listened.

Yasotay and Baatar started to walk their horses to the right, following in the same direction the bear had run. Baatar dismounted and walked on foot, listening intently.

"You should be careful," declared Temujin with a grin. "I do not want to explain to Jamka how a ghost bear ate his cousin!"

Tacotan added, "Yes, be careful. They may be ghosts, but one can anger them, and their wrath is horrible."

Yasotay clearly heard something and lifted his hand for silence! "It almost sounds like the faint yelping of a dog," said Yasotay. "Mhmm, mhmm." *That was most surely yelping*, thought Yasotay, and it was barely audible.

Baatar asked, "Did you hear that?"

Yasotay said, "Yes, I heard something. It's very faint, but what is it?"

"Over here." Baatar walked toward a large outcropping of rocks and hopped up on them.

Yasotay and Baatar slowly moved toward the sound. The remainder of the party stayed where they were, watching the two move toward the yelping sound.

Yasotay was still on his horse following Baatar, who was climbing over boulders on foot; his horse had been left with the others. The yelping was getting louder and louder with each step.

Baatar stopped atop a large rock and climbed up on a ledge. Both could now hear a consistent cadence of yelping. The sound came from where a rock was split, with some small bushes growing between the two rock faces.

"Here's where the noise is coming from," said Baatar, peering into the crack before exclaiming, "It's a little pup with his foot stuck! The little fellow must have fallen into this hole here." With that, Baatar reached into the crack, grabbed the baby bear's paw, and set it free. He then lifted the little bear by its hind leg out of the crack and high up in the air. "I got him," exclaimed Baatar.

"Haha," the group cheered. They had been watching Yasotay and Baatar from a distance, enjoying the entertainment on an otherwise non-event-filled trip.

Like the mother, the small brown male bear had a white streak on his neck. Thankfully, he had stopped his yelping and was now looking around in amazement at everyone. Baatar brought the small brown creature down, then held it like he was cradling a baby in his arms.

"You seem awful friendly for a little ghost," said Baatar as he scratched his neck and belly. The little bear looked up at Baatar's smiling face, and it seemed to Baatar that he was smiling back.

"You're holding him like he's your baby," Yasotay teased. "Don't nomads name their babies!"

"Baabar, I will call you Baabar." The little bear barked once, then again, and at a different sound and pitch from the earlier yelping.

The remainder of the group was farther down the hill but overheard him and were laughing at Baatar. "You should keep him; maybe it's a good omen for my wedding," said Bourtai.

"We should go; that mother bear could be…" Temujin started to say but was interrupted by Borchu.

"*BEAR!*" yelled Borchu, pointing up the hill, his big cheeks and normally squinting eyes gone large.

Everyone looked uphill simultaneously and saw the mother bear barreling down that slope like a bolt of lightning.

"That's trouble," said Baatar, who appeared oddly calm in voice and movement.

"Come on, Baatar, let's GO!" yelled Yasotay, spinning his horse around and slowly trotting toward the others. Fully aware of the drama unfolding, they had already begun to move away. Borchu's short, stout arm lifted his crossbow from his side, and Temujin strung an arrow from his quiver.

Baatar jumped off the rock, still cradling the bear in his right arm, and ran down the hill. Yasotay had his horse in a trot headed away from the advancing bear. Looking back, he saw Baatar running toward him with the bear still nestled in his arm.

"The bear, put down the bear!" yelled Yasotay.

"I'm running away from the bear. What are you talking…" responded Baatar, running behind Yasotay and his moving horse.

"Baabar! Put down the baby bear, put down, Baabar!" shouted Yasotay.

Finally realizing what Yasotay meant, Baatar slowed his running enough to place Baabar on a rock. He hesitated for a brief moment, making sure he was set down safely. Then he scrambled away, running toward Yasotay. Running and jumping with his arms now free, he slapped them on the top of Yasotay's horse's ass and vaulted up, grabbing Yasotay by the waist. Realizing he had him, Yasotay rode hard to put distance between them and the charging bear and to catch up with the others riding ahead.

Looking back, Baatar could see the mother leaping right past baby Baabar, still sitting on the rock where Baatar had left him. After a couple of steps, the mother bear slowed and then stopped her advance.

Temujin, who had turned to look back and aim, lowered his bow. Borchu, too, put his crossbow back at his side. They stopped as Yasotay approached them and held Baatar's horse for him. Baatar swung off Yasotay's horse and onto his own without touching the ground.

"Well, you can tell everyone you saved and named a ghost!" exclaimed Yasotay.

"Came close to getting mauled by one too!" Temujin laughed.

"I was glad I could help and also make a friend," said Baatar. He was still a young man, and that fact shone through with the childish grin on his face.

"From what I could see, that mother bear didn't seem too friendly," added Borchu.

After all the excitement, everyone was back to riding down the trail. The four of them lingered for a moment. Looking back, they could see the silhouette of the mother sitting on her haunches and the baby bear walking atop the rock, sniffing around. This left a vivid image in Yaso-tay's mind of the love a mother bear has for its cub.

"Most mother bears will go to any lengths to protect their young," explained Borchu. All four riders, one at a time, began to peel away, trotting toward the main group.

"Yes, most mothers are ferocious protectors of their young, it's part of their being," said Yasotay, the last to turn and follow the group.

It had been three years since he had ridden a horse for an extended period, and Yasotay was certainly feeling it. This long ride to get Temujin's bride consisted of two full days plus the morning of the third day to get there and then three full days of riding to rejoin the clan. Riding with the horde had been exhilarating for him. It made up for the rash on his backside and the aches in his body, which were killing him. The clan had moved, and they planned to meet them in the valley within the shadow of Mother and Father Mountain.

As Yasotay and the nomads traveled, he found himself reflecting on the events of the past few days. While he wasn't sure how long he would stay with them, he had already learned so much from this unique culture. Despite his experiences studying with great masters and reading about different historical periods and events, this nomadic lifestyle completely differed from any other culture he had studied. It felt like he had discovered a cultural enigma and was exploring uncharted territory. While the Mongolian way of life was raw and challenging, it was a true test of human survival at its most basic level.

The valley between Mother and Father Mountains geographically narrowed toward the northern end. The valley, with many trees, shrubs, and other vegetation on the east side, was primarily a wide-open pasture perfect for grazing, lush with green rolling hills. But there was one unique distinction: a large rock that looked like it had been dropped into the valley by the hand of God. It was the same type of rock, though not as large, as those that encircled the valley on the slopes of Mother Mountain to the east and Father Mountain to the west. All of them were made from the same reddish-brown granite as the obelisk-shaped rock in the middle of the valley.

They arrived late on the third day. The valley was in the deep shadow cast by Father Mountain yet was still undeniably beautiful. It was the perfect place for a wedding. This was the valley where Temujin and his family had suffered through the Mongolian winters for as long as he could remember.

"My father took me up there when I was very young," said Temujin, riding alongside Yasotay. "We climbed up that big green hill to touch the rock for luck." Temujin's face smiled with this sweet remembrance.

"I remember one winter after my father died, and before my half-brother Bekter passed away, all my brothers and I were playing up there, shooting arrows into a dried-out animal skin hung from a string on a stick. We were laughing and having fun when suddenly an arrow shot from somewhere behind us broke the string. We turned to see this odd-looking old man who had shot the arrow standing there. We had previously seen him around camp. My mother had told us to stay away from him. 'There's something wrong with him,' she'd said. We were all very young and scared.

"After a long stare, he said to us, 'You boys are weak; you need to be strong. Your father is dead, and you will be too. You are fragile and will be killed before your next birthday if you don't toughen up!'" Temujin's shaky voice expressed the baffling look on his face. "We didn't know what to say; who was this man, and why did he say that to us? He left as quietly as he came, but I remember from that point on…our play was different. We all seemed to focus more on honing our skills…archery, horse riding, wrestling, and sword fighting." Temujin looked out across the valley, "This valley brings back many memories!"

Up ahead, the small collection of gers could be seen. Their distinctive shapes, first small, gradually grew larger and larger as they drew near. The circular forms of the nomad's traditional dwelling, covered in layers of white felt, appeared like pearls scattered across the landscape. There stood the Nine Tails of the Yak prominently displayed next to the entrance of Temujin's ger.

Temujin looked directly at Bourtai and proclaimed, "*We are home.*"

CHAPTER SIX

Valley between Mother and Father Mountains, fall, 1178 CE

The clan's winter camp was situated at the narrow northern end of the V-shaped valley. The northern reaches of the valley, in the tip of the V formed by Mother and Father mountain, was a short horse ride end-to-end. To ride to the southern end of the valley, at its broadest point, could take half a day or more. Mother Mountain, accompanied by her peaks-in-waiting, rose in the east, but the range was situated on a diagonal from north to southeast, while Father Mountain and his peaks were on the valley's west side and were also located diagonally in terms of compass points from north to southwest.

A small stream, little more than ankle-deep, flowed along the valley's east side. It was called the breast milk of Mother Mountain, which the land suckled from her snowy peaks. A thick blanket of green grass covered the valley, but all other plant life, every tree, bush, weed, and shrub, sprouted within twenty paces of this stream's crackling course. As Yasotay walked along the waterway, a wafting odor of rotten eggs combined with a tinge of fecal matter had driven Yasotay to this morning's exploration in the woods—escaping this odiferous situation was critical. His desire to live as a simple soul had led him to these nomads. With them, he could experience life and grow as a person without the meaningless demands, mind games, and mischievous jealousies of his previous life. It's what drew him to them, but it also created his current predicament.

A very small clearing came into view and immediately struck him as *the ideal location*! There was a cluster of bushes and small shrubs where the stream's flow jagged left, creating a small pool in the otherwise naturally shallow stream. Yasotay required privacy, and this spot afforded him the needed concealment. "Perfect!" he exclaimed. There were several large, flat, moss-covered rocks readily available. "These could be useful!" he said aloud. He realized that with a little effort, all he had to do was stack some rocks to make this site ideal for his purpose.

Removing his thick brown-leather boots, Yasotay rolled up his pant legs, preparing to wade into the stream. His brown hair had grown much longer, and the fine bristles of a wispy beard had started to form on his chin. His face revealed some apprehension that grew with every step he took toward the water's edge. When his bare feet touched the water, they were instantly numb. He thought, *It's too cold this morning. I'll build it now and return later in the day!*

Near the pool to the west were three large glacial boulders stacked one atop the others. The two lower flat stones were fully covered in deep green moss. Yasotay noted that this three-rock arrangement looked similar to the obelisk rock standing in the middle of the valley. Each rock was as wide as the wheel on an oxen cart. Stacking large flat stones he found around the site, he built a small dam just past the narrow bend in the stream.

Building this private bathing spot reminded him how he would receive an annual care package of personal hygiene products from the emperor. Every New Year's celebration came with a wonderous gift basket filled with spiced bath bean, sponges, toothbrushes made from the finest horse hairs, and clove-scented lotions. These baskets would be delivered to a couple hundred or so of the Jin elite as a gracious gift from the emperor. Fortunately for Yasotay, the remnants of what remained from his last gift basket was tucked away in his wooden chest. Bathing three to four times a week and brushing his teeth daily were habits that had been disrupted when he joined Temujin. And, as he was well aware from all the evidence, the nomads didn't believe in bathing. More than didn't believe; they thought that taking a bath could anger Tengri, who would send down bolts of lightning to punish those who disobeyed. Yasotay was concerned that if Tengri didn't punish him for bathing, the nomads just might. So, it was best to be hidden and do this in secret.

Yasotay had done his best to assimilate the nomad's ways and immerse himself in following their customs. He intentionally avoided dwelling on trivial cultural differences and instead emphasized their mutual beliefs. He recognized that the importance placed on family, friendship, and respect for elders were noteworthy shared values that stood out.

While his nasal passages had become more tolerant of the malodorous nature of the nomads, his own rancid stench was another matter. It had been six weeks, the longest period ever, that he had gone without a proper bath, and he intended to have one—*today.* After adding several smaller, flat stones to his barrier, the water level began to rise, along with Yasotay's relief and a smile. The water and terrain had formed into a small quasi-oval tarn. This small natural crater filled to a little over knee deep, which was plenty. Knowing that the water would be slightly warmer later in the day, Yasotay decided, *I'll come back, get in, wash up quickly, and I'm out,* he exclaimed as the freezing water created tiny bee stings at the bottom of his knees. He placed the last couple of rocks in place for reinforcement and considered the task finished. Yasotay stepped out shivering and dried his feet with a rag. After pulling on his boots and promising himself to return, it was time to track down Baatar for his first nomad archery lesson.

"I think it best if we start at the beginning," said Baatar, standing in an open field within sight of the camp. The queue of braided brown hair on the back of his head was decorated with rings of silver. He had small, matching bands of silver hanging from the two braided tendrils that started at the top of his head and ran along either side of his youthful face.

"Yes, I prefer that approach. While I've been trained on the bow and arrow, these weapons are different. I told Temujin and Borchu I'd join the archery competition tomorrow, and I would prefer not to make a fool of myself," said Yasotay. He had quietly returned to camp and sought out Baatar, who led him to a makeshift archery range with two wooden stands, each holding an animal fur target.

"Here is a *rox*," Baatar said, holding out his hand to reveal a polished piece of bone. It was the same as the one Baatar wore on his thumb. Yasotay had asked him about it when they met. "You will use it to hold and release the string to fire the arrow," explained Baatar, his brown eyes lighting up. "It works like the trigger on a crossbow. This one is for you to use." Yasotay put it on, and it fit tightly around his right thumb.

"The key to releasing the string and hitting your target is concentration. You must control your breathing and stay focused! We will start you off with a beginner's bow, which is much smaller," said Baatar with a grin. He pointed toward a couple of small bows among the eleven or so that Hassar had so graciously loaned them for today's training. Yasotay noticed that all the bows were complex in their design. They were crafted from blending materials together. These weren't just made from one piece of bent wood but from an elaborate combination of multiple parts. Hassar's bows were leaning up against a simple wooden rack, neatly aligned. "Try that one," Baatar said, pointing, "the one on the end."

Yasotay picked up the bow and inspected it closely, noting, *This is very different from any other bow I have ever handled. It's a little small but looks deadly, nonetheless.*

"If I teach you the bow, will you show me how to use your ball-and-chain weapon?" Like everyone, Baatar had heard Temujin's story of his escape by the river and how Yasotay's wonderous and mysterious weapon had struck down three of his captors. To date, Yasotay had been very reserved about showing the weapon to anyone and was less than forthcoming in actually demonstrating the device.

"We shall see. Let's continue with this bow first!" responded Yasotay, examining the excellent weapon in his hand closely.

"As you can see, we have two targets twenty-five paces away." Baatar explained that "each bow is made for the size and strength of its user. The bow frame is built from wild goat horn, wood, and several pieces of small animal sinew, all glued together. You see, a curved horn bone is cut perfectly down the middle. Then, a wooden grip is carved, shaped, and sized to fit one's hand. The wooden handle is securely attached to two matching curved horn pieces." Baatar paused, pointed toward the curved portion of the bow, and continued, "The sinew from small animals is layered with glue onto this part of the bow to give it strength. The glue is made from animal cartilage, ligaments, bones, and hooves, all boiled down into a strong, sticky substance. It took many layers of sinew to make my bow this strong." Baatar motioned to the bow in his hand. "Once dry, it is ready. This layering process gives the bow greater strength than any other method!"

"So, can they get wet without falling apart?" asked Yasotay.

"Yes…and no. The bow can get a little wet. We wrap the curved portion of the bow with bark from the white birch tree or in leather. It helps repel water, but it's best to keep your bow dry." Looking closely at Baatar's bow, Yasotay could tell he had put a great deal of time and craftsmanship into his weapon. It was undoubtedly the best-looking bow of the bunch.

"The arrows are made with the tail feathers of birds instead of the wing feathers, which do not fly as straight. Here, let me show you!" With that, Baatar slid an arrow from the quiver at his side, nocked it while setting his feet shoulder distance apart, and took aim at the target. He pulled back, held the string taunt for a brief moment, and then released it with a barely perceptible *Twang, Whoosh…Thong.*" The arrow flew straight and true into the round white center of the fur-covered target.

Yasotay had noticed that the nomads had a unique way of holding the arrow and releasing the string. The arrow was placed on the opposite side of the bow from how he was taught to draw and fire an arrow. These bows were nothing like the ones he shot as a child or any he had seen during his time with either the Song or the Jin. Their blended components made for a much more accurate and powerful weapon. Baatar's detailed description, coupled with everything he had read about them, rattled around in Yasotay's brain, leading him to speculate that the nomad's version of the bow was clearly the next step in the development of the bow and arrow. It was more accurate and powerful; and, in the right hands, much more deadly!

Baatar explained, "There are two main touchpoints of the string at each end of the bow. One is the point where the string loops through a notch in the bow." Baatar pointed to a small post immediately past the loop. "The other is this post, called a *tovh.*"

"This is important! Notice there is a tovh at each end of the bow. When the string is aligned with the tovh at each end and is seated properly, it gives these bows much greater accuracy," Baatar insisted. "If the tovh is missing, or the string isn't seated properly, you miss, but when aligned properly…" Baatar quickly nocked and shot another arrow with a smooth, lightning-fast motion. *Twang. Whoosh. Thong.* Baatar's second arrow joined his first in the center of the target.

"Instead of holding the bowstring, you nestle it in at the back of the rox, and then the arrow shaft is not on the hand's knuckle side of the string but on the thumb side so that it can be fired from horseback," said

Baatar, showing Yasotay how he was holding his hand with the arrow. "Here, now you try,"

At that moment, they both heard someone approach and turned to see Tera's caramel-colored eyes glaring at them as she stormed up to where they stood.

"Good morning, Tera. How are you today?" asked Yasotay.

"That bow is too small for someone his size!" boomed Tera, ignoring Yasotay's greeting. She appeared furious, emitting irritation from her red hair. She strode toward Hassar's bow collection and seized the largest one from the rack. "Here, Yasotay…use this one. It's probably too small since you are much taller than most, but it's better than that child's bow he gave you." They both stared at her dumbfounded. "I teach all the children how to shoot and ride and would only give that bow to a young child. I know what I speak of," proclaimed Tera, handing the bow to Yasotay. Bobbing her head to the side, she removed a strand of hair from over her eyes.

"Yes, and that's why I started him with a child's bow, to teach him how we shoot the same way I learned, the same way we all learned," Baatar said while Yasotay stood there holding both bows, watching the two debate the issue.

"You're a child, and unlike you, he is not a child!" Tera exclaimed with no small amount of attitude. "He needs to learn properly, which means the bow needs to fit his frame." She was slightly taller than young Baatar, and using that advantage, you could see the fire in her eyes as she spoke down to him. She was enraged for some reason, and Baatar appeared to be the dried dung for her flames. His face turned bright red, and he stood quietly motionless as she continued. "You just don't understand what you're doing!" Baatar didn't react or respond. "His left arm holding the bow needs to be FULLY extended!" she added.

Trying to break the tension, Yasotay chimed in, "Let me try this." Setting the smaller bow on the ground, he grabbed an arrow from Baatar's quiver and moved to the firing line. Nocking the arrow, Yasotay planted his feet properly, pulled back on the string, and took aim. He couldn't help but notice how difficult pulling back on the string was.

Twang. Whoosh. Thong. The arrow hit the outer edge of the target, well outside its center where he had aimed.

"There, see…pretty good shot," Tera insisted. "You just need to clear your mind and work on your form. Get comfortable releasing the string using the rox. Your draw elbow should be pointed opposite to where you are aiming." Tera demonstrated the movement and how her elbow was up, extended back, and level with her right draw hand, which was at her face.

"Thank you, Tera. I will work on my form." He turned to the young man. "Did you see that, Baatar, I hit the target? You are an excellent teacher!" Yasotay felt sorry for him as he withstood Tera's reprimand in silence. His face was flushed, shoulders hunched over, and there was an awkward silence.

Tera finally perceived the maladroit moment and that she was the cause. "I must go! I have chores to do," she spun around and walked away in a huff.

Once Tera was out of earshot, Baatar finally spoke again. "What did I do or say for her to treat me that way?" He could barely be heard over two fighting dogs yapping loudly in the distance.

"I'm not sure," said Yasotay.

"Is it my imagination, or does she seem infuriated with me?" he wondered aloud, lining up and taking another shot at the target. A third bullseye.

"No, you're right, she seemed pretty mad…I wouldn't worry about it," said Yasotay.

"She is my betrothed. Is that the treatment I am to expect from her once we are married?" asked Baatar, the tendrils of his brown hair hung down, framing either side of the frustrated look on his face.

Yasotay's face softened. "I must admit, Baatar, that I am unaware of women! Well, what I mean is that my interaction with them has been very limited and often confusing. But I do know her father said she was not pleased with the fact that he had chosen her husband for her. I sense that she would prefer to choose for herself," he said, his voice trailing off into speculation.

"Or is it that she does not care for his choice?" Baatar asked in a matter-of-fact tone.

"I don't think that's true, Baatar," Yasotay said, feeling like his words were not getting through. "Tera is a very strong-willed person. I believe she objects to not having a voice in the decision. It's not you!" Yasotay released another arrow, his broad shoulders slumping as this one missed the target completely. This rox is going to take some getting used to.

"Either way, she hates me!" exclaimed Baatar, shooting another arrow into the center of the target. "Also, you dropped your elbow on that last shot. Just like she said not to do!" The look on the young man's face reminded Yasotay of a wounded puppy.

They took turns shooting arrows into the targets. After they had both taken about ten shots, the two of them walked over to retrieve the arrows.

"You know what, I think that elbow trick she mentioned really does work!" said Baatar sarcastically. "I clear my mind, focus on my form… and look!" He waved his hand toward the tight grouping of arrows at the target's center and said, "Wisdom applied!"

Yasotay lightly laughed. Pulling the arrows from his target, he said, "Yes, wisdom…a dish that matters not how it's served, as long as you consume it." He paused and had another thought. "Or it might consume you!" he added, smiling broadly.

"I guess I prefer mine with a little more honey and a lot less horse leavings!" Baatar managed to force a grin across his face.

Yasotay pushed him with a playful elbow. "You're a good man, Baatar!"

Baatar smiled, liking that Yasotay had called him a man. Both men looked at Tera, who was about a hundred paces from their target area, fussing with the animal fence outside the family's ger. Yasotay was taken by the palpable longing in Baatar's long gape. They continued shooting and retrieving their arrows. After seven rounds, Yasotay consistently hit the center of the target right along with Baatar. The fighting dogs were now in a barking war that echoed through the valley.

"You're doing well, Yasotay. It appears you have gotten the hang of this. You learn quickly. Next, we must practice shooting from atop a moving horse. I can round up some horses, and we can…"

With a shift of the slight breeze, Yasotay suddenly detected his own stench, whereupon his gaze was drawn upward to check the sun's position. It was high in the sky, and one thought crossed his mind: *It's time!*

Yasotay interrupted Baatar. "Thank you for the lesson. I am already feeling it in my arms and chest," he said, stretching his arms to his side. "I have some chores to help Altan with…maybe we can work on that another time?" Yasotay was already turning to leave.

"Didn't you say you will compete in the archery competition tomorrow?"

"Yes. Temujin insisted that I try to compete in at least one of the three skill competitions. So, between wrestling, horse racing, and archery, I picked archery!" said Yasotay. "My logic is simple. First, everyone in camp is a better rider than me, even the children. Plus, the inside of my legs hasn't healed from my last long ride. Second, your wrestling looks very different from the fighting styles I know. I saw Altan practicing with someone and throwing them to the ground like a bag of feed. So, while the bows are significantly different, archery seemed the obvious choice!"

"If the fixed target shooting ends in a tie, which it often does, the matter is decided by shooting from atop a moving horse," said Baatar. "Have you ever done that?"

"I doubt that I will get that far. Hassar is the favorite to win the competition. I'm just trying to please the groom and have no illusions of winning the competition, Baatar."

"I plan to compete in the horse race, and unlike you, I plan to win! I will prove to Tera that I am no longer a child but a grown man!" proclaimed Baatar. Ten thousand thoughts of what to say filled Yasotay's head, but not one word came to mind worth saying.

"Thank you again for your help. I don't doubt you will do fine in the horse race tomorrow. I will be cheering for you to win!"

"You should take that bow with you and use it tomorrow. Hassar said to let you pick whichever one you would like to use," Baatar said.

"That's kind of him. Thank you. I will." Yasotay grabbed the bow and walked back to Altan's ger. Tera was still outside, and Tata stood within arm's reach of her, hovering over her like a shadow. She was still reinforcing the fencing, which penned the family's small flock of goats and sheep.

"Does she follow you everywhere you go?" asked Yasotay, walking up behind Tera, who was still on her knees, fussing with that section of fencing.

"She and I see things the same way. It's what makes us close," said Tera, reaching out and scratching between Tata's ears just the way she likes.

"I feel like you two may be getting too close," Yasotay said in a playful tone as he ducked into the ger. He leaned the bow next to his wooden chest, opened it, and grabbed a small wooden box and a rag from within. He was tucking the small wooden box into the fold of his deel when he walked out of the ger.

"What is that?" asked Tera, who caught a glimpse of the box.

"Oh, it's nothing, just a gift from a friend," said Yasotay.

"Where are you going?" she asked with a pout. "I need help setting up the targets for tomorrow's archery competition." In the sunlight, her hair looked more reddish than brown today. He liked it.

"I see. When are you doing that?" asked Yasotay.

"As soon as I get this fence fixed, in about half a shi."

"I'll meet you back here in half a shi." Before she could say another word, he started to walk quickly toward the woods.

"I will be back!" exclaimed Yasotay, turning and waving.

She noticed he didn't break his stride or slow his pace. *He was acting...odd.*

As Yasotay approached his hidden bath area, he noticed his dam had created a nice-sized little tarn that was certainly big enough for his purposes. *That water still looks cold!* He thought to himself, seeing tiny icicles hanging from the underside of rocks around the pool. Yasotay stood on one of the larger rocks to the right of the pool and could hear the water rippling over his makeshift dam as he removed his clothing.

He neatly folded and placed each piece on the rock at the pool's edge. Naked and holding his small box high, he slowly stepped into the deep part of the pool. Chills ran up his legs and into his torso. The water here came more than halfway up the length of his thigh. Yasotay reflexively brought his arms in toward his torso and shivered. *I was wrong...this water is FREEZING cold!*

Reaching over, he placed the box atop the pile of rocks that formed the dam. It contained his bath bean and a toothbrush. For the past six weeks, Yasotay has had no opportunity to use the bath bean short of cleaning his teeth. Dipping his hand into the open box, he retrieved a small cloth covered in bath bean and began rubbing it over his chest and arms. Keeping the cloth wet, he dipped his cloth repeatedly into the bath bean, then scrubbed his whole body with it. He moved quickly because he needed to finish the task at hand and get out! Splashing cold water on his torso to remove the bath bean's sudsy layer made him feel even colder, if that were possible.

Finally, after a few moments of rubbing the bath bean on his face and hair, he crouched down and plunged into the icy cold water until fully submerged. Yasotay remained underwater momentarily, wiping bath bean off his face and head till he could stand it no longer. He stood up quickly, throwing his head back and taking a big breath. The water whipped from his head and across the bushes surrounding the pool. He heard the bushes rustling, which gave him pause, and he stood motionless, waiting to see if someone was there. Standing there naked and shivering cold, he was unsure what it was and kept quiet for a long moment. Then, after hearing nothing, he stepped out of the water and back atop the moss-covered boulder. He reached over, grabbed his toothbrush, which already had plenty of bath bean on it, and brushed his teeth vigorously.

Once he was finished with his teeth, he again entered the water and used the bath bean to wash under his armpits and between his legs again. Then, feeling that the task had been completed sufficiently, he stepped out of the water and back atop the moss-covered boulder. Yasotay grabbed the small dry rag he had brought and began using it to dry

himself off. The cold air stung his naked body, but the bath bean's laven-
der and clove scent made it a blissfully tolerable experience. *Finally, I no
longer smell like a three-day-old corpse*, he thought. Then he picked up
the stinky deel he had lived in since the day he arrived, telling himself, *I
need another one of these!* and put the dirty deel back on.

Yasotay arrived to help Tera with a smile on his face and time to
spare. After stopping by the ger, he was ready to help Tera prepare
the archery competition targets. There were five or six targets similar to Baatar's. These were well-made targets, each marked with the
same-sized white bullseye painted onto the fur. Tera grabbed one of
the targets and began walking toward where Baatar had set up his
archery range.

"Grab one of these and follow me," she ordered. Yasotay gathered
up two targets, one in each arm, and dutifully followed her. The targets
were animal hides covering a wicker wheel filled with grass. Each wheel
was attached to three wooden poles that worked like a tripod to stand
upright. Tera marched right past where Baatar had lined up Hassar's
bows on a makeshift rack.

"Over here. We will place the firing line here." Tera stuck a stick into
the ground and, digging her heel into the dirt, made a short line. "The
targets need to be lined up in a row down there!" she said, pointing
them at a different angle than Baatar had used on his shooting range.

"You smell funny!" she blurted.

"What?"

"You smell funny. What is that?" Tera asked. "You smell like, like…
food!" she laughed.

Yasotay felt embarrassed. "I just couldn't stand the…never mind,
where do you want this?"

"Fifty full paces from this firing line," answered Tera. Yasotay began
counting out his paces.

"Forty-seven, forty-eight, forty-nine, and fifty," Yasotay announced
and marked the spot by digging his heel into the ground and placing
a target precisely at that spot. Then, as Yasotay walked back, he came
within comfortable speaking distance of Tera.

"I don't understand. Please explain?" Tera asked. "What couldn't you stand?"

Yasotay realized she would persist with these questions and resolved to be honest with her, "I needed to take a bath, so I took one in the stream over there."

She could see by his body language that Yasotay was uncomfortable talking about this. "But why? Wasn't it cold?" she asked with a look of bewilderment. "Why would you do that?" She paused. "What about the spirits of the water? Couldn't you have been put to death for offending them? If Tengri didn't kill you with a bolt of lightning first!"

"I understand your concern, and it was icy cold...I just like how I feel afterward...it's better!" Yasotay said, stammering. Not only didn't nomads take baths, but they also appeared to have trouble comprehending the slightest reason for them!

"So, what do we do next?" he asked, attempting to change the subject by holding up the other target he still carried.

"Now step off fifteen paces from here, head that way, and mark it." Tera pointed him perpendicular to the line he had previously just stepped off.

"Fourteen and fifteen," Yasotay said, then dug his heel into the dirt.

"Mark that spot with a stick. That is the other end of the firing line. Now, fifty steps that way and place the other target there." Oddly, there was a brief break with the incessant bleating of the sheep in the background.

"I see what you're doing. Once I've set up this target, we have our four corners and will place the remaining targets between these two, which we have already measured, and then draw our firing line, and we're done!" Yasotay explained, content with his assessment.

"Yes, that's right.... Is there some religious reason why you get wet when it is so cold?" asked Tera, "Won't you freeze?"

Yasotay didn't answer her. Instead, he counted off the fifty paces and placed the other target. Then he began the long walk back to the ger to get the remaining three targets. When he returned, Tera had already set her target in line with the others. She was now scuffing the end of a long staff along the ground in a straight line to mark the firing line.

"I want to learn more about why you do this bath thing," she said pointedly. Yasotay felt mildly agitated. He wanted to change the subject.

"Fine, I'll explain it to you all you like, but please, let's keep this between you and me. Your people view bathing very negatively. It's hard enough trying to *fit in* here without people knowing that I bathe, considering how they feel about water spirits and Tengri sending down lightning bolts."

"You have my word!" she promised with a satisfied smile as if she had won some unrecognized point in their game of words, "I will say nothing, and you will teach me about this bath thing you do!"

"Good!" responded Yasotay. "Now, please, before we speak more about that, explain the nomad's formal wedding ceremony to me?"

"Our weddings are a confirmation of the union between a man and woman's family. They allow everyone to bestow their best wishes on the couple. First, the groom's family formally beseeches the bride's family to part with their daughter, which is followed by the exchange of gifts. Then, the actual marriage ceremony is performed. Finally, there are the celebration festivities."

"Yes," said Yasotay, "I saw the black sable coat that Tacotan and Sechen, Bourtai's parents, had given Temujin."

"Temujin's mother, Houlun, has made a traditional deel for Bourtai, and she will dress her new daughter in it for the wedding. Additionally, Temujin's people will give the couple a new ger, a new home to reflect their new union. This ger will have a large piece of white felt laid at its front entrance. Bourtai will boil the bride's tea and oversee the preparation of the bride's food, which will be offered first to both mothers and then to the family elders. Gifts will be given, games played, and a large celebration will honor the newly married couple."

"It sounds like an all-day celebration," Yasotay said with a smile. "I must ask…are all nomad weddings done in this way? This seems like a very large event with the ceremony, the games, and the celebration!"

"Yes, sometimes a celebration lasts two or three days," said Tera. "Temujin is our leader, so this wedding has additional meaning for the future of our clan. Music will be played, everyone will drink, and yes, to us, family is everything!"

"I have noticed that!" said Yasotay. "This is not something I am used to."

"You mean family? Are your parents alive? Do you not have a family?"

"Yes, my mother died, or not my mother, but…it's hard to explain." Yasotay had not talked about Mana to anyone since her death. "My mother is wealthy and powerful. Mana, one of my mother's many servants, raised and cared for me. She was more like my real mother. We did everything together, and one day, Mana was gone…murdered."

"I'm so sorry," Tera said. Her face softened, and her eyes looked watery while she placed her hand on Yasotay's shoulder.

"I have never been close with my real mother and never met my father, but Mana was family to me, my only real family." Yasotay paused for a moment.

Tera sensed that he was holding back from saying something, something more, and then he continued.

"I watched when Temujin's mother's face lit up on our return; her love for him was clear for all to see. It made me think of my Mana, who would light up the same way with me…every time."

"Yes, well, I hate my father…or, at least, when he doesn't listen to reason," responded Tera, her face flushed. "I have no interest in marrying BAATAR!" Tera's face blushed with anger. "He is forcing me to do something I don't want to do!"

Yasotay could sense the emotion and feelings of frustration in her voice. "Baatar is a good kid!" Once spoken, Yasotay realized his mistake as soon as the word came out of his mouth.

"Kid, child, yes, you are right. He is a CHILD!" exclaimed Tera, getting louder and more animated. "My father is more stubborn than Tata!"

"You and I know no one is more stubborn than Tata!" Yasotay said in a lighthearted and placating manner, trying to soften the conversation.

Tera was flustered, but she gave his jest the smallest of smiles, then continued, her tone lower, "He just won't listen to me. Baatar is a child. I am a grown woman…would you feel any differently if you were me?"

"I would do my best to respect my parents' wishes," said Yasotay, feeling awkward when considering his relationship with his mother. "This is what Confucius taught us: filial piety…our duty to respect, obey, and be attentive to our parents' wishes."

"Is that what you are doing now, your mother's wishes?" That fire was back in her eyes.

"This is different," protested Yasotay, with the effort of someone struggling to convince himself of that difference.

"Is it? How? Your mother is rich and wanted you to run away and live with us, nomads?" Her words dripped with sarcasm while her knuckles turned white, gripping the stick she used to mark the firing line.

Tera noticed the scar on his chin was red again as he spoke. "You don't understand. It was different. She lied to me. I couldn't trust a word she said, and instead of confronting her, I left!" said Yasotay in a bland, emotionless tone. "My mother doesn't know where I am, and the only reason she would care is because she's not controlling me!"

Tera grew silent momentarily, thinking this through. She dropped her hands to her sides, the stick limply trailing on the ground. Finally, in a lowered voice, she said, "Then you understand my problem. She doesn't care; she just wants to control you. You made the difficult choice, which is why you're here with us now!"

"Your father wants what's best for you. He does care," said Yasotay. "Baatar is a good young man who won't remain a child forever. It is the way things are!"

"Baatar is not the *way things are* for *me!*" Tera fumed. She spun, and her stick whipped around with her as she stabbed it into the ground at her side. She walked back toward the camp, stabbing the ground angrily with every other step. Over her shoulder, she barked, "We are done here!" As she stormed up the hill toward the main encampment, Yasotay noticed large white clouds moving in over Father Mountain.

The sun was climbing the backside of Mother Mountain as Yasotay gathered his morning thoughts. It was Temujin and Bourtai's wedding day, and Yasotay was sitting on a rock about two hundred paces or so south of the camp, performing his morning ritual. As usual, he sat on one side of his blanket with the other over his head, back in his warm cocoon. He loved this spot because it afforded him a view of the valley as the first rays of sunlight danced on the valley floor. Yesterday's conversation with Tera did not end well. He was concerned that the example of him going his own way would cause Tera to do something drastic. It seemed unlikely she would leave, but she certainly inferred she might. While he could sympathize with her, their situations weren't the same. As it was everywhere, Yasotay knew that choosing a husband for a daughter was a father's responsibility. Altan was just doing his duty. He loathed to entangle himself in this issue between father and daughter. Both were headstrong people, and Yasotay was merely a guest in their ger. It was best to stay out of the fray and respect the natural order of things.

Bands of sunlight began to break through from the back of Mother Mountain, casting streaks of dark shadows across the valley. The giant obelisk could be seen now to his right, and the camp, still in shadows, was to his left. The valley's plants had begun to wilt and die since the season was changing. The first hard frost had come recently, the season was changing. The crisp smell of fall permeated the air, accented by the faint odor of plants dying in the natural order of things.

Walking back to the camp, Yasotay watched the buzz of activity as people were up and moving earlier than usual. Preparation for the day's celebration seemed to be paramount in everyone's mind. This was an important day; Temujin, their leader, was to be wed in a family celebration the likes of which Yasotay had never seen. While he had witnessed massive Jin celebrations with fireworks and thousands marching in formation, this was different—more intimate—because it involved a tight-knit group of people who cared for each other. Yasotay was honored to be among them and felt a little jealous of the love and support afforded Temujin. He walked into the ger and was greeted by a wave of heat and the visceral, slightly metallic smell of freshly cut meat. Tera, working with her mother Sarnai, was stoking the fire. From what he could tell, they were planning to steam a large slab of lamb in an even larger pot.

Tera called out, "Yasotay, can you help me?" Her caramel eyes had lost their fiery glare from yesterday. "We are preparing lamb for Bourtai. She's concerned that more people than expected will arrive, and she won't have enough food. You can help by bringing her the two chickens in the cage outside."

"Yes, I am happy to help," Yasotay said, placing his blanket on his wooden chest and squeezing sideways to pass Sarnai, carrying a portion of the butchered lamb.

"I separated them. Bourtai needs only young chickens, and we only had two," explained Tera.

"Oh, why only young chickens?" Yasotay asked.

"It's a wedding ritual that the shaman recommended," answered Tera, distracted with many things on her mind.

Yasotay walked outside and found the cage with the two small chickens. Dutifully, he carried the cage to Temujin's new ger. As he walked up, he could see the bride and groom outside. Temujin's red locks of hair were bouncing as he attempted to hold down a small chicken struggling for its life. Bourtai was standing over him holding a knife in one hand while the other hand rummaged around inside the abdomen of the spry and terrified chicken. Temujin had a serious look as he held on with two hands, doing his best not to let it get away. The chicken's head thrashed about, wings flapping, feathers floating in the air. This chicken was putting up a darn good fight, and after a few moments, Bourtai pulled her bloodied hand from inside the chicken and proclaimed, "I got it!"

"Here, let me see," said Temujin, who looked quizzically at the small bloody lump in Bourtai's blood-soaked fingers. "It looks good to me!"

"Here, see, it's perfect!" Bourtai held out the small chicken liver in her bloody hand to Houlun and Tacotan, her brown hair stuck to the side of her round face, sweaty from the struggle. The mothers of the bride and groom inspected it closely, and both nodded in agreement.

Yasotay reluctantly held up the cage and said, "Bourtai, I have these for you from Tera."

"It doesn't look like we are going to need them," said Temujin, handing the still-thrashing chicken to Tacotan, who quickly and humanely ended its ordeal with a quick twist of its neck. Then, holding the chicken by the head, she cut it off. The beheaded chicken fell to the ground. It was finally free and still surprisingly lively as it bounced to its feet and ran off. Tacotan, still holding the head, gave chase. Three giggling children followed the headless, liverless chicken and Tacotan in a parade around the back of the ger.

"Please tell Tera I said thank you," said Bourtai.

"So, what was that about?" Yasotay asked Temujin, who was smiling broadly, as his mother Houlun and Bourtai filed back into the ger. Houlun following the bride's every step.

"It's a tradition for the bride and groom to find a lucky mark on a chicken's liver," said Temujin, "We would have had to keep killing chickens till we found one. Fortunately, our first chicken had the lucky liver! We will hold one more ritual here in a moment, and then we're off to watch the first competition."

"Yes, archery is first, and Hassar is by far the best," Yasotay said. "I've seen him shoot. No one will beat him!"

"You sound like you've already lost before nocking your first arrow!" Temujin insisted.

"I will try my best, but Hassar is amazing. So, what is next for you?"

"Eating, drinking, and other than that, I have no idea," Temujin said with a smile, wrapping his big arm around Yasotay. "Today, I am told what to do, and I do what I am told! As long as I have a drink in my hand, I am in perfect balance with nature!" Temujin and Yasotay looked down at the groom's empty hands, which he held out in front of them. Their heartfelt laughter echoed through the camp as they parted ways. Yasotay went to prepare for the archery competition, and Temujin went to find a drink!

Baatar had previously explained the simple rules of the archery competition. Yasotay needed to fire ten shots at the target. The goal was to have more center shots than your opponent. There was no pausing between shots, so once you started, you must finish. Nock, pull, fire, nock, pull, fire. Only the briefest pause was allowed for aiming once the arrow was nocked and drawn. That was the rhythm that each participant tried to keep with all ten shots. Each person went head-to-head against someone else—only one battle at a time. If you won, you were matched up with another winner, and the two of you would go again. If you lost, you sat down and watched. If you tied, you did another ten shots each. This was repeated until the matter was decided.

Tacotan and Houlun had organized comfortable and prominent monarchical seating for the bride and groom to watch the competition behind and to the right of the firing line. This vantage point provided a perfect view of each contestant and their shot. Jamka arrived just moments before the competition started and offered his deepest regrets to the couple for being late.

"My *other brother* has finally arrived," announced Temujin. "And how did the hunt for our Taichiud friends go?"

"They remain elusive and cunning," said Jamka. "My spies tell me they are still looking for you and some ghost!"

"It's no matter what they're looking for," said Temujin confidently, sitting next to Bourtai in his seat of honor, "what matters is you didn't miss out on the drinking!" A chorus of laughter accompanied this boast. "Here, take a swig of this and get in there. You must join the archery competition!" With talk of serious matters put aside, Temujin and Jamka took a large draw of ayrag from a leather-covered bladder.

"If that's the case, I need to know, where is Hassar?" asked Jamka, wiping the drink from his mouth with a joking smile. When he spotted his rival standing near the firing line, he exclaimed, "No, we cannot allow him to participate…he cheats!" pointing at Hassar.

"What?" asked Hassar in surprise. Temujin laughed at the interchange, knowing full well that Jamka was teasing the young man.

"Yes, I say no one as skilled as you should be allowed. Maybe we make him shoot standing on one leg…to make it fair," teased Jamka, which elicited another chorus of laughter.

The competition began, and the participants were quickly winnowed down from eight to four. Hassar didn't miss a shot. As a display of his skill, all his shots were taken with his left foot raised in front of him, his right knee slightly bent, and his shots were still smooth, quick, and accurate. This elicited another chorus of laughter and cheers from those watching. He was the only one to score a perfect ten. Yasotay had won his first head-to-head, missing only one of his ten shots. The final four remaining were Baatar, Hassar, Jamka, and Yasotay. Temujin asserted his position of honor and paired Baatar against Yasotay and Hassar, Temujin's younger brother, against Jamka, his childhood best friend.

"That's fine, Temujin…pitting me against your brother," said Jamka, then looking directly at Hassar, he added, "I would prefer you to shoot with both feet on the ground. Grant me the dignity of claiming you required both feet to beat me!" More laughter came from the crowd.

"Please accept the honor of going first," invited Hassar with a nod. Yasotay wondered if this was a sign of respect or done in jest. At times, it was difficult for Yasotay to tell the difference. Jamka quickly rattled off nine perfect shots. On the last one, he seemed to hesitate briefly and missed the center mark by the smallest of margins.

"Alas, I left you an opening, which is all you need," said Jamka, "the victory is yours for the taking." He then waved his arm toward the firing line.

Without another word, Hassar took a confident stance at the line and, with complete self-assurance, quickly and gracefully pumped ten arrows into the dead center. Jamka took the loss gracefully, joking about having to sit with the losers. His gregarious nature livened up the party and made everyone laugh a little louder and drink a little more. Temujin seemed to feed off his boisterous antics to play a game of one-upmanship with his friend—who could garner the loudest laughs? Every joke was answered with another.

Next up was Baatar versus Yasotay. Yasotay went first and placed eight out of ten arrows in the center, missing his first shot high-right and his last shot low-left. Baatar followed. His motion was clunky and awkward, and his results showed it. He was lucky to get seven out of ten. His mind was obviously elsewhere. So, the final match was between Hassar and Yasotay. Yasotay held no hope of winning; Hassar was gifted with deadly aim.

Hassar started the match with his third perfect set of ten. Yasotay followed with his first set of ten to hit the target's center. He was getting used to the new bow. Having practiced archery in the past, it wasn't all new to him. They both shot another round of perfect tens, with the cheers from the gathered crowd getting successively louder. With each perfect score, the seriousness of the competition and the weight of the moment increased. Yasotay sensed they were now at an inflection point. They tied again with two more perfect scores. That was three ties, which meant the competition would be decided by shooting at a moving target from a galloping horse.

Excited at the prospect, Temujin jumped from his seat to mark off the direction and spot of the firing line. With a look of sheer joy, Yasotay could tell the groom loved every moment of this competition. Temujin explained the tiebreaker, "This is the line which the shooter must ride across before shooting at the target," he pointed to the line clearly marked on the ground. "You cannot stop your horse while shooting. You cannot start shooting till you pass the line. The target will be thrown in the air as you pass the line, and the goal is to hit it with as many arrows as possible before it hits the ground!" Temujin held up a small round lattice cage made from wood and stuffed with grass. "This is your target!" It had a rope attached like a tail, and Temujin began to swing it in a circular fashion. "I will show you!"

"Does this remind you of something, Yasotay?" Temujin said with a grin while spinning the target as fast as he could. He let it go, flinging it high in the air. A group of small children in bright red and yellow deels ran after the target as it landed and bounced on the grass-covered field. One child pulled at another's deel, trying to get the advantage of reaching it first.

Yasotay watched, thinking about the timing needed to get off more than one shot. He wished he had stayed for the "shooting-at-an-airborne-target-from-a-moving-horse" lesson Baatar had offered. Unfortunately, for Yasotay, this would be an impossible feat. Or at least it seemed that way.

Seeing the apprehension on his opponent's face, Hassar kindly offered to go first. He was already on his horse. As he surged forward, he nocked his first arrow and had another in his draw hand parallel to his bow. Yasotay thought, *That's interesting.* He rode up to the starting line, guiding his horse with his knees. Temujin was standing at the line, spinning the target. Hassar drew his arrow back precisely as he crossed the firing line at full speed. At the same time, Temujin released the target into the air. Hassar's first arrow hit the mark perfectly, dead center. It affected the trajectory of the target, but that didn't matter. Since the arrow was already in his hand, his second shot was immediately after his first. It caught the target cleanly again. Hassar's third shot was not as fast since he had to pull the arrow from his quiver, but it still pierced the target moments before it hit the ground. Cheers went up from the crowd. What an amazing series of shots. Hassar was showing off, and everyone loved it! The target bounced on the ground and was again chased down by the children fighting to reach it first. The three arrows were still in the target as the one lucky child carried it back to Temujin.

It was evident to Yasotay that the brothers had played this shoot-the-moving-target game in the past. Many times! Yasotay knew well the skill required to master a weapon and shoot three arrows like that. He didn't believe he could pull off three shots on this moving target. His guess was it would take him a great deal of practice to accomplish such a feat. Yasotay's goal was simple: do his best and get at least one arrow into the target. Getting two off would be great, but he wouldn't try the two-fisted arrow trick shot that Hassar had pulled off. He'd end up accidentally shooting himself or someone else. No, one-nocked arrow, drawn when he crossed the line, and he should get one good shot off. You never know. Maybe he'd have time to get a second one off. *Sure,* he told himself, *I'll lose, but I might not look like a total fool.* He had a game plan, and now he just needed to execute it.

Yasotay had located and saddled the gray-and-white mare he had ridden on the trip to collect Bourtai. After a week of riding, he felt he knew this horse or, more important, the horse knew him! Yasotay apprehensively held the reins in his draw hand as his horse galloped toward the firing line. Building up speed, he approached the line. Temujin released the target into the air. As Yasotay crossed the line, a rather unfortunate thing occurred. He forgot to release the reins, so when he pulled back on the bow, he inadvertently also pulled back on the horse's reins suddenly and hard, causing the horse's head to pull hard to the right as it skid to a complete stop. Yasotay was wrenched half off the horse to his left, pointing the bow down and back. The impact of Yasotay's body against the horse's side dislodged the half-drawn arrow, which rocketed off toward Temujin's left foot. Before he could react, the arrow skipped off a rock in front of his foot and careened into the gathered spectators, where the bride and the elders sat.

At that same instant, Yasotay flipped completely out of his saddle and landed flat on his back. He landed hard with a giant thud. Meanwhile, a young man in the crowd had reached out his hand to stop the arrow in a natural defensive reaction. Or, one could say he caught it. The arrow penetrated the center of his palm, stopping halfway through. Surprised by the occurrence, he held his arrow-pierced hand high in the air as if he had caught a prize.

Everyone was stunned and held their collective breath as the mishap unfolded. It happened so fast that it took a moment for everyone to realize what had happened.

Finally, coming to his senses, Temujin yelled, "Great catch!"

The crowd erupted with cheers and laughter. Tera and Baatar ran over to Yasotay, who was trying to get up—slowly.

"Are you all right?" asked Tera, taking Yasotay by the elbow to help him up.

"I'm fine," said Yasotay, attempting to dust off his deel, "other than my pride."

Baatar could see that though he was a little dazed, Yasotay was fine. Then, he added, "I hope the horse droppings softened your fall." Baatar pointed toward Yasotay's arm.

"Ahh, great!" exclaimed Yasotay, holding up his right arm, covered in fresh horse dung. "How is the one who caught the arrow?"

If it weren't for the red streak running down the back of his hand, no one would know he had just been shot. The flesh around the arrow had been perfectly perforated.

"He's fine. Look at him. Temujin is parading him around," said Tera, motioning toward the crowd where Temujin was showing off the injured nomad and holding his arm in the air, arrow clean through his palm.

Hassar rode up and, from atop his horse, asked, "Yasotay, are you harmed?"

"No, I'm fine. Congratulations on your victory, Hassar. You truly are amazing with that bow!"

"Huh, you wouldn't know I'd won. The person with the pierced hand seems to be the winner here today." Yasotay smiled then grimaced in pain as he walked back, watching Temujin's antics with the young nomad as he shared his drink with him, joking and carrying on while the laughing crowd cheered.

With the break between events, everyone went to get a drink and have some food. It was a festive occasion, and next up were the wrestling matches. Several people approached Yasotay to share their own harrowing tales of errantly flying arrows.

"I accidentally shot my brother in the leg when he was eight and I was ten," said an elderly woman who stepped over to Yasotay. Given the nomad's cultural focus on archery, this seemed to happen at one time or another in all their lives.

The wrestling matches began once Temujin had taken his position with Bourtai. Yasotay stood toward the back of the crowd to watch. Currently, though, the groom was face-to-face with Jamka and horsing around. Each had a good grip on the other's deel. Playfully, they were trying to pull the other to the ground. Nomads seemed to love wrestling, and none more than Temujin. Jamka was quick and moved to his opponent's right. Getting low, he got his shoulder under Temujin. He humorously tried to lift him off his feet, which was no small task. Temujin laughed, then took a big bite from the leg of lamb he still held in his right hand.

"Arrgggh," grunted Jamka.

While Jamka wasn't small, Temujin was too big and heavy for him to pull off that wrestling move. He jovially groaned again under his friend's weight. Laughing, they both stood up and shook hands. With the fake wrestling match concluded, Temujin bent down and grabbed his leather bladder, which never seemed too far out of reach.

"If you want to wrestle here today, my friend, you'll have to pick someone willing. I'm just going to eat," Temujin said, thrusting the leg of lamb up, "and drink!" He then lifted his bladder high before taking a long swig from it.

"No more wrestling for me," said Jamka, holding his back in mock pain.

"We are in for some good matches today!" stated Temujin confidently.

"Yes, and my wrestler, whatever his name is, should do fine," said Jamka, laughing. "He's young, but I've heard he's good." Jamka paused, trying to clear his mind. "Yarru, that's it! Yarru is his name."

"I think old man Altan will be our lion today! Hopefully, this contest will at least be competitive. Unlike the ending to the archery…that was much more bizarre than competitive!" said Temujin, looking over and spotting Yasotay in the crowd.

"Your friend Yasotay almost shot you!" exclaimed Jamka.

"Yes, but that was his first attempt at shooting an arrow from a horse." Temujin stepped over to Yasotay, patting his friend on the back. "I can say confidently, Yasotay, you will only get better shooting at moving targets!" This joke got more laughs from Jamka and everyone else within earshot.

"Not one of my finer moments!" said Yasotay. "Thankfully, I didn't kill anybody, and the only consequence from the incident was a hole in a hand and a sore backside." Yasotay rubbed the small of his back.

"So, what are the rules of this competition?" asked Yasotay. "It's my first nomad wrestling match!"

"Simple, get your opponent to the ground," quipped Jamka. "The only things allowed to touch the ground are the palms of your hands and the soles of your feet. And there is no time limit."

Now, Yasotay was standing next to Jamka, who was seated beside the bride and groom. A drumbeat, light at first, then louder and louder, grabbed everyone's attention. The crowd, which seemed more significant than the one in attendance for archery, had collected in a U shape.

Wearing the customary upturned boots, the four wrestlers paraded past them into the center of the field. Each participant began to slowly flap their arms like they were the wings of a bird of prey. Then, all four wrestlers, in turn, slapped their hands against their thighs, slapping their inner thighs twice and their outer thighs once.

"This is their *call to battle*," explained Jamka to Yasotay. "While this is a smaller event, you could have twenty or more wrestlers at a large Naadam. That shorter one there is my Yarru."

Then, two wrestlers, one of them Altan, moved to the side while the other two remained in the center of the field. Yarru's opponent wasn't someone Yasotay knew. The two combatants stayed in the center of the implied arena. Both wrestlers flapped their arms toward the east twice and toward the west once. They took deep, loud breaths and then crouched down. They again slapped their thighs twice more and, in unison, turned and faced each other. The match was on. Both men immediately grabbed the other's shoulders. The bigger man tried to use his size and strength to twist Yarru's shoulders and turn him to the ground. But Yarru was too quick. Stepping his left leg forward, he hooked it behind his opponent's foot. In a flash, he was off balance. Realizing his error a moment too late, the bigger wrestler took the roll, falling to the ground, and the match was over almost as quickly as it started.

"He's with me! Great move, Yarru." Jamka was loud with his congratulations, cheering, "Yarru! Yarru! Yarru!"

"This seems to take more technique than one would imagine," said Yasotay.

"Technique and position. A bigger man doesn't necessarily have the advantage," insisted Jamka, "although size can help if used properly!"

"I like this young man, Jamka. He's quick and smart!" said Temujin. The next match was between Altan and a younger, taller opponent. This match lasted considerably longer, with Altan coming close to forcing the young wrestler off balance several times. Finally, after multiple attempts, Altan spun the young man, stepped into the turn, and flipped him over his hip onto his back. The momentum carried Altan over him as well, and he landed on top of his opponent with a big thud for the win! Lying there heaving and making an odd retching sound, it was a while before the young wrestler caught his breath, and the field cleared for the final match.

Once Yarru and Altan finished their ceremonial "bird of prey" dance, and with two slaps on either thigh, the final match started. Altan was clearly stronger and more experienced, but Yarru was quicker, and his speed made up for his lack of skill and strength. This match dragged on, and when Altan tried the move that worked in his previous opponent, Yarru was too quick for him and deftly escaped the throw-down. The struggle continued until Altan had the advantage, grabbed Yarru, lifted him off the ground, and flipped him down hard. The crowd roared for Altan.

"Altan was much stronger, but you must admit young Yarru did well!" Jamka stated.

"Yes, I agree," Temujin said. "So, we have been friends for a long time, haven't we?"

"Yes, mostly," quipped Jamka with a smile, anticipating a joke from his childhood friend.

"So, I know your competitive nature very well. First, you knew beating Hassar was out of the question, so you abandoned any hope of winning the archery contest. The wrestling you would have loved to win, but you only had a young prospect whose name you couldn't even remember. So, that means that you're betting on winning the horse race, and you have brought one of your fastest riders and best horses."

Jamka interrupted Temujin with a grin, "*Two* of my best…and that's not counting Baatar, who is as quick as lightning."

"Two or, better yet, three of your best riders because you couldn't leave here without at least one victory!" Temujin playfully protested.

"Old friend, you know me too well," said Jamka. They both laughed heartily, enjoying the moment.

"And that is what should concern you," said Temujin with a devilish grin.

The starting line was decorated on either side with red, blue, and yellow ribbons on the top of tall stakes. The ribbons were gently fluttering in the soft breeze, and the audience was ready for the final competition of the day, the horse race. There were twelve riders in total, three of whom were from Jamka's clan, including Baatar. All the riders were lined up and ready to go. Tera was a late addition to the field, riding her father's beautiful white mare with small black spots. Even its white tail had a black tip as if dipped in an ink well. One of Tera's many chores was to tend to all her father's horses, and her mother once observed, "When she rides that horse, it's as if she and the horse are one."

The race was a simple out-and-back, going around the large black obelisk-like rock in the middle of the valley. The starter held a stick with a narrow red flag. All riders had their eyes on that ribbon. Once the race was on, it was a mad dash to and around the rock and back to the start/finish line.

Tera sat on her father's beautiful horse with a furrowed brow, eyes slightly squinting, pursed lips, and a tense-looking jawline. Yasotay could see she had that same fire in her eyes from the other day. He had overheard her telling her mother, "It's all in good fun." But Tera didn't look like she was having fun. She looked deadly serious. It appeared to Yasotay that she had something to prove. It was as if Tera didn't want Baatar, *the child,* to win. She couldn't allow him to be declared a winner competing among adults. Whatever the case, she was clearly in it to win; determination was written all over her face.

Ready! A moment later, the red flag hit the ground. The racers were off in a mad chorus of "yahs" and whips slapping horses' backsides. Tera and Baatar, on his brown colt, got off to early leads. Since they had been at opposite ends of the starting line, they rode parallel though a good distance apart and were quickly out to a two-horse length lead ahead of the rest of the pack.

Tera was riding hard, and Baatar was doing his level best to keep up with her. As the race progressed, with the horses heading toward the large rock, it quickly became a two-horse affair. By the time they reached the obelisk-like rock protruding from the ground, Tera and Baatar were ahead of the rest of the field by five or six horse lengths. Making the turn and coming back up the valley toward the finish line, Tera seemed to have a slight lead. They were riding hard. While Yasotay knew she was a good rider, the skills she displayed today surprised him. Baatar was not quite neck and neck with her as they were about seven horse-lengths from the finish line. *She's going to win*, thought Yasotay.

Then, all of a sudden, Tera's horse hitched an odd step, and a loud *SNAP* was heard. She pulled back, and the mare put its weight on its hind legs, sliding. She tried to bring her weight off her right front leg, but her momentum carried her forward, and the mare was forced to put weight on that foot. That was all it took. The horse went down hard. Baatar crossed the finish line without a word from the crowd; all were stunned at what had transpired.

Tera's mare, which had been in the lead had gone down just before crossing the finish line. It crossed the line on its belly with legs extended awkwardly. Tera was in midair, still holding onto the reins. Twisting, she fell heavily onto her right side and ended up in a pile three paces from her horse.

Altan and Yasotay ran to help her. Baatar immediately reined in his horse, jumped off, and ran back to the finish line, where Tera initially lay motionless. As they reached her, she was already trying to sit up.

"Are you hurt?" asked Baatar.

"No, I'm not. What about the horse?" asked Tera.

They looked over at the mare, already back up, standing on three legs. A blood-smeared, sharp white bone poked through the skin of her lower leg, and blood streaked down to her hoof.

There was a long pause as they looked at the horse and its damaged right front leg dangling just above the ground.

"She'll need to be destroyed," Altan stated with a tone of loss. Though her leg was fractured, she was still somehow standing. She snorted air loudly through her nose, sweating profusely. She was in obvious distress.

Tera's shoulders were hunched, and she looked beaten and depressed. Yasotay couldn't help but feel for her. She had made a noble effort in the race but came up short and lost her father's best mare. They both knew it was a costly loss for Altan.

"Are you sure you're not hurt?" asked Yasotay, conscious of not wanting to appear more concerned than Tera's father and her betrothed.

She felt the gentle tone of empathy in his voice. "I'm fine, but for some stupid reason, I wanted to win that race," Tera admitted aloud, tears welling up in her eyes. "And I killed that beautiful horse because I wanted to win." She smacked her hand on her leg in frustration, "that was foolish!"

"You didn't kill the horse," Altan said caringly in a kind voice. "You gave it a good effort, Tera! It was just bad luck."

"Thank you, father," she said, which were three more words than she had spoken to him since Baatar had arrived in camp.

It was a short walk to where all the food and drink had been set out for the festivities. For Yasotay, it was just a little further walk to his secret bathing area to remove his current stench. The midday sun had made him begin to smell ripe. Thanks to his failed attempt at shooting a target from horseback, the smell of horse dung had become an ever-present aroma about him that he had to remedy. Now that the competitions were complete, the festivities moved on to the heavy eating, drinking, and storytelling. How ironic that the last time he stole away for a quick bath, he missed out on archery training. Training that could have kept him from requiring an immediate bath at this inopportune time. It was late afternoon and getting cool quickly, though not yet freezing. If he left now…. First things first, he needed a clean deel, so he needed to collect it from his wooden trunk. He had to go there to get his bath bean anyway. He could get all his stuff, hurry to his little tarn, wash, and run back in minimal time, and the nomads would be none the wiser. That was the plan. Now, it was time to move!

His bath felt refreshing in a cold yet clean way. Yasotay quickly scrubbed his hair and face, dunked underwater, and then sprang up, creating a splash, his head moving upward toward the sky. But then, his eyes caught something. *Was that a female form?* Stabilizing his stance and wiping the water from his face, his eyes focused. It was…it was Tera, standing there naked in his hidden bathing area, watching him. While Yasotay had never lain with a naked woman, he had certainly laid eyes on one before. He had frequented the public bathhouses during his stay in the Song Empire, so he was quite familiar with a naked female body.

But this one was perfect…his gaze finally released his mind to speak, "What…what are you doing here, Tera?" He couldn't help but admire her perfectly curved body and its tussle of fine reddish-brown hairs in her nether region. *If she is caught naked with me, it would cause us both huge problems.* His immediate thought was *we should both get dressed and leave.*

"I want you to show me how to do this," said Tera with a mischievous grin. "But that water must be ice-cold," she added. She knew why she was here and what she was doing. Tera was proving to Yasotay that she wasn't a child; she wasn't like Baatar. "You promised you'd teach me," she whimpered with a cute little pout.

"How to do what?" asked Yasotay, whose initial shock was beginning to wane. He was now trying to rationalize their nudity while rubbing the back of his neck. This felt awkward. Then, words from somewhere popped into his head: *They felt no shame in their nudity.* Next came images from the public bathhouses in the South, where nudity in mixed company was common. *It wasn't shameful; it was just people bathing!*

"What are you doing with that...what is that?" Tera pointed at the small wooden box perched on the rock.

"That's what I use to wash with. It's called bath bean, a dried powder made from ground beans, peas, and spices which, when mixed with a little water, creates a cleaning paste used for bathing." Yasotay paused for a moment. "How did you know I was coming here?"

"I'm sorry, but I followed you yesterday and saw you," replied Tera, sitting on a rock closer to where Yasotay stood. "I could smell you in the ger afterward, and I really like that smell. Can you help me to smell like that?"

"I guess I can show you. Are you sure it's...all right?" At that moment, a frog jumped across Tera's knees, which were in front of Yasotay, who reflexively put out his hand to catch the little frog. But he closed his hand too soon, and it landed on his closed fist. The frog quickly turned and jumped the opposite way toward Tera's face. She screamed and jumped off the rock into Yasotay's arms, who was still standing in the pool of water. Her abdomen smacked into his face. He caught her body with his arms just underneath her buttocks, and she slowly slid down into the pool until his face was even with hers and the length of their bodies were pressed against each other. They finally separated once she gained her footing.

Stunned, Tera stood there with the water up to the top of her inner thighs. Yasotay was still holding her up from under her elbows, and then it struck her like a lightning bolt. "This water is *cold!*" she screamed the last word loudly.

"Yes, it is." Yasotay laughed aloud—his naivete kept him from fully grasping the gravity of the situation. So, he thought, *Why not explain proper hygiene to her*? He didn't actually know how the nomads would look upon him teaching Tera how to bathe, but he believed, *It was certainly something they all needed to learn*!

"Can you show it to me quickly because this water is icy cold?" asked Tera, her arms pulled tight across her chest, her teeth chattering, her caramel-colored eyes begging for relief.

"Yes, a quick bath.... So, I remember when I was a child, my Mana would sing, "Scrub the pits to stop the PHEWs!" He demonstrated *phews* by pinching his nose and scrunching up his face. Yasotay struggled with not staring at the beauty of her naked body bobbing in the water as she laughed at the visual of him acting the child. "That means scrubbing under both armpits and your leg pit until the stink and dirt are gone." Yasotay took the rag and rubbed it under his arm. "Understand?"

"I don't have a rag," declared Tera, her arms still hugging her upper body. She was shivering, and her nipples were painfully hard. She looked over and noticed that Yasotay's were too. "Mine are for milking. At least, hopefully, someday. Ever wonder what yours are for?" With that, she reached out and touched his rock-hard nipple with the tip of her finger.

"Tera, stop that!" he was jolted by a lightning-bolt sensation from her touch. Jerking away, and in a serious tone, he said, "Look here." He took his rag, put it under water, and squeezed out the water with his hand. Then he dipped it in the bath bean and handed her the rag. Tera knew what he wanted her to do. She washed under her arm with the bath bean, just like Yasotay had explained to her.

"Now what?" asked Tera.

"Wash the other one," he said and motioned to Tera's other armpit. Tera dutifully scrubbed under her other armpit.

"Now you have to rinse it off. Splash water to rinse the bath bean off," instructed Yasotay, splashing water under his arm and showing her how it was done.

She splashed very little water because it was so cold. Yasotay noticed she still had splotches of bath bean paste under her arm and on her side. Attempting to be helpful, he splashed a large handful of water under her arm. But the water was freezing cold, and he splashed more than he meant. Sucking in hard, it took her breath away. Tera took this as intentional and splashed Yasotay back with a big wave of water. Within moments, it turned into a playful, freezing-cold splashing war. Each frozen splash of water received one in return. Then, they both began laughing and grabbing each other's arms to stop the splashing. In the tussle, they both knelt in the freezing tarn with just their heads above the waterline.

"I think it's better under the water, or I'm getting used to it," Tera said with a smile. "But I am COLD!" Whisps of her breath were visible.

"I am too," shivered Yasotay. "By the way…it might be best if you don't tell anyone of this!" You could almost see his breath as he spoke with the water line right beneath his chin.

"Are you serious? Of course not…no one must know about this," Tera quickly replied. "My father would kill me." Then, thinking for a moment, she added, "No, actually, he would probably kill you first!"

"Are you serious?" Yasotay asked. The expression on his face went from playful to fearful. "I am indebted to Altan. The last thing I want is to dishonor him."

"Don't worry. I won't say anything," she said with a smile, "How would he ever know?"

"Maybe we should go!" urged Yasotay, "Yes, I think we should go. I really don't want to cross Altan!"

"I am going to finish this first. You promised to show me. Where is that rag?" Tera found the rag, squeezed it out, and stood up to dip it into the bath bean. The water came to the top of the hair tuft above her leg pit. Using the rag, she scrubbed the bath bean in the front as she looked down and then from behind, arching her back to reach it. Yasotay couldn't help but watch. His mind wandered briefly, admiring the movements of her perfect female form. All of a sudden, he felt something within him stir, growing into a sense of embarrassment.

"It's done…we must go," Yasotay said, coming out of the water in a flash and drying himself off.

Noticing his "problem," Tera said with a mischievous grin, "I guess nipples aren't the only thing that gets hard." Though still a virgin, she had been raised around animals and knew what that was for!

Yasotay was already putting on his clothes as Tera stepped out of the pool. Her arms were across her chest, and she was still shivering. Then, they both heard a noise, like twigs snapping.

"Shhh," Yasotay whispered, half-dressed. Naked, Tera was standing there dripping wet. Her arms wrapped around her abdomen. They looked at the bushes and, for a moment, stood motionless.

Then Yasotay broke the silence and said quietly, "Quickly, get dressed, and let's leave." Once clothed, Yasotay led the way, peering past the bushes and motioning for Tera to follow. Tera stopped and went back toward the pool to the rocks. Grabbing the small box of bath bean, she said, "That was fun. We will need this again!"

Over fifty people stood around, talking, laughing, drinking, singing, dancing, and eating. The evening had set in, and most of the well-wishers had gathered around a large fire built for this occasion. Yasotay slipped unnoticed into the crowd. He wore a clean deel and felt somewhat refreshed after his bath. After a tumultuous day of fun and games, the bath certainly helped. He looked forward to an evening of eating and drinking with his new friends.

"Yasotay, there you are. I was looking for you," Temujin said in a loud voice over the crowd's conversational chatter.

"I'm here," said Yasotay. "Just had to change my clothes."

Temujin smiled. "Good. I am ready now," he announced as he stepped up on a log, putting him a head above the gathered crowd.

"I have something to say," bellowed Temujin, and the crowd grew quiet.

"Upon my father's death, my mother was fleeced like a spring goat. This theft was done by some of the same people who swore allegiance to my father. Those first couple of years after his death, my brothers and I helped my mother the best we could, but it was hard, and we lived through great hardship. All we had were meager scraps of food to live on, and we were assaulted from all directions. My brothers and I were repeatedly mistreated by those who did nothing but take what little we had. And, because of my birthright, I was taken captive again and again." Temujin's face bore the weight of his message.

"Upon my first escape from the Taichiud, I returned on a terrible day. My father had had over a hundred horses, and almost all of them were taken." Raising both hands with his thumbs tucked in, he continued, "But! We managed to keep the *eight* best horses!" He emphasized the eight, then paused. The crowd was silent. "These eight horses and two goats were all that remained from my father's immense wealth. Everything else had been taken. Then, on that day, horse thieves stole our remaining horses. The cowards took our last shred of hope for surviving the winter. All that was left was an old mare my brother, Belgutai, was out riding. I was only eleven years old, but when Belgutai returned, I jumped on that old mare and chased the thieves as far as I could. After days of tracking them, I came upon someone on the side of the trail milking a mare. This was Borchu, who aided me in my time of need." Temujin paused and bowed slightly to Borchu's short, stout frame standing to his left. His squinty face smiled in return. Temujin continued, "He gave me the use of a fresh horse and rode with me to find and retrieve my stolen horses. After that, he left his family to serve mine. To be part of my family and be by my side, a true friend, my first *nokhor!*" Temujin raised his bladder of drink and took a big swig. Then he held it out to Borchu, who took it and drank from it.

"My latest adventure with the Taichiud brought another stranger into my life. He is not a nomad, yet in my time of need, when I was injured and on the run, he helped free me and put his own life in danger when it was not in his best interest to do so. Yasotay, you are a true friend!" Temujin again raised his bladder and took another big swig. Then he handed it to Yasotay, who drank from it.

Raising his drink, he spoke again, "To Mother Houlun and Mother Tacotan and the rest of my family, your strength and wisdom have brought us to this moment. We thank Tengri and our ancestors for watching over us." Temujin raised his bladder, took a swig, and handed it to Houlun, who drank from it and gave the bladder to Tacotan. Then, it was passed around to Temujin's brothers.

"And, finally, to my wife Bourtai. I am a hunter, and you are my precious dove-tailed sable, a treasure I will always cherish. It is an honor to make you my kin. May we have many children and many years together!" Temujin again raised his bladder, this time to a round of cheers. Handing it to Bourtai, he stepped down while she took a drink.

At one point, feeling the celebratory nature of the moment and a little drunk, Yasotay stepped up to address the crowd with a bladder of drink in hand. "When I first heard of the nomads, the words I'd heard to describe your people, well, weren't very kind." He paused for a moment. "Now that I have met you myself, the words that come to mind are sweetness, warmth, honor, bravery, family, and friends. The nomads are the most noble, down-to-earth people I have ever met, and it is truly my honor to be a guest among you and learn your ways!" This tribute garnered a roar from the crowd. Yasotay continued, "Among my people, we have an ancient tradition that the work is only half done after the drinking, so always remember to leave a little for the last," Yasotay handed Temujin the bladder and added, "lest you leave nothing for the bed!" That brought another round of cheers from everyone. Yasotay stepped down from the log, laughing and sharing drink after drink with those in the crowd.

Baatar stood outside the gathered crowd, with his back to the darkness. He was staring coldly at Yasotay and glared at him. So much so that Yasotay made his way over to Baatar. He could tell from the young man's body language that something was wrong. He held anger in his eyes, his jaw was clenched, and his right hand was on the hilt of his dagger. Walking through the collection of well-wishers, Yasotay stepped up to him and asked, "What's bothering you?"

The silence between them stretched for several moments while Bataar's eyes never left Yasotay's. Then, in a low, hissing voice, Bataar said, "I know what you did. How could you?" Without another word, he broke his eye contact and walked past Yasotay from the darkness of their encounter into the light of the celebration. Yasotay was left staring into the night, contemplating the implications of his accusation.

CHAPTER SEVEN

Southern Steppe, late winter, 1178 CE

W inter on the steppe was cold, hard, and dry. So dry, in fact, Yasotay observed that the air drew out all moisture from within one's body, so much so that it seemingly reached into every orifice to extract every last drop. After weeks of enduring this misery, Altan finally introduced him to the ancient tradition of applying animal grease to the skin. The grease was made from rendered fat, boiled down, and scraped off the top of the brew. This practice, he was told, "has been around forever." Yasotay quickly realized it provided two main benefits and caused one minor problem. The benefits were that it helped your body retain heat and thoroughly treated the problem of dry skin. The minor issue was that it made washing any part of your body extremely difficult because water just ran off your skin. The truth was it was too cold for a bath anyway, and after the incident with Baatar over his last bath, he didn't want to think about another one right now.

Yasotay had bigger problems to consider. As he looked out into the vast darkness during his morning ritual, he could see whispers of the coming sunrise. The wind whipped through the barren wasteland, attacking every fold of his tightly drawn cocoon. Huddled within, Yasotay was trying to understand why Temujin, an honorable, loving family man, would succumb to fits of rage-filled violent revenge. Was it a flaw in his character? *"Hamartia,"* exclaimed Yasotay aloud, remembering the Greek term for a fatal flaw. Then, dismissing that notion, he cleared his mind of everything that had happened so far on this trip. He moved on to the thought: *What's my role in all of this? Do I really want to be involved in these blood feuds?*

The steppe was yet consumed by darkness and full of fantastical mirages for Yasotay to view within the depths of its blackness. It worked as a mirror drawing from his mind what he had stored there and flashing the scenes of the slaughter he had witnessed. While he couldn't see the faces, Yasotay could feel the pain, smell the blood, and hear the screams of grief over lost beloved ones. He heard moans in the dark that haunted him, and he couldn't remove the luminous images from his head.

The slaughter had occurred just three days earlier. Temujin and his brothers, Hassar and Belgutai, along with Borchu, Altan, and Yasotay, had left the valley between Mother and Father Mountains, heading south. They rode with a force of fifteen horses to escort Temujin, whose mission was to show respect to a significant person in his life, his father's *anda*. Temujin was on a political errand to see his father's blood brother, Togru.

The great Togru led the powerful army of the Keraites. His empire covered a vast portion of the steppe and lay north of the Jin and Western Xia Dynasties. This empire was on the southern border of the Merkit, the Tatar, and most of the remaining nomadic groups, including the

Borjigin, Temujin's birthright. Togru's army numbered in the tens of thousands; thus, he was a force to be reckoned with on the steppe.

On the first day of their trip, they proceeded at a brisk pace. The weather was cold and very dry but tolerable for travel. Toward the end of the day, they encountered another group of travelers who had set up a temporary camp. Their exchange started with the usual pleasantries, but once Temujin discovered their names, the massacre of the small encampment of twenty men, women, and children began. Yasotay had witnessed death but had never seen anything like this slaughter. He felt that how Temujin, Hassar, and Borchu had acted toward these people was indefensible. Up to that point, their previous trip to retrieve Bourtai had been the only camp massacre Yasotay had seen, and that was after the fact.

Yasotay witnessed this one unfold firsthand in front of his very eyes. As soon as Temujin raised his sword, the extermination began. When it started, Yasotay jumped from his horse, not knowing what to do. He watched in horror as Hassar pumped three arrows into a pregnant mother and her two boys. The last killed was the youngest, shot in the neck while bending down to hold his mother's head. Yasotay recalled Hassar's rapid arm motion during the archery competition, but instead of watching in awe, this time, he recoiled in disgust.

Temujin slid down from his horse and began to hack his way through one person after another. Borchu's stout frame followed behind him, protecting his back and finishing off anyone Temujin had struck down if need be. People were running, yelling, and screaming. A few men tried to muster a response to the attack, but then Altan and Belgutai also jumped into the fray. They killed everyone. This assault was brutal butchery—and Temujin, Hassar, and Borchu were the most vicious. They seemed to revel in the destruction. Then, in a matter of moments, it went from total chaos to complete quiet. He could hear the lone, delicate song of a small bird and some goats bleating. The extermination was complete! Temujin walked back to his horse, his face red with blood and rage, his sword arm also covered in it. Hassar was retrieving his arrows while Yasotay stood there, motionless. Deeply unnerved and in a state of shock, with only a simple one-word question formed in his mind, he asked it aloud, "Why?"

"Because they deserved it! He said his name was Chuluun, son of Temujin Uge, and he was a Tatar," explained Temujin, the blood in his hair barely perceptible as it mingled with the red knots of head hair.

The beleaguered look on Yasotay's face didn't change. "But why?" he asked again.

"He is a descendant of one of the Tatar rats who poisoned my father," insisted Temujin. His face was solemn, and with a voice cracking in anger, he spit out, "That's why!" He stared into Yasotay's eyes for a brief moment and then stormed away. Yasotay left it at that; he was at a loss as to what to say in response.

The sun had risen, and Yasotay, still in his cocoon, had spent the whole sunrise ruminating on this traumatic encounter instead of enjoying the glorious display of a new day. Killing women and children for revenge just seemed wrong. He concluded that while he disagreed with Temujin's handling of Chuluun, son of Temujin Uge, and his clan, Yasotay decided it was a cultural dispute. He had no interest in getting involved in such revenge-driven cultural disputes—and revenge, Yasotay realized, seemed to motivate most of the conflicts among the nomads. Yasotay knew they would be packing up and heading out shortly, so he folded his blanket and walked the short distance back to their makeshift camp. Temujin insisted that no more than half a day's ride remained to reach Togru's encampment; they expected to be there sometime later that day.

True to plan, by midday, they were approaching Togru's camp. Viewing it from high ground, they could see that it was still a good distance away. It looked like the valley had a large infestation of small, round, and white ant mounds. As they neared, the smell of burning dung hung in the air. Two sentries met them, interrogated them about their purpose, and then let them proceed, only for them to encounter another group of sentries along the way. Each time they came to a new sentry post, Temujin explained, "My name is Temujin. I am the son of

Yesugei, the anda of Togru, and I am here to see my blood father." Each time, the sentry took a long look at the men and then escorted them to the next checkpoint.

The camp had thousands of tents, gers, and wooden structures. Finally, they were ushered into a ger connected to a larger structure. This one, by far, was the largest and completely different from the others that dotted the landscape. It was explained that all swords, bows, and weapons had to be left outside the main doorway. Additionally, they were instructed to remove their boots once inside. Once through the narrow entrance, they walked into a large open room adorned with statues and paintings. Many rugs were thrown about, covering the floor and hanging on the walls. The carpets were caked in mud and dirt close to the entrance, where they took off their boots but were pristine further inside. The fine wool rugs of sky blue, deep scarlet red, and beige patterns were all different but clearly made by the same craftsman due to their unique patterns and similar hues.

There was a large number of people in clusters scattered about the room. The crowd left a large open space in front of what appeared to be a throne on a small dais. Yasotay took note of what appeared to be two separate shrines on either side of it, each consisting of small tables holding candles and adorned with stone statues. Above the tables was a large wooden cross, and to the right were various banners. On the left hung a painting of Jesus of Nazareth. In it, Jesus is standing at a door, holding a lantern, and knocking. There were also several large stone carvings. One looked like The Madonna, but Yasotay didn't recognize the others. The glow from the hundreds of white coccus candles littered about the room gave off sufficient light to create a comfortable atmosphere. Yasotay was very familiar with the odd, musty smell of these candles, made from the secretions of insects. They reminded him of Chang's library, where he would always find solitude and escape.

Among the people in the room were men who looked like merchants, standing with their backs against the walls; fake smiles and bland looks abounded. Borchu nudged Yasotay when he recognized one of them. "I know him," whispered Borchu in a hushed voice to

Yasotay about the man in the odd-looking yellow hat with two large feathers, one brown and one white, in it. Yasotay took note of him.

On the dais sat an oversized wooden chair, and in the chair sat a bearded man wearing a long, dark wool cloak flowing down to the floor over a white silk tunic. Two gray chin puffs hung low from his face and were decorated with metal clasps. The wool cloak on his shoulders was embroidered with gold leaves and gem-encrusted branches. He wore a white ecclesiastical zucchetto skullcap with fine gemstones, the white silk tunic visible in the center of his chest. The clothing perfectly framed the small metal cross on a plain leather twine around his neck. Three attendants, each holding a large metal cross and wearing brown-hooded cowls, stood in his shadow at the room's far end. The older man got up from his throne and walked straight to Temujin, his cloak floating across the top of the carpet, holding out his arms.

"My most honored Togru, how are you?" said Temujin, meeting him halfway and placing his arms under Togru's, holding him up under his elbows in the customary gesture. The *zolgokh*, as it was called, was more than a form of etiquette. It was a respectful gesture that reflected one's values of humility, gratitude, and honoring one's roots and traditions.

"It is a relief to see you alive, Temujin. I had heard rumors of your escape. I am pleased to see they were true!" Togru replied.

"You are a father to me, Togru. It is a relief to see you healthy and strong. And your clan is strong, the strongest in the land!" proclaimed Temujin, bowing three times to display his deep respect.

"You honor me with your deference, Temujin."

"I brought you a gift as a further display of my respect," exclaimed Temujin, reaching into a large sack Borchu carried. He pulled a black sable jacket from the sack and presented it to Togru. This was the black sable overcoat with the finely polished metal clasps and leather hoops that Bourtai's parents had given Temujin as a wedding gift. The black fur seemed to shimmer in the light of the room's hundreds of candles.

"You honor me," Togru said, examining the large black jacket closely. It truly was a beautiful coat. Running his hand along the soft fur, Togru admired the gift. "This is beautiful, my dear young man…thank you." Togru motioned to an attendant, standing in the shadows, who immediately stepped over, retrieved the coat, and took it away.

"I have come to you to inform you personally of my wedding to Bourtai," said Temujin. "But first, if I may, let me introduce my companions. You know my brothers Hassar and Belgutai, and I believe you've met Borchu and Altan. And this is Yasotay, the southern wolf who helped me escape captivity from the Taichiud."

Each man slowly and formally approached Togru and paid his respects as Togru held out his arms in the customary way…Yasotay, last in line, finally reached Togru.

"So, you are the one who freed Temujin?" asked the old man. His brown eyes seemed to have a sharp edge. Yasotay reached out his arms for the sixth and final ritual.

"Temujin freed himself. I just gave him a helping hand," answered Yasotay, squeezing Togru's elbows; by now, he was well used to the zolgokh.

"I know of what it means to receive help when in need…Temujin's father helped me when my brothers forsook me. Because of that, I hold his family in great esteem!" proclaimed Togru, stepping over to place his arm around Temujin.

"Your father was a dear friend to me, my blood brother, my anda. You are like a son to me!" exclaimed Togru, showing genuine warmth and caring for the young man.

"You honor me," said Temujin. Looking around, he pointed to the painting hanging in a place of high honor. "That is beautiful… what is it?"

"It is a painting of Jesus the Almighty, standing upon the threshold and knocking on the door of those who don't believe!" said Togru. Yasotay could tell by the hushed tone with which he described the painting that it was his pride and joy.

"Yasotay, have you ever seen a painting like this?" asked Temujin, his green eyes marveling at its detail. Yasotay could still see streaks of blood on the right arm and left shoulder of Temujin's deel.

"No, but I believe it's based on The Book of Revelation, chapter 3, verse 20 of the Bible…'Idoú, stékomai stin pórta kai chtypáo.' It's greek and it means, 'Behold, I stand at the door and knock,'" answered Yasotay. "I agree it is a beautiful painting."

Togru crossed his arms over his chest. "How do you come to know of these things?" he demanded, with a look of bewilderment and in a contentious tone. "What gives you the right to speak the holy words?" Yasotay noticed Togru's body posture had changed. He had been very welcoming a moment ago. He now appeared much more guarded and suspicious. Yasotay wondered if he had offended him!

Yasotay flashed a quick, tense smile. "I…just know of…I can read, I have read…" said Yasotay, groping in a stuttering voice for answers, instantly regretting having said anything. *I need to change the subject.* Yasotay asked, "So Temujin tells me you're a Nestorian Christian. Is that correct?"

"Yes," answered Togru, his brown eyes peering down his nose. He asked, "Have you heard the words of our savior Jesus Christ?"

"Yes, I have read them," answered Yasotay awkwardly, stumbling over his words. "I have read the Bible."

Togru's face seemed to flush white. "Only the holy men have read from the book! You're no priest; are you a demon? Are you saintly or satanic?"

"I'm no holy man!" responded Yasotay, "nor am I a devil. I have read many holy books."

One could see that Togru's mind was struggling to comprehend this odd young man. Taking a moment to gaze at Yasotay, he then asked suspiciously, "Do you know what this is?" He lifted the cross from around his neck.

"It's a cross…a Christian cross!" he answered. Yasotay knew of this type of cross and its secret compartment but chose not to identify it. *It seems like Togru needs to assert his superior knowledge in religious matters.*

"It is a special cross, a Reliquary Cross, made of two halves, a front and a back connected with a hinge. A secret compartment lies in the middle and holds an artifact of supreme importance," explained Togru.

The look on his face was serious. The rasp in his voice indicated that he was speaking of something of great importance to him.

"What is it? What does it hold?" asked Temujin. Togru now had the undivided attention of everyone in the room. Temujin's companions leaned forward to see the magical object and hear what Togru would say.

Togru lowered his voice and spoke reverently as he explained, "The holiest of men, Jesus Christ himself, was hung from a cross. This Reliquary Cross holds a shard of wood from the actual cross on which Jesus was crucified!" Slowly, in a measured fashion, Togru opened the cross around his neck. Yasotay could tell that Togru knew how to draw out the moment for effect. And, he obviously held this artifact, genuine or not, in complete reverence. The cross opened, and inside, on the vertical axis, was what looked like a small brown sliver of wood. After briefly showing it, Togru closed the compartment quickly and delicately. He placed the cross back on his chest. Yasotay looked around at the five faces of his fellow travelers, and they all looked in awe. He wondered if they actually knew what Togru was talking about. It was as if they were in a trance. Was it the size of his army, the vastness of his empire, or the confidence he used when speaking about his religion that commanded their respect? Yasotay didn't know, but Togru certainly knew how to captivate an audience.

"Temujin, we must talk," Togru said, changing the subject and placing his arm around Temujin again. "I am suspicious of the Taichiud, as you should be too!" he quietly said as he guided Temujin toward the left side of the dais. "My friend Ahmad has told me they are planning an attack against you," said Togru. "Ahmad, come please tell Temujin what you know!"

A chubby man in a green deel with bright, delicate yellow flowers embroidered on the cloth stepped forward from the group of people with their backs against the wall.

"I was told that you killed two men during your escape from the Taichiud," Ahmad said. "Is this true?"

"Yes," said Temujin, looking over at Yasotay, who nodded in agreement.

"This greatly upset the Taichiud leader. It was his son you killed," explained Ahmad.

"So, what does this matter to me? I was defending myself," said Temujin.

"The Taichiud are planning to capture you again; this time, they intend to kill you!" Ahmad persisted. "They know of your trip here. I told Togru you would arrive soon, and here you are."

Temujin looked at Togru. "Is this true? Did you know of my coming?"

"Ahmad told me of your plans yesterday. That you would be arriving today to pay your respects and deliver me a black sable jacket," Togru said with a discerning expression as his sharp brown eyes softened, if just a little. The candlelight made the tiny gems on his skullcap glitter.

"How can this be?" asked Temujin, with a look of surprise and concern. "I told no one! The only people who knew of my trip were from my own clan and maybe those who attended my wedding!"

"The Taichiud have spies everywhere, and so do the Tatars and the Merkit," answered Togru. "You have a spy within your camp! You must take a different route home or take an escort, which I am happy to send with you."

"We came from the southeast and then headed west to avoid the Merkit, but we ran into Tatars from the east who had strayed a little too far west for their own good," said Temujin with a smile. "It was Chuluun, son of Temujin Uge—the man involved in the poisoning of my father." Temujin paused for effect, then said in his deepest baritone voice, "I slit his throat with my own blade."

"May he rot in the darkness of hell and suffer eternal damnation in the lake of fire," said Togru, walking back to the throne and taking his seat on the dais. "You have done your filial duty. Your bravery and honor, Temujin, is without question."

Yasotay wondered if that were true, based on what he had witnessed. He said nothing.

"You and I share the same enemies," responded Temujin, head bowed in respect. "I will help you in any way I can. Just speak to me of that which you desire of me."

"I have put much thought into this, Temujin," answered Togru. "You are young and brave. Now that you are freed from bondage, you must be clever and remain free. You have married, which is good. Now, you must build a family!" Togru stood up. "But this will take time. And your clan is too few now. It would be to your advantage to bond as anda brothers with your lifelong friend Jamka."

"Jamka is, indeed, a dear friend. When we played together as children, we swore allegiance as blood brothers even then," answered Temujin. "Can I ask why you feel this way, why you see this as so important?"

"Jamka is Jadaran, related to your family through a mythical shamanic bond. The Jadaran are a much larger and more capable clan. Your father's warriors were scattered to the wind after his death and must be replenished. Our strength is in our numbers," answered Togru. "How many warriors do you have?"

"Twenty-two!" Temujin replied apprehensively. Yasotay was sure he was included in that count.

"Jamka has thousands of warriors, and more are joining him every day. The Jadaran frequently camp close to you. This would be a good alliance for you, Temujin!" said Togru. "While you may have the courage of a lion and the strength of a bear, your clan is vulnerable due to its small size. Pairing with Jamka…yes, you must consider this, my son!"

"I don't know if Jamka would want to join forces with me," said Temujin. "I cannot expect him to honor a vow made as a child."

"He came to me to pay his respects recently, and we spoke. I am confident he would consider it an honor to become anda with his childhood friend," said Togru.

"I appreciate your advice," said Temujin, with a genuine smile and a slight nodding of his head in agreement. "You are a wise man. I will speak with Jamka about this when I see him again."

"Good boy," said Togru. "Your safety and the safety of your new wife is of great importance to me, Temujin," continued Togru. "This bond will benefit you and your family. You need to produce children. Build a larger family, young man! Back then, my plan with your father was simple. I would control the south and the west, and he would control the north and the east by splitting up the lands that the Tatar, Merkit, and Naimans now control. They are still our shared enemies!"

"Yes, they are. I share the same enemies as you!" answered Temujin, "They are our enemies too!"

"Come," Togru said as he rose, motioning for them to follow him, "we must eat and celebrate your coming victories."

They walked through a different entrance that, like the main hall, was also carpeted with many rugs. Each was about five chi tall and four chi wide. The rugs were also outside and used as a walkway to connect this structure to an even larger one. They walked into this ger, and at Togru's insistence, they sat on several small gray and brown pillows. There was enough for each of them. Togru joined them, sitting slightly higher on a sizeable yellow pillow set aside for him.

Togru barked, "*HEMEN!*" and within moments, several men and women entered with bowls and dishes of food that were laid out in front of Togru's guests. Then, two men and one woman entered the ger as the food bearers left. Each of them held an odd-looking instrument consisting of a trapezoid-shaped wooden sound box with a long wooden neck at the end of which was carved a horse's head. Yasotay had seen and heard this instrument before. It was called the horsehead fiddle. It had two strings made of horsehair. One of the three began to play.

"This is a fascinating instrument," said Yasotay. "With an amazing and unique sound! Is it true that one string is from the hair of a mare and the other from the hair of a stallion?"

"Yes, and the story behind the instrument is extremely interesting," said Altan, speaking directly to Yasotay while everyone listened.

"Please, if you would, tell the story," asked Yasotay, as the melancholy music from the horsehead fiddle echoed through the ger.

"As I was told, a great emperor sent out his most noble warrior to conquer new lands," Altan began. "With many victories, and after many years of courageous battle, the warrior found himself far away from home with few friends. Lonely, he met and fell in love with a beautiful princess from a distant land." Altan paused. "One day, the emperor summoned the noble warrior back home. In recognition of his heroism, the emperor offered the great and noble warrior a feast where everyone would celebrate his many victories. But he could see the heartbreak in his warrior's eyes. The noble warrior told the emperor about his lost love from a distant land. He was deeply touched by the man's love, and in consideration of his bravery, the emperor gave him the most prized possession in his empire, a winged horse."

Altan paused again for effect. "So, every night from atop the winged horse, the warrior flew to his princess, only to return each morning to attend to his duties for the emperor. One day, an evil neighbor saw him riding this wonderful horse. She was possessed with jealousy. 'Why should this man be the only one to have this winged horse?' So, she took a knife and cut the wings from the horse. The noble warrior was heartbroken, knowing he would never see his love again. So, he fashioned a fiddle from the horse's bones, skin, and tail. This fiddle symbolizes the friendship with his horse and the noble warrior's love for his lost princess. He used his horsehead fiddle to play poignant songs about his lost love."

"That's a beautiful story," said Yasotay, "very touching, especially with the fiddle playing in the background. It sounds like a horse galloping." The sound from the fiddle filled the ger.

"It's a bunch of horseshit," said Temujin. "I heard the same story, but that he used the fiddle to play love songs for his lost horse! Who did he love more, the horse or the princess?" This taunt got a chuckle from those eating and listening to the stories.

"There are other versions of the story, but this one is my favorite," said Altan, taking a bite out of a piece of boiled meat.

"Temujin, I assume you'll wait until tomorrow morning to leave?" asked Togru, eating from a bowl of what appeared to be dates.

"That was my plan, but based on what Ahmad has told us, we must change our route home," answered Temujin, cutting off a large chunk from an even larger leg of lamb. Temujin seemed capable of eating whatever was put in front of him. He had a voracious appetite.

"Again, I offer you an escort if that will help?" said Togru, still fussing with the dates in his bowl.

"No…but you show me great respect with this offer. It is better if we move as a small group and as quickly as possible," responded Temujin. "There are only six of us, but we fight like twenty." He paused, gauging his host's reaction, then continued, "We will leave tomorrow before sunrise, and moving quickly, we will stay away from the main routes."

"I am concerned for your safety, Temujin," said Togru. "But I under-stand…you are the Blue Wolf, and you will find a way!"

They listened to the horsehead fiddle musicians, who took turns playing their songs. Togru and Temujin spoke privately for well over half a shi. The other five travelers listened to the musicians, as each one had a slightly different sound and style than the other, which explained why there were three of them instead of just one. As the night grew longer, the travelers were finally offered a place to sleep, which they gladly accepted. Before leaving, they all bade farewell to Togru in a sign of respect—a bow and kiss on their host's hand for his hospitality. Then, after being reunited with their boots and weapons, they were shown to another ger where they could stretch their weary legs and sleep for the night.

The following day, they were gone before dawn. Yasotay watched a beautiful orange-and-red sunrise from atop his horse as the different route home meant they made slower progress. Temujin took them on a much less traveled path over rugged terrain, where only a few of their numbers could pass. It was narrow and, in many places, treacherous. It wasn't until midmorning that they stopped at a convenient place to water the horses and refill their water bladders.

"Back at Togru's camp, did you see the one man wearing the red boots with blue pants and green top?" asked Borchu, whose eyes appeared to squint from the sun even more than normal.

"What are you talking about?" asked Altan.

Yasotay was bent down, filling his bladder. "Yes, in the gallery of the dais room, I remember him. He wore an odd-looking yellow hat and had a pointy mustache."

"Yes, the man in the yellow hat with the feathers who stood out from the crowd," said Temujin.

"Yes. He's sympathetic to the Merkit," said Borchu.

"Are you saying he is a Merkit spy?" asked Temujin.

"No, I don't know that for a fact. I know of him and was told he was originally from the West. From what I recall, he travels a lot, and someone said he was a Merkit. I recognized the mustache."

"We have Merkit to the west, Tatar to the east, Taichiud to the north, and spies everywhere in between," said Temujin. "Thankfully, we have Togru to our south, or we would be cornered like a fish in a bowl!"

"Yes, it's troubling to hear we have a spy among us…possibly within our clan," responded Borchu.

"It's not definite that we have a spy," cautioned Altan as he adjusted the saddle on his horse.

"Then how did they know of the sable jacket?" asked Yasotay. "I didn't even know Temujin planned to give that jacket as a gift."

"Many others in camp knew," answered Altan.

"I know, maybe it's Nugai. He travels all the time. He is a trader," Hassar interrupted.

"I seriously doubt that Nugai is a traitor," said Altan.

"Trader, traitor, what's the difference," quipped Hassar with a grin, "both look to take advantage."

"Let's head out!" Temujin said. "I want to get home as quickly as possible. We must go east the rest of the morning to avoid the Merkit. Then we can finally head north toward home."

Borchu was done checking the tie-down on the six rolled-up rugs that Togru had given Temujin as a wedding gift. He jumped up onto his horse, and with the others, he followed Temujin through the rocky rolling hills of the steppe.

After a while, as he rode along, Yasotay's mind wandered. *Do I really want to stay with these people?* This was the big question burning in his mind.

He had left the Jin Empire because of all the corruption, backstabbing, and lies. He tried to drown it out with his studies, but that didn't work. He left Chang's library to look for a new life, a new purpose, to see and experience for himself all the amazing things he's read about. To Yasotay, the nomads were fascinating—a large, unwritten book. For the most part, they were very family-oriented, quite jovial and celebratory, and they seemed to share only one common cause…survival. But then, both man and beast all shared this immutable goal. Yet for the nomads, it seemed much more acute, very much like in the Greek parable of the sword of Damocles. Death seemed to hang over their heads at every moment. They lived with that mindset—that death was potentially around every corner—constantly fighting to survive.

While life wasn't perfect with the nomads, it was exciting and very different. Yasotay felt obligated to Altan for all he had done for him. He had shown great kindness by inviting him into his home. Yasotay had done everything he could to repay their kindness. He had grown fond of Tera, Sarnai, and her young son Erden. Living with the four of them had been like living with the family he never had. But this life out here on the steppe was hard. And then there was Temujin! Ever since being reunited with his clan, he had begun to take his birthright and its leadership role very seriously. He seemed to want this, but Yasotay couldn't help but wonder to himself, *Is he ready to lead? What will become of the Borjigin under Temujin's leadership? Will he continue to kill innocent women and children like he did with the Tatar group they met on the road? He slaughtered them because someone was related to the man who may have been involved in his father's murder. This seems insane. Do I want to get involved in other people's blood feuds?*

CHAPTER EIGHT

Valley between Mother and Father Mountains, early spring, 1179 CE

Yasotay watched as the full moon was setting in the southwest sky. It was moments before sunrise, and he could see something moving in the darkness. It appeared to be a lone gray wolf. Its long legs and stealthy narrow frame slinked along a stone's throw away from where Yasotay sat, tucked away in this morning's cocoon. The wolf looked like it was searching for something. The flushed radiance of the moonlight created an odd blue glow across the valley. It made the wolf appear dark blue as it crept along. He assumed the wolf didn't see him sitting there or hadn't deemed him a threat, so it chose to ignore him. Then, abruptly, the wolf stopped dead in its tracks. It was peering south.

It didn't move a muscle other than to curl his upper lip. Yasotay could see it was revealing a pearl-blue row of dangerous-looking teeth. Then suddenly, he turned and quickly scampered away to the north. Yasotay focused, listening, looking, and trying to discover what had spooked the wolf, but he could hear nothing.

Yasotay realized that this was the third full moon of the new year. Spring would come soon. It was just around the corner. The relentless chill of the winter winds was beginning to subside. "I think it may be time!" he said aloud.

The winter had passed quickly thanks to the mundane routine of daily tasks and the tight-knit, intimate environment within Altan's family ger. Tera seemed to have called a truce with Altan. The home atmosphere was relaxed and pleasant throughout the cold winter. Such an intimate family experience was new to Yasotay, something he sensed he had craved yet didn't know why. His gaze was now absorbed by the orange glow of the rising sun behind Mother Mountain, which became brighter and brighter while his memories of the past winter warmed him.

It was the normalcy of it all, especially playing with the toddler, Erden. Most days, everyone stayed inside the ger. Its warmth drew you in from the bitter cold outside. Most of their time was spent playing *shatar*, a variation on a game from India called Chaturanga. It was played on a square board of inlaid, equally sized smaller squares in two alternating colors, one light and the other dark. Yasotay, Altan, Sarnai, and Tera spent days playing against each other. Each side had sixteen pieces; one game could last half a day or longer. Arguments regarding the rules, all in fun, were part of every game. Yasotay enjoyed spending time with Altan, Sarnai, Erden, and, of course, Tera. He recognized that he cared very much for her. Too much, he felt, and this had become a problem for him. *I can't get too close*; he reminded himself. Their mutual attraction was palpable, but Tera was promised to another—a young man whose family was a good match and who could help Altan's family survive.

The relentless family pressure seemed to have made Tera succumb to her fate with Baatar. *It's probably for the best,* Yasotay told himself.

Brooding about it had become a daily distraction. Magnetically drawn to her, Yasotay often contemplated what settling down with someone like Tera might be like. His flights of fancy were always resolved by the inescapable fact that Tera had no choice—and neither did he!

Yasotay's mind raced through different scenarios, and then, like a pot reaching its boiling point, he involuntarily blurted out, "*It's time to...leave!*" This brought the following thought: *Tera will want to leave with me!* Was this another fantasy, or was it the outcome he truly desired? *Would it be what she wants?* Either way, it would be a big problem. *Tera wouldn't do that. She wouldn't leave her family. Where would we go?* He cared for Tera, and this feeling ran deep. He had never cared for anyone in this way. But he couldn't act on it and betray Baatar. A brotherhood had developed between them. *He is like a little brother to me.* And he wouldn't do that to Altan either, so it was best to leave—and soon. *In the next couple of days!* Maybe he would head south and get away from this bitter cold. Yasotay had learned that Baatar would be returning today or tomorrow. Removing himself and allowing Baatar to build a relationship with his bride-to-be would be for the best. *It's decided.* He would wait until Baatar arrived, say his goodbyes, and leave. Yasotay felt a wave of relief come over him. He knew this was the right thing to do.

It had been a while since Yasotay had last seen Baatar. It was at Temujin's wedding when the bathing incident and subsequent unfortunate confrontation had occurred. It took a good deal of pleading and explaining before Baatar understood. At first, Yasotay did his best to explain that he was simply teaching Tera how to bathe herself, an everyday activity among his people in the South and one that Yasotay had participated in since he was a child. Yasotay even offered to show Baatar how to bathe if he'd like, saying, "It's good for you! There is nothing improper or wrong in bathing." Yasotay added confidently, "The Qur'an, the holy book of the Muslims, says Allah loves those who keep themselves pure and clean." He hoped these beautiful words from a revered deity would convince Baatar's young and impressionable mind that there was nothing inappropriate about showing Tera how to bathe.

"No, it is wrong. I must tell Altan!" Baatar would not relent. Finally, Yasotay explained that Tera could be put to death if Baatar told anyone in the clan of this. In the end, he promised not to speak of it. Fortuitously, Baatar had to leave for home the next day, so Yasotay didn't need to address the issue any further.

Yasotay's departure would unfold over the next few days, removing him as an impediment between Baatar and Tera. Yasotay assumed that while Temujin would be angry with him for leaving, it was still for the best. That was a problem for another day, but today, he needed to help Altan with a chore. Late last fall, all the horses were set free to roam through the mountains during the brutal winter. Tata, like the other asses, stayed close by the ger. To Altan's irritation, Tera kindly covered her in a blanket.

"Why don't you just have that ass join us in the ger?" Altan asked sarcastically with the insufferable look only a father shows his daughter. "And why waste one of our few blankets on that ass?" Working hard to hide his grin, Yasotay shared a look with Tera, knowing they shared the same thought—they knew why!

Now that it was early spring, Altan and Yasotay's task was to round up the herd of roughly one hundred horses meandering along the base of Father Mountain. The sun was blazing through the peaks of Mother Mountain, and Yasotay knew it was time to head back. So, he got up, folded his blanket, and went looking for Altan.

"Morning, Altan," said Yasotay. His lanky, lean limbs moved slowly and smoothly as he walked.

"Ah, there you are. Fine morning. Are you ready to leave?" asked Altan, maneuvering his stout frame and short legs over one of the many fences he'd made to keep the goats in their pen.

"Yes, I just need to drop off this blanket and grab my staff."

"You don't need a staff, just a willow branch to smack their backsides. We are rounding them up, not beating them!" teased Altan. He enjoyed ribbing Yasotay almost as much as Yasotay liked the fatherly figure Altan had become to him.

This wooden staff was Yasotay's favorite weapon, ideally sized just a little taller than him. His swift movements with it made his training opponents appear to be standing still. Coupled with its added length of reach, it gave him an advantage over most combatants with a sword or other weapon. Opponents didn't realize this advantage until it was too late. He used the length and speed of his staff strikes to his advantage. Fast as lightning, the end of his staff would connect with an enemy's throat, groin, eyes, or instep long before he was within sword-striking distance. Most strikes were meant to hurt and get opponents to recoil, flinch, hesitate, and shift their focus toward their injury for only a brief moment. Usually, this was all Yasotay needed to strike a finishing blow. Yasotay had experience in hand-to-hand combat, having studied various arts since he was old enough to remember. His travels and royal standing gave him access to several masters of these arts.

"I have learned that a light, loving touch with a firm staff works best," Yasotay replied with a grin.

Altan laughed. "Like the switch we use on children." He paused. "Speaking of which, Tera was looking for you! Hurry and gather your things because rounding up the horses will take all day," Altan said, chuckling to himself.

"I will be right back." Yasotay blushed as he quickened his step toward their ger, fearing that Altan knew his feelings for her. This notion made him uncomfortable.

Stepping into the ger, he placed his blanket beside his wooden chest. Tera was the only one inside.

"Good morning, Tera. Your father said you wanted to speak with me?"

"I was wondering," said Tera. "It's getting warmer during the day now, and I was thinking we should take another bath…"

"Tera, you know that was a mistake. Baatar is coming. He'll probably be here today!" said Yasotay. "Also, I have something to tell you!"

"Oh…" Tera said, her caramel-colored eyes softening, hopeful her instincts were wrong and he wasn't leaving.

"I am leaving in the next few days!" explained Yasotay with a resigned look.

Tera paused momentarily. She had had a feeling this was coming. With a slight crackle in her voice, she asked softly, "Where are you going?"

"South," answered Yasotay. He knew she was hurt, sad, and disappointed...so was he. They both just stood there, knowing each other's thoughts.

"YASOTAY!" Altan bellowed from outside, "It's time to go!"

"I have to go," explained Yasotay, "I have to help your father."

"What?" Tera asked, looking befuddled, awoken from her trance.

"I'll explain when I get back," said Yasotay, "I promise!" he said, trying his best to be reassuring.

Outside, Altan rumbled again, "Let's go."

"We'll talk later, I promise," said Yasotay as he left the ger. The last he saw Tera, she was slapping her leg in frustration, and her head tossed back as if to prevent tears from falling from her eyes. Yasotay knew from her reaction that it would be a difficult conversation. Living with her these past months, he had come to know her temperament well.

Altan and Yasotay walked in silence for a while toward the base of Father Mountain. Hints of spring were starting to appear in the valley. Blue, red, and yellow weeds and wildflowers were popping up everywhere on the mountain's plateaus, ledges, and mantels.

The terrain along the range that comprised Father Mountain was populated with the sundry plant life of its ecosystem. Peashrub, poppy, and Siberian elm were mixed in with thousands of larches, the most prevalent tree in the cordillera. They walked along a green carpet of grass that encompassed the base of the range, thinning in its far southern reaches. Due to its location directly north of the Gobi Desert, the valley experienced limited annual rainfall. In sharp contrast, the mountain range received a substantial amount of precipitation. Among the numerous peaks, the most prominent, referred to by the locals as "Father Mountain," stood prominently before them. The other peaks consisted of a series of rugged, smaller rock formations extended along the chain of summits.

"Altan, may I ask how you came to marry Sarnai?" asked Yasotay.

"Her father and my father came to an agreement!" answered Altan. "Sarnai's father was very poor!"

"So, her marriage to you and your family helped Sarnai's family?"

"Yes, it did." Altan paused. "As you have come to learn, life on the steppe is hard! We do what we need to do to survive." They walked along in silence until they reached Father Mountain's hilly grass-covered base.

Finally, Altan broke the silence. "Have you noticed she is taken with you?"

That statement caught Yasotay off guard. "What, well, no…yes, but Tera and I are just friends."

"That is not what I asked," responded Altan with a wry grin.

"Yes, I see that," answered Yasotay with a slight pause. "Altan, I have grown to care for your family. You have treated me like one of your own…the family I never had!"

"It has been our pleasure, Yasotay." Altan walked side by side with him before pausing and turning to Yasotay. Gazing at him with those steely gray eyes, he added, "You are a man of honor. I see that in you!" They continued walking up the mountain, and before long, they could see some horses grazing over the rise.

They found a handful of horses gathered in a small ravine between two large earth mounds. Each man picked a horse and hopped on it bareback. "Altan, I must leave in the next couple of days. I want to thank you for inviting me into your home and for the kindness you've shown me." Lightly tapping the backside of his horse, Yasotay drove it toward the others there.

"It sounds like you have someplace to go!" said Altan. Then, the tone of his voice became serious. "You will be missed, Yasotay. And you'll always have a place to rest your head if you ever find yourself back with us." Altan paused for a moment in thought. "Have you thought about how Temujin will react to this news? He seems to like having you around."

"Thank you, Altan, that is very kind of you to say," responded Yasotay, "And yes, I have thought of Temu—did you hear that?" Both men did, indeed, hear a faint noise. At first, Yasotay thought it was a wounded animal. Then, a high-pitched "Aarrgghhhhhh!" rang out. It sounded like a woman's blood-curdling scream.

"What is that?" said Altan, and then they heard another scream.

They abandoned their task and rode hard back toward camp. Steering with their knees and holding tightly to the horses' manes slowed their progress. When they broke through the tree cover, from their higher vantage point, Yasotay saw hundreds of warriors on horseback. They were gathered in a group near the large black obelisk south of camp and positioned just outside the arrow range of the camp. Yasotay and Altan had to pick their way down a steep mountainside path.

They stopped their downhill progress for a brief moment. They had a clear view of the scene below them from where they stood. The invaders were releasing three- and four-man attack squads, one at a time, from the main body of warriors. These squads were riding hard toward their camp through a hail of arrows, no doubt from Hassar and the others in the camp. Once they arrived, the warriors began swinging their swords and briefly causing chaos, only to turn around and ride back to the main group. It seemed to Yasotay like some sort of bravery rite-of-passage stunt. Some only rode halfway there, releasing an arrow toward the camp before riding back. Based on the large number of warriors, they could have easily overwhelmed the camp's sixty-five men, women, and children. But for some reason, they chose to play this childish game of torment. Why?

"It's the Merkit," said Altan, with a clear seething undertone to his voice. He knew this clan well. Yasotay and Altan continued their mad scamper down the mountain and soon found themselves behind the large grouping of warriors. Altan cut the corner and led them to the northern part of camp. Altan assumed that Temujin and his nineteen or so warriors would gather at the furthest point away from the frontal attack to plan a counterattack. As they approached, Yasotay saw Temujin and two others atop horses. The rest of those who could fight were on foot. Hassar led the effort to shoot arrows at the raiders as they drew near. The rest of the clan were either hiding or holding swords and axes, prepared to fight back. Most of the clan's horses remained on the hillside, which was extremely unfortunate.

"Temujin, it's the Merkit!" exclaimed Altan in a huff, riding up next to him.

"For some odd reason, they're taunting us. They have hundreds of warriors who could easily overwhelm us," said Yasotay. Just then, Baatar rode up from the east side with two other riders.

"There are at least five hundred, maybe more, to the south," Baatar said. "We came up from behind them and around to the east." *Thunk.* Just then, an arrow sunk into the thigh of the horseman to the right of Baatar, who let out a growl of pain.

"We came up from behind them around the west side," said Altan.

"Their flanks are open!" Yasotay and Temujin said at the same time.

"The Merkit taunt me! They are playing a game, toying with their prey. I say we attack their flanks," said Temujin with a look of total frustration. The man with the arrow in his leg broke it off with a grunt, leaving a portion still lodged in his leg. Another wave of four Merkit horsemen rode up and shot arrows at anything that moved. A sword fight broke out between two men on foot against some of the raiders on horseback. Each wave of raiders was becoming more and more aggressive.

"We only have eight horses. Are you saying to take four horses each and attack both flanks? We are nineteen against hundreds!" Yasotay said in a deadly serious tone. "I think we should protect the women and children and fight these bastards as they come."

"I agree, Yasotay." said Temujin. Setting his anger aside, he looked directly into his eyes and said, "Get Bourtai and the other women and take them north to safety." He then turned to Borchu. "Let's kill these bastards." Temujin rode over and swapped sword strikes with two raiders. Borchu joined in; soon, he was wildly swinging his sword by Temujin's side. Yasotay jumped off his horse, exclaiming to one of the men, "Here, you're probably better at fighting from a horse than me." He promptly jumped on and rode off to join the fray. Hassar had a group hidden behind a ger, shooting a barrage of arrows at the approaching raiders. Within moments, all the others were embroiled in the battle.

The camp was in chaos as the aggression escalated. People were running about frantically. A goat with an arrow in its belly went scampering past. Another wave of raiders had opened all the pens and forced the animals out. The raiders were playing with them. One raider started randomly shooting arrows into the sides of the gers. Another let one fly, hitting an old man who was helping a young child to safety in the back. Yasotay saw that and charged him on foot with staff in hand. The raider saw him coming and nocked an arrow, drawing it to fire. Yasotay had closed the gap. He took a big step hard right, then another hard left. The shooter tried to readjust his aim left and then right, but it was too late. Yasotay thrust out his staff and jabbed him hard just under his chin. The arrow released from his bow but missed its mark. It hit a ger, leaving only a hole in the felt side. The raider fell off his horse with a hard *thud* in a pile, making a gurgling noise.

Finally, arriving at Altan's ger, Yasotay ducked inside. Tera was there alone, holding a sword in her hand. Her hair looked more red than usual and was tussled about her head. You could see the stress in her eyes. This method of attack was terrifying to those in the camp awaiting annihilation. But it was clear that she was ready to fight whoever entered her ger. Seeing Yasotay, she dropped her sword, moved quickly to him, and gave him a big bear hug.

"Where are Erden and Sarnai?" asked Yasotay. Tera pulled away. She could see the concern on his face, which was heartening for the briefest moment.

"I don't know. They were out tending to the animals when this all started," said Tera. "Where is my father?" she asked. Yasotay could tell she was relieved he was there with her.

"He is fine. Look, I saw Tata outside. We will ready my cart and take as many north to safety as we can."

Tera nodded in agreement, and they hurried outside into the chaos. Arrows were flying every which way. Yasotay led Tera as they crawled over to Tata, peering up only enough to see the four black socks on Tata's legs. Yasotay brought Tata to the cart behind the ger, and they quickly worked together to harness her to it.

"Wait here with Tata. I'll go find the others," yelled Yasotay over the uproar of screams, animal sounds, and battle cries. *Thunk.* An arrow lodged into the side of the cart.

"I'll be here," Tera said as Yasotay ran off, ducking low through the hail of arrows.

Yasotay ran into Altan, who was fighting off two raiders at once. Yasotay came up from behind, struck the knee of one with the end of his staff, and smashed the other end into the second one's throat. The knee strike made the first raider hesitate briefly, and Altan stuck his blade into the raider's chest. Both limp bodies went down in unison.

"Have you seen Sarnai and Erden?" asked Altan, wiping his blade on a fallen man's pants.

"No," answered Yasotay. "Tera's with Tata at the cart. I am looking for them now and will send them north if I can find them!" Yasotay was speaking rapidly. Altan could tell he was upset about Sarnai and Erden.

"I will find them! Taban and her four children are in there," Altan said, motioning to the ger on their left. "Get them to safety!"

"I will." With his head down, Yasotay ran to the door and pushed open the felt door flap. Taban, pregnant with a large swollen belly, swung a huge club at him and barely missed his head. "Ahhhh…" Multiple children were crying at the same time. Yasotay hadn't seen the club coming as his eyes hadn't yet adjusted to the dim light. Luckily, she missed.

"Wow, wait, Taban. It's me, Yasotay," he said, reacting late to the object hurling past his face. "Altan sent me. Come, I'll take you and your children someplace safe!" There were three young children and one older girl of eleven. The children were all huddled together at the farthest point from the entrance. Yasotay had seen these children playing around camp.

"Come!" she commanded, reaching her arms to her children, and the two smallest ran to her. The other two followed their mother, holding onto her deel. The children were scared, quietly weeping. Taban whispered to them, "Shhhh, be quiet. You will be fine."

In a calm voice, Yasotay said, "Just follow me, and everything will be fine." He hoped he sounded convincing. But Yasotay's mind couldn't blot out the images he had seen from previous massacres. *They can easily overrun us. Kill us all with half their force. Why are they doing this?* He asked himself. These questions were haunting him. Taban had a death grip on the back of Yasotay's deel as she and her group of quivering children followed him, cowering from arrow fire to the cart where Tera was hiding beneath the cart's bench seat. Tata stood there, strapped to the cart, as if this wasn't different from any other day. The children piled into the back. Tera joined Taban on the front bench. They had room for maybe one or two more people. Just then, Bourtai ran up, crouching to avoid catching a stray arrow.

"Where is Temujin?" asked Bourtai as two arrows whizzed over her head.

"He's over there fighting," said Yasotay. "He told me to get you to safety. Hop in," he said, motioning for her to get in the cart.

"Here, sit up front. I'll sit in the back with my children," said Taban, sliding, with her big belly protruding, from the front bench to the cart bed. Her children closely huddled around her. The fear of getting hit by an arrow terrified the children. There was very little room in the back for more people to sit. Bourtai climbed up onto the bench with Tera.

"This cart is full," declared Yasotay. "Head straight north as quickly as you can. I'll find another cart and help Altan find Sarnai and Erden."

"No, I want to stay and help you find them," responded Tera. She was pleading with him. Her body leaned toward him.

Yasotay was about to voice his objection when two raiders dismounted their horses and ran toward them. Swords held high, each screaming a battle cry.

"Just go. I promise I'll find them," he said, then immediately ducked the swinging sword of the first charging raider.

"Tata, GO!" yelled Yasotay, touching his staff to her hindquarters. She bolted forward as Tera and Bourtai struggled to hold on to her reins. Yasotay flipped his staff around and crashed the end into his assailant's nose. The shot made him cover his face with his hands, which gave Yasotay all the time he needed to trip his feet out from under him and deliver the fatal blow to the man's throat. Yasotay had been practicing these moves since he was young, which was now paying off. His training from the martial arts masters of the Jin and Song dynasties was reflected in how he conducted himself during combat. His exceptional fighting skill was evident to anyone willing to notice. Muscle memory was an amazing asset that, coupled with his natural speed and agility, gave him a distinct advantage. He made short work of every raider he encountered.

The other raider had run past Yasotay, chasing after the moving cart. The children in the back screamed in unison as the hurtling raider charged at the back of the cart. With a flick of his wrist, Yasotay threw his kusari at the legs of the raider. Wrapping around his legs, it tripped him, and he went down hard, slamming his head against the back of the cart.

Tera guided Tata north as the children's screams turned to sniffles as they departed the chaos.

Tata guided the cart with the seven women and children to the north. Running at full speed, she carried them to the northern reaches of the valley. The level grassland gradually narrowed into a meandering, mountainous gorge at the farthest northern end of the valley. This winding pass was unsuitable for carts. It's much too narrow. Typically, travelers navigated this route in a single file, making it less than ideal for groups larger than thirty or forty. Several stretches of the path provided perfect opportunities for an ambush. There were numerous accounts of people being trapped in the pass that led you to the western side of Father Mountain. Like all of Temujin's people, the Merkit knew the narrow mountain pass well. When the Merkit force came up the valley from the south, they had anticipated that Temujin would send those he wished to protect there. So, the Merkit had sent a small group of warriors to the camp via the route around Father Mountain to head off anyone fleeing. It took a little over half a day longer than the southern route from the Merkit camp, but they had planned for this delay. The group was told, "We will attack at high noon. So be in place and be ready! And remember, they may all flee en masse, so be ready and follow the plan."

Trees, bushes, and boulders created a small cathedral-like clearing at the entrance to the narrow northern pass. As Tera entered the clearing, she slowed the cart. Tata snorted loudly and shook her head. Tera said, "What's bothering you, Tata?" Then, out of nowhere, they appeared, and immediately, the cart was surrounded by warriors on horseback.

Tata reared up on her hind legs. "Whoa, settle down," a slender warrior on horseback said, grabbing Tata's reins and blocking the cart from moving further. Another warrior took hold of Bourtai to pull her down from the cart seat.

"How dare you!" yelled Bourtai, "What do you want?"

"I'll wager that's her," said one of the warriors, "that's his wife!"

"Can you believe that! He sent his wife north just like the three chiefs said he would!" said another warrior with thick black hair and a long, scruffy black beard.

"Are you sure? How can you tell?"

"That one in the back with the four children isn't her! Temujin was just married a couple of months ago. He didn't get busy that fast!" said another warrior, who got a hearty laugh from the gang of men. Their antagonistic, bawdy laughter and general appearance unnerved the children, who were cowering in the back of the cart and clinging to their mother.

"You!" said the one who looked like their leader, pointing at another warrior. "Ride south a little way and watch for anyone else coming!" Their leader wore a striped red-and-yellow top with red pants and dirty yellow boots. The warrior immediately rode off.

Next, one of the rougher-looking warriors pulled Tera down from the cart. He grabbed Tera's chin with his dirty hand, leering into her eyes, and asked, "Are you Bourtai?" His bad breath caused Tera to gag reflexively. Her head bobbed to help hold back the revolting acidic bile climbing up her throat. Recovering, she spat in his face. Initially, this didn't elicit a response, but then he quickly raised his hand and back-handed Tera hard across the face.

"This little filly is going to be fun to break!"

"Answer up! Which one of you is Bourtai?" the leader demanded. Both women stood there defiantly.

The Merkit, with the bad breath, grabbed Tera by her red hair and yanked her head up. Blood trickled from her mouth, a slight moan escaping her lips. Then he snarled, "We'll have you both moaning like that soon." Two of the other warriors laughed and flashed lascivious sneers.

They all paused, awaiting a response, but neither woman said a word, not a single sound.

"We don't have time for this!" The leader exclaimed, "If that's what you want, then…fine! There are only two or three woman at the right age in their camp. We'll take both of them. She must be one of the two!"

"We only have one extra horse," said another warrior. "Doubling up riders will slow us down on these steep trails!"

"Unhook that ass and put one of them on it. That animal can keep up," said the leader. Turning to the women, he spit out, "I'll get you two to talk!" he threatened with an assured tone. "Your cowardly friends will be coming soon, so we must do this later!" The menacing look he gave Tera caused a loud gasp from the older girl in the back of the cart.

"What do we do with the rest?" asked the one with the black hair and beard, looking down at the children huddled around their mother.

"Leave them in the cart," said the leader. "Let the bird fly, and then we get out of here."

The Merkit warriors tied Tera and Bourtai's hands, placing Bourtai on the extra horse. Tera was made to climb on Tata. Finally, they released a white bird from a wooden cage that immediately flew high and headed south. The warriors atop their horses turned their heads skyward, watching the bird fly off.

"Let's go," said the leader once the bird was out of sight. He whistled sharply; moments later, the rider sent south rode up.

"It's still clear. No one is coming," said the scout. "I saw the bird flying south to its mate just like the old man said."

The warriors mounted back up on their horses and prepared to leave. Their leader motioned to two of the warriors to take the two prisoners and lead them down the narrow pass. The warrior leading Tera and Tata said, "She's going to have a rough ride on that ass bareback all the way back to camp."

"She looks like she can handle it! I'll wager it's not the biggest thing she's had between her legs!" said another, eliciting another round of laughter.

The leader turned to four warriors following behind him in single file. "I want you four to set up that log we found and hold off anyone that comes up this path. The rest of us will continue on with the captives. You need to give us time to make it through the pass, and then you can follow. We will meet back at camp if you can't catch up!"

"We know the plan," said the Merkit who had hit Tera. He was finally wiping Tera's spit off his face. Moments later, they were all out of sight, the cart left behind with Taban stroking her belly in a reassuring circle and using soothing words to calm the nerves of her children.

Dodging between seven or eight gers, Yasotay searched for Sarnai and Erden. They were all empty. He found most of the other women and children in two gers toward the back of the camp. He went looking for Temujin, who was on horseback fighting raiders alongside Borchu.

Yasotay could see Temujin and Borchu were getting tired. They needed a break. Yasotay poked the raider in the back that Temujin was brandishing swords with, which made him hesitate. It was all Temujin needed as he buried his sword in the side of the man's neck. He fell from his horse to the ground. The raider fighting Borchu bolted off and headed back toward the south.

"What's the plan?" asked Yasotay. "We can't kill all five hundred like this!" Yasotay hopped on the fallen warrior's horse and pulled up next to Temujin.

"We've lost three men so far. The way I see it, we have three choices," Temujin said. "We can keep fighting till they kill all of us. Or we can charge them head-on or retreat up the Northern pass with most of us on foot." Temujin shook his head. "All bad options!"

"Why are they playing this game...taunting us but not mounting a full attack? It doesn't make sense!" said Yasotay as he looked up to see a white bird flying directly south toward the main body of the attacking raiders.

"We don't have a choice. We fight in place while we move our women and children north through the pass to escape," said Temujin.

"Look," said Yasotay, pointing toward the sky. No sooner had he spoken than a horn blast echoed through the valley. Without warning, the Merkit army turned and galloped off to the south. The advance squads, still fighting, stopped, turned, and raced to catch up with their comrades. Hassar, standing alongside Temujin and Yasotay, took a wide stance, drew back his bow, and let an arrow fly high toward the retreating raiders. They all watched as his arrow fell just to the side of a man on horseback. "Wait!" said Hassar, nocking another and drawing back his bow. He hesitated, aiming for a moment, and let another fly. They eagerly tracked the flight of Hassar's arrow as it came down and lodged in the left shoulder of one of a handful of warriors left in view. Moments later, all that was left of the raiding Merkit warriors was a big cloud of dust that hung in the air.

"Hahaa, nice shot, Hassar!" exclaimed Temujin over the cheers of the others watching its flight.

"I don't understand," said Yasotay. "What was the purpose of that attack?"

"They were trying to embarrass me," said Temujin. "The Merkit are belligerent people."

Borchu rode up to Temujin, "It looks like we have lost four, and three are injured," said Borchu.

"How many of the Merkit?" asked Temujin.

"We killed thirty of those cowards before they ran, or we would have killed more!" insisted Borchu. "Should we pursue them?"

"No, we stand and wait and gather horses and weapons should they return!" said Temujin. His deel had blood splatter up his arm and across his chest. A single drop of blood had landed on his cheek and left a blood trail down his face.

Temujin turned to Yasotay. "Who taught you to fight with a stick like that?" he asked. Staring directly at Yasotay, he said, "You fight men with swords, with just a stick! I have never seen anyone fight like this!"

"I fight to survive, just like you!" answered Yasotay, "I learned this fighting style from the masters I trained with in the past. I know the sword, but I prefer staff!"

Suddenly, an injured Merkit warrior, previously thought dead, jumped up to their right and started hopping toward a horse, trying to get away, "You, there, where are you going," said Borchu, who dismounted and stepped toward him, raising his sword to strike.

"Wait, Borchu," yelled Temujin. "Bring him here!" Borchu grabbed the Merkit raider by the long tendrils of the woven hair on his face and dragged him over to Temujin. Pushing him down into submission, kneeling him in front of Temujin and Yasotay, who were still on horseback. Borchu stood behind the kneeling wretch.

"What was the purpose of this attack?" asked Temujin, his green eyes glowing with rage.

The warrior said nothing. Temujin nodded at Borchu. Using the pommel of his sword, he smacked hard on the side of the warrior's leather hat!

"Why did they attack, then withdraw?" asked Temujin again, this time in a menacing tone.

"I am Burak," the warrior said, conceding something so as not to receive another dose of Borchu's persuasion.

"Tell me, why did they attack this way? Why did they do this?" asked Temujin, knowing Burak was following orders. Borchu smacked him again.

Burak started laughing, very low at first, then growing into maniacal laughter. "Congratulations on your recent marriage!" He snickered with a wide grin.

"Can I have that for a moment?" Temujin asked, motioning for Yasotay's staff. Temujin took the staff and poked hard at Burak's face, catching him flush in the mouth. His head jerked back violently.

"I can see why you like this stick," proclaimed Temujin. "Borchu."

Burak was choking on blood while fingering his mouth to identify his remaining teeth. Borchu, standing behind him, brought his sword up and thrust down, burying the point where Burak's shoulder met his neck, pushing the blade into his torso. He pulled his sword out, and the body slumped over.

"Where is Bourtai?" asked Temujin, his voice filled with concern.

"I sent her north in a cart with a group of women and children," answered Yasotay.

"Was Tera with her?" asked Sarnai, who had walked up with Erden in her arms and Altan at her side.

"Yes," answered Yasotay. "They took Tata and my cart!"

"Come, we must find them. NOW!" ordered Temujin. "Borchu, stay here. Send someone for me if the Merkit return. Scavenge whatever you can from the dead and make sure everyone has a horse just in case they return." Borchu handed Temujin whatever arrows he had left in his quiver. Altan jumped on a stray horse. Temujin wheeled Bourtai's beautiful white horse around to go—the same horse he had given Bourtai as a wedding gift—and took off in a dead gallop north. Yasotay and Altan followed him, and all three rode hard toward the entrance to the northern pass.

Covering the distance as quickly as possible, they finally came to the abandoned cart. Taban was sitting on the ground leaning up against a cartwheel as two of the younger children were playing with sticks, holding them in the air as an older child walked underneath them. Yasotay could tell it was Taban from a distance due to the hump of her large belly. They all froze when they saw Temujin, Yasotay, and Altan riding up from the south.

Temujin skidded his horse to a halt. "Where is Bourtai?" he demanded.

"They took her," replied Taban. She shifted to her side, grabbing the wheel and trying to pull herself up. She struggled to lift herself. "It was a trap!"

"How do you know this?" asked Temujin, his eyes narrowed, looking down at her as she finally got to her feet.

Holding the wheel for support, Taban said, "I overheard the Merkit warriors saying that. There were ten of them waiting for us when we arrived."

"And Tera?" asked Yasotay.

"They took her too. They said Bourtai was who they were after, but when the two wouldn't tell them who she was, they took both of them," replied Taban. "They are taking them to the Merkit camp. This was their plan all along, to take Bourtai."

"They did this for revenge," raged Temujin in a low and menacing voice, "those worthless dogs. Come! We will catch them and slit their miserable throats." Temujin pulled on the reins of his horse, and Yasotay and Altan turned toward the narrow north pass.

"Wait…there is more!" Taban said. "They have set another trap!"

The three stopped and turned their horses toward her, waiting for an explanation.

"As I have said, there are ten of them. I overheard the leader say four warriors were to stay behind to block the way. They knew you would follow. They lie in wait just up the pass. Four sit with plans to ambush you. They were told to let no one pass."

"We shall see about that," said Temujin, turning to leave.

"Wait!" said Yasotay, "did they say anything else? Think…"

"The four are just up the path a short way. The leader wanted them to stay in place and fight you off while he got the women to the other side of the pass. He said they would all meet up at their camp."

"Temujin, as you know, that pass is narrow with numerous blind corners. We can't follow on horseback. We are sure to ride into their trap!" said Altan.

"What are you suggesting?" asked Temujin.

"We could go slowly on foot!" interjected Yasotay. "We find their trap instead of falling prey to it, overtake their position, then use their horses and pursue!"

"Yes! This sounds better than riding headlong into a trap that we know awaits us," claimed Altan.

"Let's go," said Temujin, sliding down off his horse. He and Altan both checked their weapons. Each had a sword, bow, and quiver full of arrows. Temujin kept a dagger in his boot. Yasotay carried only his staff, a small sharp blade he mainly used for eating, and his kusari in its small leather pouch. Yasotay took the time to harness the horse he rode to the cart so Taban could take the children back to camp.

"You are a prince, Yasotay," said Taban, climbing aboard the cart. As she guided the cart toward safety, one of the younger children in a bright red deel sitting in the back stood up and raised both hands over his head. Yasotay did the same in response, leaving smiles on their faces.

Yasotay ran to catch up with Temujin and Altan, who were already hurrying down the path…quietly. The three moved cautiously along the winding trail, peering around each corner. The trail had quickly narrowed, with boulders, trees, and rock faces on either side. There was a small dried-up creek bed to the right side of the path, with the occasional large tree growing along it, but there was nothing but a rock face to the left. They cautiously made progress up the trail.

Suddenly, an arrow whizzed past Altan's right arm and nicked it, and all three of them instinctively lunged to the left, toward the rock face and away from the arrow's path. Whoever had shot that arrow gave away the advantage of his position. Had he waited, all three would have been in firing range, scrambling for cover.

"I guess we've found them," grimaced Altan, holding his left hand over the upper part of his right arm. Blood began soaking his deel around the hand. They were now hidden behind a large slab that had fallen from the rock face eons ago. They could advance no farther. Temujin slowly peered around it, trying to catch a glimpse of the attackers, and then quickly pulled back—an arrow flew past where his head was moments ago.

"Great, so now what?" asked Temujin. Yasotay was helping Altan wrap a piece of cloth around his arm to stop the bleeding.

"Well, looks like we go up!" Yasotay said and pointed up the rock face.

"We're going that way?" questioned Temujin, looking up at the jagged wall that rose high above their heads. It looked as if the side of the mountain had been sliced off, leaving a craggy rock face of hundreds of ledges climbing into the sky.

"We have no choice," replied Yasotay. "We climb. They will keep their eyes on the trail and won't be looking up. As we move across the wall past them, we can take the advantage."

"Please…show me the way," said Temujin, sarcastically as he waved his arm at the towering rock wall Yasotay proposed they climb.

Yasotay drew on the training of his youth, running, climbing, and jumping on boulders in the mountains near the Purple Cloud Temple. As a teenager, this had been one of his favorite diversions from studying. He would run all day in the woods, climbing large hills and jagged rock faces, always carrying his staff.

Yasotay jumped up and grabbed a small purchase with one hand on the lower rock face. Lifting his body and swinging up his arm with the staff, he wedged it between two rocks and used it as a grip. He kicked his leg up, pulled himself there, and then moved up again with a big step using his free hand. Temujin and Altan stood there watching in amazement. Yasotay was at least twenty chi above them, hanging on to the side of the rock face. He looked down at Temujin and Altan, who hadn't moved.

"Are you coming?" asked Yasotay with a grin.

"As soon as I grow a tail," answered Temujin. "You're like a monkey!"

Patting his belly, Altan said, "I need to grow more than a tail to climb that."

"I think I can move across the wall from here and find a spot to get a shot off," said Yasotay. "Here, take my staff." He bent down, dropping his staff to Temujin. "Give me your bow and a handful of arrows."

"Are you sure you can reach them?" asked Temujin, reaching up as high as he could to hand Yasotay his bow, but he couldn't quite reach it. Yasotay moved down to a lower ledge to be within reach.

"I think so. I just need to climb up over that rock ledge. I should be able to see their hiding spot from the other side," said Yasotay, studying the various ledges that lined the rock face wall.

"What can we do?" asked Temujin.

"I will call down when the way is clear," answered Yasotay. "When I yell, you come running!"

Yasotay tucked the five arrows into his deel and slung the bow over his shoulder. "Do you want more arrows?" asked Temujin.

"This should be good." Yasotay straightened the bow on his back. "I need my fingers for climbing." He held out his hands, wiggled his fingers, gave Temujin a quick smile, and was gone, climbing the rock face with the ease of a mountain goat.

After traversing several difficult spots requiring careful, deliberate positioning, Yasotay reached a point high above the trail and to the north of his friends. He stopped climbing to assess the scene below him. He had a good view of where the warriors had positioned themselves for their ambush. He realized they were actually in a perfect spot. There was no way someone could move along the path from the south without affording the ambushers numerous free shots from cover. He could see their arrow tips poking out from their concealment. Yasotay couldn't see the warriors as he wasn't at the right angle, but now he knew where they were hiding. He would have to climb up higher and then come down past them. He started to make his way over the top of an especially large ledge, but before long, he was climbing down to a perfect view of them in their little hideaway. Moving as quietly as possible, he took position.

He had reached a vantage point where all four warriors were clearly in view. They were below and to his right and had four horses to Yasotay's left. He was about twenty-five chi above and behind them, almost in a diagonal. With their backs to him, Yasotay had the element of surprise, but it was still four against one. Three of them had their bows resting at the ready, and their attention was focused down the trail where Temujin and Altan crouched just out of sight from them. The fourth warrior fumbled with a large leather bag on one of the horses. The men had placed an old log next to a large boulder, blocking the path and giving them more protection. Yasotay didn't have time to waste. They needed to reach Bourtai and Tera. The raiders who had them already had a significant head start.

Looking closely at the rocks jutting out from above the ambushers' hideaway, he devised a plan. Yasotay could hear them talking.

"You are such an idiot," one of the ambushers said to the other. "I can't believe you couldn't wait!"

"It was an accident! It slipped out of my hand," replied the second one.

"You have an excuse for everything. You're such an idiot!" berated the first ambusher.

Yasotay quietly maneuvered along the ledge. It was close to and above where the three lay in wait. He knew his odds were better up close against three than shooting at them with a few arrows. Not willing to wait any longer and more confident in his hand-to-hand fighting skills compared to his proficiency with a bow, Yasotay jumped directly into the middle of them. He first crashed Temujin's bow over the head of the man in the center. Next, he kicked the bow out of the hands of the one to his left, which disoriented him while he turned and throat-punched the one to his right. He caught him clean, that's two down, two to go…

Turning back to the one on the left, who now had his sword in hand and was pulling back to take a big swing at Yasotay. To his misfortune, he was much too close. Yasotay quickly pivoted to his left out of the way and placed his right hand under his assailant's swinging right arm, pulling him forward and off balance. The warrior was already lurching when Yasotay tripped him, so he stumbled even more. Grabbing the back of his head, Yasotay slammed it against the rock ledge. He fell in a heap on top of the man he had been criticizing just moments ago. *Now, where's that fourth one?*

He stood frozen twenty-five paces away, standing beside the horses and watching the whole show in shock. It had all happened so fast. Yasotay bent over, grabbed a bow from the ground, and found an arrow. Then, realizing he had grabbed Temujin's broken bow, he threw it to the ground and grabbed another. By the time Yasotay had nocked and drawn the bow, the fourth man had hopped on a horse and was riding hard down the pass just as he tried to take aim.

"Ahhhh," Yasotay yelled after him. The fleeing Merkit was now around a corner and out of sight. "Temujin, Altan, come on…" Yasotay shouted. The other three horses, untethered intentionally, had followed the fleeing warrior some distance up the trail.

"No!" yelled Yasotay, seeing the other horses follow as he ran after them. He would have to catch the horses before they could follow after that warrior. It took a short while, but after a hundred paces or so, he caught up with the three riderless horses that had slowed to a stop. Yasotay could still hear the hoofbeats of the fleeing warrior, but he was out of sight. So he jumped on one of the horses and led the other two back to Temujin and Altan.

Temujin stood on the log that the warriors had placed on the trail. As Yasotay rode up, he asked, "I see three bodies and three horses...I thought there were four?"

"One got away!"

"It could be worse. We have three horses, so let's track him down," said Temujin, throwing Yasotay his staff. "What happened to my bow?" Temujin picked it up wide-eyed. He held the broken remains of his bow in the air awkwardly. He held it up even higher, showing it to Yasotay.

"Sorry, that one to your left broke it with his head," answered Yasotay. "Just grab one of those on the ground!"

"Yes, we must go!" exclaimed Temujin, who stepped toward a horse, saying under his breath, "Shitty Merkit bow." Temujin spat on the ground. "I would rather use my blade!"

Suddenly, they heard a deafening noise that sounded like the mountain was falling down around them—a large tree crashing to the ground. They could hear birds crowing and limbs breaking.

"That's up ahead. Let's go!" said Yasotay, and within moments, all three were racing up the pass.

After a short ride, they could see a tremendous larch tree lying across the trail. This old tree's stubby branches and massive trunk totally blocked the way. While they could climb over it, getting a horse to the other side was impossible. The girth of the tree was as wide around as two people. It would take days of work with several axes to clear the pass.

"How did he do that so quickly?" asked Altan, staring at the large mass of tree limbs and branches. The top of the larch tree, with its millions of needles, was now at their feet.

Yasotay positioned his horse next to the rock face, stood on the horse's back, and climbed up the rock to get a better view. "There, you can see it. They were ready for us. Knew we would pursue, so they chopped on that tree until only a handful of strokes were left," explained Yasotay. "It must have been their backup plan. The last one who escaped us rode up, swung his axe at the tree a handful of times till it fell, and rode off knowing we couldn't follow!"

"How do you know this? Something you read about in your library?" asked Temujin.

"What's a library?" Altan said.

On their ride back toward the valley between Mother and Father Mountains, they stopped where the Merkit had pulled a log across the trail. The three of them lifted and threw the log to the side so they could pass. They rolled the dead bodies over to the side as well, got back on their horses, and continued down the pass toward the valley.

"So, I heard you were leaving?" Temujin blurted out, looking at Yasotay.

"Yes, but how did you know? I just decided earlier today and only told Tera and Altan," said Yasotay. He knew Temujin wanted him to stay, and Temujin seemed always to get his way.

"Tera came to me and wanted me to convince you not to leave," answered Temujin.

"Well, my plans have changed. I'm not going anywhere unless it's to the Merkit camp to get Tera and Bourtai!"

"What you did back there...your climbing ability...the way you fight. We are going to need your help!" exclaimed Temujin.

"I give the two of you my word. I will do everything I can to get them back," assured Yasotay, "This is my fault. I should have gone with them...to protect them."

CHAPTER NINE

Northern reaches of Khamag Mongol Territory, spring, 1179 CE

Yasotay's sleep had become increasingly challenged since Tera was taken. Thoughts of her ill-fate filled his nights with sinister scenarios. Most nights, he found himself lying prone and playing that fateful day over and over again in his mind. *What could I have done differently? I should have taken them myself. I could have stopped this.*

When the three of them, Temujin, Altan, and Yasotay, returned from the northern pass, everyone was in favor of readying the horses and going after Bourtai and Tera. But, as Yasotay calmly explained, the problem was that the Merkit were still directly west of their position.

"Since we can't go directly over Father Mountain, pursuing them through the northern route would require six axe-wielding men and a very long day," said Yasotay.

"How did we let this happen!" roared Temujin. His emotions seemed to be getting the best of him.

"That tree was massive!" insisted Altan.

"If everyone in camp helped, we might be able to clear that tree in less than a day, but that still leaves us over a day behind them…unless we clear the tree tonight!" Yasotay paused, then continued. "Going around the mountain via the southern route means we must chase behind hundreds of Merkit warriors, surpass them, head north again somehow, and catch up to the kidnappers before they reach the Merkit camp and its thousands of warriors. And, we have at most just over a dozen who can ride and fight," said Yasotay.

"How did we let this happen!" Temujin shouted again, this time angrily slapping a tray of food off the table. He was in great distress over the capture of his wife. He often cycled into these fits of rage, cursing and blaming others. It was apparent his pride was hurt. After a good deal of irrational back-and-forth banter, Yasotay convinced Temujin to calm down and think through the situation.

"Together, we will come up with the right solution!" said Yasotay.

Finally, Temujin was able to assess the situation they faced rationally. "We need a bigger army!" he said, trying his best to keep his emotions under control. "The Merkit have thousands of men!"

"A small group that's well-versed in working together and operating quietly could possibly…a small ninsha team could rescue them, but we have no such team." Yasotay paused, then admitted, "I agree, we need more warriors."

"My father's blood brother, Togru, has many warriors," said Temujin. "But his advice was for me to team with Jamka, which so far I've ignored. How can I ask him for help when I dismissed his counsel?"

"You can't at first," said Yasotay. "So we approach Jamka for help? If he turns us down, you can go to Togru and ask for his help with your head held high."

Temujin insisted, "Jamka is my oldest friend. I am confident he will help us." The remainder of that evening and all through the next day, they continued to debate their next step. With clearer heads prevailing and a sensible plan, a small group of eight riders and twenty or so horses headed south three days after the raid. Traveling along the east ridge of Mother Mountain, they then turned northeast and deep into Khamag Mongol territory. Temujin's goal was to convince Jamka and the Jadaran Clan to join his cause and help him retrieve his wife and Altan's daughter. Yasotay found it painfully ironic that they were traveling further away from the Merkit Camp and thus further away from saving Tera. The journey seemed longer due to harsh winds and bone-chilling rains plaguing their travel. Finally, on the evening of the third day, they arrived at Jamka's camp.

After exchanging muted pleasantries, Temujin told the story of the trickeries that had befallen them, sparing no details of the attack and kidnapping. He held back nothing and told all the particulars of how the Merkit had manipulated him into sending his wife north, thinking it to be safe, only to send her directly into their arms.

Hearing the story repeated caused Yasotay's stomach to turn over. He could see from the red hue of Temujin's face that he was experiencing a new level of embarrassment and rage with the retelling of the story. The voice in Yasotay's head rang out: *WE HAVE TO FIX THIS!*

"Even if I were to join forces with you, would it be enough?" Jamka asked, his face filled with concern for his good friend.

"I believe it would," Temujin said confidently. "I must save her!"

"I volunteer to go!" exclaimed Baatar loudly. Everyone looked over at him briefly. His face was flushed with anger, framed by the two braids hanging down either side of his face.

Jamka ignored the young man's interruption and continued, "How many are the Merkit?" he asked, looking directly at a tall, slender elderly man in a gold-colored deel decorated with a bright pattern of tiny pink and yellow flowers. He was obviously one of Jamka's counselors.

"The Merkit have roughly eight thousand warriors!" answered the counselor with the self-important air of someone who knows such things.

"And how many warriors do the Jadaran have?" asked Jamka, even though, as they all knew, Jamka was well aware of the size of his own army.

"You have twelve thousand five hundred and thirty," answered his counselor in a matter-of-fact tone.

"Half of my men is the most I dare take on this mission. I must leave warriors to protect our camp. I do not trust that the Tatar won't attack in our absence!" Jamka paused, contemplating. "I believe we need twice that amount to assure a victory against the Merkit," he added. "We would be attacking a superior force on their own land, which they know very well!"

Temujin looked disheartened and sighed. Jamka understood his old friend's reaction. He continued, "You have traveled far. It is late. You're tired. Let us speak of this plan in the morning. My people will show you to a place to rest!"

At first, Temujin looked like he had been stabbed in the gut. Recovering quickly, he said, "You are right, my friend." His body slumped, resigned to the fact that Jamka spoke the truth. He wasn't thinking straight and needed to rest. "We have ridden for three days without rest, and a place to lay our heads would be greatly appreciated."

"Show them to my private quarters," ordered Jamka. The man with the gold deel stepped forward from Jamka's side and held his arm out, directing Temujin and his men. "Please follow me!"

Baatar stepped forward and insisted, "Yasotay, I must speak to you privately! I will bring you to the others once we have a moment...to talk." He motioned to Yasotay to follow him.

Temujin and his men were shown to a large ger used as guest quarters. It was comfortably appointed with food, several benches, blankets, and plenty of room to sit or sleep. It was a private space for them to get some rest. Within moments of entering the ger, most of the men had claimed their space and were fast asleep.

The ride was torturous, with the Merkit riding hard as though a pack of wolves was chasing them. The quick pace made the full-day ride seem a blur to Tera. Her only comfort was knowing her father, Yasotay, and Temujin would come for Bourtai and her. Tera anticipated that these men would beat them until they got their desired answer: Which is Bourtai?

Upon reaching camp, they pulled the two women off their horses, tied their hands behind their backs, and threw them into an empty ger. Tera smiled as her last glimpse of Tata was of the devastating back-kick she landed to the middle of the chest of one of the warriors who had foolishly lingered behind her. As they dragged Tera facing backward into the ger, her smile immediately disappeared; she had a good idea of what was coming next.

The beating began. They had no questions at first—the Merkit were looking to soften them up by repeatedly slapping them hard across their faces. With their hands tied behind their backs, Tera and Bourtai had no way to protect themselves.

Suddenly, the beating stopped, "What is your name?" said Bourtai's tormentor, giving her a moment to consider his question. "What is your name? SPEAK!"

Bourtai's eyes darted between Tera and her persecutor. "Don't say a word!" insisted Tera through blood-smeared teeth. She was sitting up, her hair matted, blood drooling down the right side of her mouth. Her left eye had a large red swollen mark.

With surprising speed, the man reached down and swung his hand, slapping Tera hard in the face again. He proceeded to beat Tera while Bourtai watched. His attack was so sudden and fierce that Bourtai's body convulsed from the sounds. "And these are your first words?" giving Tera one last slap. "Haven't you had enough? You stay out of this," the man growled with a low, gravelly voice.

"Now, what is your name?" he asked Bourtai again. His foul breath reeked of spoiled meat and sulfur. He raised his hand and struck her hard, catching her flush on the right side of her face. "You're going to answer me, or I will beat you worse than I just beat her." He raised his hand to Bourtai again. Seeing Tera's brutal beating, Bourtai had had enough; she knew their defiance was pointless. Cringing, she said, "I am she. I am Temujin's wife, Bourtai."

"Finally. But do I believe you?" He asked Bourtai, raising his hand again.

"Yes, yes, you can. I am Bourtai, wife of Temujin, son of Houlun and Yesugei of the Borjigin clan."

He stared at her long and hard. "I believe you," he said, lowering his hand. "You are going to Chilger."

The man released the collar of Bourtai's deel. Then, pulling a rope from his pocket, he reached down to tie Tera's legs together to stop her kicking. He kneeled on her hips and slid down, sitting on her legs; after a good deal of wrangling, he finally tied her ankles together.

"You just keep fighting like that. This should be entertaining," he said, pausing for a moment, then continuing, "They sold you to Darmala, that fat pig!" Turning his head away, he spit on the ground. The man stood over Tera and talked to her as if they were conversing. "Your friend here is going to a good man who will care for her if she is nice and warms his bed. It will be good for her, don't worry." Towering over Tera, he said, "But that disgustingly fat pig Darmala won't be as kind to you." He reached down to lift her off the ground. Tera violently jerked away and kicked hard with both feet, just missing his right leg.

"Easy, easy now. I have a feeling this is going to be an unpleasant experience for both you and Darmala." Laughing aloud, he grabbed Tera and tossed her over his shoulder. She started bucking so wildly that the man let her fall to the ground. Tera hit hard on her side, knocking the wind out of her.

"You should fight Darmala like this, not me!" He looked over at Bourtai and said, "You come." Bourtai rose and followed him out of the ger. As she left, she took one final look down at Tera, still lying on the ground and breathing hard, her face smudged with dirt. She looked defiant.

Walking silently, Yasotay followed Baatar outside the ger over to where their horses were standing. As they walked up, Yasotay saw an ass with four gray socks mingled in with the horses. It immediately brought Tata to mind, and he suddenly felt a pang of guilt over being so preoccupied with Tera that Tata's plight hadn't occurred to him. Someone as dangerously ill-tempered as Tata captured. That would be trouble for both her and her captors!

Finally, Baatar turned to face Yasotay. "How did they capture her? Why did you let them take Tera?" he blurted out. His face was flush, and the rims of his eyes were bright red. "I thought you were this great warrior; why couldn't you save her?"

"I understand you're upset, Baatar…it's just as Temujin has explained: the Merkit planned every aspect of this kidnapping. We were outnumbered and outsmarted in every way," said Yasotay. "Tera was taken because they didn't know which one was Bourtai. They wanted Bourtai!"

Baatar paused, the color coming back to his face. "So, what do you plan to do? You know they will sell her to someone as a wife."

"Tera will never stand for it," said Yasotay. "She is too strong-willed to allow that!"

"Which means they will either kill her or make her a sex slave once they realize she's incorrigible!" exclaimed Baatar.

"Don't you think I know that," said Yasotay in frustration. "Yes, that fear has crossed my mind. But we can't let worry distract us. We need our wits to win her back."

"Then what are we going to do?" asked Baatar adamantly.

"…everything I can to return Tera to her family," Yasotay replied.

Baatar nodded his head, seeing the resolve in Yasotay's eyes. The man wore his determination like body armor. That and all of Temujin's stories about Yasotay's abilities gave him hope.

"Are you as good a warrior as they say?" asked Baatar, his eyes wide, staring at Yasotay in wonder and hope.

Looking at Baatar's expression and hearing his inquiry, Yasotay couldn't help but think, *This is something a child would ask.* He paused, then responded, "I have heard the stories…often standing right beside

Temujin. If they were untrue, I would not allow the claims to stand!" Yasotay said, "The man has a gift for glorifying the facts, but other than that…"

"So, you climbed a cliff face like a monkey?" interrupted Baatar. "And you killed three men in the dark with that ball and chain?"

Yasotay chuckled. "My point exactly; I have never seen a monkey climb a cliff face, nor has Temujin! But I did climb up a rock wall to get behind those who lay in ambush!"

"And you killed three of them at once, jumping down into the middle of them, breaking Temujin's bow over their heads!" said Baatar.

"Listen, I know you love these battle stories, and I heard you volunteer for our mission to save Tera and Bourtai. But you should consider staying here and helping to protect this camp. I am concerned for your safety." Yasotay hesitated with this next point. "You are too young for such battles! I promise I will do everything I can to rescue Tera!" pleaded Yasotay.

Baatar suppressed his anger about the "too young" comment and said, "Good, because if you're as good as they say you are, then I will need your help! I won't stay behind. I'm going with you to save Tera!" insisted Baatar, slamming his fist down into his open palm. "If I have to go alone, I will do that! I will be the one to save Tera! I am her betrothed; it is my duty."

Yasotay could see the sheer determination on his face and hear it in his voice. He had never seen that hand gesture before but understood it meant the young man was adamant! "I see." Yasotay paused. "Baatar, we are friends. Is that true?" he asked.

"Yes, yes, we are!" answered Baatar.

"I want you to hear what I'm saying. I will do everything I can to save Tera, but right now, preparations have to be made. I would prefer to go in with a small team and steal them back. Temujin, however, is convinced we need an army."

"I understand," said Baatar, "speaking of being prepared, I made something for you!"

"Well, thank you. I also consider you a friend. I promise I will help you, but you must do me one important favor!" explained Yasotay.

"What?" asked Baatar.

"You must stay close to me during the battle and do as I say!" replied Yasotay, his facial expression and voice deadly serious. He slammed his right fist into his left palm, as Baatar had.

Hesitating for a moment, "I understand!" Baatar murmured his pledge in a far-off voice.

They walked back together in silence, the wind kicking up. Baatar guided him to the guest ger and left him with a simple, "Good night!" Yasotay went inside and sat on the ground with his back against the wall. Altan had lain down atop his blanket with his head close to where Yasotay sat.

"What did Baatar want?" asked Altan in a low voice, trying to be quiet. Most of the others were asleep already. Altan couldn't sleep; he was curious about what Baatar had to say to Yasotay.

"He is concerned for Tera," answered Yasotay.

"As am I," said Altan.

"He is too young. I think it best he stays here. That's what I told him," said Yasotay.

"Did he agree with you?" asked Altan with a smile.

"No, as you would expect," Yasotay said, shaking his head. "We need to move quicker. This gathering of a large army is taking too long."

"Yes, I agree. Tera's strong nature will be a problem for her!" said Altan. "They will keep Bourtai as a prize, but Tera will be meat for the mongrels!" The look of despair on Altan's face alarmed Yasotay.

"I disagree; Tera is smart. She will see the situation for what it is and do her best to survive!" said Yasotay in the most reassuring voice he could muster. But, he wondered, *Did he believe that?* "To commit, Jamka needs to believe we will win!" Yasotay continued. "Temujin should tell Jamka that if he joins us, we will next go to Togru and request his help."

"It will take days to assemble and move half of Jamka's army, over a week to travel to Togru, and who knows how long to assemble such a joint force and march on the Merkit," said Altan, sounding exasperated. "We will be lucky to attack them by summer!"

"All we can do is wait…A storm is moving in," said Yasotay as the wind whipped against the outside of their ger. It had started to whistle and howl through the camp.

"Yes, I noticed a storm coming in from the west. Let us hope it passes soon!" responded Altan, looking as if he were ready to fall asleep.

A short time later, Jamka's counselor, still wearing his golden-colored deel, poked his head in their ger, holding a candle and looking around. Seeing Yasotay still awake, he said, "Come outside; you will want to see this!" Altan's eyes popped open. Borchu and Temujin were also awake enough to hear him. All four rose and stepped out the entrance.

The moon was full and still high in the eastern sky. It cast ominous shadows over the vast open plain. Large groups of clouds that looked like huge puffy cashmere clumps could be seen in the night sky to the east. It was what appeared in the western sky that the counselor had called them to see. Yasotay looked westward and saw what looked like a wall of clouds, more brown than white, rolling directly toward them. This cloud wall was hundreds of chi from the ground to high in the sky. Its vast moving mass traveled much faster than its white, puffy relatives, which dangled motionlessly near the rising moon.

"What is that?" implored Yasotay, yelling over the noise of the wind. He had never seen such a sight firsthand. He quickly realized the difference between reading about sandstorms and the sight of one barreling down upon you!

"That is a sand cloud, and it's headed our way. It will overrun the camp shortly!" said the counselor in his distinctive, matter-of-fact tone. "I suggest you return to your ger and ensure the entrance is closed properly. There are ropes around the felt door flap on the bottom and top corners. Don't forget to close the crown flap and douse the fire. Make sure it is secure!" The tumbling sound of the wind and the imposing view of the brown cloud wall bellowing in from the southwest was hypnotic. But the intricate details of its smaller bulges churning in the moonlight and its sheer size were *amazing*. The sandstorm's astounding beauty and sheer power demanded one's attention.

The wind was now blowing even harder through the camp. It led the pace in front of the sand-churning mass headed right for them. Yasotay, Borchu, Altan, and Temujin returned to their ger and secured it as they were told, preparing for the sandblasting it was about to endure. They took up their positions on their sleeping mats and waited for the storm to hit.

Looking at Temujin, Yasotay asked, "So what would have happened if we were traveling to Togru when this storm hit?"

"That would be what one would call a terrible night!" said Temujin. Altan laughed lightly at first, then Temujin and Yasotay joined in with low chuckles as the storm engulfed their ger. The walls shook from the thundering winds and pelting sand, and everything went dark black.

Yasotay stood in front of the prisoner, sitting on the ground with hands tied behind his back and legs extended flat on the floor. The prisoner wore a hanfu, but it was not of this century. It was from the Tang Dynasty hundreds of years ago. They were in the emperor's palace, in Mana's room. Someone had placed a sack over the prisoner's head, and Yasotay had questions for his captive. *Whap!* Yasotay smashed his staff down hard on the prisoner's shoulders. Asking again, he demanded, "Where is she?" He had been at this for days, and his patience had come to an end.

All he could hear in reply was a very faint whimper. A thought occurred to him: *All he needed to do was apply the right amount of pressure.* Yasotay slammed his staff down on the prisoner's other shoulder. *Whap!* Again, a muffled whimper that could barely be heard. *How much of this can someone take?* He thought.

"WHERE IS SHE?" Yasotay raised his voice and asked again, slamming his staff down hard against the prisoner's back. *Whap!*

Yasotay was becoming infuriated. The beating wasn't working. He was feeling very discouraged and anxious.

"It's a simple question!" he yelled. Using the end of his staff, he popped the prisoner hard in the middle of the head. *Knock!* It made a hollow sound. He believed the strike had landed right on the forehead. But he wasn't sure. Did it even matter?

Again, there was no answer. Yasotay felt the anger building up inside. He was at wit's end. He needed an answer. He needed it—NOW! Her life depended on it.

"You need to answer! You need to answer! You need to answer!" Yasotay growled in a most insistent, sinister voice. "WHERE IS SHE?" he shouted again.

Yasotay dropped his staff across the prisoner's legs. Then he jumped in the air and onto the staff, crushing the prisoner's knees. "AAAaaah-hhhhh," Yasotay yelled. Again, not a sound was heard. He was beyond incensed, sweat dripping from his brow; he couldn't wait any longer.

Throwing his staff clattering to the floor, he screamed, "You're going to tell me where Tera is…I MUST KNOW WHERE TERA IS!" Then, pulling a knife from inside his boot, he straddled the prisoner's legs, "Or I'm going to slit your miserable throat!" Ripping off the man's mask, he pulled back in horror, confounded to see his mother's face—Princess Jia.

"NO, NO, no, no, no…"

"Yasotay, wake up," Hassar said, shaking his shoulder. "Wake up. You're having a bad dream!"

His eyes peeled open, "Hey? What? I'm fine. Really, I'm fine," he exclaimed, "everything's good!"

Yasotay sat up, soaking wet from sweat, and shook his head, trying to clear the cobwebs. He had a peculiar taste in his mouth. He wiped an odd crust from around his eyes.

"That was a scary dream," said Hassar, holding a candle in his left hand, Yasotay's shoulder in his right. "The way you were jerking your body, I thought you were killing someone, maybe yourself!" Yasotay looked around the ger. All the others in his party were awake and looking at him. Temujin sat across from him, eating from a bowl; he gave him a nod. Standing behind Hassar, Altan had a concerned look on his face. There was an odd mist in the room, a very fine brown haze on everything, including on and around the candle in Hassar's hand. He could hear the wind whipping around the outside of the ger.

Suddenly, there was a pounding on the ger's entrance flap. A cascade of sand rushed in when they untied a portion of it and pulled it back. It was the counselor covered in sand dust, his bald head and face sheathed in a cloth sand shield. If you looked closely, you could see his eyes. He unwrapped the scarf from his face and said, "I hope you are faring well. If you need anything, let me know."

"I will," said Temujin.

"We are trying to save as many animals as possible," explained the counselor. "It is morning but still black as night. Jamka is busy at this moment with other matters. He asked me to apologize for not being able to meet with you now."

"We understand," answered Temujin. "Tell him if there is anything we can do to help, my men and I are at his disposal."

"I will relay your message. We fear this storm may last a while," said the counselor. "Again, if you need anything, please let me know. I will come by later this evening to check on you. If you choose to go outside, I highly advise you to bundle your face. People have died due to exposure to sandstorms."

"No, we are fine and appreciate your hospitality," Temujin responded.

"Where would you advise that we…relieve ourselves?" asked Altan sheepishly.

"Cover your face, and I will show you the way," said the counselor, who shook the sand off his scarf and rewrapped his face with it. Altan coiled a scarf around his head and over his eyes and mouth and followed the counselor out into the sand cloud.

The sandstorm lingered on, hiding the rising sun. Finally, the sun started to break through the fine clouds of floating powder. Jamka came to see his visitors with his golden-deeled counselor.

He briefed them about the storm damage and discussed his concerns about the war plan. "As I said, I am troubled about the size of our army. Six thousand men attacking an army of eight thousand, even with the element of surprise, is…unwise," said Jamka.

"I agree. That is why we must first go to Togru and ask for his assistance," said Temujin. "His army is vast, and if he joins with us, our odds will be greatly improved."

"Why do you believe he will help us and our cause?" asked Jamka.

"Togru is my blood father," answered Temujin. "My father came to his aid when he was in need. He will come to my aid when my family is in need. He is someone I can rely on. After those Tatar bastards killed my father, he was the only one to help with aid and advice. Togru told me that forming a partnership with you would be advantageous for both of us. I can protect your southwest border with the Tatar, and you protect the northeast. We work together for mutual benefit while protecting our flanks from the Tatars."

Jamka nodded his head. "If Togru can give us ten thousand warriors, we can easily smash the Merkit and return your wife to you."

"Yes, I know that Togru will help us if we go to him together as a team!" said Temujin confidently. "Seeing you and me riding at the head of six thousand warriors will convince him that together we can crush the Merkit." Temujin added, "Togru hates them almost as much as he hates the Tatar!"

"It is settled. Once we have dug out from under this sandstorm, I will ready my men, and we will take our petition to Togru," answered Jamka.

Jamka rode in front, leading his six thousand two hundred and twelve nomadic warriors as they traveled southwest across the arid plains of the sand-covered terrain he called home. The sandstorm had killed thousands of animals, mainly the smaller ones. It affected goats, dogs, and sheep far more than horses, camels, and oxen. It also killed off some of the elderly and the very young within Jamka's clan. The counselor told Yasotay that some seven hundred animals and fifty people were choked to death by the blowing sand. But what haunted Yasotay was the loss of valuable time the sandstorm had cost. The delay only protracted their mission to save Tera and Bourtai. He knew with certainty that they had to move quickly if they were going to save Tera. Bourtai would be kept alive as a prize, but Tera…

Yasotay and Altan understood that saving Tera wasn't the main reason behind the undertaking. For Temujin, it was about recovering his wife and redeeming his pride! Yasotay believed this kidnapping was more humiliating to Temujin than being forced to wear the cangue around his neck for eternity. The Merkit had meticulously planned and executed a deception that had undermined Temujin's leadership. It made him *the fool*. Though he would never admit it, Yasotay could tell that it made Temujin doubt himself. You could see his humiliation when discussing the kidnapping—his fits of rage over otherwise irrelevant things were an obvious byproduct. It was affecting his relationship with his companions. He would blow up, yelling and screaming, for one reason or another. He did this with every member of their eight-man group, except with Yasotay. He noticed his exclusion and wondered why. He wondered how he would react if the irrational outburst were directed at him.

They rode at a brisk pace. Looking back, Yasotay could see the massive dust cloud the thousands of horses produced. It was later in the day when, up ahead, Yasotay could see three men on horses that stood in the middle of their path, waiting…

"Who are they? Do you see them?" Yasotay asked Temujin over the roar of the galloping hoard.

"They are Tatars," answered Temujin. "This could be trouble!"

"Three horsemen against six thousand?" asked Yasotay.

"There are more than three thousand a day's ride from here!" said Temujin, "and look!" He motioned to his left. Yasotay hadn't noticed that on the hillside to his left were hundreds of warriors sitting on horseback, perfectly blended into the terrain, many with arrows nocked watching them from a distance. Jamka lifted his fist high in the air, and the mass of moving horses came to a slow rolling stop.

"We do not want to fight the Tatars today," said Jamka, conferring with Temujin and his trusted captains, who were gathered around him.

"Are you sure they feel that way too?" asked Temujin. "I ask because they look ready to fight!"

"I will negotiate with them. Temujin, and I mean this with no disrespect, but I think it is best that you stay behind and blend in with the group. We have no interest in war with the Tatar at this time. I feel your presence will only serve to enflame them further."

"I agree, my brother," said Temujin, turning his head and spitting on the ground. "The Tatars will feel the edge of my blade soon enough, but this is not a fight for today!"

"I will speak with them; Baatar and Sukh, join me!" commanded Jamka, wheeling his horse around and heading toward the three waiting Tatars. Yasotay wondered about the choice of those two contrasting riders. Sukh was a hulking bulk of a man who carried a giant axe over his shoulder. His horribly scarred face and knobby, cracked hands made clear he had seen many battles. Yasotay had noticed this large leather-clad mass earlier; the man looked more menacing than anyone he had ever met. Then you have Baatar dressed like a young prince in a colorful deel, with perfectly braided hair, a fair complexion, and slight of frame. He was, in every way, the opposite of Sukh. Baatar accompanied Jamka, Yasotay assumed because he was trying to give his young cousin negotiating experience. The purpose of Sukh joining him was obvious... *intimidation!*

Jamka, with Baatar and Sukh following closely behind, went to speak with the three Tatars two hundred paces ahead of their stalled advance. Yasotay looked closely along the ridge, where now an even larger number of Tatar warriors stood watching. Most of Jamka's riders just sat there staring straight back.

"I would guess there are over seven hundred Tatar warriors on that hill," said Yasotay to Temujin.

"If not more," answered Temujin, sitting atop his white steed. "They can see we are too large an army for the force that they have here. I'm sure they sent a rider to notify the Tatar generals to get more warriors, though it would probably take at least a day to get them here. This band is a scouting group that is patrolling their northern border. The Tatar have over forty thousand warriors in total. Let us hope they choose to negotiate. While I would enjoy cutting their numbers down by seven hundred, just not today. We must meet with Togru and assemble our army to attack the Merkit and retrieve my Bourtai."

The envoy rode up to the waiting Tatars. Their conversation was brief. Before long, Jamka, Sukh, and Baatar were riding back to their army. And the three Tatars rode off toward their warriors, watching from the hillside.

"They said they had no desire to fight with us today!" exclaimed Jamka. "They are looking for you, Temujin! They say you killed Chuluun and fifty of his family and friends a while back!"

"They speak part of the truth. We did kill Chuluun; I killed him myself, but unfortunately, his family was less than twenty!" answered Temujin with a grin.

"Then it is good that I told them I had not seen you and thought you were still being held by the Taichiud," explained Jamka. "The old man asked about the big one on the white horse." Temujin was the only rider on a white horse and stood out from the others. "I told him you were Sukh's brother." The group of them laughed.

"To me, Sukh is what we all should all aspire to look like…I am proud to pose as his brother!" said Temujin, bowing while holding his hand to the side in jest to more laughter.

The horde of troops got back underway and made good progress for the rest of the day. Yasotay could see that this army loved Jamka. He was a strong leader, and they willingly followed him. Yasotay, Baatar, Temujin, Altan, and Jamka rode within earshot of each other.

Yasotay, riding next to Jamka, asked, "From what I can tell, your army has a distinct chain of command from you down to each individual rider?"

"Yes, everything is organized into groups of ten," Jamka said. "I have twelve main captains who each command a *minghan* of one thousand warriors. I give all orders directly to the minghan commanders. They, in turn, give their orders to their ten *zun* lieutenants. Zuns are troops of one hundred. They give their orders to their ten *arban* sergeants. Each arban is ten riders. So ten arbans to a zun and ten zun to a minghan. Twelve thousand warriors under the direct control of my twelve minghan captains and me."

"So this is how so many ride as one!" said Yasotay.

"Yes, and there is even one more level, a *tumen*," said Jamka, riding along at a comfortable talking pace. "A tumen consists of ten thousand riders! I will someday lead many tumen of men!" Jamka smugly stated, his chest heaving. Yasotay could tell he was a proud man who aspired for more.

"Don't forget generals," interrupted Temujin. "A general can have many tumen under his control."

"It has been many years since we have seen all the nomads under one banner. You are talking nearly one hundred thousand warriors riding for one leader!" said Jamka. "That, my friend, would be a difficult feat to accomplish. One would need to unite all the clans! Very difficult!"

"My ancestors rode across these same plains with such a force," bragged Temujin, "and it is my destiny to do the same."

Jamka narrowed his eyes, then smiled. "Well, we won't need a hundred thousand warriors to rescue your wife, just another eight to ten thousand from Togru. That should ensure our victory," said Jamka with pompous delight.

Temujin seemed to deflate. As intended, Jamka's comment clearly bothered Temujin. Yasotay noticed how Jamka has been goading Temujin over the past couple of weeks. Yasotay could tell that Temujin was undoubtedly seething inside. He knew Temujin well and recognized how he would hold back from confronting his friend about his snide remarks. None of it sat well with Yasotay. It wasn't his place to interfere.

"I can assure you we will get the additional men from Togru!" insisted Temujin, with his brow furrowed, as he smacked his horse's side and pulsed ahead of the group.

"I hope he is right," said Jamka to those still listening. "Our success depends upon it!"

"Togru has a great army. He has many tumen…Temujin is like a son to him. Togru is his blood father," said Altan, "I am confident he will give us the additional support we need." Altan said this loud enough to ensure Jamka heard him.

They rode in silence for the rest of the evening. Yasotay could sense the friction between Temujin and Jamka. Nothing that couldn't be forgiven. But he could see Temujin needed to show Jamka he was his equal. These two have been competing for many years. The only way for Temujin to be Jamka's equal is by convincing Togru to provide the necessary warriors for the attack on the Merkit. Yasotay supposed that Jamka could probably conjure a thousand reasons to attack any number of other clans. The spoils of victory were a temptation difficult to ignore. Jamka was willing to attack the Merkit for Temujin—with one condition. Like many other leaders on the steppe, he realized long ago that you could lose everything in attacking a mightier foe. Jamka's approach was to wait and see what Togru would do—it made perfect sense. Yasotay thought to himself, *Jamka is nobody's fool. He will not take unnecessary chances just for Temujin's wounded pride.*

CHAPTER TEN

Southwest Khereid Territory, late spring, 1179 CE

As they rode, six thousand strong, the sound of hooves echoed through the valley, filling the air with a deafening roar. Dust swirled around them, with clumps of dirt flying about. The sense of invincibility that Yasotay had felt during his first ride with Jamka's horde was now gone. While Yasotay rode the arduous distance from Jamka's to Togru's camp, he realized the once-exhilarating feeling was replaced with a deep, hollow emptiness. He felt they were headed in the wrong direction to where *he* needed to go! They had already experienced a significant delay. The storm and resulting damage at Jamka's encampment were horrible and breathtaking. So many animals were just buried in the sand. Getting Jamka's army dug out and underway took much too long.

At times, he held on to the silly notion that Tata would somehow protect Tera. But as the trail rolled on, Yasotay found no solace in that whimsical notion. *The longer we wait, the less chance we have of finding Tera alive.* It was just that simple. This singular thought haunted him day and night. Yasotay knew Bourtai was a trophy, but to the Merkit, Tera was *chattel.* He needed to act quickly.

Finally, the horde of horse-riding warriors reached the far outpost of Togru's camp in the late afternoon of the seventh day. As they approached the outpost, the lead minghan commander coordinated the groups of riders to set up a temporary camp down from the outpost. It was a short ride to Togru's main camp for the small party of riders that continued on: Yasotay, Temujin, Borchu, Altan, Baatar, Jamka, his counselor, and Sukh with his intimidating hulk of a body and large axe. They followed Togru's sentry through the myriad of checkpoints and handoffs, questioned each time, and finally arrived at the main structure. Like their earlier visit, they entered the first ger, left their weapons outside, and removed their boots. Sukh had no interest in taking off his boots or laying aside his axe, at least not in this camp. He didn't fully trust these people, so he waited outside.

Once inside, they found several people standing around, huddled in smaller groups of five or six. Unlike before, when people stood with their backs up against the wall, they were now milling about the room, talking. Togru was nowhere to be found in the main hall. Yasotay searched around the room for anyone familiar. He noticed one of Togru's three retainers, the ones who were previously carrying the large metal crosses on his last visit.

This retainer recognized Temujin and approached him. "Welcome. I am Yandas. How can I serve you?" asked the small bald man in the brown-hooded cowl.

"I am Temujin, son of Togru's blood brother, and I am here to see Togru!" The impatient tone of his voice showed that he had had to state this too many times that afternoon.

"I remember you, Temujin son of Yesugei, welcome. I am sorry to say that Togru is attending to other matters at this time," answered Yandas, bowing his large bald head apologetically. He had a long facial scar that ran from the corner of his left eye down past his mouth. His stark white complexion and severe lack of facial hair gave him an odd appearance not easily forgotten.

"Do you know when he will return?" asked Jamka.

"He is expected back in the next few days." Yandas, smiling large, only with his mouth closed, showed no teeth. "I apologize for the inconvenience. I can provide you with sleeping quarters, but your army must stay at the outer boundary and approach the main camp no further."

"I understand," said Jamka. The tendrils of his mustache framing his mouth and chin swayed as he bobbed his head in agreement.

"Temujin, we all heard the story of your wife being taken. Is this true?" asked Yandas.

"Yes, the Merkit have deceptively deprived me of my bedmate," said Temujin.

"I am sorry to hear that, but I know someone who may be able to help. He has information about your wife's captivity," reported Yandas, which grabbed the attention of Temujin and his companions.

"Who is he?" asked Yasotay, interrupting.

"It's the Tumed, right over there." Yandas motioned toward a man wearing a heavy deel overcoat of blue with a dark-brown pattern. He had short brown hair with a beard worn close to his face and wore a cylindrical fur-trimmed hat that came to a point. He was talking with two others with their backs toward the newly arrived group.

"I would like to speak with him," said Temujin, intently staring as he headed in the man's direction.

"If you need anything further," Yandas said. He bowed deeply, displaying the entirety of his bald head, "Please inform me when you wish to retire. I will show you to your quarters when you are ready."

With that, the group led by Temujin walked up and stood behind the two people speaking to the Tumed. They looked directly at him, which drew the Tumed's attention.

"Hello, I take it you are Temujin," the man said, "and friends..."

Temujin nodded, and the Tumed turned to the other two men he'd been engaged with. "If you will, please excuse me!" he said, bowing, and then he moved to their left to speak with Temujin's group alone.

"I know what you're interested in," exclaimed the Tumed. "But, you understand, I am a very poor man and don't want any trouble!"

"So, what is that supposed to mean?" asked Temujin, "What do I care? I want to know about my wife," Temujin blurted out.

"You want money?" said Yasotay, more a statement than a question. The man smiled. "He's saying he wants money in exchange for information, Temujin!"

"How much?" asked Jamka, who stepped forward, ready to play the negotiation game.

"I hate to make you bother with such trivial matters," the Tumed feebly claimed.

"Here, take this," Jamka said, pulling a silver bracelet from his wrist and handing it to him.

"I am most honored by your most gracious gift," he said, taking the offer and bowing in appreciation.

"What news do you have for us?" insisted Temujin, who was tired from the long ride and just wanted answers.

"Two women were brought into the Merkit camp a couple months ago. At first, they said nothing. They were beaten until it was determined which of them was Bourtai. Once she was identified, the woman was immediately given to Chilger," explained the Tumed.

"Chilger, who is Chilger?" asked Temujin with a bewildered look.

"As was explained to me, many years ago, your father stole a bride. Chilger is the son of the man whose bride your father took." explained the Tumed.

"Just as I thought. This is about revenge...revenge for my father's misdeeds," responded Temujin in a low and menacing voice. "I will have this Chilger's head on a stake!" he insisted loudly with a scowl.

"Do you know where this Chilger is keeping her?" asked Jamka.

"She is held in Chilger's ger," answered the Tumed. "She lives as his wife!"

Yasotay knew that look. That last statement enflamed Temujin's face bright red. All his facial muscles tensed up, and two large veins throbbed visibly on his forehead. Even his red hair seemed to percolate with anger. Yasotay knew of Temujin's tendencies, most notably his anger, which could boil over into fits of uncontrolled rage. But surprisingly, Temujin kept his emotions under control for now.

Yasotay asked, "What happened to the other girl?"

"The one who was not Bourtai?" asked the Tumed, "The other young girl...she is pretty too. They call her the honey badger because she is the difficult one!"

"Yes," said Altan, "the difficult one!" His voice trailed off.

"She was beaten and then sold to Darmala!" answered the Tumed offhandedly. "He paid a pretty price for that prickly princess. I know this because I overheard Darmala complaining about her to Usun and Beki. He was annoyed that he had paid so much for such a wild filly. Said that he would sooner have an angry honey badger in his bed than her!" The Tumed smiled and sighed. "That's where she got her name. Darmala's business is selling camels. He knows nothing of these things. Beki told him to beat her more, which he did, but she still fought him. Finally, sick of his complaining and wanting his money back, Usun promised to help him sell her to a slave trader on the Silu. So that's what he's doing. He'll end up making more money than he had originally invested."

NO! thought Yasotay, who felt like he had been punched in the gut. He looked over at Altan, whose face was blank; he looked stunned, trying to fathom her fate but couldn't.

"Where have they taken her?" asked Yasotay, breaking the silence after the initial shock and leaning in toward the Tumed.

"Nowhere yet. They are waiting for the buyer to arrive. I know this because I heard Darmala complaining about having to feed her until he comes and takes her away. He is such a fool...why complain? He stands to make good money!"

There was an awkward silence. Looking down at his feet, Baatar mouthed his rebuke but said nothing. This news washed over him, stirring an uncomfortable wave of emotion.

"Can you draw a map of the Merkit Camp?" asked Temujin.

"As I told you, I am a poor man!" the Tumed implored again.

Yasotay could feel the anger building inside him toward this vulture. He wanted to say: *Just give us the information we need, and we won't kill you!*

"We can discuss further payment, but first, I want to know what ger this Chilger lives in. Where is it?" demanded Temujin. He and Jamka took the Tumed aside to discuss the Merkit camp and its position in the valley. Yasotay, Altan, and Baatar huddled off to the side.

"What is this Silu?" asked Altan.

"It's a network of interconnected trade routes that cover the great expanse between the East and West, North and South," Yasotay explained. "Some of the trails are more dangerous than others. Large cities are located along the main routes, many surrounded by great walls. Everything from silk and wool fabrics to all types of scents, spices, and all manner of animals, including humans, are bought and sold along these routes," the matter-of-fact way Yasotay explained this only added to the shock of the incomprehensible situation that Baatar and Altan were experiencing.

There was a long silence while everyone thought about the Tumed's statement. Finally, Baatar blurted out much too loud, "I think he's lying! I mean a slave trader…I never heard of such a thing!" Baatar seemed to be in denial.

"When I was younger, I was asked by the head priest to decipher a book he had bought, which was written in Turkish. After carefully reviewing the manuscript, I found that it was a ledger of sales transactions. The book was from a merchant in the city of Turpan."

"I have heard of Turpan," said Altan. "It is to the west at least thirty days travel from here. It's a famous city where they brought water from the mountains to the desert by building the *Karez* tunnels."

"That is correct, Altan, the ancient wells of Karez. Now, this ledger showed the wide range of goods the merchant sold, and I remember being asked, 'What is the most common thing sold in Turpan?'" Yasotay hesitated and gave them time to prepare!

"Well?" asked Altan.

"The most lucrative and common goods this merchant sold by far were humans. He sold all manner of weapons, carts, wagons, and wheels, but what he sold most were slaves!" Yasotay whispered so lightly that Baatar and Altan strained to hear him.

"He said she is to be sold but hasn't been taken…yet," Baatar reminded everyone, "but what does that mean?"

"I would guess it means the buyer is coming to them," said Yasotay, searching for answers, "Whatever it means, we need to move quickly; instead, we sit and wait!" Yasotay bemoaned. They could hear the anger in his voice.

"Well then, let's go *now!*" Baatar was emphatic.

"Let's speak with the Tumed again. He may know where this Darmala is holding her," said Yasotay. Altan agreed, and motioning with his head, the three men rejoined Temujin and Jamka, who were still squeezing as much information from the Tumed as they could afford.

"This is good," said Temujin. "Your description of the camp was helpful." Temujin was pleased with what they had discovered and seemed done with the Tumed.

"I have one last question," said Yasotay, interrupting the Tumed's departure. "Do you know where the other woman is being held," he inquired.

"I am a poor…" the Tumed whined again.

"Yes, we know you're poor, here…" Baatar handed him a silver bracelet from his wrist, very similar to Jamka's.

"Blessings upon you, my young…" the Tumed started to say.

"Yes, just tell us the location." Baatar insisted.

The Tumed paused for a moment to collect his thoughts. "The Merkit Camp is north of here. No one can get within twenty *li* of the southern border without alerting them. You can't go around to the east without going through the narrow pass at the top of the Mother and Father Mountains. You cannot go west into Bayad-controlled land. The only way from here is to go directly north. Darmala is holding her at the northern end of the camp. He is one of their richest traders, and you cannot miss his lavish ger, or his large herd of camels, or him for that matter. Darmala is a man of great wealth, which is only exceeded by his great girth. He is as fat as one of his pregnant camels." The Tumed flashed them a crooked grin; he seemed to enjoy insulting Darmala. With a brief bow, the Tumed left. The seven of them stood awkwardly, looking at each other.

"We need to leave for the Merkit camp soon!" said Yasotay, coming out of his trance and looking like he was ready to go.

"No. What we need right now is patience," said Temujin. "The Tumed told us the Merkit are awaiting our invasion. They know of the six thousand that left the Jadaran. The Tumed also said the Merkit do not believe Togru will get involved."

"Can we trust what this Tumed says?" asked Yasotay.

"That is unclear, but I must convince Togru to provide us with at least six thousand warriors. With that size force, we will easily over-whelm the Merkit," said Temujin, "The Tumed is sure of it, and so am I!"

"We need to leave now!" responded Yasotay.

"We can NOT!" answered Altan loudly. Everyone became quiet and looked at him. "I love my daughter, but we cannot!" Altan said in a low voice with a dejected look, "We cannot attack without the additional men!" Yasotay could see the pain written on his face but knew he spoke the truth.

"Yasotay said we need to leave now. To save my betrothed, to save Tera!" pleaded Baatar.

His cousin reached out and gripped his arm. "Her father is right! We must not risk it! A direct assault on their camp with too small a force is too risky. When Togru returns, we will beseech him for more men, and then we will ride after Bourtai and Tera with a force that *cannot* be stopped!"

Yasotay nodded. "I understand that's the best approach." He then calmly continued, "But I must leave now! Just me. I don't need thousands of riders. I will steal one person…someone they don't care about! Tera is no prize to them; they intend to sell her off. I will pay this Darmala a visit, cut this throat, and get her back!"

"I agree," interjected Baatar. "Let's go!"

"Wait, Yasotay!" insisted Temujin. "You seem to forget that we have a battle to wage, and I need your help. I promise we will do everything to save Tera, but I must first convince Togru to give us warriors and then plan an attack to rescue Bourtai *and* Tera. I need your help with that. We are better off working together than separately. Yasotay, you promised me that you would help me. This is the help I need! I don't need you running off and getting yourself killed. Trying to sneak past the whole of the Merkit army is a fool's errand. Your chances of rescuing Tera will be better with a force of twelve thousand warriors riding with you against them!"

After a long silence, Yasotay said, "Temujin, I gave you my word to help save Bourtai, and I will honor that, but we need to move quickly!" Everyone stared back at him. Yasotay continued, "I have a thought. How many days is it to the Merkit Camp from here?"

"It's a three-day ride," answered Temujin, "and that's three full days."

"It took at least five days to prepare Jamka's army for travel. I am guessing it will take Togru's army at least that many days to get ready. If I leave here tonight, I can get there in two days, scout their defenses, and return long before the whole army is ready," stated Yasotay. It was obvious to everyone listening that Yasotay would not, could not, sit still. He clearly felt compelled to plunge forward *immediately*.

"If I leave now, the whole trip is five days. I will shorten the time by traveling all night. If you want me to help you plan, I will be of more assistance if I can see their camp, assess their readiness, identify the placement of their sentries, and return to help you plan our attack in four or five days. Togru may not even return before then," said Yasotay, convinced by the soundness of his plan.

Temujin thought for a long moment. "Fine, Yasotay, I understand. I have seen you get by on less sleep for more days. If you say you will return, then you will return. I will go along with your plan," he said.

"You can take three of my best horses," said Jamka. "Temujin, I think this is a good plan…gathering as much information as possible before we strike."

"'If you know the enemy and know yourself, you need not fear the result of a hundred battles!'" quoted Yasotay with a smile. He enjoyed quoting the masters even when nobody knew the reference.

"Sun Tzu, from the Art of War!" said Temujin, smiling in return.

Yasotay said in surprise, "That is correct!"

"You see, I am listening when you speak endlessly on these long journeys," said Temujin with a hint of sarcasm.

"I will ride with you, Yasotay!" said Baatar.

"No, I'm sorry, but you cannot come with me," insisted Yasotay, who then turned to Altan. "I know you want to come, but truthfully, it's better I go alone."

"I was with you on the northern pass. I saw how you climbed over the mountain. You go where few of us can follow. I respect your wishes," replied Altan.

Baatar kicked the dirt in frustration. Jamka turned to him. "You cannot go. This trip is too dangerous," he insisted. "You must listen to Yasotay!" Jamka knew that young Baatar looked up to Yasotay. "You will only serve to slow him down! And get both of you caught."

Baatar said nothing. They had all heard the stories of Yasotay's ability to accomplish extraordinary feats, which was precisely what they needed right now. With the issue settled, Yasotay excused himself and walked toward where his boots were awaiting him.

"Jamka, I will accompany Yasotay to camp and see that he gets the horses he needs. I will sleep tonight with the warriors in the field. Do you have any messages for the minghan commanders?" asked Baatar.

"Yes, tell them to get comfortable. We will be staying here for the next three to five days. I will return to meet with them in the morning," said Jamka. "Make sure he gets three of my best steeds for his travels."

"As you wish, I will handle it," said Baatar, quickly saying their goodbyes. Baatar followed Yasotay out to their horses.

"Temujin, let's get Yandas," said Jamka, "to show us where we can sleep. I am tired from the trail and need some rest."

Yasotay and Baatar rode quickly toward the temporary camp that Jamka's forces had established roughly five li from Togru's camp. The sun was on the edge of the horizon, glowing a brilliant orange. The remainder of the sky was a deeper orange, with a ceiling of blue clouds, the bottoms of which held a deep orange hue. The trail was well-worn, winding through the fields of dead grasses and bushes. You could see green sprouts beneath the dead growth, stretching to replace their ancestral remnants.

"I know what you're planning!" insisted Yasotay, slowing his pace. He had a severe look on his face.

"Plan…what plan are you talking about?" asked Baatar, making his best effort to play dumb.

"You say that you came to get me horses and sleep with the warriors. But you plan to wait till I leave, then you intend to follow me!" said Yasotay. He sounded irritated, not wanting to play this silly game. "Don't deny it…it's the truth."

Baatar started to say something but then slumped in his saddle. His slouching shoulders showed he had given up on the ruse. "The truth be told, I am confident I would not slow you down. I am not like Altan. He is old. I don't question that he is a good fighter, but he is not as quick as us. He has left his days of youth behind. While I may not fight like you, I can run as fast, hide as well, and ride even faster. I can help. This trip is all about riding, hiding, and observing, and I can do that as well as you. As a matter of fact, I can ride better than you and shoot a bow as well as you. So why not take me?"

"You seem to have a well-thought-out piece of logic…and yet if I still say no, will you respect my wishes?" asked Yasotay. "Remember, you were already deceitful once, and I knew!"

"I guess you must first tell me no, and then...*we will see* once you leave!" answered Baatar in a playful manner with a wry little grin.

"Uh-huh," muttered Yasotay under his breath, thinking.

While riding in silence, both men were assailed by their worst fears about Tera's troubles. These thoughts starkly contrasted with the beautiful orange glow of the sunset on the sea of clouds overhead. As they approached the temporary camp, Yasotay slowed and announced, "I need to stop for a moment and relieve myself!"

"That sounds like a good idea. I could use a moment myself," said Baatar. "Oh, I wanted to give you something!" Baatar had a large leather bag attached to his saddle, where he carried his bow. He opened it and inside were two bows. "I made this for you!" Baatar pulled out a bow and handed it to Yasotay. It was a beautifully crafted weapon. It had a leather grip that was comfortable in his hand and a bright white tovh at either end of the bow where the ends of the string were seated. It was an example of true nomadic craftsmanship.

"If you can, I would rather you not break this over someone's head!" said Baatar. "I spent many days making you one of the best bows on the steppe!"

"This is a remarkable weapon," said Yasotay, humbled and appreciative of the gesture. But, while holding the bow in front of him, he realized, "I cannot take this. It's too much. You are too kind."

"You can, and you must. I spent months making this bow for you! I included a small change that makes its draw a little tighter. Its power is amazing. I think you will love it," said Baatar, beaming with pride. Yasotay realized that Jamka was right. Baatar looked up to him; you could see it on his face. He was thrilled that Yasotay was so impressed with his work.

After a quick nature call and a minor alteration to the rider's situation, the two were back on the trail headed toward the camp. Though now, they proceeded much slower than before...something was different!

"I know you're mad at me...for now...but remember not coming with me is in your best interests, Baatar!" said Yasotay, "and you know that I will make every effort to save Tera. I think you should accept your

EYE OF THE NOMAD

situation as I plan to do myself and press on. You can certainly understand the solid *logic* in my counterargument…can't you?"

"UUUuuummmmm," muttered Baatar, who could not speak
because Yasotay had gagged him. He had tied Baatar up like a goat,
ready to be sheared. Yasotay bound his hands and feet into submission
and threw him belly down over his horse, which was currently "riding"
alongside him.

"I knew you would agree! And I truly love this bow. It is a piece of
craftsmanship like few others. You should be very proud," insisted Yasotay with a broad smile.

"Uuumm, um, um, ummm, um," said Baatar, his face glowing red
with anger straining to be heard.

"Yes, you are welcome; you deserve it. It is lucky for you that I had a
clean piece of cloth for that gag in your mouth," said Yasotay. "Trust me,
you do not want to know where the only other piece of cloth I could have
used for a gag has been!" Yasotay made a funny, wincing look on his
face. "It would not have been good!" Baatar kicked and screamed, none
of which amounted to much. Yasotay rode into camp with a big smile on
his face, searching for and finally finding one of the minghan captains.

"Careful, you need to be careful, or you will fall off!" said Yasotay to
the wriggling Baatar. He then turned to the general. "Hello, good evening. Jamka asked me to hand this young man over to you and tell you
and your men to make themselves comfortable. He said we will be staying here for at least three to five days," explained Yasotay. "Additionally,
he said he would return in the morning to deal with young Baatar here
and his inappropriate behavior. But in the meantime, your instructions
are to keep him tied up until he arrives."

"UUUuuummmmm, um, uuumm," grunted Baatar.

"He's been bucking like that all the way from camp! And I need
some horses. I must run a quick errand. Jamka told me to take his fastest steeds. Can you help with that?" Yasotay asked with a smile, patting
Baatar on the back of his head. "Uuumm, um, uuumm," grunted Baatar
in short bursts, trying desperately to be heard. "Remember, Jamka was

clear to keep him restrained and safe...he will deal with him in the morning!"

"Yes, Yasotay, if you will come with me," said the minghan leader. "You, warrior, take Baatar here, get him off that horse, and make him comfortable, but leave the restraints on!" One of the warriors walked up to lead Baatar's horse away.

Yasotay couldn't help but take some parting jabs. "I truly hope you don't mind, Baatar, but I have borrowed your quiver of arrows. You see, I have this beautiful new bow and may need them. I want you to remember that 'all deceit has its punishments and rewards.' I believe that saying is from a holy book; I can't recall which.... Anyway, be safe, my friend, and *we will see* once I return!"

After collecting the horses and his gear, Yasotay caught the last bright orange rays of the setting sun as he headed down the trail. The colors had nearly faded away, and all that remained was the shadow of an orange glow as Yasotay traveled on, riding hard directly north on the trail to the Merkit camp. Yasotay didn't actually have a plan, but he knew he had to go.

Back at camp the next morning, Jamka finally began to untie Baatar. "So, I am waiting to hear what happened?" asked Jamka after giving him a drink of water. There was a long pause, and Baatar didn't say a word. "Since it appears you're having trouble with explaining yourself, let me take a guess: you told Yasotay, or he figured out that you planned to follow him. I'll bet he knew, as did I, that it was odd for you to willingly choose to sleep in the field instead of in a comfortable ger with blankets and pillows. Since he did not want you following him, he tied you up and instructed the minghan captain to make sure that I dealt with you in the morning...did I miss anything?" asked Jamka.

Baatar hesitated for a moment, remembering the consequences of his last deception. "No, my cousin...I am sorry," Baatar reluctantly muttered, dropping his head in shame and disappointment.

Yasotay rode through the first night. He could clearly see the beaten trail by the moonlight running off to the north. A trick he learned from Temujin during their longer trips was to hook his deel sleeves into the saddle, which gives a rider enough stability to nap while riding overnight. Though Temujin had warned Yasotay that he had seen several people fall too deep into sleep, only to find themselves woken up the hard way. It may not have been real sleep, but it was rest. Yasotay didn't know why, but ever since he was young, he had never required much sleep. Late in the evening of the second day, Yasotay stopped and slept on the ground for one shi. Coupled with the light naps he had taken while moving, he found himself in the saddle and alert, looking ahead for the first sign of a sentry.

He started to slow when he smelled a dung fire. After proceeding cautiously for a short while, he could see the faint smoke trail spiraling into the night sky. It was dark out, but the slight amount of moonlight was of some help. Yasotay tied off the three horses just off the trail and crept as close as he dared to the burning fire.

He could see one guard was sitting up, wide awake, whittling a piece of wood with a small dagger. Yasotay assumed that this guard had pulled the short straw and, as a result, had late-night duty. From what Yasotay could count, seven other similarly dressed men were lying asleep on the ground. At least ten or eleven horses were tied off to the far right side of the camp. Like the whittling guard, all seven were close to the burning fire. There was no chance of riding his horses past these guards. He wasn't sure, but he assumed they were Merkit. If they were to wake, it would mean trouble. The Tumed had said that the first line of sentries was twenty li from the Merkit Camp. It was long past midnight, and Yasotay was hopeful the distance was much shorter because now he was traveling on foot.

He snuck around the guard post, giving a wide berth to the collection of men and horses, and worked his way past them back onto the trail a short distance away. He knew that he didn't have much time until the sun came up. And due to the flat, open nature of the terrain, making him an easy target, Yasotay had few options—so he ran.

Keeping a solid pace for a short amount of time, he started to slow when he sensed he was coming upon another collection of sentries. This turned out to be a much larger group of warriors, with two guards awake, one pacing back and forth and another just sitting at the fire and staring into the darkness. Behind them, Yasotay could see, even with the limited light, a large valley with hundreds of gers laid out in front of him. He found a very inconspicuous spot, away from the warriors, to rest and await the sunrise. He wanted a better view of the camp, and unfortunately, the only way that would happen was for him to patiently await daybreak.

It was a while until the first light of day illuminated the Merkit camp. He could see a river to the west and a mountainside to the east. The gers were spread out across a wide area. Yasotay saw there was no way around to the northern side of the camp without going directly through the camp itself. There were sentries posted at short intervals along the trail. This would be a problem since word of an attack would spread quickly through the camp. A surprise attack would be difficult, if not impossible. The result would be that warriors at the camp's northern end would have the time to prepare for a fight or the best chance of escaping the battle.

Yasotay left his spot as dawn broke. He hoped to get a head start on the sleeping guards, who were beginning to stir. He had acquired a good sense of the camp's layout and sentry postings. He thought of trying to sneak past the sentries to the east, going around to the north that way. There was this fat camel salesman whom he wished to pay a visit to, but Temujin was right! It was too risky. Even if he did reach Tera, he would have to steal a horse or a camel and evade the thousands of Merkit that would be chasing them. Hopefully, he would get his chance soon. Yasotay committed what he saw to memory, and unless he wanted to lose his horses, he needed to head back the way he came. Resigned to return to Togru's camp, Yasotay ran back up the trail. He noticed a small stream of smoke rising skyward to the east and another further up to the west. The Merkit appeared to have guards stationed on either flank of the forward guard posts and further back too. Yasotay made a mental note of this layout and kept running.

As he approached the furthest outpost, the one he had first come upon, Yasotay spotted only two sentries when originally there were eight. This meant six sentries were patrolling the area. Yasotay darted quickly and quietly around their little campfire to where he had left his horses. As he crept closer to the spot, he found one of the sentries standing there with his back to him, looking through the bags on his horse. Yasotay crept closer. Using the end of his staff, he tapped the man's shoulder. Slightly startled by the poke that interrupted his rummaging, he turned to look around. He never made it all the way. Using the end of his staff, Yasotay popped him hard on the side of his jaw. He went down with his forearms pointed up, hand in the air in an awkward position, trying to stop something that had already happened. This one was going to need some undisturbed rest. Yasotay didn't want to chance another sentry coming upon him, so he collected his horses and quietly headed south back to Togru's camp. The return trip was long and relatively uneventful. He passed just a few travelers going in the opposite direction.

Yasotay arrived, as he predicted, on the fifth day. Jamka's army was still stationed a short way from Togru's camp, and Jamka was there meeting with his lead minghan captain.

"Yasotay, it is good to see you made it back," said Jamka with a smile.

"Is Togru back?" Yasotay asked.

"He returned yesterday evening. Togru had gone to negotiate with the Tangut. But thankfully, he has returned. Temujin wants you to join us this evening. Temujin and I are to become anda! We are to swear it in blood tonight. He gave me the gold belt that Togru had given his father when they became anda." Yasotay could see the wide leather belt trimmed in gold with a solid gold clasp around Jamka's waist. A skilled craftsman had made this belt. It was of immense importance to Temujin, Togru, and now Jamka, who wore it proudly.

"That's great." Yasotay paused. "And Togru. Did he commit warriors to our cause?"

"He promised that we would talk about it tonight. Togru is interested to hear what you uncovered," said Jamka, shoving his thumb under his belt, apparently satisfied with it. "I left Temujin to speak with Togru while I worked on readying the troops for battle with my ming-han leaders."

"I take it Baatar is fine?" Yasotay asked, curious about the young man, not seeing him approach.

"You said it was a clean rag?" interrupted Baatar, walking up to them.

"No, I said you were lucky I had that rag because my other rag…" Yasotay smiled, glad to see Baatar wasn't holding a grudge.

They shook hands. "You will be happy to know that I have your quiver here with not one arrow shy from when I borrowed it," proclaimed Yasotay.

"That's fine. I have more," answered Baatar. "Please keep them!"

"Were you able to gather any information regarding sentry positions and the layout of their camp?" asked Jamka.

"Yes. I can draw a map of the camp and the locations of the sentries, along with rough numbers. It's a large camp with thousands of gers spread over a wide area. There are three main Merkit groups. When coming to the camp from the south, there is a river to the west and mountains to the east. Our options are limited. When I say spread out over a large area, I mean a vast area. If we were to try to attack from the west, we would have to cross the river…twice."

"Attacking from the west would also require us to move through Bayad territory," added Jamka, "Not wise!"

"And to the east is the mountain range crowned by Father Mountain. So, unless we are to fly, an attack from either the east or west is out. Our only approach is from the south. We will first have to contend with several sentry outposts because if we want to maintain the element of surprise, we must stop them from riding off and notifying the camp to prepare for our approach," explained Yasotay.

"This is all good. Additionally, did you identify where all the sentries are located?" asked Jamka.

"Yes, we can discuss that in detail with the group. When are we meeting with them?" inquired Yasotay.

"Later today."

"Good, so I can get some sleep," Yasotay said in relief.

"The minghan captain has a comfortable spot for you over there," Jamka said, motioning to a small, shaded area that looked like the perfect spot for getting some rest without the worry of falling from your horse. "I will be working with my minghan leaders all afternoon. Rest, and I will wake you when it's time to leave."

"Thank you, Jamka." Yasotay yawned, stretching his arms over his head. "I could use a nap. I had little time to sleep these past five days!"

"I understand," said Jamka with a chuckle, recalling the distance Yasotay had just covered in such a short time. He had traveled that way many times in the past, and it was difficult. Yasotay fell fast asleep soon after setting his head down. Jamka gave him most of the afternoon before waking him to join Temujin. Jamka and Baatar rode with Yasotay through the various sentries to Togru's main hall.

"It's good to see you have returned safely," Temujin greeted Yasotay warmly. "I've spoken with Togru several times and am confident he will help us!"

"This is good news," Yasotay said, encouraged that progress had been made in his absence. "I have some valuable information that we should discuss regarding the enemy's sentries and camp layout."

"Yes, good, but first, we need to talk with Togru. He was asking about you," said Temujin.

Just at that moment, Togru entered the ger. The various groups scattered about stopped talking and turned to watch him as silence crept into the room. His robes hung low, covering his feet, making it look like he hovered across the room. Those who had gathered in the room gave Togru a wide berth. The protocol was only to approach him if he called upon you, and in that case, you were expected to come quickly. Togru didn't hesitate with formality. He moved straight over to Temujin and Yasotay, who stood beside Jamka and Baatar. Stopping in front of Yasotay, he extended his arms in greeting. Yasotay placed his hands under Togru's elbows, showing the customary respect.

"It is good to see you have returned, Yasotay," said Togru in a friendly voice. "I hope your scouting trip bore good results…what did you learn?"

"I learned that it will be very difficult to attack the Merkit camp by surprise but not impossible. I agree with the common belief that using overwhelming numbers and attacking from the south is best…I have an idea of how we may still use a surprise strategy to our advantage. Sentries are located on the main trail into the camp from the south twelve to thirteen li from the camp. They are stationed throughout their southern border, which means they are there intentionally to detect and communicate any large attack from the south to the main camp," explained Yasotay. "We must use an approach that shuts down their lines of communication with a smaller force that targets these sentries."

"You sound like someone who has a plan," observed Togru. "Please continue!"

"I do! Our best approach is to send two small teams, no more than twenty riders each, ahead of the main force. Traveling in stealth, they will neutralize the forward sentries. Upon approaching the outskirts of the Merkit camp, they will await the remaining force to join them. This approach could improve our ability to surprise the Merkit and ensure a quick and decisive victory. Since the two kidnapped women are being held in two locations within the large camp, we should have those same two groups of riders focus solely on finding the prisoners, one team searching for Bourtai, the other for Tera. At the same time, the bulk of our warriors will be directly engaged with the enemy," explained Yasotay.

"How large of an army do you feel we require to assure our victory?" asked Togru, who was thoroughly engaged by Yasotay's clear and concise description of the situation and his approach.

"They are spread out over a wide area, which will fracture our forces. I feel confident an additional eight to ten thousand riders will be more than sufficient," answered Yasotay. "As we've been told, the Merkit have eight thousand warriors, at most. With ten thousand additional warriors, we would have twice their number!"

"And you believe that these numbers, along with your planned element of surprise, will defeat them?" asked Togru.

"Yes," answered Yasotay. "I do."

"Do you agree with your friend, Temujin?" asked Togru, shifting his gaze to him.

"This is the first I have heard of this plan since Yasotay's return. Regarding the Merkit camp's layout and advance guards, I agree that we can successfully take their camp by attacking in numbers. I am confident that ten thousand more riders will suffice…if Jamka agrees!" responded Temujin.

"Wise answer, Temujin. You always hear from your anda before making a final decision," said Togru, pleased with his response. "And what say you, Jamka?" asked Togru.

"I agree with Yasotay's assessment and his approach to the attack," answered Jamaka.

"Good, then it is settled. I will assign a tumen with ten thousand men to join your efforts. Together, we will deal with the Merkit," responded Togru, turning and walking to the dais to sit in his chair. "I have needed to deal with these pesky Merkit people for many years." On his way, he stopped and made the sign of the cross before the painting of Jesus knocking on a door. As he sat, one of his aides brought him a bowl of water. Using it to wash his hands, he then dried them with a white cloth draped over the aide's arm. Next came another aide with another bowl of water. Togru sat, and this aide knelt before him and washed his bare feet. He toweled them dry with another white cloth. The eyes of everyone in the room were fixated on this washing ritual.

Yasotay's mind drifted to the memory of his last bath. It was the one with Tera. The image of Tera standing there naked and repeating that silly children's rhyme came vividly to mind. He glanced over at Baatar, who was staring at him, and it immediately made him feel uncomfortable. It was as if he could read his thoughts.

After an intentional dramatic pause, Togru continued, "So, now that our plan for the attack on the Merkit has been decided, next is the matter of the blood union of Jamka and Temujin as anda brothers. Do you still intend to commit to each other in the bond of blood?"

"Yes, Togru," answered Temujin and Jamka simultaneously as they stepped forward.

"Good. Your first act as blood brothers will be to defeat the Merkit," responded Togru. "Yandas, if you would, please."

Yandas was waiting to be called upon, standing on the side of the dais. He held a large platter with two decorative daggers and a small bowl of ayrag, the traditional fermented mare's milk drink. Yandas walked toward Temujin and Jamka, holding the platter out before him. Both Temujin and Jamka took a blade from the platter. Taking the daggers in their left hand, both men pulled the blades across their right wrists. They then grasped each other's upper right forearms with their right hands. This commingled their bleeding wounds. Yandas took the bowl of ayrag and hovered it beneath the pair's wounded embrace. Droplets of blood mixed into the ayrag, and when Yandas felt he had gotten enough, he placed the bowl back on the platter. Next, he handed each of them a small strip of white cloth. Temujin took a strip of cloth and carefully wrapped Jamka's wound. Once done, Jamka did the same, wrapping Temujin's wrist. Temujin reached over and grabbed the bowl of ayrag.

"I make this covenant to Jamka, my anda, my brother whose blood now flows in me!" Temujin raised the bowl to his lips and drank from it. When done, he handed it to Jamka.

"I make this covenant to Temujin, my anda, my brother whose blood now flows in me!" Jamka said, then drank from the bowl, placing it back on Yandas's platter. Jamka's blood had already begun to seep through the white cloth around his wrist. Both men grasped each other's arms again, now also clapping their left hand on the other's right shoulder as they had done so many times in the past. The in-unison claps made a loud smacking sound, and everyone in the room cheered with big smiles. This was a joyous moment for the two…for everyone.

"Let us eat and celebrate this union of blood, and we will toast our upcoming victory," announced Togru.

Those who'd come to witness the ritual began to file out of the main hall. A smaller group funneled into an area where food awaited their arrival. Boiled lamb and horse, along with curds, herbs, and cheeses, were provided along with copious amounts of ayrag. Togru's entourage thinned out from thirty-five or forty to five or six. Altan, Baatar, Borchu, Jamka's counselor, and Yasotay followed behind Temujin and Jamka.

"So, I must ask, the formality of the ritual appeared well planned. Did you practice this custom earlier?" Yasotay was curious.

Jamka answered, "Yes, Togru explained the anda ritual earlier today. He planned the ceremonial part of the ritual once we expressed our interest in becoming blood brothers."

"Soon, we will ride north and destroy the Merkit," said Temujin, looking directly at Yasotay. "This plan of yours to send advance squads... I like it. I should head up the first group, and Altan or Baatar can lead the second. It makes sense to have Jamka lead the main force while I lead the rescue. You, Yasotay, will ride with me. Once we neutralize the sentries, we will save Bourtai. Altan, Tera's father, and her betrothed Baatar will be tasked to find and save Tera." Temujin hesitated and, in a meek tone, said, "As long as Jamka approves of this approach?"

"Yes, you're recommending I lead sixteen thousand men into battle. I would be a fool or a coward not to agree!" said Jamka with a smile and a pat on Temujin's back.

Yasotay was distracted thinking. He desperately wanted to present some logical reason why he should be part of Altan's squad, looking for Tera, but he couldn't find one that wouldn't betray the secret of how he felt about her.

"I don't think Baatar should even participate, let alone lead an advance group into battle," argued Yasotay.

"I agree," Temujin said in a low tone, not wanting Baatar to overhear. "He's too young, but do you honestly believe you can stop him? What are you going to do, tie him up again?"

"No, I'm just saying I agree Altan should lead the second group. I would rather have Baatar with me or leave him with Jamka. You certainly should lead the first group, but with Altan in charge of the second group, it will be difficult for him to keep an eye on Baatar. I strongly recommend that Baatar stays with his cousin Jamka, who is his family."

Yasotay would have trouble trying to recall the rest of the night. He could remember drinking with Jamka and Temujin and toasting their coming victory over the Merkit. He was still exhausted from the five days of constant riding. This, mixed with the alcohol, made the remainder of the night a blur. He did remember talking to Baatar, who was, again, insistent that he would be the one to save Tera. Yasotay grew bored as he listened to Baatar ramble on about bow designs and other things that, at that moment, held no interest in Yasotay's mind. He needed more sleep.

Later that evening, Temujin explained that it had been decided. Altan would lead the second group, but Jamka would not refuse Baatar from riding with Altan. Yasotay wanted to fight this decision; *Bataar was going to get himself killed.* Yasotay had accepted the fact that Tera couldn't be his, but there was nothing that was going to stop him from doing everything he could to save her. He certainly didn't want to see Baatar get killed. Yasotay strongly questioned young Baatar's involvement in this rescue. He sensed that Baatar would be more distraction than help. He hated the part of himself that whispered in his mind, *if Baatar is killed, then Tera is mine!*

CHAPTER ELEVEN

Merkit Territory, late spring, 1179 CE

It was four long, excruciating days of waiting for Togru's army to get ready to depart. The logistical aspects of gathering provisions and planning supply lines took much longer than Yasotay expected, but he couldn't argue with the results. Their army was impressive. Sixteen thousand warriors were riding to save Bourtai and Tera, whereas six weeks ago, they had less than twenty riders.

It was late afternoon on the third day of travel when they came upon the first visual marker Yasotay had placed in his mind. He had calculated that this spot was roughly twenty-five li from the main camp and well over ten li from the first group of eight Merkit sentries he had discovered last week. It was the perfect place for an invading army to camp, with only a short ride in the morning to their target. Yasotay remembered this spot from the distinct bowl-shaped hill, with veins of rock jutting out from the hillside and grass that grew everywhere the rock was not. There were two wild camels, a cow, and a bull standing at the foot of the hill, grazing in an open field large enough to host an army three times the size of their horde.

"Temujin, this is the spot. We are just under half a shi horse ride from the main Merkit camp," announced Yasotay. Temujin and Jamka were riding alongside him with Baatar, Altan, and Borchu close behind, "It's roughly quarter a shi ride to their forward sentries," he added.

"Here is where we camp for the night," said Temujin. With a signal from one of the tumen leaders, the rolling wave of horses and men came to a slow stop. With no more than a hand motion, the empty valley, where only two camels stood moments ago, was now filled with sixteen thousand men setting up a camp spread out at the base of the hill. Once they were settled, Yasotay, Temujin, Altan, and Jamka met with Jamka's counselor, the two tumen commanders (one was Jamka's and the other Togru's man), and Baatar.

As Yasotay began to outline his plan again, all eyes were fixed on him. "We are twenty-five li south of the main Merkit camp," said Yasotay, drawing a line in the dirt with a stick. "The camp is here," he said, drawing a cloud at one end of the line, "and we are here," where he drew a cloud at the other end. "There are forward sentries posted here, under twelve li from their main camp." Yasotay drew an X roughly a third of the way along the line from them. "A main sentry post is here," he drew another X much closer to the Merkit camp, "which is only two li away from the main camp."

"How many again are in their forward sentry post?" asked Temujin.

"There are only eight to ten sentries at the post here," he pointed with the stick. "We can assume they send out regular patrols from this forward post during the day. Then, they have roughly one hundred men stationed here at the main sentry post closest to the main camp," Yasotay added, using the stick to point to the X closest to the Merkit camp.

"I watched their movements, and the men from the main post patrol this wide space between their forward sentries and their main sentry post here two li away from the camp." The others nodded their heads. "As I told Togru, we will send two squads of twenty riders to approach the forward post in secrecy from both sides." Yasotay pointed again with his stick.

"The two groups will verify that the Merkit defenses are still as they were six days ago," explained Yasotay. "We will send one rider back to the main group to notify Jamka to ride. The two advance squads will neutralize the eight forward sentries and then spread out, slowly working their way north toward the main Merkit Camp, dispatching all those they may come upon."

" ... without alerting the others," Temujin emphasized.

"Once notified that all is as planned, Jamka will lead the army's charge from here. The horde will ride hard directly for the main camp. They will face no resistance until reaching here!" Yasotay pointed to the X closest to the Merkit Camp, "They will easily overcome this post, and once they have regrouped, go on to attack the heart of the Merkit camp by surprise, overwhelming it and assuring our victory. While this attack is underway, the advance groups will work to find and rescue the two hostages."

"Yasotay and I will lead the first team to rescue Bourtai. Altan and Baatar will lead the second to save Tera," Temujin added.

"We need to identify forty men who will ride with the two rescue groups," said Yasotay.

Temujin looked at the two tumen leaders. "You each can provide twenty of your best men?"

"Yes," they both answered, one immediately after the other.

"Do we have any questions?" asked Temujin, who paused momentarily. "Good. Have the forty men join us at the northern end of camp, now!" Temujin paused and thought a moment, then asked, "Have we set up sentries around our perimeter?"

One of the two tumen leaders stepped forward. "Yes, Temujin, we have established a perimeter. No one passes to or from the Merkit camp tonight."

"To our success," Temujin proclaimed, raising his sword, which resulted in a large cheer from all those listening.

Yasotay could tell that Temujin was comfortable being in charge. This battle, including the inner workings of a large combat force, was the first he had ever been called upon to manage. From discussions of how the attack would proceed to what enemy units they could expect to engage in and how the terrain could give advantages, Temujin was in his element. It was his first real chance to prove he could lead an army. He needed a decisive victory to establish his reputation as a great leader of men. Many were watching Temujin to see how he performed in a leadership role, and Temujin knew it. Temujin, his ego on full display, had confided in as much, saying, "I am a born leader of men." Yasotay wondered what was more important to him: saving Bourtai or wielding such immense power?

"I can break her!" insisted Guiyu. His short, slender, and wiry physique appeared to be coiled like a snake, arms crossed at his chest, right leg over his left, sitting on a bench in Darmala's ger. "You will see. It's just a matter of time…and the right amount of…" he stammered with a menacing look, searching for the right word while nervously switching his left leg over his right, "…encouragement."

He had a raspy, harsh tone with a heavy Turkish accent. "It's like breaking a beautiful wild horse," Guiyu explained. "The horse knows it's a magnificent creature, and because it knows that, it does not easily succumb…it takes time, pressure, and persistence." He spoke in a slow and deliberate tone. "Some break easier than others…but they all break!"

"She has been nothing but difficult!" said Darmala, exasperated, the rolls under his chin jiggling. "I have beaten her so many times my arms are tired!" he added, licking the juices from his chubby fingers one at a time.

Guiyu thought to himself, *Darmala looks like someone who would tire getting up from a seated position.* Darmala dropped a lamb bone into a bowl, sitting next to his large carcass of flesh.

"Did you leave any permanent marks?" asked Guiyu. His beady eyes darted to the fat, smelly man whose gluttony appeared to have no limit.

"No, of course not!" said Darmala. Rolls of blubber around his waist shifted to his right as he reached into a bowl to grab the bone end of another lamb chop. His four servants knew that he liked the bowl to be full of his favorite foods. He would keep it just out of easy reach. It was a foolish notion, but he believed it would help reduce the amount of food he ate.

"If she is young and pretty, there is value in that. If you disfigured her while trying to break her," insisted Guiyu, "it reduces her value to my buyers." Guiyu paused, "It's pristine, young nubile bodies...that is what sells!"

"You said you are also looking to buy some camels?" asked Darmala. "I have some of the finest camels in the land."

"Yes, but let's first see the girl, and then we can talk more," replied Guiyu.

Guiyu had just arrived after a long journey. It was late evening, but he was still ready to do business. He had come through the Altai Gap, the only mountain pass along the wall of mountain ranges that ran north from Manchu to Afghana. Guiyu traded in all kinds of wares, and his most common route was between the Naiman territory in the east and the Kara, who controlled the Altai Gap and the city of Turpan to the west. Rarely did Guiyu travel this far east, but he had heard of Darmala and his large herd of camels and felt he could make some fortuitous trades. Guiyu's caravan comprised seven large wagons filled with a wide assortment of goods, forty camels, a handful of horses, four servants, and twenty hireling fighting men. At least four camels pulled each wagon. Guiyu found that camels were the best animals for transporting his traveling marketplace instead of horses or oxen. Camels could cover long distances over rough terrain with minimal effort, carry heavy loads, and survive on limited vegetation. They could also travel for many days without water and were the perfect beasts of burden for Guiyu's purposes.

"Please, follow me. I will take you to her," instructed Darmala, throwing a lamb bone aside as he struggled to rise from his seated position.

"Trust me, she will welcome the notion of willingly warming someone's bed once I have introduced her to the art of submission," declared Guiyu, standing up and revealing his diminutive stature. "I have never had one I couldn't break!" His voice projected a far more sinister nature than his small physique exhibited.

They found Tera in a ger a short distance away. Her hands were tied behind her to a large stake driven into the ground. She was sitting there with her legs in front of her. It appeared she had been trying to escape by pulling on the stake behind her back. Working it back and forth, it was almost loose. She was but moments from tearing herself free.

Darmala, understanding the situation immediately, stuck his head out of the ger, yelling into the night air. "She is escaping! I told you to watch her closely, and now she's escaping! Where are my three worthless sons!"

Guiyu walked behind Tera and, using his foot, pushed the stake back into the ground and stepped on Tera's hands in the process.

"Aaahhh," yelled Tera through her gagged mouth. She jerked her fingers out from under his boot.

"You see, Darmala, this is the problem right here. Look how comfortable she is...you're giving her too much freedom." Guiyu pulled a cord from his pocket and wrapped it around her feet. Driving his foot into the side of her shoulder, he rolled her onto her belly. Placing his knee on Tera's back, he quickly untied her hands from behind her back, freeing her from the stake. Roughly maneuvering her free hands, he immediately tied them up behind her head. Next, he ran the remaining cord from her feet to the cord around her hands. *And pulled*! Tera was fully stretched out on the ground with her tied-up hands connected to her tied-up feet behind her. Guiyu had done this before.

"AAAHHhhhhhhh," screamed Tera, her face reddened with pain. Holding her breath, she was in an excruciatingly uncomfortable position of submission.

"See, you stretch to the point when they yell out in pain, and then you tie it off there!" Guiyu quickly knotted off the end and ensured she couldn't reach it with her fingers. "This is how you leave them tied up!" Tera could be heard lightly grunting under the stress this position put on her shoulders, back, and legs. For the first couple of moments, she thought she would pass out. Next, Guiyu inspected her body like someone buying a goat or a horse, opening her deel to squeeze her arms, legs, and breasts. Next, he pulled her top up and pants down and ran his hand across the skin of her taut belly. He admired her torso for a lingering moment. He proceeded to run that hand across every curve of her perfectly tense, light-brown body. Then, smelling his fingers, he licked the tip of his index finger with a quick double-flick of his tongue. A relaxed smile slowly crossed his face.

"Some minor bruising, nothing major!" said Guiyu, holding Tera's straining face in his hands. He removed her gag to inspect her teeth, lifting her lip. "Her teeth look good," her face sneered as she experienced this degrading assessment of her physical worth.

"She is pretty. That should…" Just then, Tera turned her head to the side and bit at Guiyu's hand. He quickly moved it. Darmala flinched; he was startled by the *crack* her teeth made crashing together.

"Ah, so you have some spirit, don't you!" said Guiyu, roughly placing the gag back over her mouth, and then he slapped her hard across the face, which made Darmala jump again.

He grabbed Tera's face in his hand and came close up, face to face with her! "If you bite me, I can assure you it will be the last time you bite anything with those teeth." His foul breath caused Tera to experience a wave of nausea. Guiyu then stepped back and considered her for a moment. "I see why you call her Honey Badger." Guiyu reached over and pulled on the cord, which was already fully taut. This elicited a loud "AAAaaahhhhhh." Tera's face went flush red again and then a deathly white. This time, for a short moment, she did pass out.

"You will yield…I can assure you of that," Guiyu said, his voice low and grave. "The ride back to Turpan will be long and painful for this one. I will turn your Honey Badger into a kitten wanting nothing more than to cuddle!"

"Come, let us return to my ger, and we can have a drink and discuss the price for my camels," implored Darmala. "You mentioned you're leaving tomorrow?"

"Yes, this trip has taken longer than I expected. I will take this one off your hands. I like how she looks…I may train her to warm my own bed!" Guiyu said, laughing harder than necessary at his own words.

Yasotay woke up well before dawn. Today was finally the day! He grabbed Tera's blanket and went out to find a spot. Perched high on a rock, the valley filled with a sleeping army was nothing more than a shadow in the night. The waxing quarter moon shone brightly, giving everything in the small cauldron-shaped valley at the base of the hill an odd glow. In his solitude, his mind began to paint a picture of the upcoming battle, contemplating the possible outcomes. Questions flickered through his mind like the distant dancing stars that sparkled in the heavens. Then, a gentle hush descended on the chatter of thoughts in his mind until the silence seemed to fill his little cocoon and all the world around with two simple words: *Save Tera!*

Returning to camp, Yasotay checked the side bags on his horse as men began to assemble. He watched Sukh strapping a third axe to his horse.

"Seems to me you have enough axes, Sukh," Yasotay said in a hushed and friendly tone.

"They are like my children. They all want to come along for the fun," said Sukh, sounding deadly serious.

The forty men mounted up and left quietly, heading directly north. Temujin and Yasotay led the first group of riders, with Altan and Baatar riding with the second group. Each group of twenty traveled light with only one horse for each rider and no supplies to weigh them down.

Last night, Yasotay had a long conversation with Altan and Baatar regarding their specific strategy for saving Tera. The decision was for their group to ride around the right side of the camp to find the camel trader at the north end. Yasotay had noticed on his scouting trip that many more gers were set up closer to the river to the west than along the mountainside to the east. He assumed these spots were reserved for the more influential families in the Merkit tribe.

"When we finally reach the camp, if your group can circle around to the east, you should encounter less resistance and may get to the northern end quickly to find the camel trader," said Yasotay, "Don't forget, it's a fat man named Darmala. He has a very large collection of camels and three younger sons."

"We understand," said Altan.

"So, what is your plan?" asked Baatar with a young, quizzical look on his face, "Where are you going to be? Do you plan to help us?"

"I will be going with Temujin to the middle of the camp to look for Bourtai," said Yasotay, "As soon as we find her, I will come to help you find Tera!" promised Yasotay in his most convincing tone. Yasotay couldn't help but respect the young man's singular focus on saving his betrothed and proving to everyone that he was an able, grown man who could do it!

As Yasotay rode at the head of the group of riders alongside Temujin, wild thoughts of potential outcomes raced through his mind. Aside from the obvious fact that he wanted Tera to be rescued, he was concerned for Baatar. His desire to prove his love for her was reckless. *'In war, The Way is to avoid what is strong and to strike at what is weak.'* Yasotay knew full well that recklessness was a weakness others would exploit, and they were going to war. On the other hand, if Baatar did save Tera, Yasotay believed that Tera might even see Baatar in a new light. *Well, I guess only time will tell.* He smiled at the thought of Baatar saving the day just as he recognized where they were and brought the group to a halt.

Reining his horse to a stop, Yasotay whispered, "Let's go, slow and quiet, shadows in the night." With that, the riders dismounted as planned and fanned out on foot, creeping quietly north. It didn't take long for them to locate the forward sentry camp. Then, very quietly, they took up positions around the sentries as they slept. As Yasotay expected, one of them was awake. With the others holding their position, in a flash, Yasotay had crept up behind the awake guard and yanked him from his perch atop a rock with a quiet, muffled jerk. Everyone paused for a moment, waiting to see if the others would wake up. The anticipation made moments seem like a lifetime; then suddenly—"Alarm!" screamed a sentry returning from patrol. He jumped into the center of his sleeping cohorts and yelled again, "Alarm!" This second call immediately drew a hail of arrows from the stalkers. *Thwock, thwock, thwock* came the whistling sound of twenty arrows hitting their mark, piercing the otherwise silent setting. Those lying asleep were peppered with arrows. The returning sentry just stood there, axe in hand, not hit by a single one. He looked around, surprised at the volume of arrows shot at those sleeping, but as he drew a breath to yell out again, ten arrows quickly filled the center of his chest. *Thwock, thwock, thwock.* Two awoke screaming from the pain of being shot, not yet dead, as the patrolling sentry's body fell to the ground. Both appeared to try and stand up. Sukh was ready and charged into the center of the killing space, dispatching the wounded sentries with two big swipes of his axe. Four others joined Sukh, with sword in hand, giving every prone Merkit sentry a just-in-case poke with their swords.

"Good," said Temujin in a low voice, "Altan's group will fan out and slowly sweep to the right of the trail, while my group will sweep to the left. Where's our runner?"

"Here," a young man called out with his arm raised.

"Tell Jamka everything is as expected. The path is clear for his full advance north toward the main Merkit camp," said Temujin.

"Yes, Temujin," replied the young man, dropping his head in a quick bow before jumping up on his horse and riding hard south.

"Everything is going as planned. The main group should reach the camp at sunrise," explained Yasotay.

"Good, then let's go," said Temujin. With that, the two groups split up, fanned out, and began the slow sweep toward the main camp. They were looking for any scouts patrolling the area. It was still dark, but the sunrise was coming soon. They need to move quickly to maintain the element of surprise. Seeing no sentries, they covered a good deal of ground in a short amount of time. As they slowly crept forward, it wasn't long before Yasotay smelled something odd. It smelled like urine. He motioned for everyone to hold up. Looking ahead in the dark, he could see very little except the shadows. He slowed to barely moving and then stopped.

"Do you smell that?" Yasotay whispered to Temujin.

"Smell what?" asked Temujin.

"It smells like piss," said Yasotay. "I think we've stumbled into a *lavare*."

"So what? You smell piss," said Temujin, "and what the hell is a lavare?"

"It's where warriors are told to go to relieve themselves. It's best to keep it in one area with a large group, usually downwind."

"So what?" asked Temujin, "people have to piss." Temujin's head jerked suddenly, realizing what Yasotay meant once he said it.

"Wait here and let me go see," said Yasotay.

Temujin nodded his head and held up his hand, motioning for everyone to move back a few steps. The minghan captain and two arban lieutenants relayed the message down the line. Yasotay crept forward and saw an unexpected sight. Moments later, he returned and beckoned the minghan captain. He and his lieutenants approached where Yasotay and Temujin were crouching down.

"There is a camp of thousands of men no more than two hundred paces ahead," whispered Yasotay.

"You never said anything about an army positioned here!" proclaimed Temujin in an exasperated tone.

"The Tumed did warn us. He said the Merkit knew about the six thousand that left the Jadaran," said Yasotay, emphasizing his point a bit too loud. "They must have set a trap!" he whispered adamantly, struggling to keep his voice low.

"A trap? How do you know this?" asked Temujin.

"It makes sense. These Merkit have been ahead of us at every turn," said Yasotay. "Consider for a moment from their point of view. They know an attack is coming from the south, and there's only one main route from there to their main camp. My guess is they've set up their forces to lie in wait on both sides of the trail. Their plan is simple; we come rambling down the trail and walk right into the middle of hell!" Yasotay's hushed voice rose in pitch and slightly in volume. "They want to put us in the middle and catch us in a crossfire. It will be a slaughter. It makes perfect sense!"

"We must warn Jamka!" Temujin and the minghan leader said in a whisper at the same time.

"Jamka needs to split off three or four thousand riders round to the east and west sides of the road and engage the would-be ambushers. Otherwise, if they continue on the trail, they will be caught right where the Merkit wants us: in their kill zone," Yasotay's drawn brow clearly spoke of how gravely he viewed the situation, annoyed at himself for not anticipating.

"I will go warn Jamka," said one of the two lieutenants.

"No, you stay here with your men. I will go. It will be better coming from me," explained the minghan leader.

"Agreed, you should go now," whispered Temujin emphatically. With that, the minghan quickly and quietly walked his horse another fifty paces before jumping on and heading in a mad dash to intercept Jamka and the main body of riders.

"What about Altan and Baatar? We need to warn them," asked Yasotay.

"You go warn them. I will stay here and await Jamka's men," said Temujin. Yasotay nodded in agreement and was off on foot to find Altan and Baatar.

Moving with all due haste, Yasotay quickly scrambled toward the trail and up the large rolling hills. He could see how the trail meandered among these hills, creating a long ridge on either side of the path for a stretch. Yasotay realized, *This is their spot.* With archers on the high ground, an invading army approaching from the south would be trapped like fish in a barrel. Fortunately, the Merkit's plan was discovered before this disaster. Suddenly, as Yasotay reached the top of the eastern hill, he could hear arrows whizzing through the air.

Crouching low, he crept downhill and approached Altan's group. They were directly engaged in trading arrows with Merkit warriors. From his vantage point, he could see the shadows through the darkness, and as he had suspected, thousands of warriors were also stationed on this side. Arrows were flying wildly in every direction as the Merkit warriors were shooting at shadows. Then, their fire would focus on where the return fire originated. It was still dark, but it didn't appear that many, if any, were hitting their marks. It wouldn't be long before the Merkit realized their force was a hundred times the size of Altan's small group. With the light of day, the Merkit would fully engage them and quickly overrun Altan's position with sheer numbers.

Diving behind rocks and running from cover to cover, Yasotay finally reached Altan and Baatar. "I came to warn you that there may be warriors lying in wait!" said Yasotay, his back up against a large rock where they had taken cover. "...but it seems you already know!"

"One of our men walked right into the middle of their camp," Baatar confessed. "We didn't see them till it was too late."

"We need to move," said Yasotay. "The sun will be rising shortly. Once they can clearly see our position and ascertain our numbers, they will flank us and quickly overrun us!"

"Have you warned Jamka?" asked Altan as an arrow bounced off a rock and landed on the ground between them.

"Yes, we sent the minghan captain to warn him," replied Yasotay. There were more and more arrows coming at every moment. They had taken cover behind a series of large rocks, sparse trees, and thick underbrush just south of the encampment. The time had passed for them to make an escape up the hill and back to the south. They would be exposed to a hail of arrows.

Yasotay could see a shadow moving to his right. It was a group of Merkit trying to flank their position. The sun would come up any moment now. Yasotay proclaimed to Altan, "We need to start moving to the south...*now!*"

The minghan leader rode hard, reaching Jamka and the troops after a short ride in the black of night. Racing toward them with his hands waving in the air, he stopped the oncoming mass of horses to explain the situation to Jamka.

"The Merkit have set a trap!" explained the captain. "We need to split off two groups of at least four thousand riders each to directly attack those lying in wait on either side of the trail!"

"Did they tell you anything else?" asked Jamka.

"We need to hurry. Our advance teams are outnumbered a hundred to one and will soon be discovered if they haven't been already."

Jamka called over the tumen commander and explained the situation. "We will split into three," said Jamka. "Each of you will take four thousand along the east and west sides of the trail. I will lead the larger body of our forces up the center, and we will see who sets the trap!"

The two tumen leaders quickly organized the troops directly under their command, and within moments, all the riders were underway. Jamka had ordered a hard charge in the hope of reaching them in time.

Yasotay had started to move their fifteen remaining warriors south away from the Merkit troops that were finally advancing on their position. The receding darkness had unveiled their small numbers. Arrows were flying everywhere. Their position was untenable. Three of them had already been killed, and with two badly wounded, a quarter of their forces were disabled.

"Altan, we've got to move, or we'll die here if we don't!" said Yasotay as he fired another arrow at their tormentors.

"We need to carry the wounded...*look!*" said Altan, pointing toward the east hill.

A bright strand of light sprang out from between the hills to their right, initially blinding Yasotay. The sun was rising, and a good bit of detail, previously hidden in the darkness, began to appear. He looked up to see an orange haze illuminating hundreds of riders, thundering in from the south. Coming over the hill was a swarm of Jamka's riders. The invading forces engaged the ambush encampments on both sides of the road. The Merkit positions were pelted with thousands of arrows and stormed by hundreds of riders who appeared to come from everywhere. Within moments, hundreds of Merkit were killed, and both entrenchments quickly overrun. Many arrows chased after the large number that scampered away, but the surviving Merkit warriors were quickly gone like the shadows of dawn.

Temujin, on horseback, crested the hill, looking for something. He recognized Altan's group and rode to where they sat on their horses. They all watched Jamka's main force head up the trail toward them unopposed.

Next, Temujin rode directly up to Jamka when he came into view, stating, "The Merkit are a bunch of cowards. Come, my blood brother, let us ride together into victory!"

Jamka smiled a wide grin, "Yes, my brother!" With that, the whole cavalry of sixteen thousand rode hard into the Merkit Camp.

The sun had just risen, and the Merkit camp was not ready for the devastation about to be unleashed upon them. The invading forces met minimal resistance, easily hacking their way through the first line of the camp's gers. Upturning anything in their way, the wave of riders plowed through, shooting, slashing, and burning whatever they encountered. Every type of carnage was on full display. Thousands of arrows were buzzing through the air, some incoming from what little resistance the Merkit could muster. Yasotay tried his best to remain aware, but all was in chaos. Atop his horse, pressing quickly into the camp's interior, he realized it was all a game of chance. Getting hit with an arrow from an unforeseen angle was a real fear.

It was the sheer butchery that Yasotay struggled with…women and children were being raped, beaten, and chopped to death indiscriminately. The assault upon the innocent was grotesque. Moreover, the haphazard way the nomad leaders allowed their troops to engage the enemy was startling to Yasotay. This wasn't the organized warfare that Yasotay had read so much about. There was no glory in this.

Most people were running every which way. Some riders sent arrow after arrow into the interior of the encampment and at those fleeing, pummeling whoever moved on foot with a hail of arrows. Others used their swords to slash anyone they could reach from atop their horses. The camp was overwhelmed—the element of surprise had worked beyond their wildest dreams. The Merkit were being absolutely devastated. This was Yasotay's first real battle, and it was a massacre.

He personally wanted no part in the bloodbath. The killing of innocent women and children seemed barbarous to him, but he did have a purpose for being here: it was to save Tera.

"First group, follow me," Temujin yelled as he rode hard toward the center of camp. Yasotay quickly followed along with the other riders. Their task was simple. They needed to find Bourtai. The Merkit were fleeing in droves in whatever manner they could quickly muster. They hacked their way through the throngs of people, not stopping to engage them. Temujin stopped and looked around as they reached the center of the primary collection of gers.

"We need to start checking the gers," he said. "How else can we possibly find her in all this madness?"

Yasotay looked around at the anarchy. The Merkit were being exterminated.

"Everyone, start checking inside the gers!" commanded Temujin. Those following him dismounted and started searching for Bourtai.

Temujin grabbed a woman who had darted out of a ger, trying to run past him. "Where does the man named Chilger live?" he asked the woman, holding her chin up and putting her face to face with him. Terrified for her life, the woman responded, "I don't know who you mean." Temujin dragged his knife across the woman's throat and threw her aside.

"I will find her if I have to slit every throat in this camp!" proclaimed Temujin. He was frustrated and had not anticipated how difficult it would be to find his wife amid all the chaos, with everyone running and screaming in panic. After searching multiple gers, they found most of them were empty. Yasotay did his best to avoid getting hit by arrows or stabbed by the remaining sword-wielding Merkit warriors who were still fighting.

"What else can we do?" asked Temujin of Yasotay, who returned the question with a lifted eyebrow and a shrug that clearly stated to Temujin, "I have no idea!" They mounted their horses, surrounded by a scene in total disarray. The chaos and sheer pandemonium were palpable; people were everywhere, all running in different directions.

Suddenly, Temujin yelled at the top of his lungs, "Bourtai, where are you, Bourtai!" Yasotay's initial thought was that this was a waste of time. "Bourtai, where are you, Bourtai!" Temujin yelled again. Then, with no better idea, Yasotay decided to join in, calling out, "Bourtai! Bourtai!"

Then they heard someone shout, "Temujin, Temujin!"

"Shhh, wait, you hear that?" asked Temujin.

"Temujin, Temujin!" They looked around and saw her in the back of a cart, a hundred paces away, being pulled slowly by two oxen. Struggling with her hastily tied restraints, she freed herself, jumped off the cart, and ran toward them.

Temujin spotted her, wheeled his horse around, and kicked his steed in her direction. Weaving his way through the insanity, he finally reached her. Bending down, he scooped her up and placed her between him and the pommel on his saddle. She immediately hugged Temujin with a grip so tight that it initially startled him.

Yasotay slowly rode over to the couple, giving them their moment. Finally, he said, "I am glad to see you safe, Bourtai!"

Bourtai began to cry uncontrollably, still holding Temujin tight while the frenzy continued around them. Finally, Bourtai caught her breath, and in a broken voice, she looked directly at Yasotay and asked, "Did you find Tera?"

Temujin turned to him and said, "You should go and see if you can find your woman!"

Pausing in thought for a brief moment, Temujin stroked her hair. "I am going to remove Bourtai from this mayhem!" Without a word, Yasotay immediately spun his horse around and bolted off, heading north.

"Tengri be with you!" Temujin yelled after him.

Yasotay waved his hand without looking back as he rode hard through the pandemonium—north!

The invading force had already penetrated the entirety of the Merkit camp. There was still sporadic fighting and arrows flying in every direction. Riding past one burning or collapsed ger after another, Yasotay could tell the battle was already starting to wane, and the havoc that had been caused was difficult for him to comprehend. Due to being outmanned, the Merkit had been unable to fight back in any meaningful way. Whenever a Merkit jumped on a horse and attempted to engage an invading rider, three other invaders descended on him. It was a total rout with all the confusion, anarchy, and tumult accompanying such a battle. It was one of the most intense moments in Yasotay's young life. He had never experienced a maelstrom like this, but he couldn't get caught up in it. He had to find that camel trader!

Yasotay could see a collection of gers. Behind the gers was a large area with over a hundred camels standing as if nothing was happening. In front of the gers, Altan and Baatar were on foot, fighting three men with swords. They were holding their own, but two against three was a challenge. As Yasotay approached, he drew his bow and shot three rapid arrows from atop his horse while charging the melee. Each struck one of the three men. The first one landed under the raised arm of the one fighting Baatar. The other buried itself into the hip of one fighting Altan. The distraction gave Altan enough advantage to strike his opponent with a finishing blow. The third arrow caught the last person in the foot as he tried to run off, causing him to fall. With one fluid motion, Yasotay jumped off his horse and crashed his bow into the side of his face, smacking him out cold.

"You're here," said Baatar. "We were wondering if you were coming or not."

"Have you checked the gers?" asked Yasotay.

"No," answered Altan. "We had just arrived while these three were loading their cart. We were delayed, more resistance than we expected."

"So, let's start. I'll check these three. Check those two over there," Yasotay motioned Baatar toward a collection of gers to his left.

"I'll check these three over here," said Altan, moving to Yasotay's right.

Baatar came out of his second ger with a frustrated look. "They are both empty!" he exclaimed.

"So, are these!" said Altan. "Where is Yasotay?"

"I don't know!" answered Baatar.

"Wait. Isn't that Tata?" asked Altan. "That ass over there tied to the fence." They could see Tata a short distance away. She awkwardly kicked the fence she was tied to and pulled on the reins tied to her head. Altan said, "That's Tata for you! Always fighting something."

"If it isn't her, it must be her sister because that ass is certainly acting crazy like her," said Baatar, like Altan trying to make light of the disappointing situation.

Yasotay came hurrying out of his third ger, "Nothing...mine are all empty!" The frustration in his voice was evident.

"Ours too," answered Altan. He looked around. "Hey, did you notice all of the camels are gone?"

"They must have scattered with all the commotion," said Baatar.

Yasotay thought, *Where could she be? Did they take her already?* Yasotay was looking around, sick at the idea that they must have taken her days ago. The gers were all empty, and the camel owner was gone! The place looked abandoned except for a handful of horses and some goats walking around. The feeling of loss and dread came over Yasotay.

"They must have taken her days ago!" said Altan solemnly.

"Now, what do we do?" asked Baatar.

"They have probably taken her to Turpan. It must be at least a month's trip, maybe more," said Altan.

"I'm going. Let's go!" insisted Baatar.

"We shouldn't act in haste," insisted Yasotay. "I agree we pursue them! But let's think this through!"

"We must first go find Temujin and Jamka," said Altan, "but I agree we must pursue."

"No, we should get started…now!" proclaimed Baatar.

"But which way? There are thousands of people fleeing in every direction," said Yasotay. "Do we check those dead and fleeing, or do we assume she has already been taken to Turpan?"

"We will need provisions," insisted Altan, "and will want to take additional men!" Altan's voice became low and grave. "We may never find her!"

Suddenly, they could hear a banging or knocking sound, "Knock, knock, knock."

"Yasotay, we weren't sure, but isn't that Tata tied up to the fence over there?" asked Baatar.

Yasotay was getting ready to respond to Altan when he looked over, smiled, and exclaimed, "Yes, yes, I believe it is her!" Distracted by this discovery, he forgot his train of thought and quickly walked over in stunned amazement, placing his hand on her head. He stroked between her ears. Tera always insisted that Tata preferred that way of being caressed, as if she could read Tata's mind. This time, Yasotay did it to try to soothe her; she seemed highly agitated.

"Hey Tata, how are you? Easy girl! You look fine…easy," Yasotay tried to calm her down, but she resisted. Tata kept bucking her head and pawing at the fence where her reins were tied. "Easy girl! She's acting like she's going to explode!" exclaimed Yasotay. She just kept lifting her left leg and kicking at the fence where her reins were tightly secured.

"Easy, easy, Tata, easy, easy," Yasotay said, almost getting stepped on. He'd seen her mad, but this was more than that; she was acting crazy. Giving her what he believed she wanted, Yasotay reached over and unknotted the leather strap that secured her to the fence. As soon as he did, she bolted off in a full run.

"Wow," said Altan.

"She sure is in a hurry!" proclaimed Baatar. "Where's she going?"

"Come on," Yasotay said, running to his horse and agilely jumping on. "I know you'll think I'm crazy, but those two are inseparable…two souls, one spirit…I'll bet she's after Tera!"

"Yaaah," Yasotay yelled and rode after her. He rode at a breakneck speed north, away from the Merkit camp.

Baatar and Altan jumped up on their horses and followed. Yasotay rode at a maddening pace. Even so, he still struggled to keep up with Tata, as Altan and Baatar struggled to keep up with him. He trailed behind Tata by at least seven or eight horse lengths, and Altan and Baatar trailed Yasotay by the same length. They were all riding at full speed, chasing this crazy ass who seemed to be pulling away from them.

Yasotay then noticed a large plume of dust ahead. It was from a massive collection of camels all loping along at a good pace, but not as quickly as Tata was chasing them. Their speed was more of a trot, a pace replicated by a series of carts in a long caravan that followed them. In the front of the caravan were over a hundred camels, with a handful of riders keeping the pace and galloping alongside. Behind the herd were seven large carts in a row, each pulled by four camels. The carts seemed to be heavily weighed down and had two drivers each, trying to keep up with the rigorous pace of the unburdened herd.

Yasotay slowed, keeping stride with the back of the last cart in the caravan. Baatar and Altan caught up with him and adjusted their pace so all three rode two or three horse lengths behind the caravan. The two drivers leading the last cart couldn't see them because they were following so closely.

All three were watching Tata, who was galloping alongside the cart immediately in front of the rear cart. All of a sudden, female hands bound at the wrist reached out from the cart toward Tata's head.

"Look, that has to be Tera!" said Baatar as he and Yasotay both galloped faster toward Tata and had now pulled alongside the last cart. Just then, Yasotay ducked under a long pole that stabbed at his head from a hole in the side of the cart. Then an arrow whizzed by him, and then another. Yasotay returned fire and hit one of the drivers of the second to last cart. Next, someone started shooting arrows at them from the cart up ahead.

Altan shot back. The caravan's defenses seemed coordinated. It was apparent they had experience dealing with bandits or other miscreants accosting their caravan. The carts were manned with at least two, if not four, people either shooting arrows or poking long staffs at anyone who dared to come alongside. The solid wooden walls of the cart gave them some protection. The small windows, set at various heights, were to be avoided. Long poles for poking riders off their horses and shooting arrows came from them. Other than that, it appeared the caravan planned to fight off all who came near and keep moving!

"Go save her. This is your chance. Save Tera!" Yasotay yelled at Baatar while shooting an arrow. Baatar nodded, and then, ducking his head down further, he encouraged his horse to pick up its pace and move toward Tata alongside the second cart. Arrows continued to fly all around them.

Altan hit the driver at the front of the last cart with an arrow to the chest. He slumped over and then fell from the moving cart. The guard sitting next to him dropped his bow and grabbed the reins. Arrows were still coming at them from the carts up ahead, but it appeared that the trio had neutralized the closest threat. Altan was hit with a lucky shot in his leg with an arrow fired from a cart further up the line. Suddenly, someone swung open a trap door in the sidewall of the trailing cart and jumped out, grabbing Yasotay by the shoulders and pulling him off his horse. They both landed on the ground hard.

Baatar finally came alongside Tata. He could see Tera. She was in what was nothing more than a large cage on wheels made of wood and metal, obviously used to transport prisoners. The driver was staying low and keeping pace with the cart in front of him. The other man who replaced the driver Yasotay had shot was out of sight. At least four or five people were in the cage with her, all cowering low so as not to be hit with arrows. Tera was the only one standing, reaching out. Baatar looked closely for a cage door but couldn't see how it opened.

"Baatar!" Tera cried out.

"The door," yelled Baatar. "How does it open?" he screamed, as an arrow just missed him, careening right past his face.

"Here, use this to cut the cord on your wrist," said Baatar as he reached out and handed his dagger to Tera.

"The roof. The latch is on the roof!" Tera yelled back. The din of the camels and the sounds of the moving caravan make it difficult to hear. Tera took the dagger and began cutting the cord around her wrists.

Altan nocked, drew, and shot repeatedly at anyone who stuck their head out from the two carts, the one ahead and the one immediately behind the cage cart. The drivers of these carts stayed low and did not stop. Arrows came at them erratically, shot from the carts further ahead.

Baatar jumped from his horse and onto the outside of the cage. Stepping on the crossbars and grabbing the higher ones, he crawled up to the cage's roof.

Fortunately for Yasotay, the guard who had jumped from the cart and yanked him to the ground had miscalculated. Instead of driving him down, he grabbed him while flying by, and so Yasotay landed on top of him, the back part of his shoulder driving into the chest of his assailant, which cushioned his fall. Yasotay could hear the man's rib cage popping and cracking when he landed on him. Rolling right over him and landing on his feet, Yasotay took a quick pause, realized he was fine, retrieved his horse, and was back chasing after the rolling caravan. Luckily, it was moving slowly enough that Yasotay's horse could easily catch up to it again. What this caravan did not do was stop. It just kept rolling on, no matter what.

Yasotay caught up to where he could see Baatar on top of the cage with Tera inside. Arrows were flying from Altan toward the carts ahead, whose riders sent volleys in return. Tera and Yasotay's eyes met in all this mayhem, and she smiled, the same crooked little grin she had given him so many times. This time, it felt different. It hurt like a stab in the heart.

Tata was still running alongside the cage cart. She had an arrow sticking out of her left front leg but had not missed a step. Baatar pulled and banged at the latch on top of the cage. Suddenly, an arrow flew from nowhere and struck Baatar's right arm. He grabbed his arm, and just then, they hit a bump that knocked Baatar off balance. He fell off the roof but managed to hold onto the side of the cage with his left arm. Baatar was dangling by one arm from the cart with an arrow stuck in his other arm. Both Yasotay and Altan returned fire. They figured the arrow had come from the cart immediately ahead of them. They sent arrows, one after another, into any window and crack in that cart. Yasotay nocked, drew, and fired repeatedly. Baatar regained his footing and climbed back on the roof of the cage cart.

Baatar returned to working the latch. Yasotay couldn't help but think that Baatar's efforts to open this gate with an arrow stuck in his arm were heroic. He was proud of him. Finally, Baatar yanked the latch free and threw open a metal fastener, and the cage door dropped down with a large BANG, slamming onto the ground. It bounced up and then fell as it was dragged behind the cart. Baatar broke the arrow stuck in his right arm with his left hand and winced from the pain. He climbed down the cart's side and hopped back on his horse, which was still running alongside. Tera stepped out and climbed along the outside of the cage. Altan and Yasotay vigilantly watched the other carts, expecting another arrow to come flying their way. Yasotay could see the bruises on Tera's arms and legs and felt anger rising within him. Baatar reached out his hand, and an arrow almost hit it. Tera hung from the side of the cart, holding on with just one hand and one foot. She jumped, landing with a thud on Baatar's lap. As soon as he had her, they peeled away from the caravan. While slowing their pace dramatically, the procession continued charging along and was soon out of firing range.

Finally, they stopped! Tera jumped down from Baatar's horse.

"Tera!" cried Altan, "My daughter!" Altan jumped off his horse and hopped toward her with an arrow in his leg. He and Tera embraced, holding each other for what seemed like an eternity to them.

Yasotay drew a sigh of relief. Everything considered, this raid and rescue was a great success. *Thank God it's over*. Yasotay walked over to

Tata, who had slowed and stopped with them once she saw Tera was free, and gave her a big hug. "Good girl, Tata, Good girl!"

Tera then ran to Baatar, jumped in his arms, and gave him a huge hug, "My Hero!" she proclaimed loudly with a big smile.

"Ouch," cried Baatar, flinching from the broken arrow still sticking out of his arm.

"Oh, I'm so sorry. Look, there's a hole in your sleeve," said Tera.

"There's a hole in my arm, with the tip of an arrow still stuck in there," said Baatar.

"I can help you with that." Yasotay jumped down from his horse. He looked through his bag for some salve he had for such wounds.

Tera walked up to Yasotay, not waiting for him to finish fishing through his bag. She gave him a big hug from behind him and whispered in his ear. "Thank you. I don't know what you did, but I know it was everything!"

"It was Tata who saved you, Tata and Baatar!" exclaimed Yasotay. He pulled a small leather pouch from his bag, and they walked back to Baatar. Tera helped him take his shirt off. Yasotay looked closely at Baatar's wound.

"Look, they never even slowed down!" said Baatar. They could see the caravan far off in the distance, still moving briskly.

"I guessed they have learned that when you're attacked, the one rule, no matter what, is to keep moving!" exclaimed Altan as he stared off into the distance.

"Here, bite down on this," said Yasotay, holding up a broken arrow. "This is going to hurt a little!"

Baatar took the arrow and bit down on it.

"Tera, hold the wound open for me," Yasotay said. Next, he placed the tip of his knife in the entry wound next to the arrow and pushed it down. Then he pulled up. Baatar's face turned red and then white, and he yelled loudly, his eyes rolling up in his head. The arrowhead popped out with a little blood splatter on Tera and Yasotay's faces.

"Don't let him fall over," Yasotay said. Tera caught Baatar under his left arm as he staggered.

"Wow, there, we got it," said Yasotay. He quickly wiped some salve on the wound and wrapped it tightly with a cloth. Tera held Baatar, who was a little wobbly. He drank some water, but it took him a few moments before he shook it off.

"We need to return to the camp and find Jamka and Temujin," said Altan.

"Didn't you get shot in the leg?" asked Yasotay. "I remember looking over and seeing an arrow sticking up from your leg!"

"It went clean through my leg and struck the side of my horse!" Altan said in astonishment. "I had to break it off and pull it out, or it would have kept stabbing my horse!"

"Let me put some of this on it. It will stop the bleeding and ease the pain!" said Yasotay.

Yasotay knelt, applied some salve, and bandaged Altan's leg. The arrow had, indeed, gone clean through his leg. He had already pulled it out, so all Altan required was a little salve and a good bandage. Finally, Yasotay turned to Tata, who had been shot too! A crossbow arrow, considerably shorter than a regular arrow, protruded from just above her front right leg. Tera gave Tata a big hug and whispered something in her ear. She held her head high as Yasotay quickly yanked the arrow out of her leg. Drips of blood ran down her leg. Tata lifted her head like she wanted to rear, but Tera held her tight, and Tata's fear quickly passed. Using the same ointment, Yasotay put a glob of the salve on Tata's wound, which would stanch the bleeding. Tera walked her around in a circle, and she seemed to be moving fine.

They mounted up and headed back toward the carnage at the Merkit camp. Tera rode bareback atop Tata. She insisted, even after everyone offered her their own saddled horse to ride.

"Her leg is hurt, and I am less of a burden to carry than any of you!" exclaimed Tera.

"There is no coming between those who share one spirit!" declared Yasotay.

"I would wager that I am less of a burden than you!" Baatar said.

"Don't worry, Baatar. You may be small now, but you will grow big and strong!" said Tera.

She then leaned forward and hugged Tata's big brown neck. "I understand Tata; she wants me to ride with her." Tera then reached over and placed her hand on Baatar's thigh, which elicited a large smile from him.

"Inseparable," stated Yasotay. "Those two are inseparable!" This declaration further elicited a smile from everyone.

They rode slowly back toward the Merkit camp. They could see a small bit of fighting still going on as they approached. Most of the Merkit warriors, along with many of the inhabitants, had fled the camp in the early moments of the invasion. The last remnants of brave Merkit warriors were still fighting for their lives. A group of them had hidden in a small, wooded area near the river. As Altan, Yasotay, Baatar, and Tera rode back toward camp, these last vestiges of the battle were to their right. More than three hundred of the invading warriors, led by Jamka, were posted in a field fifty paces from a wooded area at the far end of the crescent-shaped field. They were shooting arrow after arrow into the thick bushes where the remaining Merkit holdouts fought on and returned fire.

The trees and underbrush formed a wide, half circle around a large field where a handful of gers still stood. Each of them was covered with arrows sticking out every which way. This had become the last line of what little defense the Merkit still held. Jamka's warriors were making a sport out of it, taunting the seventy Merkit men, women, and children who were hiding in the bush and firing off the occasional arrow.

"Jamka, Jamka," Baatar yelled out and waved, riding slightly ahead of the other three.

Yasotay, Altan, and Tera were looking at Jamka, but his back was to them and at least a hundred paces away. Baatar was waving his hand and calling out to get Jamka's attention when Yasotay saw a black flash whoosh past his right eye.

It went by so quickly that Yasotay was immediately startled. He heard the *whizz, thunk,* and felt an odd feeling in his gut. Then, Yasotay saw that Baatar had a black feather sticking out of the back of his neck. *That looks wrong!* he thought. Just then, Baatar's head turned, trying to look back, and Yasotay saw the tip of the arrow protruding from the front of the boy's neck. Drops of blood dripped from the tip. The arrow had pierced Baatar's neck. He grabbed the end of the arrow protruding from under his chin, and a large gush of blood shot out from his neck. He started to topple, falling from his horse—everything was happening in slow motion. Yasotay lunged forward, jumping off his horse to catch Baatar and soften his landing. He caught him in time as he fell out of his saddle.

As he eased the boy's body to the ground, Yasotay went to the ground with him. Then he looked up to see where the arrow had come from. Across the field was Temujin, holding a Merkit with a bow in his hand from behind. He had his arm around the archer's head and his blade at his neck, ripping across it and leaving a red line. Temujin released him, and the Merkit just stood there, blood squirting from his neck for a brief moment. Then he dropped his bow and landed face down, falling like a tree.

Yasotay's attention returned to Baatar as he gently and carefully placed Baatar's head sideways on his lap. After piercing the back of his neck, the arrow exited the front left side of his throat. Baatar was gurgling blood, trying to speak.

"It's fine, Baatar," soothed Yasotay. He knew there was nothing he could do for his fallen friend. "You're going to pull through, Baatar!" he consoled him, his voice crackling. Tera had jumped down from Tata and was kneeling next to Yasotay. Tears began to well up in both of their eyes.

"I'm sorry! I'm sorry…. Tell Tera I'm sorry, I let her…" Baatar's eyes rolled to the back of his head. Blood gushed from around the arrow and pulsed slower and slower. Yasotay knew he was gone and could feel his life and spirit leave his body. This was the closest Yasotay had ever experienced the death of someone close to him as it happened. Tera cried torrents of tears while leaning her head on Yasotay's shoulder.

Jamka turned and recognized Tera, Altan, and Yasotay hovering over someone on the ground. He wheeled his horse around and rode toward them, seeing it was a warrior who had been hit. Jamka slid his horse to a stop. Yasotay looked up and saw Altan glaring into the distance at Borchu, Temujin, and Hassar, who were running up to them.

"What happened?" asked Jamka. Then he realized who was on the ground. "NO! Not Baatar!"

"It was a Merkit archer," claimed Temujin breathlessly, winded from having run a good one hundred paces. He pointed back up the hill. "He was up there. I couldn't reach him before he got off a shot… but I did slit his miserable throat."

"Yes, we were working our way through the thicket trying to flush out the remaining Merkit, and one of them got off a lucky shot," said Borchu.

"What a shame; he was a good kid," said Hassar, who looked down upon Baatar's face of death.

Tera was still crying. Altan stood there glaring at Temujin, not moving a muscle or saying a word!

Jamka jumped back on his horse. "Where is this ARCHER!" he bellowed with a deadly sneer.

Borchu pointed back up the hill to where Temujin had left the body. Jamka rode hard for a hundred paces, flung himself from his horse, and began viciously stabbing the corpse of the Merkit warrior. He was infuriated, stabbing again and again and again. He then let out a wild animal howl and fell to his knees. Having worked himself to exhaustion, with all emotion drained from him, Jamka slowly stood up, got on his horse, and rode back to where Baatar's body lay. They had all observed Jamka's outburst in stunned silence.

The group stayed there for a long while, mourning their friend. Tera was still crying softly, holding onto Yasotay's shoulder while he held Baatar's lifeless head on his lap. Yasotay had reached down to close his eyelids out of respect. Jamka returned, dismounted, and knelt on the other side of Baatar, facing Yasotay and Tera.

"He was so young!" Jamka said, staring into his face, which did look young…young and innocent. "Cousin. I knew I should have kept you by my side!" insisted Jamka.

"He saved me!" Tera said in a matter-of-fact tone. "Baatar rescued me from the slavers. He jumped on a steel cage within a rolling caravan, with arrows flying everywhere to save me." Tera leaned over and kissed him on the forehead. "My hero!"

"He insisted on going after you. He was determined to save you." proclaimed Jamka. "I could not deny him that!"

Yasotay nodded his head. "Yes, there was no stopping him, Jamka."

Tera wiped the tears from her face. Borchu, Temujin, and Hassar stood there with their heads bowed, watching this scene unfold. All except Altan, who still had not moved a muscle and had not said a word!

"What will we do with him?" asked Yasotay to nobody in particular.

"He stays where he lays!" answered Jamka. "That is our way."

The group lingered around Baatar's dead body for a while longer. Jamka returned to his men. The taunting games they had been playing were over. Three hundred men were ordered into the woods and thicket to finish off any remaining resistance. More than half of the inhabitants were fortunate enough to have fled, and the rest were carcasses lying in and around the camp.

Altan still hadn't said a word. He was stony-faced and silent. Yasotay had asked him, "Are you hurt?" Altan said nothing. He was obviously distraught, but they were all disturbed over what had happened to Bataar. Yasotay walked away. The warriors were told to gather all the animals, collect valuables from the camp, and assemble back in the field where they'd camped the previous night twenty li south. There, they would divide the spoils. Yasotay left the scene while Tera, Tata, and Altan were still standing over Bataar's body, lost in their grief. Later, they followed the others back to camp.

When they arrived at the camp, there were thousands of warriors at the site. Some cared for the few wounded, and others were cooking food. But most were sitting around laughing and enjoying the day. It was well past noon, and the air in the camp was jovial. Their victory had come quickly and gone smoothly. This celebration severely contrasted with the mood of Tera, Yasotay, and Altan.

"Tera!" yelled out Bourtai.

"Bourtai," replied Tera in relief and somewhat disbelief. She jumped down from Tata, and the fellow survivors embraced. They held each other for a long moment. Each was very happy to see the other had survived their brutal confinement.

"I worried that fat man who took you would chop you up and eat you!" said Bourtai, laughing, which got Tera to finally break a smile.

"Altan, where is Baatar? They said you went to find Tera with him," asked Bourtai. Altan did not respond. She looked at him as he stared off into the distance, seemingly not hearing a word she said.

Yasotay answered for him. "Baatar was killed by the Merkit."

"Pfft," scoffed Altan, turning his horse around and riding off in haste.

"Altan seems broken up over Baatar," said Bourtai.

"We are all heartbroken. But my father has acted this way since it happened. I tried to get him to talk," explained Tera, "but he had nothing to say."

"He just needs some time," said Yasotay. "He felt responsible for Baatar, as did I, and Altan undoubtedly feels that he let him down. Let you down."

"There was nothing he could have done," sighed Tera.

Late in the afternoon, Temujin, Borchu, and Hassar were standing outside a ger in the center of what remained of the devastated Merkit camp, drinking ayrag from a bladder.

"Are you ready for another ride?" Hassar asked Temujin with a big smile.

"He needs to get back to Bourtai," teased Borchu. "Did you save a ride for her?" he asked, laughing loudly, taking a large swig from the bladder.

"I can ride, my friend, as many times as I like!" said Temujin with a wry grin. "Don't you worry about my vigor...and give me my bladder back!"

"If you will excuse me, I am ready to ride another mare," proclaimed Borchu as he strolled into the ger, where they held six young Merkit women captive for their amusement.

"Don't forget to tie her back up once you're done," Hassar yelled after him, "the last one you rode took off because you didn't tie her down."

"I don't think he cares," said Temujin, taking another swig from his bladder. "I don't think I care either…there are plenty of pretty young mares tied up in other gers."

"Hey, it's Altan…" said Temujin, seeing him approach on his horse.

At that moment, Altan was looking around, searching for someone. When he saw Temujin and Hassar, he immediately wheeled his horse around and rode up to where they stood.

"Altan, would you like some…" The man slid off his horse, rushed up to Hassar, and punched him in the face HARD!

"Stop, Altan," yelled Temujin, "what are you doing?"

Hassar immediately hit the ground. Altan stood over him and turned his head to look directly into Temujin's eyes, glaring!

"Why did you hit Hassar? Why would you do that?" asked Temujin, rather sheepishly now. He knew why. Temujin tried to keep up the ruse. "What's upset you? Why did you hit Hassar?" Temujin avoided Altan's gaze.

"He shot Baatar in the neck with one of the Merkit arrows," answered Altan loudly. "I saw your little deception, Temujin. You stood there holding a blade to the throat of a Merkit warrior who just happened to have a bow in his hand after Hassar made the shot! It was all make-believe! You slit that Merkit's throat, in sight of everyone, blaming it on that man who was now dead!"

"Quiet your voice!" Temujin said in a low and ominous hiss. "You speak very dangerous words, my friend."

"Speak," Altan said in an equally low and ominous voice. "WHY? Why did you kill that boy?" The look in Altan's eye told Temujin it was best to tell him the truth. He looked around, making sure nobody could overhear what he was about to say.

"It's simple; now Yasotay will stay!" answered Temujin in a low voice. "I know you love him, and so do I. But it is your daughter he truly loves. I know you have seen them together! Everyone has. They are the perfect couple! He would never have stayed if Baatar lived to marry Tera," insisted Temujin. "Yasotay felt he was coming between them. Your daughter was what kept him here this long, and Baatar's claim on your daughter was the only thing making him leave. We can't have Yasotay leave us."

"You killed Baatar so that Yasotay would stay with us, with you?" spat Altan, almost trying to convince himself of this truth.

Temujin responded in a low voice, talking quickly, "Your family and mine have looked out for each other since our great-grandfathers rode together. Keeping Yasotay here with us is in both of our best interests! Nothing is making him leave now. It's just a matter of time before he asks for your daughter's hand in marriage. Realize this man is a weapon. It's not just his warrior abilities. You saw what he did at the Northern Pass. You have been fighting longer than me. Who fights like that?" Temujin paused. "His knowledge of warfare is what makes him so valuable. He knows the ways of those who antagonize us from the South and even those beyond. He is a strategic thinker, one who can help me return our clan to the glory of our past, and he will also make a great son-in-law for you!"

Altan dropped his head. Looking down at the ground, he repeated, "So you killed that young man to keep Yasotay here?"

"Altan, you believed in me and my family while all the others abandoned us. I did not do this to hurt you or your family. This is in your family's best interests; it is in all of *our* best interests," insisted Temujin. "Look in your heart...you know what I say is true!"

Having calmed down, Altan moved from standing over Hassar. Temujin reached out and helped his brother from the ground, dusting him off and checking his chin.

"This was not Hassar's decision. It was mine!" said Temujin. "I told him what to do, and he obeyed me. If you want to be mad at someone, you can be mad at me! But, as I said, I acted in our clan's best interest. Realize that this man can and will help me fulfill my destiny. The question is...will you?" Temujin now looked into Altan's eyes for the truth. "I can't have you saying anything to anyone about this. No one knows, and it must stay that way. Are we agreed upon this, Altan?" Temujin rested his hand on the sword at his hip.

"Like Jamka or Yasotay?" asked Altan.

"Exactly like Jamka or Yasotay," warned Temujin. "It's best you say nothing to anyone!"

Altan paused for a long moment, then begrudgingly said, "I understand."

CHAPTER TWELVE

Jadaran Territory, late fall, 1180 CE

Yasotay sat motionless in his cocoon, not wanting to disturb her. It was well before sunrise. After tossing and turning for what seemed like an eternity, he had gotten up and retreated to his morning spot. His inability to sleep was caused by the importance of the day. *I am marrying Tera!* It made him feel somewhat antsy to think those words. Eighteen months had passed since Baatar's death, and Yasotay still thought about him, especially today!

He had seen this owl previously, a large brown bird with pointy black eyebrows that lived among the tall pine trees. Yasotay was sure it was a female because they were considerably larger than the males.

And this owl was huge! Her large frame stood in one spot, frozen. A full moon hung in the sky, giving them both a good view of the vast hunting ground.

She had not moved a muscle, but this morning, he could tell she was hunting. Yasotay was doing his best not to break her concentration. He remained utterly motionless and focused on silencing his breath. He noticed her head move slightly with the faintest hint of a rustle. She was judging the distance from her prey. Yasotay enjoyed observing predatory hunting techniques. He honed in on the outline of the beautiful eagle-owl perched above and to his right.

Suddenly, the owl dropped from the tree without a sound. She flew in a broad rising arch lifted by the air current and then dove at the last moment, razor-sharp talons forward. She snatched a small rodent from the ground and flew upward again with a heavy flap of her wings, making the first sound since she had left her perch. Yasotay couldn't see much, but from what he could, he made out her radiant orange eyes and the long, ominous shadows she cast from her outstretched wings. She returned to a nearby tree. The black-and-brown vertical stripes on her white chest could be seen when she turned in just the right direction. And he could see her catch squirming, some small creature, a mouse or vole of some type.

The eagle-owl was becoming one of his favorite predators. This reminded him of how the orchid mantis was Master Lu's. The two were so different one could hardly compare them. The only thing they had in common was speed. The mantis uses deception and patience to lure in its victim and then strikes with amazing speed. The deception is in its appearance; it looks very similar to the pink orchid, a plant its victims naturally gravitate toward. So, while the eagle-owl uses hearing and stealth, the orchid mantis is primarily about deception with a good measure of patience. What they share is their speed when striking. Master Lu's school was based on the principle that different animals, like the orchid mantis and the eagle-owl, could be used to teach predatory proficiencies.

Yasotay had always thought he would someday like to establish a martial arts school. He had a preference for training in smaller groups of ten or fewer, which he viewed as more manageable. So Yasotay had started a small training program to teach hand-to-hand combat to the nomads. His sessions quickly became very popular and were quite competitive. He also encouraged Hassar to conduct advanced training with the bow. Yasotay worked with Hassar to establish promotions for those individuals who had begun to exhibit high-level skills.

Temujin supported these new training regiments, even personally attending one of Yasotay's classes. His clan had grown to over eighty people, more than three times its size when Yasotay joined them two years ago. Temujin and Jamka had been inseparable blood brothers these last eighteen months. Living, eating, and traveling together, like family, they often shared the same ger. This created a strong bond, and they lived like family during these past months. Despite this and everything appearing to be fine, Yasotay could perceive some animosity between them.

Yasotay had to cancel teaching his hand-to-hand combat class because today was the *big day*. He and Tera were to be married this day! A flash of sunlight shot out through the mountain range with a single strand of bright light that blinded Yasotay momentarily. Once he looked away, his eyes slowly adjusted as daybreak began to illuminate the open plains. Yasotay stood up, folded his blanket, and headed toward their ger.

Now, to address my first and most important task this morning. Yasotay had to find more young chickens! Since chickens were rare, this wasn't something easily accomplished. At least, that was the task given to him last night. Tera's mother, Sarnai, felt it would be bad luck if they didn't execute the wedding ceremony flawlessly. This included the chicken liver ritual that Yasotay found so odd, overtly superstitious, and, most important, incredibly wasteful of chickens, which were very few and far between. Sarnai had gone out of her way to ensure everything was perfect for Tera's special day. So Yasotay needed to acquire more chickens because he wanted to please Sarnai and didn't want to ruin Tera's wedding day. *Hopefully, the ceremony will proceed with no problems.*

"Yasotay, did you get extra chickens?" asked Sarnai as soon as he entered the ger.

"It's as if my mere presence brings the thought of chickens to your mind!" teased Yasotay with a grin. She was busy cooking boiled lamb over a fire and seemed preoccupied with the multitude of other preparations on her mind.

"Good morning, Yasotay. It's such a fine day, and…did you get more chickens?" Sarnai repeated her question. Having lived with Yasotay for a good while now, Sarnai was comfortable with his fun-loving nature and sarcastic barbs.

"Good morning to you, Sarnai, and no, not yet. I am going now… where's Tera?" Yasotay was curious about the whereabouts of his bride-to-be. For the past couple of days, she had seemed very anxious and was constantly busy.

"She is setting up the new ger Altan made for you two," answered Sarnai. "She seems in a big hurry to move out of our home. I guess she's excited about starting a family of her own."

"I share in her enthusiasm. So, I am going to find some chickens with extremely well-endowed livers…or, at least, we can hope!" exclaimed Yasotay with a big smile. He liked teasing Sarnai with his off-hand comments.

"Don't you worry about wasting chickens. We are going to have a happy and healthy marriage, even if the two of you have to rummage through the innards of every chicken in camp!" she said with a smile. "You will find the perfect liver!"

"I have no doubt," Yasotay said, and with that, he was off to find more chickens. The first logical stop on his quest was Temujin and Bourtai's ger.

Temujin called out to him as he approached, "I was warned you would be stopping by looking for chickens!"

"Yes, it doesn't surprise me that you were forewarned. I am, indeed, in search of a chicken who happens to be in possession of the perfect liver!" said Yasotay. He noticed Bourtai, holding Jochi, step out of their ger. "Good morning, Bourtai…and Jochi."

"Good morning, Yasotay. Are you looking for something?" Bourtai kidded, shifting her weight while holding the one-year-old on her hip. He smiled.

"While we have some chickens, I cannot vouch for the quality of their internal organs," said Temujin with a laugh. Yasotay couldn't help but chuckle along with him, considering the absurdity of this particular ritual.

"As you know, it's better to be a chicken's head than a phoenix's tail," said Temujin.

"Are you quoting on the merits of leadership by Su Qui from the Warring States period?" asked Yasotay with a smile.

"Yes, as I have told you, you talk a lot, and as a habit, I do happen to listen…occasionally. Come, let's have a quick drink!" insisted Temujin.

"You are starting very early with challenging my wits and my constitution." said Yasotay, "Is it going to be that kind of day?"

"It's your wedding day. It's a celebration, so…I am happy for you and Tera…drink with me!" Temujin was not to be denied. He pushed the bladder of ayrag into Yasotay's hands. He took a long swig from the bladder and handed it back to Temujin, who did the same.

"You are right, Temujin. Traditions are a good reminder," conceded Yasotay. "They connect us with those who came before us and provide a future connection for those yet to come!"

"As always, my friend Yasotay, the great philosopher!" said Temujin, bowing and extending an outstretched arm. "Please let me show you the way to my chickens and your happy future."

They found two chickens of the appropriate age. Placing them in a small wooden cage, Yasotay thanked Temujin for the chickens and the drink and walked the thirty paces to Jamka's ger. He found him standing next to a small collection of horses, talking to one of his tumen commanders, his back toward Yasotay as he approached.

"Who gave you those orders?" Jamka asked in an irritated voice.

"Temujin told us to speak with the minghan captain and coordinate preparations for tomorrow's departure," answered the tumen commander.

"I give the orders of when my people move out, not Temujin…he is *not* my equal!" barked Jamka. Then, seeing Yasotay, he told the man, "We will speak of this later." Jamka turned to face Yasotay with a big smile. "Ahh, may the blessings of Tengri be upon you, Yasotay." He paused and then remembered. "Wait. Aren't you getting married today?"

"Yes, and the reason for my visit. I am in search of young chickens with healthy livers."

"Ha! I should've known. We may have one or two. Let's see if we can help," said Jamka with a wide grin, motioning for him to follow.

After his two visits, Yasotay now had three more chickens to go along with the five Sarnai had saved. Thanks to her attention to every minute detail, the wedding ceremony would go as planned.

The soon-to-be bride and groom were convinced that their union was the next step in their blossoming relationship. But it took them a while to speak about what had happened to Baatar. It took even longer before they could openly discuss their feelings for one another. They had to work through the pain and guilt they both felt first.

Yasotay couldn't remember having ever spoken with her father about Baatar and his death. Altan was always tight-lipped about the subject when it was brought up. Still, to this day, he hadn't said a word about Baatar, how he felt about what happened, or about his death to Yasotay, Tera, or Sarnai. This fact had concerned Yasotay when he had gone to Altan months ago to ask for his daughter's hand. He didn't know what his response would be, but Yasotay knew that Tera was the one for him. He had always sensed their instinctual attraction to each other. It was now clear to him that he deeply loved Tera.

"Altan, I need to speak with you," Yasotay had asked respectfully. At the time, Altan was sharpening his knife. He motioned with his elbow for Yasotay to sit on the log across from him.

"I would like to marry Tera, and I am formally requesting your blessing," said Yasotay with a sheepish look.

Altan's response was simple. After a long pause that appeared to be a search for the right words, his knuckles turned white on the hand that gripped his blade. "You have it!"

That was all Altan could muster at the time. Yasotay could tell that something was bothering him. He assumed it was what had happened to Baatar. Yasotay, too, felt bad about the boy's death, but Altan still seemed to carry pain from it. The planning began as soon as Sarnai and Tera heard of Altan's blessing. However, Yasotay had no one from his family to stand with him, so adjustments to the ceremony had to be made. In Mongolian weddings, not just the individuals but also the two families were considered to be *getting married*. So, it was decided that Temujin and Bourtai would act as Yasotay's family.

More than one hundred people were invited to Yasotay and Tera's wedding ceremony and celebration. It had a festival-like atmosphere with games and plenty of food and drink. While Sarnai was a stickler for details, she kept the ceremony itself as simple as possible. Yasotay was told to ride up on horseback so that Altan and Sarnai could formally greet him.

"Welcome, come inside, hurry, you're too slow!" said Sarnai.

Yasotay had been forewarned of this traditionally abrupt greeting by the parents of the bride. He quickly jumped down off his horse and entered the ger. When he walked in, Yasotay searched for Tera. To his left stood Temujin and Bourtai, wearing their best clothes with big smiles. He turned to his right, and standing there in a beautiful cream-colored deel was the love of his life. She wore a silver-colored belt cinched around her narrow waist and an embroidered veil with a silver band on her head that matched the belt. Her mother had toiled for days on end to make the garment perfect. Her deel had intricate tiny loops of brown embroidery around the collar and along the seams. Tera wore a red veil that was also intricately embroidered with flowers and leaves. Woven tendrils adorned with tiny flowers draped down from her head on either side of her face. Gaia, the Greek goddess of the Earth, never looked as enchanting as Tera did, thought Yasotay.

This was the first time he had seen her in a couple of days, and he realized she had intended it that way. His first sight would be of her in all her glory.

"You are absolutely beautiful," said Yasotay with a big smile. He could see a single tear rolling down her cheek. "I love you."

"I love you too!" gushed Tera.

Sarnai paused for a moment, allowing the gravity of their moment to sink in, and then she diligently moved the proceedings along. Next was the gift exchange and the search for that perfect liver. Yasotay gave Tera a large white and brown cashmere blanket.

"This is wonderful. Thank you…Tata will love this blanket," said Tera.

"Actually, I thought that it would be a fitting blanket for our wedding bed. I was in search of a blanket when I met Temujin…who brought me to you. And the first thing you ever gave me was a blanket," said Yasotay, "so the gift of the blanket has much meaning for me. But if you would prefer to give it to Tata, I would understand." The little scar on Yasotay's chin was glowing.

"No, It's perfect. I love it, thank you," said Tera. Then she walked over and, with her back to him, lifted something and carried it back to Yasotay, cradling it like a child. "I got this little fellow for you."

In her arms was an adorable Bankhar puppy with dark-brown fluffy fur and large floppy ears. He had a light brown spot above each of his expressive eyes with patches of light brown around his snout and mouth and on his legs and chest. He also had an area of white fur right where his neck met his chest.

"This little fellow will grow up strong, loyal, and protective. He will be a great help with managing our sheep and goats," said Tera. "I hope you like him."

Yasotay lifted the dog from Tera's arms and held him face-to-face. The dog reached out with his long tongue and gave Yasotay's face a big lick that made everyone laugh.

Yasotay laughed, trilling his lips, "Pbbbt …I think he likes me."

Next, they were fortunate to find a perfect liver, and thankfully, they only had to sacrifice two chickens. And finally came the tying of the hands and the head toss. In the yarn ritual, the couples' wrists were tied together with a piece of blue silk yarn, symbolizing their union, and it had the additional benefit of warding off evil spirits. The last ritual before they embarked on feasting, singing, and drinking was the *khoorog*. Yasotay called this ritual *the head toss*. It was the offering of a sacrificed sheep's head to the groom from the bride's parents.

Among various Mongol tribes, the most revered sacrificial animal is the sheep. It's regarded as a magical creature whose wool, skin, bones, and meat are believed to possess cleansing and fertility-inducing properties. And the most sacred part of this sacred animal is the head. It was Yasotay's role to accept the cooked sheep head from Tera's parents and eat a piece to show his courage and commitment to their marriage. Once he took a bite from the sheep's head, the ritual concluded with the bride and groom together throwing the head up through the crown or roof hole of the ger. They had only three tries to accomplish this feat. This ritual was supposed to bring prosperity to the newlyweds.

Yasotay took the sheep head from Sarnai and took a bite, trying not to show his distaste and looking away from what he was biting. His teeth raked across the side of the small cooked skull that didn't yield much meat. But Yasotay chewed what little meat his teeth had scraped from the skull and, with an odd look on his face, motioned to Tera for the head toss. They aligned themselves under the hole in the ger and attempted their first toss. Tera was caught off guard, their throwing motion uncoordinated, and the head bounced off the side of the crown, falling back to the ground. The Bankhar puppy immediately went to the head and started sniffing at it.

"That's not for you, or not yet," said Tera, picking the sheep's head from the ground. "Let's try this again." On the second try, they missed again.

With the final throw, Tera and Yasotay had their timing down, and this time, the head sailed clear out of the ger. Sarnai went outside and retrieved the head, giving it to the puppy to chew on, which Yasotay learned, oddly enough, was also a Mongolian custom.

The day was filled with unforgettable moments that would remain in Yasotay's mind, but Tera's flame burned brightest for him. Her frequent smiles and laughter were coupled with how absolutely stunning she looked in her wedding deel.

Tera and Altan had prepared their new ger by placing the newly-wed's bed at the northern end and leaving a large plate of food near the hearth. The final step was the shaman blessing the ger by taking a piece of food from the plate and making an offering to the gods by throwing it out of the crown. She did this while chanting an unintelligible prayer.

After all the day's festivities were complete and the formal wedding ceremony over, a small group sat around a fire, talking, drinking, and laughing. The mood to drink and continue the celebration seemed to hang on for several days. Several large logs were lying around the fire for seating. In many respects, these were the last days of summer. They would be leaving soon for their winter camp.

"Yasotay, why did you pick days before we leave for the winter grazing grounds to be wed?" asked Jamka in a slurred voice. "I would rather sleep in for a week after a celebration like this…especially with a new wife in my bed!"

"It was my choice," interrupted Tera. Her caramel-colored eyes looked tired after the long day, and Yasotay knew she would like nothing more than to wish everyone a good evening.

"The shaman predicted Tera will bless us with a grandchild next year," said Sarnai. Altan sat by her side in his usual stoic fashion.

"Already thinking grandchildren, are we?" interjected Temujin, who, surprisingly, seemed relatively sober.

"Yes, and your mother Houlun was happy to see Jochi arrive, wasn't she?" asked Sarnai.

"It seems that she would have preferred to *see* him a few months later!" interjected Jamka, laughing loudly. Some of the others, those close to Jamka, joined in on the laughter.

"And what do you mean by that?" asked Temujin, not finding his comments humorous. Yasotay had seen that look before. It was a face that told him that Temujin was irritated and, if pushed, he might enter the next stage, which Yasotay calls—exploding rage.

"Jochi is the result of Bourtai being more of a honey pot than a honey badger!" Jamka's drunken, snide comment was delivered with slurred words and a big smile. He was trying desperately to be funny but was a bit too drunk to realize his comments verged on dangerous. A roar of laughter erupted from Jamka's loyal followers. Temujin knew full well what Jamka meant by this comment since it was he who recounted the tale of Tera's kidnapper's nickname for her. None of those loyal to Temujin laughed or smiled. They awaited Temujin's wrathful response, having seen it so many times. Yasotay was embarrassed for Temujin and fearful of how he might retaliate.

Temujin paused for a long time, and suddenly, his shoulders slumped. Then he replied with a clear and even voice, "Yasotay, Tera, congratulations!" Temujin acted as if nothing had been said. "Bourtai and I are going to retire. We have a long day ahead of us tomorrow. We wish all a good evening!" And with that, the two rose to leave. Bourtai shot Jamka a poisonous glare as she followed Temujin.

Yasotay noticed that everyone there looked stunned, except for Jamka, who sat there in a deep drunken state. Whatever he expected, even Jamka, drunk as he was, could tell he had crossed the line. Once Bourtai's pregnancy was revealed, gossip regarding the baby's paternity spread through the camp like wildfire. Even Tera had pointed out to Yasotay that Bourtai gave birth to Jochi seven months to the day since they were rescued from the Merkit.

The long-standing friendship of the "blood brothers" had been tested by eighteen months of slights and minor jabs in jest, but this felt more grave. Months ago, while at the Merkit victory celebration, Jamka, again in a drunken stupor, said that Bourtai had "gotten fat" during her captivity. At the time, nobody, including Temujin, seemed to associate his comment with a possible pregnancy. Temujin didn't show near the control then, cussing and carrying on. It occurred to Yasotay that maybe *Temujin is developing the self-control necessary to be a good leader.*

As Temujin and Bourtai turned to leave, one of Jamka's men said, "Tucking tail and running, are we?" Like a wild animal, Temujin lunged at him in a flash. The man who had made the quip had been sitting on a large log. Trying to avoid the onslaught, he quickly jerked his head back, and his butt slipped off the front of the log. Then, he tried to squirm away from the attack. Temujin grabbed his head with both hands and slammed it hard against the log three times. The last blow affixed the man's head to the log by piercing his eye socket on a pointy branch sticking out of the log. The impact popped his eyeball out of his head. A red-and-white string kept his eyeball from rolling away as his head was impaled on the log. Temujin turned back and gave Jamka a blazing look as the man's dying legs twitched. Nobody said a word except for the dying man, who made an eerie sound, "Shee, shee, shee, shee," as his body convulsed. At least thirty people watched as he went deathly silent and motionless. All Yasotay could hear was the fire crackling. Temujin stepped away from the body, took Bourtai's hand, and walked away, making an unhurried exit. Bourtai said, "Good night," smiling. Her scowl had changed to a smug look, but no one noticed because all eyes were transfixed on Jamka, who brooded with his head down.

It was moving day, and everyone was up early and packing for the long journey ahead. Before midday, they were headed south toward the Jadaran winter pastures. It was a three-day trip, and the resulting caravan stretched for as far as the eye could see. Jamka's clan was well over twenty thousand strong, with twice as many animals—horses, goats, sheep, oxen, and camels. Moving a group this large required a great deal of coordination and planning. It was a monumental effort. Two tumen commands directly controlled all activities within the chain of command. For the past eighteen months, Temujin had worked side-by-side with Jamka, leading their army. Since they became anda, Jamka treated Temujin as his partner, as one would a brother. Collaborating with him on all major decisions, the two agreed on most of them, often working as one.

The task today was to ensure everyone was packed and on their way. Usually, Jamka and Temujin would wait and join the rear of the long caravan, helping to organize those stragglers who inevitably lagged at the end. For some reason, today was different. Temujin was up early, helping those within his clan. They were the first ones on the trail. He was leading not only his clan but also the whole procession south. Others fell in line because everyone knew it was *moving day.*

Fortunately, it was a clear, sunny day, and the weather was comfortable for travel. The terrain was relatively flat, with long sloping hills falling away in front of them. Pine trees were sparsely scattered along the hillside, with grass covering everything except the large rocks strewn about the landscape as if they were placed there by giants. Two or three li up ahead was a large hillside covered in hundreds of pine trees that looked like good hunting grounds. A dirt path was cutting through the hillside and winding as far as the eye could see. Temujin rarely rode in the front, but his horse would not allow anyone to ride ahead of him this morning. Tera was driving Yasotay's cart, pulled by Tata. Tera liked the canopy on Yasotay's cart, which she put up to shade her from the sun. Sarnai and Erden rode with her, and Yasotay and Altan on horseback, directing their herds.

As the day wore on, the group was making good progress. Temujin started to ease back a little, and Yasotay noticed he began riding alongside his fellow travelers, talking with them. He seemed very upbeat, laughing and joking. Later in the day, he came around to where Yasotay was trying to manage his side of the moving herd.

"How are you this afternoon, Yasotay?" asked Temujin with a smile. Yasotay noticed he was riding the white horse he'd given to Bourtai two years ago for her wedding gift.

"Good. What about you?" he asked.

"Pleased with our progress. With his Eternal Blue Sky, Tengri has given us a beautiful day," responded Temujin. Yasotay was glad to see Temujin in such a good mood.

Just then, someone from further back rode up. "Temujin, is this the front of the line?" It was a messenger on horseback, and you could tell he had been riding hard to catch up with them.

"Yes, it is," answered Temujin.

"Jamka has given the order to stop here for the evening. We have started to set up a temporary camp about half a li back from here," the rider explained. Yasotay looked back down the line. He could see where the large group was settling in for the evening. Bourtai rode up at the same time as the messenger. The rider spun his horse around and headed back.

Bourtai turned to Temujin. "It's still early. I think we can find a better place if we keep going!" Yasotay was surprised to hear this contrary opinion from her.

This gave Temujin pause for a moment. Finally, he said, "That's my wife. She always knows what's best. Let's continue on as she said. There is plenty of daylight left for travel!" responded Temujin.

They rode on till it was almost dark and finally stopped to set up camp. Their camp was far away from the Jadarans'. Over the past eighteen months, the small Borjigin clan had become subsumed in every way by the much larger Jadaran clan. This move was the first time they had separated since the Merkit raid. Considering what had happened last night, Yasotay felt this split was probably the best approach. Yasotay was unsure who Temujin had killed, and he had no clue what complications would arise from that and Jamka's remarks. He and Tera had retired to their ger immediately after the incident, and not a word about it had been said to him since. The split of Temujin's clan from Jamka and his clan was inevitable, given the tension that had been building since they had joined together.

Yasotay worked with Tera to set up a place for them to sleep. A short while later, it was dark, and most everyone was standing around a large fire, stretching their legs after a long day on horseback. The Borjigin clan had grown by forty-five or fifty, with several of Jamka's people deciding to follow Temujin. This addition included Sukh, whose monstrous form stood beside Temujin with his axe over his shoulder. They had become good friends ever since Jamka pointed out that they looked like brothers. Over the next two weeks, Jamka would lose another one hundred seventy-five people who also defected to Temujin's clan. Jamka had thousands, so the defections weren't critical to Jamka, but he took notice of those who left to join Temujin.

Around the campfire one night, Temujin asked Sukh, "Have you ever been to the Valley between Mother and Father Mountains?"

"No, never have I been there," answered Sukh.

Temujin raised his voice a little louder. "How do we feel about spending this winter back in the Valley between Mother and Father Mountains?" Last year, they spent it at the Jadaran winter sections of the steppe.

"Yes," multiple people cried out, excited by this prospect.

"It sounds like we're going home!" said Sarnai to Tera.

Yasotay rummaged around in his wooden chest, searching for something he hadn't seen in years. His hand finally closed around it, and he had the object he had been desperately seeking. Quickly, he shoved it into the fold of his deel and hurriedly walked out of the ger, heading toward their *favorite spot*. The Borjigin clan had returned to the Valley between the Mother and Father Mountains three weeks ago. Within the first week, he and Tera had gone to the tarn, where Tera declared, "This is our favorite spot!" Tera quickly became accustomed to regular bathing and found herself quite attached to their private stream. She expressed the opinion that she believes she must bathe at least three times a week...at a minimum. Yasotay loved her dearly, but he had to admit he sometimes struggled to understand her! Her desire was complicated by the fact that he was quickly running out of bath bean. He had to make more, but first, he needed to find all the ingredients. While Tera seemed to have embraced her new bathing ritual, Yasotay did find her brushing between the toes of her feet with his toothbrush one day. In the nicest voice he could muster, he asked her not to do that! He didn't know why; it just didn't feel right.

"I was wondering if you were going to make it!" said Tera, who was already undressed and in the water.

"Your father needed a hand with the herd," answered Yasotay. "Believe me, I've been looking forward to this all day!"

Yasotay quickly stripped out of his clothes and slowly crept into the freezing water.

"This feels much colder than last week!" insisted Yasotay, with the water just past his knees.

"I hope it doesn't become too cold to use this bathing spot in the middle of winter," said Tera. "I can't go longer than four or five days without a bath."

"This coming from the person that insisted there were evil spirits in the water?" Yasotay said with a smile.

"I still believe there are spirits in the water. They're just not evil," insisted Tera. "Now that I actually think of it…I think they're wonderful." Tera splashed a big wave at Yasotay, who was still slowly edging his way into the icy water. He cringed at first, then decided to commit and plunged his torso into the icy waters. Yasotay had made some modifications to their tarn; the main one was digging out in front of the waterfall, which made it much deeper.

"So, what is that?" asked Tera, pointing at the small leather bag that Yasotay had retrieved from his chest and placed on the top of the rock within view.

"It's something for someone special," Yasotay said with a smile.

"For me? Now you have my attention! What is it?" asked Tera with a curious look.

"I guess you'll have to look and see for yourself!"

Tera clambered over the rocks at the bottom and sides of the tarn in waist-high water to where Yasotay had left the small bag. It was made from very fine, soft leather and had the Yin and Yang symbol embossed into the leather. A drawstring closure was cinched shut with decorative aglets made from tiny metal beads on both ends of the string. She climbed partially out of the water and reached for the bag.

Looking at it, Tera could tell from the detail of its design that this was something special.

"I think you put it way over here so you could see me naked!"

"I do love the view!" Yasotay said playfully, admiring her beautifully curved body. Tera seemed to glow: her skin appeared rosy, and her breasts were bigger. *Wait, what does that mean?* He thought, raising his index finger to his mouth. Then Yasotay stammered, "Are you pregnant?"

Tera quickly slumped back into the water, holding the leather bag over her head, the only thing above the waterline. The look on her face was of total surprise.

"What...how did you know?" she asked with a pouty look.

"I know every curve of your body," answered Yasotay. With that, she gave him a big hug while still holding onto the bag. They embraced for what seemed like forever. Finally, she pulled her head back off his shoulder and asked, "It was supposed to be a surprise!"

"So, I am going to be a father," said Yasotay, who seemed shocked by the revelation. He noticed Tera biting her lower lip. She was apprehensive, and he could tell this meant a great deal to her. It meant a great deal to him too. He had always wondered if he would ever have a child. *What would it be like to be a father?* He never knew his father. Would he know how to act or what to do? *What am I supposed to do? You wanted to experience life, well here it is!*

"There's something I want to ask you." Tera was still holding the small leather bag and biting her lower lip. She paused momentarily, then said, "If it's a boy, I want to name him Baatar!"

Yasotay bowed his head in thought. Finally, he responded, "Yes, I agree. I can't think of a better name. If it's a boy, we should name him Baatar!"

Tera gave him another big hug. "Thank you!"

"So, what is this?" she asked, bringing the leather bag between them. Tera pulled the cinch loose and reached into the bag. She pulled out her hand, and in it was a green statuette. It was a decorative jade dragon of brilliant green. It had a large head, a long neck, two ruby-red eyes, and a red flame coming from its mouth. The dragon's large wings were folded to its sides. A superb craftsman had made it, and Tera had never seen anything so intricate, so beautiful—so magical.

"A very special person made this for me," explained Yasotay. "Mana's husband was the single greatest stone craftsman in the Jin Empire. His work graced the homes of many of the Jin elites. Mana had him make this special gift for me. What you hold in your hand is named Longxi. She told me that it would protect and keep me safe. She insisted that Longxi would watch over anyone who possessed it. If evil were to befall them, it would be a sanctuary for their soul," Yasotay explained, shrugging his shoulders. "Mana was definitely superstitious."

"I am superstitious, too, and I want more of my own green dragon," Tera said, pressing her naked body against his, grasping him firmly.

"No, I am serious. This dragon means a great deal to me!" said Yasotay.

"I'm sorry! I understand." Her downcast caramel eyes told him she was, indeed, sorry.

"I wanted you to have this. It is the only thing I have left from the one person who meant so much to me growing up. I have always believed it watches over me. It's important that it watch over you too! This makes you a part of me."

"Thank you. I love you, Yasotay!" she declared. As they embraced, the dragon, placed on a rock, looked down on them.

EPILOGUE

Kurultai, Upper Orhon River, fall, 1206 CE

F our nomad warriors, each with a sword and bow, stood waiting near three tall pine trees toward the northern edge of the
camp precisely as instructed. They were told that Shilu would
meet them there at sunset for a special task. Everyone was aware of
Shilu's reputation. He was an old war dog and a stickler for details.
He wasn't someone you crossed or disappointed. The four warriors
were part of the newly formed Khan's Guard, which totaled over five

hundred men with the single purpose of protecting one man. These men were not standouts in any way, nor were they the best archers or riders in the Guard. Shilu had asked his superior if there were any warriors, in particular, he thought best suited for this task. The answer was an emphatic, "No…it doesn't matter who we choose. They all die just the same!"

The camp had grown quickly over the past four weeks. The *Kurultai* had attracted tens of thousands of nomads—every military and clan leader who aspired to be part of greatness. The gathering had been long in planning and was very much like a Naadam with horse races, archery competitions, and wrestling tournaments. The main purpose of the Kurultai was to name a ruler of all the nomads. For hundreds of years, the chiefs of the steppe would convene when called to the assembly by one who commanded their respect. This Kurultai was called to order by the one whom many respected, but all certainly feared. As was evident to most, there was one clear leader among the nomads.

"I heard that he's gone crazy!" stated the tall, thin warrior wearing a dark-blue deel with bright yellow trim.

"Who has gone crazy?" asked the short warrior wearing a green deel and a hat with thick gray fur.

"The one we're having to help Shilu deal with!" replied the tall warrior in the blue deel.

"So, they need four of us in full combat gear to help him control one crazy person?" the short warrior in the green deel asked. "I don't need the rest of you; I'll tie him up and drag him behind my horse…no problem!"

"I don't think so…I heard it's *him!*" said one of the other guards standing there, waiting.

"*Him* who?" asked the warrior in the green deel. Not answering, he just stood there and stared. Suddenly, an odd look swept over his face. He realized who the guard was referring to and whispered in a low voice, "Wait, you're not talking about Allaga?"

"Shhh, don't say that name so loud!" whispered the warrior in the dark-blue deel.

The sound of that name brought terror into the hearts of men; its mere utterance brought to mind one's worst fears. That wasn't the only name he was called, but it was the one most often used behind his back. They had all heard the stories of the man who was death personified. Many considered him a wolf, and others believed he was a ghost. There were many versions of the legend, and although only a few people knew him personally, everyone in the clan of more than one hundred thousand was aware of his reputation. He was the leader of the *Mangoday*— the demon of death himself!

The Mangoday was an elite force of warriors. They were a small group of a couple of hundred men who had taken a blood oath to follow this one man, Allaga, into the inferno if requested. It was said they had been *"consecrated in death!"* As the story was told, the group was formed by Allaga, who trained warriors to become machines of death. He would take over a hundred recruits into the desert for training, but less than half would return. Many didn't survive the first three days. Deprived of food, water, and sleep, those strong enough to survive the thirty-day ordeal were changed. It was believed that his training would pluck any personal thoughts about dying from their minds.

A Mangoday warrior held no fear of death. It was as if they had already experienced death and were now walking as ghosts among the living. They rarely traveled with the main army and generally made camp on the northern end of the main clan's encampment. They would show up and disappear without notice. Unlike the regular army, Mangoday forces would never violate their enemy's women, kill children, or take any of the spoils of war. They were often the first to engage in battle and the first to leave once the battle was decided.

Finally, Shilu appeared. He was a medium-height warrior wearing a thick leather vest with a blood-red deel underneath it. A sword was holstered on his left side, and a quiver full of arrows on his right. He carried a water bladder connected to a large leather belt around his small waistline.

"Your attention!" stated Shilu. "If you care to stay alive, you should listen!" He reached down and unhooked the strap holding his quiver and water bladder, letting it fall to the ground. He pulled one arrow from the quiver that was lying on the ground. Taking the bow from his back, he nocked the arrow.

"I suggest you do the same. Drop the quiver and anything else you carry that might get in your way. You probably won't get off more than one shot," explained Shilu, motioning toward the other gear the warriors were carrying.

"I don't understand?" asked the tall one in the dark-blue deel.

"It is simple: we are going into the wolf's den! Don't look directly at him or say anything. You are to stand there, an arrow nocked in your bow, and whatever you do, keep the bow pointed toward the ground." All four warriors immediately removed the quiver and other gear from their side.

"Why?" asked the tall warrior, who placed his quiver on the ground and nocked an arrow.

"Because he will kill you if you dare point it at him," responded Shilu in a deadpan voice.

"What's the plan?" asked one of the others. "Why are we poking the bear?"

"Again, it is simple. You will follow behind me into the ger and take a position, two of you on either side of me. Nobody says a word! And I mean *nobody*. Don't even clear your throat!" Shilu paused for emphasis, looking into each man's eyes. "Make sure you keep your arrow pointed *down* toward the ground!"

"How will we know when to act?" asked one of the warriors.

"Don't worry about that. If this goes bad, it will happen very quickly, and you will know when to act! If you don't, you'll probably be dead." Shilu paused in thought, "Just don't do anything stupid like saying something or pointing your weapon at him," said Shilu.

A group of fifty men gathered at roughly a hundred paces to their right. Shilu raised his left hand, still holding his bow with a nocked arrow pointing toward the sky. The distance in the dim light didn't allow them to see who Shilu was signaling, but they could see the same raised gesture from one of the fifty men being returned.

"We're ready. Remember, two to my right and two to the left. Don't say a word and make no aggressive moves. Keep the arrow nocked and toward the ground. Let's go!" said Shilu. He led them in a single file. The unadorned white ger was twenty paces away. Shilu didn't hesitate to walk up and immediately enter the large round structure.

There was one candle on a table burning in the center of the ger. Rummaging through his large wooden chest, Yasotay could only see shadows as he searched for something. Suddenly, he realized he didn't remember what that was. His mind was racing with thoughts of what had just happened. He grabbed an old leather water bladder hanging on the wall. He remembered this bladder. *It was one Tera had made for me. It has to be twenty-five years old...so long ago!* Then it hit him. He was looking for Longxi, the green dragon figurine he had given Tera. It had been years since he'd seen it, and still, he hadn't found it. He was convinced that it was taken!

He didn't have time to reminisce. *I need to leave...NOW!* Suddenly, out of the corner of his eye, he saw someone step through the ger's entrance. Everyone knew to announce before entering. Yasotay's right hand immediately went to the blade he called the Green Dragon, not Master Jing's from the temple, but a replica.

It was Shilu who had the audacity to enter his ger without permission, and he brought four others.

"What do you want?" asked Yasotay, whose eyes went cold and dead. One hand held the Green Dragon, and the other was on his hip.

"He needs to talk to you!" announced Shilu. Yasotay was facing away from him, but Shilu knew he was ready to strike.

"I don't feel the need to talk," countered Yasotay, turning to face them.

Just at that moment, Temujin strode into the ger.

The tense atmosphere in the room intensified tenfold as Yasotay noticed the shadow cast on the wall behind them. He smiled, recalling the Greek allegory about a cave and images cast on a wall, and wondered, are they the puppeteers or the prisoners? He felt like he was the prisoner who had seen the truth.

After a moment of silence, he said to Temujin, "I see you have come to tell more lies!" then he turned to Shilu. "You are all just puppets, part of the performance for all those your fearless leader holds prisoner!" Though Yasotay was looking directly at Shilu, he motioned toward Temujin.

"It's obvious you're upset. We need to talk!" insisted Temujin. "I don't know how we've come to this."

"You killed him, didn't you?" Yasotay spits out. "You had Baatar killed, didn't you?"

"What are we talking about…someone who died over twenty years ago?" asked Temujin, lowering his gaze. "Is that what you're asking me?"

"Tell me the truth," insisted Yasotay, legs planted in a wide stance. "You had him killed, didn't you?"

"I did no such thing," said Temujin, drawing his arms across his chest.

"So Hassar didn't shoot that arrow at your behest while you held a knife to the Merkit's neck to complete the ruse?" asked Yasotay, raising his eyebrows, awaiting another lie.

Temujin paused, then his shoulders slumped in resignation. "The truth, yes, but I did it for you, for you and Tera!" Temujin paused again. "Do you remember our pledge? While we shared the same road, we would allow no harm to come to the other. Over all these years, I have kept to my word. I have looked out for you, done what was best for you."

Yasotay paused; his admission took a moment to sink in. He responded with a dead calm voice, "Is that what was best for me? Or, what was best for *you*? You killed Baatar to keep me here! To help you build your *war machine*." Yasotay paused and gathered himself. "Now that you have it, what are you going to do with it? I can't trust you. I can't believe a word you say. *Nobody* can trust you," said Yasotay, his voice escalating. "I can't believe I never saw what this really was…you're not some great leader, father, or friend. You're a lying manipulative demon, a *monster*!" he screamed with his weapon in hand. Shilu and his warriors shrank back, cowering in fear.

Temujin held his ground. "You call *me* a monster? Everyone in this ger is afraid of *you*, not me." Temujin paused, beholding the terror in his men, and then laughing a brittle laugh, he said, "Look, that one right there." He pointed at the warrior in the green deel and the puddle of piss at his feet. Temujin shook his head. "You see. We know that if you wanted to kill us, we would be dead! So, I ask you, Yasotay, who is the *monster* that everyone *fears*?"

"Tuhh," Yasotay scoffed and turned. "Call me whatever you like. It doesn't change what you are. What you have become!" asserted Yasotay, calming his voice. "You don't want to better your people; they are nothing more than puppets to you. You're only interested in their control and subjugation. To you, all of us are prisoners, and you're the puppet master putting on the show." Yasotay paused, and with a gaping mouth, he took an audible breath. "You are *pure evil*!"

There was a long pause. Temujin's posture stooped a bit, and then he said, "I think it best if you go!"

Yasotay immediately turned and stepped up to Temujin, face-to-face, standing in his personal space. "You are much more afraid of the truth than me!" Yasotay paused for a moment, and in a low and gravelly voice said, "I would think that if they were to know…"

Temujin interrupted Yasotay, talking over him. "Must I remind you there are those that will come to harm…those you love! Do you not realize the danger you put them in!" Temujin growled.

"Eventually, death confronts us all. We are each faced with doing one of two things: fight with fury or cower in fear!" said Yasotay. "Your threats don't scare me, Temujin. Not like your lies scare you! I know of your lies…Togru, Jamka, Baatar, and every other person you have manipulated and destroyed." Yasotay paused and then turned quickly to leave. Temujin flinched, covering his arms across his face. "You're a coward!" said Yasotay as he grabbed his wooden chest and walked out the entrance in silence. Temujin and his men said nothing; moving from the door, they gave Yasotay a wide berth.

The sun had just set, and a soft rain had begun. The rain didn't deter the small crowd who had heard the commotion and gathered to watch. The other warriors stood around the front of the ger, waiting. Finally, Yasotay came out carrying a wooden chest. Those inside followed behind him. He walked over to an old cart and placed it under its bench. He untied Tata from a post and slowly and methodically attached her harness to the cart. Over fifty people were standing around watching him prepare to leave. They were deathly silent. Yasotay hopped up on the cart and gave one last long look at Temujin.

"It doesn't matter what you say, what you tell them. You are what you are!" said Yasotay. He gave a soft whistling noise from atop his cart, and Tata started to move forward and slowly trotted off. The rain was so light that it seemed like a fine mist instead of raindrops. The silhouette of Yasotay slowly riding away could be seen by all who witnessed his departure. Temujin stood there...seething.

While he was riding off, a female voice cried out, "Yasotay, don't go... Yasotay, Yasotay."

Temujin took the sword from his side and, in one clean swipe, lopped off her head. Bending over, he grabbed the severed head from the ground. Snarling at the small gathered crowd, he said, "His name is never to be uttered by another in my presence!" Temujin's face was flushed with anger. Turning, he screamed at the top of his lungs toward the departing Yasotay, "I don't need you. I can do this without you–I am Genghis Khan!" Temujin raised the severed head high in the air, "You will see; they shall all FEAR me! All will bend their knee to me!"

Temujin turned back to those watching the spectacle in awe and stoically tossed the severed head on the ground at their feet, saying, "I am the punishment of God!"

ACKNOWLEDGMENTS

Embarking on this journey of authoring a book has stirred up some familiar feelings from my past. The eagerness and excitement to see where this path may lead, mixed with the usual anxiety, apprehension, and nervousness that come with starting a new venture. I have been fortunate enough to experience this "new venture feeling" several times over my sixty-plus years. They mark significant milestones in my life, a new beginning if you will, and this first book is certainly no exception.

It is odd looking back over the past thirty-eight years since the idea of writing a book first popped into my head. It was about the same time I developed a love for reading. You see, the world is comprised of three distinct types of people: those unfortunate ones who cannot read, those who can read, and then there are those who genuinely love reading. While my grade school teachers taught me to read, J.R.R. Tolkien, specifically *The Hobbit*, turned me into a lover of the written word. As someone who enjoys reading, you may be curious about my motivation for starting this journey. As we all know, having a love of reading is one thing, but writing a book is a different affair. I have been asked by several people, "Why take on such a big project of writing a trilogy about an obscure 12th-century *Special Forces* leader from the ranks of Genghis Khan?" To answer this question, please bear with me as I share a short and mildly interesting story...

In the early 1980s, I was stationed on a US Navy aircraft carrier, the USS Saratoga, home-based in Jacksonville, Florida. The ship had recently completed drydock repairs in Philadelphia and was conducting one- and two-week patrols along the East Coast and the Caribbean. As someone who had never lived on a ship before, I soon learned that my daily routine revolved around one simple question: Are we in port or at sea? While at sea, it was all shift work, so the day of the week did not matter. Your daily routine was the same, every day. You were either "on duty" or "off duty." But while in port, most sailors, especially those of sufficient rank, lived the typical Monday to Friday 8:00 am - 5:00 pm work schedule. While there was some shift work, you were free after 5:00 pm every weekday and most weekends.

At this point, I had already spent over two years living in a "berthing area." I had been cooped up in a barracks or a ship for over thirty months. I was sharing a living space with twenty-five, fifty, a hundred or more sailors at any given time. For those of you who have never had the pleasure…communal living in a berthing area sucks! I required my own space, a private sanctuary away from 120-man sleeping quarters. I needed to escape the constant drone of the ship's 1MC, which regularly blared ship-related communications. Placing my head on the pillow at night, I began to imagine the constant grind of the war machine amplified, haunting me to sleep.

Simply put, I realized *I must get an apartment*. I could handle living onboard a ship when out to sea, but I needed a home to go to when in port. Most single sailors did not earn enough to afford a place alone. The customary practice was to share costs with one or two shipmates. This was my way out of the grind: find a tolerable roommate, preferably one who could tolerate me, make a deal, and find a suitable place.

Over the remainder of my time in the Navy, I had roughly ten roommates to share the rent with—some good and some a disaster. One roommate in particular was this guy from Chicago, and his name was David Pink. We called him Pinkman. He was this big hairy Jewish guy built like a brick shithouse. He operated the radar displays I was trained to repair and maintain. We became fast friends. And if his size and stature were not intimidating enough, Pinkman was also into martial arts. His daily workouts intrigued me, and he encouraged me to join him. He started me with some basic forms and, over time, introduced me to the hand dance, the staff, and his favorite, the nuncha. After a couple of months, I was all in, questioning him on all matters of form and technique. One day, after my usual barrage of questioning, he said, "Look, Nardo, there is a lot to learn about martial arts, but what I can teach you is just the tip of the iceberg; at the heart of the arts is Eastern philosophy itself. Confucius, Lao Tzu, Sun-Tzu, if you really want to learn about Martial Arts, you need to start there!" I doubt Pinkman realized it at the time, but he had put me on a path.

My budding fascination with the history and philosophies of the East has led me to read many books and articles. I started with the classics, *The Art of War* by Sun Tzu and Lao Tzu's infamous book, *Tao Te Ching*. I quickly realized that these and all other famous works from the East had wildly varying translations due to the differences in language and culture. Over the years, I grew to enjoy the stories of the great dynasties of China. They reminded me of *fantasy stories*, of a wild and mystical world filled with extraordinary people, incredible places, and unusual creatures. One particular account of how the Yuan Dynasty came about stuck with me; I found this odd story in an *Armed Forces Journal* magazine about the little-known leader of Genghis Khan's special forces unit, Yasotay. Information about Yasotay's background and history was very vague. I consider myself a research buff, so I searched for as much as possible about him. There was nothing.

Luckily, I had made a copy of the article, which told the story of how Yasotay learned to use fear to conquer a clan, a city, and even an empire. It explained how he took soldiers into the desert and trained them to be *warriors of death*. He used those warriors to decimate his enemies using brutal psyops-like tactics to build fear within towns and cities. I read it over again and again. The story inferred that Yasotay's warriors, the Mangoday, were one of the first special forces groups within any army. Vague battle descriptions of the zombie-like warriors facing death with no fear sounded like something out of Tolkien's *Middle Earth*. While the article went into some detail, many questions were left unanswered for me. I started filling in the gaps with my own ideas: What if he was originally from a foreign land? What if he was a good guy that did a bad thing? What if he unleashed hell on earth and then regretted it? The thought of me telling Yasotay's story began rattling around in my head...and it continued to do so for thirty years.

Over this time, I was fortunate enough to build a successful career as an Engineer. My success with building an engineering company afforded me the opportunity to take a couple of years off to write a book...or three. *Why I write this story* can best be explained by George Orwell's thoughts on writing: "...One would never undertake such a thing if one were not driven on by some demon whom one can neither resist nor understand." The answers to the story of Yasotay lived in my mind, and I had no choice...*I had to write it down.*

The first book of this passion project was completed with the help of an incredible number of people, and I am truly indebted to all of them. First and foremost, I must thank my family, starting with my wife, Terri, who always had a solution to my most vexing problems. Her help and support have meant the world to me. Next, I want to thank my son AJ who came up with the names of the three books and helped me organize the "big picture" of the story. Thanks to my son William who would never turn down the opportunity to *wax philosophically* on some deep or abstract thought process, many of which have found their way into this book.

I also want to express my gratitude to my author-coach, Dawn Bates, who was critical in helping me get my head out of research and start writing. She often encouraged me to "fetch a cup of tea and just start writing!" and, of course, to Pete Canalichio, who pointed me in Dawn's direction. I want to thank all those who directly worked on the book with me: my editors David Aretha, Baasanjav Terbish, Oliva Bedford, John Nelson, Marie Timell, and, of course, editor extraordinaire Steve VanVeen. I want to thank Sarah George-Moniz, Kristi Kovacs, and Max Moss for their marketing support and the wonderful graphics. I am eternally grateful for the executive support from Ron Fishbeck, Rainbow Russell, Trinity Vallee, and Donna Ripa. Fish, you da man! There were many friends and family members who inspired and encouraged me; at the risk of forgetting someone, I will have to mention

Doug Lammers, who sat through hours of my storytelling and who, if I didn't mention him, would make me hear about it ad nauseam ad infinitum (basically a nice way of saying he would *irritate me forever)*!

I want to thank my brother Robert, who also endured hours of conversation about the 12th-century Asia steppe and assured me that while he would not sit down and read the book, he would listen to the audible version on a long drive when it was made available. I won't hold my breath. ☺

Special shout-out to just some of the folks who always seemed to ask, "How's the book coming?" along with encouraging words: my sister Maryanne Patane, Lynn Walker, Ezra Oyer, Anthony Atala, Danielle and Chad Elly, Nancy Ellis, DAV (Disabled America Veterans) folks Marc Burgess, Barry Jesinoski, Dan Clare and of course the GigaTECH guys (Cory Landrum, Bill Heapes, Scott Bradshaw, Jason Landrum, Dan Moniz, and Matt Jenks). I want to express my eternal gratitude to my mother, Grace, and my father, Big Al, who recently passed away. There are countless reasons for expressing my heartfelt appreciation to them. But above all, they believed in me, which gave me the confidence to write this book.

I did my best, and I hope you enjoyed reading it, Pops!

ABOUT THE AUTHOR

Umberto Nardolicci, also known as "Nardo," has led an extraordinary life journey. He was born and raised in upstate New York and developed a passion for innovation and service early in life, which led him to join the military—a choice that would have a profound impact.

Nardo served in the U.S. Navy and was injured during his service, leaving him a disabled veteran. He remained resilient and determined, leaving the military and securing a job at Johns Hopkins University - Applied Physics Laboratory, where he began a very successful software engineering career in the Advanced Systems Design group. Throughout his time there, he worked on several leading-edge projects that leveraged the latest technologies. This experience left an indelible mark on his approach to things. From high-tech missile systems to real-time factory floor automation and large-scale healthcare systems, Nardo has worked with some of the best and brightest, building some of the most complex and challenging systems in the world.

Over the years, Nardo's dedication to storytelling, the martial arts, and his fellow veterans has been unwavering. His fascination with traditional Eastern Philosophies drew him to finally pick up a pen in 2022 and embark on a new adventure, delving into historical fiction. His novels and passion project, the War of Fear trilogy, bring to life a long-standing desire to tell the story of a little-known but amazing warrior he had read about in an Armed Forces Journal back in 1985. Nardo's commitment to his craft and his fellow veterans is evident within every page of his novels.

The pages of Nardo's novels are not just stories but powerful tools that transport readers to pivotal historical moments. His characters bring history to life and give readers a glimpse of the horrors of war, the camaraderie of battle, and the enduring spirit of those who serve. Nardo's novels are more than just entertainment; they are a means to raise awareness about veterans' struggles and advocate for their well-being, with all proceeds from his books being donated to veteran organizations.

Nardo's legacy is one of honor, compassion, and unwavering dedication to the written word and the veterans who have given so much. His journey is a testament to the indomitable spirit within all of us and the true power of storytelling.